Nine Layers of Sky

Liz Williams

BANTAM BOOKS

NINE LAYERS OF SKY
A Bantam Spectra Book / September 2003

Published by
Bantam Dell
A Division of Random House, Inc.
New York, New York

Book design by Karin Batten

Bantam Books and the rooster colophon are registered trademarks of
Random House, Inc.

ISBN 0-553-58499-5

Manufactured in the United States of America
Published simultaneously in Canada

OPM   10 9 8 7 6 5 4 3 2 1

Further praise for **Liz Williams**

THE GHOST SISTER

"A fine example of modern science fiction . . . detailed, engrossing and real . . . The virtue of this novel is Williams' ability to force the reader to confront fundamental questions about life, religion, technology, feminism, idealism, do-goodism, and free will. *The Ghost Sister* shows how high the . . . science fiction 'literary' bar has been raised. . . . A very impressive effort, and an amazing feat as a first novel."
—*Science Fiction Chronicle*

"Williams addresses difficult moral and ethical questions in a compelling novel concerned with genetic engineering and a people's struggle to transcend their limitations."
—*Booklist*

"Reminiscent of Ursula Le Guin's *Left Hand of Darkness* . . . This is the sort of SF one wishes there could be more of . . . a thought-provoking, lyrical read."
—*Interzone*

"When the time came to compile the shortlist for the Philip K. Dick Award for best original paperback, it was only right that *The Ghost Sister* was among the final six; a book that gives readers so much to think about should be rewarded. . . . Just keep your wits about you and your senses at their sharpest, because here, only the strong survive."
—*SF Site*

"Breathtaking in its elegance . . . confounds expectations while at the same time surpassing them."
—*Infinity Plus*

"Outstanding novel! I couldn't bear to put it down. I snarled at each interruption. Liz Williams has crafted a very believable world for her first novel, populated it with believable characters, and told a story that kept me turning pages all night."
—*Aphelion*

"A brilliant novel. It does what the best genre novels should do. It poses questions about life and how to live it that have no easy answers, and never pretends to provide a single one. Williams is an author to watch, and I'll not be surprised if I see this novel shortlisted for any number of awards."
—*Wavelengths*

EMPIRE OF BONES

"Reading Liz William's *Empire of Bones* is a total immersion in a marvelously realized future. Her insight into the culture of colonization, in which humans are the colonized, is both immediate and challenging."
—Sheri S. Tepper

"Crafted and polished science fiction, with an involving cast of characters—easily strong enough never to be upstaged by the astonishing and ingenious plot, sets and technology."
—Tanith Lee

"It would not surprise me were *Empire of Bones* to be hailed as an important work of feminist sf. It certainly should be hailed, and I recommend it very highly as one of the most interesting works of sf I have read in quite a while."
—*New York Review of Science Fiction*

"A fast-paced science fiction thriller that shows what could happen when First Contact occurs. The homeworld of Rasasatra's politics, culture and social structure is crafted in such intricate detail it feels as if Liz Williams is a native social anthropologist. Yet the talented writer never slows down the action while providing characters, both human and alien, that are believable and understandable inside the strong plot. . . . A great novel."
—*AllSciFi*

THE POISON MASTER

"The book's various cultures and characters are fascinating, but what makes this story unusual is its historical breadth and its consideration of the spiritual and supernatural. Part alien adventure and part existential exploration, this top-notch tale establishes Williams as an author to watch."
—*Publishers Weekly* (starred review)

"The chances Williams has taken here and her confident handling of a wide range of material promises much for her future novels [and] should assist her in climbing up the ladder to bestsellerdom."
—*BookPage*

"The cosmos according to Liz Williams in her third novel is a strange place that defies our conception of modern physics and cosmology. . . . Williams' Latent Emanation and its sister worlds are bold, exotic backdrops against which colorful characters can undergo thrilling adventures with a philosophical subtext. . . . Williams joins A. A. Attanasio and China Miéville as one of the best contemporary practitioners of a kind of imaginative literature that fuses the intellect of SF with the heart of fantasy."
—SciFi.com

"Williams handles her complex story with masterful skill. *The Poison Master* is both big in scope and tensely claustrophobic."
—*Talebones*

To Charles North, forever

Acknowledgments

I should like to thank the members of the Montpelier writing group, my agent Shawna McCarthy, and my editor Anne Groell for their invaluable help in knocking this book into shape.

I also wish to thank everyone in Central Asia for looking after us with such impeccable guerrilla hospitality over the years, particularly:

- in Almaty, Sholpan Bekmagambetova and family and Vasily of café fame
- in Kyrgyzia, Madam Rosa Utabaeva, Kyrgyz ambassador to London
- in Uzbekistan, Viktor and Kate

I should like to thank Roger McMahon, international man of mystery, for making it all possible in the first place.

And finally, let's hear it for the Britpack, and also particularly for Chris Priest, Tanith Lee, Jay Caselberg, and the Storyvillains . . .

"Try, build a palace. Furnish it with marble, pictures, gold, birds of paradise, hanging gardens . . . and enter it. Why, perhaps you may never even have the desire to come out! But . . . your palace is enclosed by a fence, and you'll be told: Everything is yours, delight in it! But only do not go one step away from here! And believe me at that same moment you'll want to be rid of your paradise and step over beyond the fence . . . all this magnificence, all this luxury will even foment your suffering. It will become offensive to you, precisely because of this splendour."

Fyodor Dostoevsky, *The Brothers Karamazov.*

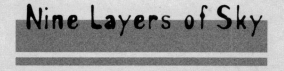

Nine Layers of Sky

Part One

One

They had reached the border early that morning, leapfrogging the grim skein of industrial towns that strung from Almaty to Chimkent. The early part of the journey now seemed remote: a grimy memory that made Elena's skin crawl with remembered pollution. It had taken almost four hours to reach the Uzbek border, crawling all the way, with the powerful wipers of the Sherpa grinding the snow into a grey slush that accumulated at the bottom of the windscreen, periodically slewing down the hood and turning to packed ice beneath the wheels.

Atyrom's sister, Gulnara, had gone to sleep on the backseat. Atyrom drove without speaking, occasionally groping on the dashboard for cigarettes. He smoked Marlboros, which Elena could not afford. Acrid smoke filled the van like the ghost of an American dream.

He offered Elena one, but pride made her say, "Thanks, I'll stick to the Polyot." She reached for her packet of rougher local cigarettes and lit up. Atyrom said nothing, but the lack of conversation was compulsory, since he insisted on playing Uzbek rock at a level that could have woken the dead. It veered from maudlin ballads to aggressive nationalistic anthems that made Atyrom pound the steering column in erratic accompaniment.

Bleary with lack of sleep, Elena stared out across the pale and endless expanse of the steppe. In summer, the land was constantly changing under the light: alternately subtle and harsh, depending on the time of day. Sometimes in summer, she and her sister would borrow her cousin's car and drive out to Lake Kapchugai, to sit by the quiet water and watch the shadows lengthen across the steppe, the afternoon sun striping the land with colors that had not changed since prehistoric times: ochre and mauve and red. Now, in late February, the steppe remained featureless beneath the snow; they could have been driving over the moon. Shortly before seven in the morning, they reached the border and the queue of traffic.

It was still snowing, and Elena could not see very far ahead. The rear lights of the truck in front of them glowed crimson, then died as the truck stopped. Atyrom gave a snort of irritation and switched off the engine. There was a sudden, shattering silence.

"How long do you think we'll be here?" Elena asked. Atyrom glanced at her with manifest contempt.

"How should I know?"

"You've done the trip before," Elena said reasonably.

"It's different every time," Atyrom answered, dismissing the issue. He settled back against the seat rest and closed his eyes. Elena decided not to argue. Atyrom was doing her a favor, after all. If it had not been for his offer, she would have had to take the train down to Tashkent, lugging the heavy bag of black-market clothes with her.

She turned to look at her friend. Gulnara was still sleeping, curled on the backseat with her face squashed uncomfortably against the doorframe. Elena watched her for a moment before fishing in the glove compartment for diversion. There was nothing but a week-old copy of *Karavan*. Gloomily, she perused the *For Sale* advertisements and the lonely hearts, but there was nothing of interest to buy and she was not interested in romance with anyone. Not after Yuri. The cosmodrome seemed suddenly very far away: another Elena, another life entirely.

It was growing cold in the cabin of the van. It had been fifteen below when they left Chimkent. She chafed her hands in the thick leather gloves and opened the door of the Sherpa. Atyrom muttered a brief protest as she stepped down. The cold hit her like a hammer, slamming its way into her lungs. Her eyes prickled and her cheeks started to burn. Squinting, Elena wound her scarf more securely around her face and trudged slowly up the line.

After a seemingly unending procession of trucks and vans, she turned the corner and saw the ramshackle customs post ahead. Blue lights sparkled eerily through the falling snow, and unease settled in an icy lump in Elena's throat. She walked up the line toward a little knot of people who were talking to someone in a Lada through the open door of the car. Elena made her way to the edge of the gathering. These were presumably the customs officials, but as everyone was bundled up under several layers of clothing, it was difficult to tell. One man had the insignia of the Kazakhstan *militzia*. What were the police doing here? A pink-nosed face peered at her like a rabbit from a burrow. Elena glanced past him, to where the driver of the vehicle sat in silence.

"Won't he get cold like that?" Elena asked inanely. The customs officer's face twitched with something that could have been a smile.

"He's not likely to get any colder." And then Elena realized that the man was dead. He seemed to stare at her. There was a hazy bloom across his eyes, like dark frost. It made her shiver even more than the cold.

"Oh, my God," she said, stepping back and slipping a little on the icy surface of the road.

"Not the only one," the customs officer said with a kind of gloomy satisfaction. He pointed to the customs post, where figures were loading stretchers into an ambulance. "Frozen stiff. Happens a lot this time of year."

"Look," Elena said. "I don't want to sound callous, but how long is this going to take?" She had no intention of emulating the driver of the Lada.

The customs officer shrugged. "We're moving as fast as we can, but the road's blocked just beyond the customs. They're trying to clear it now. I suggest you go back to your vehicle."

Elena rubbed her face indecisively, but there was nothing that could be done now for the driver, and the ambulance was there, anyway. Her cheeks felt red and raw, and her lips were already chapped. Ice crackled in her hair; she could see a frosty blonde fringe just above her eyes.

"All right," she said at last, and walked back along the line. She did not dare look through the icy windscreens of the other cars; she was afraid of what she might see. Atyrom stared at her as she climbed back into the Sherpa.

"Where have you been?"

Tersely, Elena explained, haunted by the memory of the frozen man's silent face and strange dead gaze.

"Well, too bad, but never mind," Atyrom said, with something that almost approached cheerfulness. "As long as it's not us, eh?"

Elena couldn't help agreeing with the general sentiment, but not with the way in which it was expressed. She mumbled something. Through the frosty windscreen, she could see the lights of the ambulance as it came back down the road. Presently, it was level with the truck in front and it was at this point that the truck driver chose to open his door and leap out. The ambulance veered clear of the door as the driver slammed on the brakes. The wheels of the ambulance spun, hammering it against the door of the Sherpa. There was a thunderous *bang*. The van shook and rattled, and Atyrom was flung sideways across Elena's lap. Gulnara screamed. Atyrom shouted with fury. Scrambling up, he wrestled with the door, punching and kicking until the damaged lock gave way and the door shot open.

Atyrom fell out of the van, still shouting. Elena hastily levered herself into the driver's seat and followed. The ambulance was trundling slowly down the road, the azure lights wobbling on top. Atyrom stumbled after it, bawling insults and curses.

"Are you drunk, asshole? Look what you've done to my van!"

As quickly as she could, Elena caught up with him. Atyrom was panting with rage. He shook off

Elena's restraining hand and bounded through the snow, taking long, floundering leaps like a hunting dog. Elena struggled after him. Catching up with the ambulance, Atyrom pulled open the door and dragged the driver out. Both men fell heavily into the snow.

"Hey!" Elena shouted. "Atyrom, stop! It was an accident. Leave him alone!"

Atyrom was not listening. He hauled the ambulance driver to his feet and shoved him against the side of the nearest vehicle. All down the line, men were coming out of their cars to join in the argument, and, to her dismay, Elena saw the dark-coated figure of the *militzia* man, heading purposefully toward them from the direction of the customs post.

"Atyrom, for God's sake!" she called. "You'll get us arrested."

Atyrom was shaking the driver, pushing him against the tarpaulin side of the truck.

"What about my *van*, you fucking bastard?"

Something fell out of the driver's pocket: something long and bright that Elena could not see clearly. Atyrom stared down at it for a startled moment, then gave a roar of rage and head-butted the driver. A thin spray of blood spattered out across the snow; the driver emitted a wail of pain.

"Grave robber!" Atyrom shouted.

Elena reached the irate Uzbek and hauled him back by the arms. The ambulance driver slumped back against the side of the truck as the policeman panted up. Elena caught a glimpse of a young, bony face beneath the *militzia* hat: one of those Ukrainian countenances, with cold eyes set too far apart. She pulled

Atyrom aside as the policeman swung the butt of an ancient Kalashnikov at the Uzbek's head.

"Don't touch me!" Atyrom shouted, ducking. "Don't you *fucking* touch me! Look! Look!"

Wrestling out of Elena's restraining grip, he pounced into the snow and thrust out a handful of dirty, glittering slush. The policeman stared.

"Look what this bastard's stolen! Watches! Money! *Teeth!*"

Appalled, Elena saw that Atyrom was right. A single golden tooth rested in the snow in his gloved palm, its root still stained pink.

"Stealing out of the mouths of the dead!" Atyrom roared.

The ambulance driver, wiping blood from his face with his sleeve, began to protest, but the policeman snarled, "Shut up!"

He swung the gun again. Elena reflexively ducked out of the way, but there was a hard, dull crack as the butt of the gun connected with the side of the driver's head. The ambulance driver dropped as if poleaxed, and lay still. The policeman crouched in the snow, the pale eyes glaring up at Atyrom.

"Well, what do you say, then?" he remarked quite calmly. "Half for you, half for me?"

Atyrom, evidently mollified, shrugged. "*Ladna.* Why not?"

Elena watched in horrified silence as the policeman began to pick through the driver's pockets and placed a motley collection of objects into Atyrom's waiting hands.

"What about him?" she said angrily, pointing to the driver, but no one seemed to hear. Elena knelt down in the snow and examined the man's head. The blood was already congealing, glazing like red frost across the driver's skin. Was he dead? Elena groped inside the man's sleeve. The skin felt cold and clammy. She could not feel a pulse. There was a shout from somewhere up the front of the line.

"Hey! We're moving!"

Atyrom hauled himself to his feet and began to hurry back in the direction of the Sherpa.

"Well, are you coming or what?" he said over his shoulder.

Elena pointed down at the ambulance driver. "What about him?"

"Leave him," the policeman said. He spat into the snow. "Filth."

"No! We can't just leave him," Elena said. "I think he's dead. And if he isn't, he soon will be in this temperature. And what about the ambulance?"

Atyrom looked momentarily puzzled. "So? If he's dead, there's nothing we can do about it. Are you coming or not? If not, I'll leave you behind."

Elena, rehearsing a dozen arguments, got to her feet, but as she rose she noticed something embedded in the snow, not far from the fallen driver. She bent to look more closely, and saw a small black sphere. Reaching down, she plucked it out of its icy bed. The sphere was around the size of a golf ball and looked as frail as a sugar shell, yet it was unaccountably heavy. Its matte surface seemed to swallow light. It must have fallen from the ambulance driver's pockets, along with the rest of his loot.

She remembered the dead man in the car at the head of the line: that dark, impenetrable gaze. Had the driver stolen it from that man, or from someone else? There was no way now of finding out.

Bewildered, Elena put the thing in her pocket. It weighed down her coat; she could feel it dragging at the material as she hurried back to the Sherpa, but by the time she reached the vehicle she had forgotten all about it. With the light of battle in her eyes, she climbed back into the damaged van and began to tell Atyrom precisely what she thought of him.

The argument, with Gulnara echoing Elena's every pronouncement, lasted all the way down the long road to Tashkent.

Two

Beyond the open door of the apartment block, the snow breathed a winter cold and lessened the ammonia reek of the stairwell so that Ilya Muromyets could smell his own blood. The hot, meaty odor filled the air as if the whole world were bleeding, rather than just one man. Ilya's hand fumbled to his side; his shirt was sticky and stiff. He remembered, distantly, that the dealer had knifed him. The situation, so carefully engineered, had gone disastrously wrong.

Think, he whispered to himself. *You were a bogatyr, a hero, a Son of the Sun . . . think.* Then the soft clutch of heroin took him, shutting him off from both understanding and pain. Ilya could no longer see clearly, but he could still hear. A confused blur of sound rushed around him: snatches of conversation across the city; the gulls crying over Sakhalin, thousands of miles away; a door shutting in icy Riga with a sudden decisive *thud*. All of these sounds became distilled as Ilya listened, resolving into the steady seep of his blood onto the concrete floor.

Ilya Muromyets' mouth curled in a rictus grin. The

glittering winter light glared through the door of the hallway, sharpening the shadows within. He had to get outside, bolt for what passed as home before the *rusalki* found him, but his feet moved down the stairs with a slowness that suddenly struck him as comical. He leaned back against the wall and shook with mirth, the breath whistling through his punctured lung like a ghost's laugh. He realized then that someone was watching him. He turned with a start, but it was only an old woman, clutching a bag of withered apples and gaping at him in undisguised horror. He wondered what she saw: a gaunt man with pale hair and paler eyes, like a wounded wolf.

Ilya's laughter wheezed dry. He wiped the blood from his mouth and murmured, "Oh . . . Good day, *gaspodhara*. Been shopping?"

The old woman edged past him and fled up the stairs. The slam of her steel door echoed through the stairwell. The noise stirred Ilya into motion and he staggered down the stairs and out into the winter afternoon.

He wondered why he was even considering flight. *I don't have a chance,* Ilya thought, as the sweet haze of the drug started to wear thin and reality, as cold as the day, began to intrude. He had never been able to escape the *rusalki*. His side was beginning to hurt now. His lungs burned and he could see his own fractured breath spilling out into the air.

Clutching his side, Ilya tried to run, but he managed only a few paces before the pain brought him onto his knees in the snow. The world grew dark, then bright again. Ilya began to pant in panic. He looked around. Across the street, sheltered by the wall, stood a man. His gloved hands were folded in front of him; his face was broad and pale beneath a furred hat. His eyes were black, without visible whites, and they glistened like frost in the pasty folds of his face.

"Help me," Ilya Muromyets tried to say, but the words were a whisper. The snow was searing his hands. He struggled to rise, but out on the Neva the ice splintered like breaking glass. Ilya looked up and saw that it was already too late.

A *rusalka* was rising from the river. Numbly, Ilya watched as she slid over the bank of the Neva and started to comb the ice from her hair with bone-thin fingers. He thought for a moment that she might not have seen him. But his heartbeat was slowing in the impossible cold, echoing through the winter world like a bell, and when he raised his hand to touch his injured side, the blood crackled beneath his fingers. It made almost no sound at all, but the *rusalka* heard it and her head went up like a hound's. Beneath the glistening frost of her hair, her eyes were the color of water, but then, suddenly, he was seeing through the illusion. He saw a small, pinched face beneath a fluttering flap of skin. Her hands were curled and clawed. She looked nothing like a human woman, but Ilya had learned long ago that the *rusalki* maintained a glamour to hide their true appearance.

The *rusalka* glanced from side to side with exaggerated slowness; she was playing with him. *They hear everything,* Ilya thought in despair. *If a single feather drifted down to the snow, she would hear it. She is like me.* Slowly, the *rusalka* smiled with a mouth full of needles.

"No, no," Ilya heard himself whisper, over and over again, but the *rusalka* rose like a disjointed puppet and stalked toward him. Blood filled his mouth with a rush, and he spat into the snow. The *rusalka*, murmuring, crouched beside him on backwards-bent knees and lifted up his chin so that he could look into her face.

It was the last thing he wanted to do. He could see through the *rusalka*'s eyes: all the way to the back of the north wind; all the way to the end of the world. The *rusalka* bent her head so that the cold curtain of her hair fell across his face, and kissed him, freezing the blood on his lips and breathing arctic air into his mouth. He could feel the thin spine of her split tongue, traveling down his throat, scouring it clean of blood and sealing the vent in the wall of his chest.

His lungs gave a convulsive heave. He knelt, gasping. The *rusalka* scooped up a handful of bloody snow and tasted it as though it were ice cream. A curious expression, of mingled greed and regret, crossed her face and then she sidled away, her image drawing the sunlight into itself until she was no more than a vivid shadow against the snow, and then she was gone.

Ilya raised his head and cried aloud, because she had healed him and he would live, and this was the last thing he wanted to do.

Some time after the *rusalka* had vanished, Ilya rose and brushed the snow from his frozen hands. When he looked across to the apartments, he saw that the stranger had gone. Uneasily, Ilya drew his coat closer about him and began to wander along the Neva, beside the eroded concrete fortresses of the tower blocks. A storm was whistling up out of the north. Ilya could hear the wind singing deep in the forests around the Beloye More, beyond the Arctic Circle. Patiently, he walked on, waiting for the storm to break. He felt as light and empty as air.

The last time he had been so close to death had been ten years ago, up in the Altai, and that had been the last time, too, that he had seen a *rusalka*. He had been shot during a deliberately clumsy and obvious escape from an internment camp, and he really thought, then, he had been successful in trying to die. His enemies, however, were eternally vigilant. He had watched with his dying sight as the *rusalka* slipped down out of the trees to whisper healing into his mouth, her fingers water-soft against his skin, and a new moon rising through the bones of the birches. He had pleaded with her to have pity, but she had only smiled a cold, drowned smile and made him live.

Since then the world had changed and Ilya had lost his way within it. He did not understand these new times: a day when there were no more heroes, but only the will of ordinary people. He had made and lost a fortune. If he wanted money these days, he had to work for it on the building sites or scaffolds of the city. It seemed to him that all heroes came to dust or blood or this half-life of his: enduring, like radiation. Yet he still could not resist taking advantage of the advances of this scientific age: medicine to ease sickness, drugs to ease the soul. He would have to seek out another dealer soon, to seek heroin this time, rather than a further futile attempt at death. He would go to find one of the runners who hung around Centralniye Station, and perhaps for a while he could continue pretending that he was nothing more than another casualty of the late twentieth century and not the last of the *bogatyri*.

There were no heroes anymore. Men born in the twelfth century were not supposed to see the dawn of the twenty-first. Nor were there supposed to be supernatural creatures that fed off love and blood, though sometimes Ilya watched the fanciful programs on the television and wondered whether such ideas might be gaining in strength, whether there might be a clue in this now long-standing rationalism to his own plight. Genetic modification or black magic? Behind their glamour, it sometimes seemed to him, the *rusalki* did not look so very unlike the small grey aliens that had become so popular nowadays. If one was to believe the TV, everyone in America seemed to be seeing them, and the thought made Ilya shudder.

He walked on through St. Petersburg, up the wide channel of Nogorny Prospekt. He could hear the storm now, sweeping down from the north, veering out over the Gulf of Finland. He stood still, listening with unnatural acuteness as the first wave of the storm drenched the city in a veil of ice. Thunder rolled overhead, cracking the frozen Neva with a sound like gunfire. Ilya stood quite still and let the storm break around him. Its passing left him deafened and cold, but still unmercifully alive. Doubtless it had been a warning from the forest's drowned witch-children, and when it was over Ilya sighed, then began trudging up toward the station.

The aftermath of the storm had left the city silent and deserted. The skies cleared to a pale haze and Ilya could see a crimson smear of sun far away to the west. *Time to get off the streets,* he thought. *Time to get drunk.*

There was a bar off Nogorny Prospekt that he sometimes frequented. Entering its dark environs, Ilya ordered a double vodka and felt it warm him all the way down to his heart. He put his hand inside his damp clothes, feeling furtively for the wound, but there was nothing. The storm had almost washed his clothes clean of blood. The *rusalki* were fastidious; they did not like to see the signs of a life lived hard.

Ilya drank in silence, for he had learned long ago to seal his tongue against the secrets that might otherwise be spilled. The bar was crowded. He thought, once, that he glimpsed the pasty-faced, black-eyed stranger who had been watching him by the river, but when he looked more closely, no one was there.

He stayed in the bar until midnight, drinking hard, until the memory of who and what he had been had become numbed, and he could stumble back to his meager rooms, to sleep and dream.

Three

Atyrom pawned the teeth as soon as they reached Tashkent, but by this time both Elena and Gulnara were too weary and disgusted to make further protests. They watched as Atyrom carefully counted his bounty out onto the pawnbroker's table. The teeth glittered as they fell, like the mockery of a smile. Atyrom glanced sourly at Elena and his sister, clearly expecting another barrage of criticism, but Elena, at least, had already decided that she had said everything she was going to say.

"It'll pay for the damage to the van," Atyrom said for the twentieth time, as though reasoning with children. Gulnara muttered something sour and looked away. Elena thrust her hands farther into the pockets of her overcoat and tucked her chin into her collar, though the room was stuffy in contrast to the bitter cold outside. The pawnbroker's office smelled of paraffin and despair, making Elena wrinkle her nose. Inside her pocket, her fingers curled around the small, hard sphere. It felt hot and smooth and Elena tucked it into her palm until her hand grew comfortingly warm. The thing seemed to beat with a pulse of its own, or perhaps it was only echoing her own agitated heart.

She had no reason to feel guilty, Elena told herself again. Atyrom had acted before either Elena or his sister had been able to stop him; it was not their fault. Then the pawnbroker gave a voracious grin at the sight of a fake Rolex watch and Elena's guilt flooded back, hot and fresh as blood across the snow.

Atyrom had emptied his pockets now and had begun an earnest conversation with the pawnbroker. They were speaking Uzbek, which Elena was unable to follow. A woman wearing a *shalwar kameez* came in with a tray and three little glasses of sweet tea, then disappeared. Elena stared around the room, noting the detritus of lives: old shoes gathering dust, the entrails of a radio scattered across a crumpled newspaper. She tilted her head to read the headline:

UZBEKISTAN REGAINS GLORY!

it read in Russian, with a pride that was now old, and wholly misplaced.

Elena's hand left the sphere and stole beneath her coat to the inner pocket where she still kept her Party card. She fingered the square of laminated plastic, thinking with a familiar, distant astonishment of the events that had brought her here to a pawnbroker's back room. She'd studied philosophy at university, along with astrophysics, and a memory of the *rektor* flashed briefly before her mind's eye: face flushed with enthusiasm before a blackboard, as he explained the differences between the Aristotelian notions of primary and efficient cause.

Elena allowed herself a brief, wry smile. The efficient cause of her presence here was a simple need for money—the only reason to accompany her friend Gulnara and a man she didn't like, a thousand kilometers south before the end of winter, with a vanload full of black-market clothes from the Emirates and a handful of Western videos. She was hoping for a hundred dollars: enough to pay the rent for another month and put the bulk of it into the box under the mattress.

Every *tenge* they could spare went into that box: Anna's waitressing wages, Elena's cleaning money, their mother's pension, and the results of occasional forays such as this one. The fund was growing too slowly, but if they were careful and no disasters such as illness occurred, they should have enough by the spring. The familiar thoughts crowded into her head. *And then we're out of here. Moscow first, and then Canada. Yuri told me it was crazy. What chance will I have of ever working in a space program again if I leave the country? But what's left for me here? I'd rather wait tables in Montreal than pine for an opportunity that might never come.*

Money was a good enough reason to do anything these days, Elena thought, then corrected herself as she watched Atyrom haggle with the pawnbroker. *But not good enough to trade tragedy for a few miserable dollars.* She wondered briefly how much the gold would fetch, and how a person would extract it from the teeth in the first place. Meditating on Aristotle seemed preferable.

So what was the primary cause of her present circumstances? Mikhail Gorbachev deciding years ago to drop his trousers and bend over in the direction of America? Mikhail Gorbachev being born? Elena felt, deep within her bones, that the architect of *Perestroika* was the single reason why she was here now, sipping treacly tea in a dingy room in the back streets of Tashkent, when she should have been sitting in her office at Baikonur, watching rockets reach the bright skies above the Soviet Union. She should have been what she had trained to be: an astrophysicist. Or something other than a dealer in black-market goods. At least Atyrom's videos weren't pornographic. It wasn't hard to see the funny side to the whole thing, but then, she'd always had a black sense of humor; she was Russian, after all.

At last, the pawnbroker passed over a handful of greasy dollars with a great show of reluctance, and they were shown out into the fierce white light of the afternoon. The apartment blocks of modern Tashkent were rendered into inoffensive minimalism by the snow: raw angles softened, grey concrete dimmed to the colors of a pigeon's wing. Through the bare branches of the park, the bronze figure of Tamerlane was partially visible astride a prancing horse, his mouth open in a cry of defiance against the centuries. Snow capped his pointed helmet; he resembled a savage Saint Nicholas. Elena looked up at the statue with something approaching dread, remembering old childhood threats.

Tamerlane will come for you if you don't behave.

The greatest khan of Central Asia: a ruthless, relentless fourteenth-century killing machine, riding at the head of his hordes. He had scourged the land from Baghdad to Moscow. *If anyone summed up the nature of the region—its harshness, its power—that person would be Tamerlane,* Elena thought. He was buried now in Samarkand, not so far from Tashkent. She turned away.

"Come on," Atyrom said. "Let's celebrate, eh?" The

money had restored his brutal good humor; he hugged Elena and his sister around the shoulders. Elena's diatribe at the border had, it seemed, been forgotten or forgiven. "I'll call my cousin."

Elena and Gulnara shivered outside a nearby *chaikhana* while Atyrom phoned. He seemed to be having trouble getting through. At one point, Elena could see him banging the receiver against the wall. The telephone system was a mess. Even on a good day, half of Tashkent couldn't talk to the other half.

Elena gazed around her. At a cursory glance, Tashkent looked exactly like her hometown of Almaty: the same wide streets, the same monolithically identical apartment blocks. But Tashkent, too, was changing, rising out of the ashes of the Soviet legacy as an Islamic republic. Not quite a phoenix, more like some ravaged old vulture. Elena gave a sudden shiver. The *madrasas* were reopening; Tamerlane replaced Lenin on pedestals throughout the city. The Russians had been leaving these southern capitals in droves during the last years of the twentieth century. *Perhaps they were right,* Elena thought. *Perhaps we don't belong here anymore.*

Her own sister had been talking about going back to Russia, staring theatrically out of the window like a Chekhovian heroine. "What do you mean, *back*?" Elena had asked, bewildered. "You were born here. Your grandmother was born here. This is where we're *from.*"

Now she watched as a bearded seminary student, a Koran tucked beneath his arm, picked his way carefully through the snow. *Maybe we had no right to be here in the first place.* But Elena didn't feel like a colonist, somehow. She'd only been to Moscow twice, and then only for university conferences. Russia itself was even more of a mess, and there would still be snow all winter. Canada, that was the answer. Just as cold, but thirty times as wealthy. She sighed, wondering whether Atyrom was ever going to stop talking. At last he came away from the phone.

"That's that, then. I've called my cousin; we'll go round now."

They made their slow progress back to the Sherpa. Atyrom's face grew sour as they approached; the dent made by the ambulance was very large, and very obvious.

"Never mind," Elena echoed wearily, with just a hint of irony. "The money you made from the teeth will pay for it."

"Yes, that was lucky, wasn't it?" Atyrom said, brightening. Gulnara snorted. The engine coughed in the cold air. Atyrom drove erratically, avoiding the potholes that occasionally gaped through the slush. Elena gazed out at the passing vista of Tashkent. They drove through the jumble of buildings that constituted the old town, then out past the blue plastic dome of the market. Clearly, the market was supposed to harken back to the glorious Uzbek heritage and the azure domes of Samarkand, but it looked more as though a flying saucer had landed. She thought again of Tamerlane, buried in Samarkand beneath his black jade tomb at the fabled heart of Central Asia, and felt strangely cold. Some distance past the market, Atyrom turned into a narrow side street and parked outside a corrugated iron wall.

"Our cousin's place."

Elena quickly lost track of the number of people

who seemed to be living in the house, and she never quite managed to grasp who was married to whom. There seemed to be an inordinate number of children. She drank tea, sitting on cushions around the low table, then thick syrupy brandy from the Caucasus, then more tea. The room filled with cigarette smoke. Someone stoked up the stove. Bottles of wine appeared, then food. A phrase coined by a visiting American astronomer swam into Elena's mind: *trial by hospitality.*

Rising with difficulty, she excused herself and went out into the backyard, where she stood taking deep breaths of arctic air until she started to cough. At the end of the yard stood an outhouse, and she took refuge in it, crouching by the drain in the chilly dark and listening to the sudden, unnerving silence.

The black ball was still weighing down the pocket of her coat. Elena opened the door a crack so that she could see, then examined the ball. It seemed quite solid. Experimentally, she let it drop. It did not bounce, but dropped to the concrete floor of the outhouse with a resounding *thud* and lay still. Elena picked it up and saw with alarm that a crack had appeared in the concrete. The delicate, curved surface of the sphere was unmarked, but the thing felt warmer, as if energized by its momentary flight. Elena could make no sense of it. She hoped the warmth and the heaviness were not indicators of something sinister, something radioactive. But the sphere was too smooth to be a fragment of waste, too much as though it had been made, and she could think of no analogous component of a nuclear system.

Returning it to her pocket, she went back into the chaos of the house.

———————

The next morning, Elena awoke with a head like a block of wood and a mouth that tasted as though mice had been nesting in it. She blinked, trying to work out where she was. A damp-mottled square of ceiling was illuminated by the brightness of snowlight, but the room was stiflingly hot. She could smell woodsmoke, the burnt, meaty odor of mutton shashlik, and stale wine. Craning her head, she looked down. A half-empty glass rested on the floor, inches from her face. Elena closed her eyes in fleeting pain. Across the room, two bodies stretched like beached whales beneath faded counterpanes: Gulnara and someone else, probably a cousin.

Cautiously, Elena sat up. Her head pounded with the rhythmic tempo of a thunderstorm. She winced as someone pulled aside the curtain that hid the entrance and light flooded in. One of Atyrom's relations entered: a girl, wearing a long *shalwar kameez* and carrying a tea tray. Elena greeted her with relief. She cupped the glass that the girl handed her and took a sip of strong, sweet tea.

"You've saved my life."

The girl smiled and bobbed her head. "There's more if you want it. From the look of you, you'll need it," she added tartly.

Half an hour later, fueled by tea and bread, Elena had reached a state that almost approached normality; only a nagging headache remained. Passing the open door of the adjoining room, she saw that Atyrom had also woken up, and now sat on the edge of the bed in his thermals, rubbing his head with his hands. He was back to his usual grumpy self, Elena was pleased to see. Atyrom drunk and cheerful (and singing) was a spectacle that she preferred to forget.

"Morning," Elena said. "Someone phoned for you, apparently. Left a message. I think it's about the clothes and the videos."

Atyrom grunted. "About time. I tried calling my friend for half of last night, but he wasn't in, the bastard. Never mind. Did he say when he was coming?"

"He said something about ten o'clock," Elena said, adding with a piousness not her own, "Imsh'Allah."

"Imsh'Allah," Atyrom echoed. He scratched moodily at one ankle, then began pulling on his socks. "Let me do the talking, all right? I know you brought the clothes, but I've done this before. I know about this sort of thing; I know what my friend's like. He won't want a woman butting in."

"All right," Elena said patiently, knowing better than to argue. This was Atyrom's home territory, after all. Anyway, she needed to buy cigarettes. "I'm going to find a kiosk," she said. "I won't be long."

"All right. I'll see you later."

Elena retrieved her coat from the back of the door and stepped outside. It was a beautiful day. The high, pale heavens reflected the snow, shimmering into a fierce blue at the summit of the sky. A starling rocketed across the street and into a tree, sending a shower of icicles from the branches. The day after tomorrow would be March first, Elena remembered—almost spring. She stuck her hands into her pockets and her gloved fingers met something hard. She pulled out the little ball, turning it over in her fingers. After a moment she wrapped it in a handkerchief and put it into her handbag, then went in search of a kiosk.

The place opposite the house was shut. Elena walked along the street, passing rows of faceless apartments, but it was good to get out into the fresh air after the stuffiness of the house. At last, she came to an entrance to the Tashkent subway. Down in the underpass, she knew, there would be all manner of makeshift stalls. She walked past a woman selling flowers, then a Tajik family with a pitiful array of objects: radio parts, a single shoe. They stared at her with hopeless faces. She slipped a muddle of notes into the wife's hand. They bowed their heads, blessed her over and over again. She felt momentarily as hopeless as they.

Farther down the underpass, a youth in a leather jacket was off-loading packets of black-market cigarettes. Elena bought enough Polyot for the journey home, wishing she could afford a better brand. Everyone seemed to be smoking black-market Marlboros now. With U.S. troops still stationed throughout the region, there were plenty to go round. Still, black market or not, they cost too much.

As she was handing over the money, she glanced up and noticed the name of the metro station. With no small irony, she had chosen Kosmonavtov in which to buy her cigarettes. Tucking the packets into her pocket, Elena went into the station for a look. She had been here once before.

There they all were: row upon row of cosmonauts, their faces ceramically delineated along the gleaming, indigo length of the platform, beaming from the depths of their helmets. Elena made her way to the end of the platform and stood, staring up at the image of her heroine. Valentina Tereshkova, the first woman to fly in space, gazed down the tunnel in the direction of disappearing trains. Her round face was smiling, as though she had glimpsed secrets, and the artist had painted a row of daisies around the lower edge of her helmet in a whimsically feminine touch.

Elena found herself smiling back at Tereshkova. She looked at the image for a long time, imagining that the immaculate marble confines of the metro were really part of some glowing future; that she would step outside to find Tashkent transformed, monorails sweeping across the streets, silver towers striking toward the heavens, and herself heading off for an assignment on the moon.

Yet that dream of a glorious future was already old-fashioned, she realized, more suited to the society of fifty years ago than that of today. Now, all Russians seemed to dream about was getting out, of getting rich. Without ever leaving home, she was no longer living in the same world. Reluctantly, she walked back along the platform and up into the snowy street. It had clouded over; an anvil mass threatened more snow. Elena hastened to the house.

Four hours later, with the Sherpa unloaded and two hundred dollars in their pockets, Elena, Gulnara, and Atyrom headed out of Tashkent. Elena was relieved, and not just because of the money. They were heading home. It was now four in the afternoon, nearly dark. Atyrom had taken a different route—north through Dzhambyl—and the heavy traffic had worn the snow away to a glaze over the uneven surface of the road. Mountains fell away on either side, snow-capped crags reaching up into a darkening sky. Elena watched a thin rind of sun sink down behind the line of the mountains, and then they began to descend toward the border and yet another traffic jam. This time, it was even longer. The traffic crawled forward.

"What's going on this time?" Atyrom muttered to himself. He wound down the window and peered out. "Looks like they're searching the vehicles."

"Who are? The customs people?"

"I don't think so," Atyrom said with uncharacteristic uncertainty. "Men in coats."

"What?" Elena craned past him, trying to see. The security forces almost invariably wore black, which was helpful if you wanted to know who was beating you up.

"Not KGB, then," Atyrom added. "They're not in uniform."

"Maybe they've changed their clothes along with their name," Elena murmured. "After all, they're supposed to be the good guys now." Which was true enough, she reflected, if you compared them with the *Mafiya* or Islamic fundamentalists.

Atyrom shifted uneasily in his seat. "Good thing this wasn't on the way to Tashkent."

Elena looked at him. "And why not?"

"Well . . . those spare parts I got hold of, the ones I sold along with the videos . . ."

"What about them?"

"I'm not sure where some of them came from, that's all."

"You told me they were all seconds from the factory."

"Well, yes. Most of them were."

Elena sighed. She couldn't bring herself to feign surprise.

"Good thing this didn't happen on the way to Tashkent, then," she echoed. She wondered uneasily about the penalty for handling stolen goods, and also about other possibilities. She remembered the ambulance driver, robbing the pockets of the dead: It was by no means an unusual situation among the authorities. She slipped the envelope containing her share of the money out of her handbag and tucked it deep under the seat. After a moment's thought, she slid the ball after it.

One of the men was beckoning them forward. Atyrom started up the Sherpa and they rolled along the road. When they were level with the little crew, a man leaned in through the window and said, "Open the back, please." It was a clipped, official voice, the kind that didn't even expect *nyet* for an answer, and she could not place the accent.

"What are you looking for?" Elena asked, smiling as charmingly as she could.

"Just open the back of the van, please."

Atyrom shrugged. "It's empty," he told the man, but he got out of the Sherpa and complied. Elena squinted into the driving mirror, trying to see what they were doing. The search took some time, and seemed exhaustive. They had some kind of device. She heard one of the men say, "Are you sure the scanner's working properly? We're on the other side of the border. . . ."

His companion answered, "I told you. The thing

will be difficult to detect if it hasn't been activated. But we have to try."

Elena frowned. The man came back.

"Get out of the van."

"Why? It's freezing out there."

The man jerked his head. "Just get out of the van."

Sighing, Elena got down and found herself spread-eagled against the side of the Sherpa, beside Atyrom and Gulnara. She braced herself. Her pockets were swiftly rifled. The men were looking in the front of the van; she saw one of them run a hand beneath the seats and held her breath. A voice in her ear said, "All right. You can go."

Atyrom was already impatiently holding open the door of the van. "Come on. Hurry up."

"What in the world was that all about?" Gulnara asked as they climbed into the cabin.

"I've no idea. Who cares? *Militzia.* They had some sort of scanner. They're probably looking for drugs."

"I don't think they're the police," Elena said doubt-fully. She put her hand under the seat, but to her relief, the money and the object were still there.

Atyrom shrugged and pulled away. They came level with the customs post. Elena groped in her bag for her passport, waved it at the official, and they were once more back in Kazakhstan.

"We'll press on, yes?" Atyrom said. "We can make Almaty by midnight. I'll stop in Dzhambyl and pick up some food."

"Fine with me," Elena said. She leaned back against the headrest. She felt tired and hot, though the cabin was only just beginning to warm up again. She could see her breath steaming against the glass, forming patterns as it faded. It was an effort to keep her eyes open and eventually she gave up the struggle. She began to doze, waking fitfully as Atyrom flicked through the radio stations. A white mushroom dome appeared out of the sleety darkness. Other yurts lay beyond it. Atyrom pulled off the road.

"Shashlik?"

"Please."

She watched as Atyrom stumped through the snow toward the yurts and conducted a transaction beneath the hazy lights. Soon he was back, and handed round kebabs with chili sauce. The portions were generous, but the mutton was as tough as leather. She only managed a few mouthfuls, then gave up.

"What's the matter?" Atyrom asked, frowning. "It's not good?"

"It's like eating an old boot."

"You've been eating like a bird," Atyrom scolded. "Soon you'll forget how, and then where will you be? You're already as thin as a crack. You ought to get married, have a husband to cook for. Doesn't your mama feed you and that little sister of yours?"

Her mother and Anna. Suddenly, Elena was very glad to be almost home, even though she'd only been away for three days. She smiled and said, "Yes. Yes, she does. She's a great cook."

They reached the outskirts of Almaty shortly after midnight, passing the quiet little dachas and the railway station, then the maze of dark streets. Despite promises that were now over two decades old, the Soviet luxury of street lighting had never been restored. Atyrom dropped Elena off at the corner of Ablai Khan and Mamedova Street, and with a wave was gone.

Elena turned and walked slowly down Mamedova, past the huge vent of the metro that had still never been built, past the cafe at its foot and the silent Korean nightclub, and into the courtyard of the apartment block that had been her home for over two years now. Snow covered the scrubby trees and the rusty children's swings; a single light shone out across the courtyard. Elena looked up. It was coming from her mother's flat, where the box was waiting beneath the bed.

She walked up the silent stairwell and unlocked the familiar steel door. *Moscow, then Canada. Anywhere but here.*

Four

When Ilya reached his tiny apartment, he sank down onto the iron-springed bed and reached beneath it for the sword. He sat with it resting across his knees and looked at it for a long moment: at the curve of the hilt, the gleam of the blade, waiting for memory to creep over him. He remembered the nights on the Siberian taiga, filled with small sounds: pine resin snapping in the summer sun, the rustle of dragonflies' wings as they swarmed up from the lake, the precise march of ants in the grass, and, beyond all these, the endless, ageless silence of the world.

Now his ears were filled with new sounds: the hiss and crackle of static, the grinding roar of traffic. If he listened hard enough, he could still differentiate, hearing the rumble of an army truck in Vladivostok, thousands of kilometers away, or a sudden, startling snatch of song in Murmansk, laden with cold and bell-clear through the frosty air. Ilya put his hands over his ears and sank deeper into remembering.

He was standing among the Siberian pines of his childhood, on the edges of the lake. It was long before the Soviet Union, long before the rule of the tsars. To the east stretched the long spine of the mountains, rosy with the last of the winter sun. As he watched, the light faded and the forest was folded into the dusk. Ilya crouched by the spring that fed into the lake, broke the cat-ice that had settled along its rim, and cupped his hands to drink.

The song began just beneath the edge of his hearing. At first he thought it was the voice of the forest itself, or perhaps the sound made by the stars as they flickered above the mountains. He waited, listening. The song rose and fell: high and wordless, singing of the black depths of the lake, and the starlight, and the winter air. As Ilya listened, it changed, sliding into warmth, speaking of afternoons golden with pollen and the scent of May.

He shook his head, trying to clear it, and then another sound joined the song: footsteps hastening through the long frosty grass. One of the girls from the forest villages was coming toward the lake. Her eyes were half-closed and she was smiling. She walked with sure-footed confidence. And then Ilya saw the *rusalki*.

There were three of them, perched in the branches of a pine that overhung the lake. Their long white hair was intertwined, moving as though they were still beneath the water, and their eyes were blank as ice. They looked through Ilya with indifference. Their gaze was focused on the girl. The song congealed in the twilight air, curling toward her. Ilya's sword came out of its sheath and whirled down, cutting the filaments of song in a blaze of sparks. The girl's eyes flew open and her face filled with dismay.

Ilya Muromyets stepped between the girl and the *rusalki*. Two of the beings shrank back against the tree, but the third swarmed down it headfirst, her hair floating out into the grass. She sidled out of reach of Ilya's sword and hissed. He saw pointed teeth, and between them, the grey tip of her tongue. Over his shoulder, Ilya shouted, "Run!"

After a frozen moment, the girl did so. He could hear her panicked flight as she stumbled back through the forest. Her escape seemed to bring the *rusalki* to life. The sisters in the tree dived, gliding slowly through the air and ice, to be swallowed by the lake. The third *rusalka* smiled.

"Put up your sword, Ilya Muromyets," she murmured. Ilya flinched at the mention of his name, and the *rusalka*'s smile widened. "Oh," she whispered. "Who hasn't heard of you? One of the *bogatyri*, the Sons of the Sun, the heroes of all Russia . . ."

Ilya's ears were filled with a noise like the humming of bees, as though he had put his cheek to a hive. Slowly, he let the tip of the sword fall. He could have sworn that the *rusalka* did not move, but suddenly she was standing in front of him, her hands slipping around his neck. Her wet hair brushed his face.

"Do you know what it's like to drown, Ilya Muromyets? It's the greatest pleasure of all—the warmth of water in your mouth. But we have other plans for you than drowning. Listen to what I have to tell you. . . ."

He did not wait to hear it. The ice snapped under his boots as he flung himself away from her. His sword came up to sever the *rusalka*'s throat and then her spine, which broke like rotten wood. The head flew in a great curve across the lake, scattering drops of mercurial blood, and the *rusalka*'s body shattered into slimy ice. Ilya fell to his knees, letting the heat from the sword warm him. He waited for a moment longer, but the lake was still.

Slowly, he made his way back through the forest, stopping at the village to warn the priest of the *rusalki*'s presence, and receiving the grateful thanks of the girl's family. And that, Ilya Muromyets had thought in the manner of heroes, was that.

———

Ilya looked down at the sword for a long time, remembering. So long ago that it seemed like the dream of a different man: a man who believed in God and the Zorya, a man who slew demons in the forests of old Russia. He glanced up at his reflection in the shaving mirror, at the bloodstained shirt beneath the long leather coat. In the snowlight, he looked as insubstantial as a ghost.

He placed the sword back into its sheath, lit a cigarette, and, still in his coat, went to the stove. He stood there for a moment, warming his hands. He cut a piece of bread from the loaf on the table and ate it, staring out of the window at the lights along the Neva before reaching for the vodka.

Five

It was Elena's sister, Anna, who once again suggested leaving for Moscow, one Saturday, a week after Elena had returned from Tashkent. They had just gotten off the Medeo bus and were standing outside the ice rink: Elena, Anna, and their mother. Down in the city, the air was filled with the haze of unfiltered petrol, but here on the edge of the mountains there was a cold breeze blowing, smoky with the barbecued odor of mutton shashlik. Looking back, Elena couldn't see Almaty at all, only a blur across the whiteness of the steppe, ending in the snowy curve of the foothills. She blinked. For a moment, looking out across that empty stretch of country, the city might never have existed.

At the bottom of the hill a wedding party came into view, the bride hoisting the skirts of her white Western-style dress and toiling up the road to the cafe. The sight made Elena feel cold. She pulled her thick scarf more tightly around her throat.

Then, out of nowhere, Anna said, "Why don't we just go?" The words burst from her. Her family stared at her in amazement.

"Go where, Anna?" her mother asked blankly. Anna's face was red and angry, screwing back tears.

She said, "Just—just *leave*. Now. Think about Canada later and just go back to Russia. Go home. We don't belong here anymore." She turned on Elena. "All your talk of the future and the stars, and where's it got you? Cleaning the floor at Mobil Oil. There's nothing here. There never will be."

Elena could think of nothing to say. Her sister turned and began stumping angrily through the snow toward the ice rink. Her mother shrugged, turned to Elena and murmured, "Your sister's just upset. I wouldn't worry about it. At least you've got a job. At least they *pay* you. There are people who haven't had any money since Christmas." Elena looked at her doubtfully. Her mother shrugged again, then drifted off up the hill in Anna's wake.

Disregarding the cold, Elena sat down heavily on the low wall. From here, she could see the icy peaks of the mountains, as remote as the stars against the winter blue of the sky.

She had never been a political animal. Obviously, she had belonged to the Party, but that was more for the usual practical reasons rather than ideological conviction. Any government that felt obliged to call the national newspaper *Truth* must have something to hide, Elena thought. Yet, like most Russians, she was a romantic as well as a cynic. Somewhere deep inside, there was still a part of her that believed in the Soviet Union: in the ideas behind it, anyway, if not the messy, wrecked reality.

If you were a Christian, you had heaven to look forward to. Denied that, Elena believed in the future, in tomorrow. For a while, she had really thought that they were going to make it, and even after everything that had happened, she couldn't help the hope. She still carried her Party card in her handbag: a talisman against too much change. Sitting on the wall, thinking about what Anna had said, she found herself looking at the little slip of laminated cardboard as though she had never seen it before.

The wedding party had come level with her now, the girls laughing and joking while the men, uncomfortable in their best suits, walked a few paces behind. They were Kazakhs; they and their ancestors had lived here for hundreds of years, ever since Genghis and his tribesmen had swept down out of the north. Once more she thought of Tamerlane, Genghis' even more terrifying successor, and felt suddenly out of place: tall and fair and foreign. A Russian; almost a Westerner. The wedding party glanced at her as they passed, and she thought she caught the word "Round-eye."

They were all a little drunk, she thought, trying to make excuses for them, but she still felt blank and strange. A few years ago, no one would have given her a second glance, but now she had become a foreigner in her own country.

This *was* her home, wasn't it? But people weren't even sure who they were anymore. Fifteen years ago they had all been Soviet, and now . . . Sometimes it seemed to Elena that the only way to go was up and onward: into space, into the future, trying not to make the same mistakes.

The wedding party had reached the terrace of the ice rink now, and were arranging themselves for a commemorative photograph. Far ahead, Elena could see the retreating figures of her mother and sister, heading into the cafe and the warmth. There seemed nothing to do but go after them.

———————

That night, when the chatter of her mother and Anna began to grate on Elena's nerves, she stepped out onto the balcony for a cigarette. She remembered her father doing the same thing when he had bothered to come home. Occasionally, if he had not been too drunk, she had joined him. In summer, the night air had been loud with the sound of cicadas and the distant music from the cafe: Turkish pop with a heavy bass beat. Yet it felt claustrophobic, hemmed in by the trees.

Now, behind the winter-bare branches, Elena could see the snowlit switchback of the Mountains of Heaven, stretching all the way to the Chinese border, and felt that she could breathe at last.

After the trip to Tashkent, the money had gone into the box under the bed. Elena, Anna, and their mother counted it every evening over tea, in a ritual that never varied. They had almost five hundred dollars in total. Another hundred would get them to Moscow and a rented apartment for a couple of months, plus the visa fees for Canada. Elena was trying not to think about the airfares. *We'll manage,* she thought. *We'll have to.*

She had placed the ball inside the jewelry box on her chest of drawers. In odd moments, she took it out and studied it. It remained hard and unnaturally heavy, although its warmth had changed to an icy chill. It numbed her hand so much that she could not hold it for more than a few minutes.

As a scientist, she was intrigued by it. She still had no idea what the object might be, though she had spent as much time as she could afford on the Internet at the library, searching for possibilities. She had called around to former contacts, seeking information, but no one had any plausible ideas. The object did not look like anything technological, or any kind of component, yet it seemed to have physical effects. Occasionally, she wondered whether she was simply imagining its weight and coldness, but these qualities seemed too definite, too apparent.

She had even gone to the museum, wondering whether it might be some ancient artifact, but it resembled none of the meager Kazakh relics behind their glass cases. Then, gradually, she forgot about it, and left it alone in its box.

Lighting a cigarette, Elena looked up toward the stars, picking out traces of the winter constellations. There was another faint light shining through the haze, traveling slowly across the sky. Elena watched it pass. She had helped to put a light like that up there once, years ago, when there had still been a Soviet Union. But that light had been Mir, now long since gone to a watery grave, and this was the new ISS, funded by the Americans and the occasional space tourist.

Mir had been the biggest project Elena had ever been involved in, a thing of which she had once been proud, but it had already become a grim joke. The Americans at Baikonur had talked about it in the same way that the owner of a new Mercedes might speak of a horse and cart: wonder, horror, a kind of contempt.

They had never grown used to the risks that the Russians had run; had never fully accepted that if you were prepared to put people into space, then the likelihood was that someone on the station would eventually be killed.

They wanted to have their cake and eat it, too, Elena thought. They did not understand sacrifice. But Mir had been a Soviet project from the outset. The Russians had put it up there, and it had stayed, long past its sell-by date. That should have been worth something to the Westerners, but somehow, it was not. Elena swallowed her bitterness in a drag of her cigarette.

The new station gave her some comfort. At least the cosmodrome was still part of something, even if she no longer could be. And Yuri Golynski had been up there, too, for a time, slowly orbiting the world. Elena had written him a letter when she'd been told that she was to leave the project in the latest round of funding cuts, giving him her mother's address and telling him he'd be welcome in Kazakhstan one day. He hadn't replied; had not even phoned at Christmas. Elena wondered whether he had even received it. She had said things in that letter that were perhaps best left uncommitted to paper: nothing romantic, just dreams, reflections on a changing world, and thoughts that now embarrassed her.

Yuri had not been amenable to romance, except perhaps in bed. Their affair now seemed improbable, as though she had imagined it: the Soviet cosmonaut hero and herself, tagging along behind, grounded now forever. She thought of Valentina Tereshkova's portrait on the Tashkent Metro: a little glimpse of a future that might never now be theirs.

The cosmodrome had been a bleak place even in summer. Once you got past Leninsk and the gantries and launchpads of the cosmodrome, there was nothing for hundreds of kilometers except grass and stones and sky. But at night, it changed. Then, if you stepped outside, you could see all the way to Andromeda and beyond; galaxies uncoiling clear and distant in the vastness of an ocean of darkness, suns like sparks on the water.

Memory took her further back. When she had first arrived at the cosmodrome, winter was just ending and the steppe had been a wasteland of snow. It was twenty degrees below zero; hurrying from one office to another after dark, she happened to look up and was lost forever. Yuri had come out to look for her and he had gotten stuck as well, standing out there in the winter darkness, staring at the miracle of the stars. After that, Elena knew there was no hope for her. She fell into the sky and she still hadn't come down.

But her sister's voice still echoed in her head: *All your talk of the future and the stars, and where's it got you?* Fired in a post-Perestroika funding crisis, that was all.

From inside the apartment, she could hear her mother. "Elena? What are you doing out there in the cold? Shall we have some tea?"

But Elena stayed for a moment, watching the orbiting spark until it disappeared behind the bare and frosty trees, and then she went inside.

Six

The dream was always the same, conjured up from memories of the far past. Ilya was standing beneath a mulberry tree as the blossoms scattered down around him like snowdrift. His sword was drawn, fiery in the afternoon sun. Before him, the long line of tombs marched up the hill above the city of Samarkand: turquoise domes crowning the baked ochre brick. Somewhere, in one of the dark doorways, the dead were waiting. The dead, and the *bogatyr* named Manas.

The challenge had come the day before. Ilya was far from his own lands, down in the south of the Bukhara Khanate, searching for the stolen son of a prince. He was uneasy here, disliking the southern heat and the dust, the way men looked askance at his pale skin and eyes, the reassuring touch of their hands to the daggers that they kept beneath their robes. But he had promised to find the boy, and it was not a promise he was prepared to break.

Ilya's first meeting with Manas had been on the previous evening, as he sat sipping mint tea in the middle of the caravanserai. It had been an ordinary enough scene: a throng of traders jostling with camels and horses, the veiled women weaving their way through the melee like ghosts. Ilya heard a hundred different tongues: Arabic, Farsi, Pashto, Kyrgyz, Kazakh, and the Turkic speech of Western China. He was assailed by the odors of dung and dust, blood and resin, opium and ash and charred meat. The towering walls and turrets of the *madrasas* loomed above his head, gold sparking in the firelight, the blue domes darkened to indigo. He was concentrating on the conversations around him, listening for a hint of the missing prince, when a hand fell upon his shoulder.

"You."

"Yes?" Ilya looked up. He saw a young man, dressed in the manner of the Kyrgyz people in a belted tunic and boots. His eyes were as black as a raven's, tinged with crimson in the light of the traders' fires. He had an arrogant arched nose, a mountain face: all sweeping angles, with a flamboyant moustache.

"You are like me."

"I am?" Ilya could see few similarities, but the stranger was grinning.

"A hero—a *bogatyr*, in your tongue. Not much of one, perhaps—it's clear that you're a Northerner—but a Son of the Sun, nonetheless. What's your name?"

"I am Ilya Muromyets."

The stranger gave a harsh crow of delight. "Why, I've heard of you! Better and better. Where's your flying horse?"

Ilya sighed. "I left him at home."

"And I am Manas, of Kyrgyzia. You've heard of me, of course." It was not a question.

"I may have come across some mention, here and there," Ilya replied as dryly as he could, because Manas was, after all, a legend in the South. It was always possible, however, that this man was not Manas, since there were all manner of lunatics making a living by passing themselves off as *bogatyri* and fleecing the peasants, but there was a quality to Manas' speech and figure, a kind of snapping elan, which struck a chord in Ilya.

Manas gave another shout of laughter. "Very well, then, we fight tomorrow."

"What? Why?"

"Things are so dull in these parts." Manas snorted. "This much-vaunted peace between the khanates. Timidity and decadence, more like, with warriors more interested in boys' arses than a decent battle. But now *you're* here in Samarkand. It is fitting that we should be pitted against each other. You, the hero of Russia, and I, the hero of Kyrgyzia—our lands are ancient foes, after all. We were born enemies. And isn't it said that only one *bogatyr* can kill another? What better place than Samarkand—the very heart of Asia, the place where Tamerlane himself lies buried? Russians are not welcome here. This place is sacred."

Ilya sighed. Manas was beaming, ostensibly cheerful. But there was a barbed note of warning beneath his words, and a glint in his eye that spoke of a real hate. Ancient enemies, indeed.

"All right, then," Ilya said. "Tomorrow it is. But in return, I'd be grateful for some information. . . ."

"Marvelous! I'll meet you in the Street of the Tombs, an hour before sundown."

And so now Ilya was here, underneath the falling petals of the mulberry tree, looking for a hero who would do his very best to kill him. Slowly, Ilya began to climb the stone steps that led to the Street of Tombs, sword drawn, surrounded by hot sun and shadows.

Seven

ALMATY, KAZAKHSTAN, 21ST CENTURY

The next day, Elena went to Gorky Park with Gulnara and the latter's small son. She had not seen her friend since the trip to Tashkent and she was hoping that Gulnara might talk Atyrom into another run. But it did not seem to be much of a possibility. Atyrom was leaving, Gulnara said, going to try his luck in Siberia. Uzbekistan was getting too repressive, policemen on every corner, foreign troops on the streets, and there wasn't much in Almaty. A man like Atyrom needed a bit of room to maneuver. Elena, thinking of the not-entirely-legal load that they had taken to Tashkent, was obliged to agree.

The trees had a faint tinge about them, and for the first time she could feel a breath of spring in the air. The sunlight lay thinly across the foothills of the Tien Shan, glimpsed across the ice of the boating pond. Gulnara and Elena, chatting as they walked, made their way toward the children's playground from force of habit; it had closed at the end of the previous year, due to lack of money. Then, turning the corner, Elena found herself face-to-face with a bronze figure beneath the desiccated leaves.

It was a ghost.

It was Lenin.

"So that's where he went!" Elena said. The statue had originally stood in one of the parks along Furmanova Street. Lenin's back had been turned resolutely away from the mountains; he clasped a manifesto to his chest. He had stood there ever since Elena had been a little girl, then one day she had walked down Furmanova and found that Lenin had gone. His pedestal was empty; he'd simply disappeared. It seemed ironic that he and his successors had caused so many people to vanish without a trace, and now it was happening to him.

A week later, Elena had walked back the same way and found another statue in his place: a scowling warrior on a prancing horse, with a bow in his hand. All over the city, the old faces were being spirited away and even older faces were replacing them: Tamerlane and Abai and Genghis. Elena was glad that they hadn't just thrown Lenin on the scrap heap. Through the trees, they could see other Lenins, endlessly repeated, a graveyard to Communism. Gulnara and Elena stared at them in silence, and then walked on.

The silence grew, and then Gulnara said, with a curiously diffident hostility, "It's not just Atyrom. All the Russians seem to be leaving, too. The Kazakhs don't want us anymore." She gave an angry sniff. "But we've given them everything. If it wasn't for us, they'd still be herding camels and living in yurts. Ungrateful bunch . . ."

There it was again, the lightning twist and spin

across the ethnic divide, but Elena said nothing. Revision of history and culture was the old Soviet specialty, remaking dreams to fit the grim reality rather than the other way around. Gulnara had a Kazakh mother, a Kazakh name, and Uzbek relatives, but she still thought of herself as a Soviet citizen. Whereas Elena's people, Russian colonists, had put Gulnara's ancestors to death not so long ago, and poisoned their lands with dumping grounds for radioactive waste and cosmodromes and concentration camps for Chechens. The Kazakhs had no reason to be grateful. This new phoenix republic belonged to them now, and where did the Russians fit in? Where did anyone? Her thoughts were once more running down a familiar and depressing track.

"I hear you're leaving Almaty, too," Gulnara said.

"Who told you that?"

"Your sister. I saw her in the Business Club on Friday."

Elena frowned. "What was Anna doing in the Business Club?"

"Same as everyone else. Dancing, listening to music. She introduced me to her boyfriend. He seems nice, doesn't he? For a German."

Elena said nothing. If Anna had a German boyfriend, this was the first she had heard of it. Usually she and her sister told each other everything. She wasn't going to say so in front of Gulnara, however. Stifling a twinge of betrayal, she muttered something noncommittal.

"So where are you going to go?" Gulnara asked.

"Canada," Elena said firmly. The more she talked about it, the more real it seemed.

"Have you got visas?"

"Not yet. We're going to get them in Moscow."

"I heard it was difficult to get a visa these days. Too many people wanting to get out."

"We'll manage."

"Do you have a job lined up?"

"No. But I'll find something. I'm well-qualified, and so is Anna."

"I might write to the embassy myself," Gulnara said. She looked around Gorky Park, at the derelict children's playground with its fading cartoon murals and rusted swings. Her mouth turned downward. "Look at it. Nobody cares. It's not like that in the West."

Elena felt a sudden surge of resentment that, given the dream of Canada, took her completely by surprise.

"How do you know? You've never been there. Sveta Dubrovina went to the States and didn't like it. She said no one knew who their neighbors were, and when she went into the supermarket she couldn't make up her mind what to buy; there was so much stuff that no one needed . . ."

Gulnara's mouth was open. "But *you're* planning to go there."

"I know." Elena sighed. "It's just that—I wanted something better for us *here*." *I wanted my "beloved work," as we used to say, but there's no chance of that now.*

"Oh, *here*." Gulnara grimaced. "There's nothing here. There never has been."

"That's not true. We knew where we were going, once. And then they decided to abolish the country."

"Well, I think it will be wonderful in the West,"

Gulnara said. She hesitated. "Do you think you'll get married again?"

Elena nearly said, *Why do you think I'm going?* But it was not altogether true and she did not want to sound desperate.

"I doubt it, Gulnara. I'm on the shelf already. At least I've *been* married, I suppose—better that than a *starukha*."

"Oh, Elena. No one would ever think you were an old maid. And you're only thirty-five. That's young over there. Not like here."

"It's all right for you, Gulnara. You're in the best possible position—divorced, with a child."

"You could have kids, Elena."

"Gulnara, you know I—"

"They might be able to do something. They have clinics for that sort of thing in the West." She fell silent for a moment, then went on, "Anyway, there's more chance to meet people, they say. My friend signed up with a dating agency—she's writing to a French guy already, and an American. They like Russian women over there. Not so pushy. And an American man would be a better catch than someone here. Or a German, like your sister has. They're all rich. And they wouldn't expect you to do all the housework. My friend says she knows an American man who *cooks*. Imagine that."

"Well, not with a Russian—easier to teach a bear to thread a needle. But Uzbek men cook. They're supposed to be good in bed, as well."

"Elena!"

"Well, that's what they say."

"But you wouldn't want to marry a Moslem, would

you?" Gulnara, herself Islamic, said doubtfully. "Kazakh men are hopeless."

"Russians aren't much better."

"And Westerners don't drink so much. They treat women with respect over there."

Elena sighed. "I like Russian men, though. They can't *all* be alcoholics. My English isn't great, though of course I'd try to improve it. I want to come home and have a conversation in my own language, not just sit and simper and flutter my eyelashes."

"You could make him learn Russian."

"I suppose so. I'd rather stay here. I've never really wanted to go and live abroad. But I'm not going to clean floors for the rest of my life, either."

They walked on in silence. By the time they reached the park gates, Lenin was long since lost among the trees, and Elena was wondering how much it would cost to sign on with an international dating agency.

Eight

The dream of Samarkand, of Manas, faded. Ilya raised himself on his elbows, groaning, and realized with a jolt of shock that the stranger he had seen by the river was sitting by the side of his bed.

He fumbled for the sword, but the man said with a curl of the lip, "Leave it." He twitched the heavy overcoat aside, to show Ilya the gun resting in a shoulder holster. "Anyway, you're in no condition for a fight."

Ilya stared at him. The man's face was as round as the moon; his eyes, embedded in the folds of flesh, were black and liquid. Immediately, Ilya thought: *He is a volkh, a sorcerer.* He did not know where the thought had come from.

"Who are you? How did you get in?" Ilya asked. His voice was still furred with cigarettes and vodka. To his dismay, it sounded querulous and old.

The *volkh* did not bother to reply. Instead, he said conversationally, "My name is Kovalin. I saw you yesterday afternoon. I watched you puking blood into the snow. I saw your savior, too." His gaze flickered down to Ilya's dirty shirt. "She did a good job. You look well enough, for a man who's been knifed. But you were stupid, all the same. That's no way to die."

"Any way is a good way," Ilya murmured, and began to cough.

"You don't sound very healthy," Kovalin mocked. "Perhaps you should take a holiday. Somewhere quiet. Why should you want to die?"

"Don't we all want what we can't have?" Ilya said bitterly.

"Ah, so that's the problem. I thought it might be something like that." He glanced at Ilya and his gaze sharpened. "How old are you now? Eight hundred years?"

"Something like that."

"You don't look it. But then, you don't look like a hero, either. I don't suppose anyone would bother to write a *byliny* about you these days."

Ilya gave a wheezing laugh. "There's an opera."

"I know, I've heard of it. But I don't like opera. I know a great deal about you, Ilya Muromyets. I know all the stories—how you couldn't walk for the first thirty years of your life, until three mysterious strangers turned up and freed you from your paralysis; how you slew the Nightingale Bandit; how you defeated the Tartars; how you fought for fifty days with the Kyrgyz hero Manas."

"You shouldn't believe all you read. It wasn't thirty years; it was only six. And I didn't kill the Nightingale Bandit, either. I thought I had, but years later I heard rumors that he still lived. . . . I fought against the Tartars, true, but it was an entire army that defeated them. As for Manas—the fight lasted fifty minutes, perhaps."

"You disappoint me," Kovalin said. "I expected such great tales."

"You won't get them from me. Why don't you go in search of the Nightingale Bandit and ask him? Or Manas? Assuming they're still alive."

"You're supposed to be the last of the heroes." Kovalin paused. "According to the stories, aren't you supposed to have a flying horse as well?"

"Look around. Do you see a flying bloody horse?"

The *volkh* smiled. "Well, what a history, nonetheless. I imagine it all merges into one in the end. . . . You must be longing for death."

"You have no idea."

"Why don't you kill yourself, then?"

Ilya looked at him with loathing. "Because I can't. Something stops me. I hold a gun to my head and my finger freezes on the trigger. I swallow poison, and it comes back up again. I clutch at a knife, and my hand won't budge an inch." Manas' words echoed in his head with the last of the dream. "Only one *bogatyr* can kill another, they used to say. I've never believed it, but I went looking for the others anyway, seeking death. I found no one. One by one, they have all vanished into the mists."

Kovalin said with sudden distaste, "You're a fool. Think of how you could have used your time. You could have been the tsar of all the Russias by now, with your powers. You could have changed history. And yet you've spent your time moping after a mortality that anyone with any wisdom would be happy to renounce. I suppose you don't even have the guts to leave Russia. Look at you. A junkie, a drunk . . . What happened to the hero you used to be?"

Ilya Muromyets did not reply. He did not want to look at Kovalin any longer. "Go away," he whispered.

"No. I've paid attention to those stories, you see. The ones that say you used to be a hero. Until recently, we thought the last of your kind had died out hundreds of years ago."

"*We?*" Ilya looked at the man, at his black gloves, his expensive overcoat, and wondered whether Kovalin was with the FSB. Ilya had met such men over and over again, first in Dzerzhinsky's Cheka, then in the NKVD and KGB. Power attracted them like spilled blood.

Kovalin shrugged. "My colleagues and I."

"And what exactly do you and your colleagues want?"

Kovalin paused. His small, fleshy mouth pursed. "Have you never wondered, Ilya Muromyets, just what a *bogatyr* might be? Or is it simply that you've never stopped wondering, but have given up all hope of an answer?"

"I've wondered," Ilya said cautiously. God knew, he had made enough efforts to find out over the years.

"Of course you have. You are one of the strangest of things, are you not? A man born in the twelfth century, who has lived hundreds of years and yet who looks to be no more than forty-five. A man with supernatural powers of hearing, who hears things no one else can. You used to be a sorcerer's dream, Muromyets. Now you are a scientist's."

Ilya looked at him, his heart beginning to pound with a long, slow beat that he had not felt for decades.

"You must have wondered," Kovalin pressed. "You

have so much more information available to you now, for perhaps the first time in history."

"Genetic engineering?" Ilya whispered, and hated the hope in his voice. For it was true what Kovalin had said. He still craved answers.

"In the twelfth century?" Kovalin smiled. "The only thing your people might have engineered, was turnips. And yet the *bogatyri* were a breed apart. You never knew your father, did you?"

It was as though Ilya had been waiting all his life to have this conversation. "No. I use a patronymic, but my mother told me he was dead, under the swords of the barbarians."

"If it is any comfort, she may not have lied. Not all the chosen women remembered what happened to them. Did you ever hear her speak of the *rusalki*?"

"Yes. She told me she used to see them in the woods by the lake, up in the trees. She was afraid of them."

"She was right to be afraid. Did she tell you of a day when she fainted in the woods after a stumble, or, perhaps, sat dreaming at the water's edge, as girls do, until she had lost so much time that she could not account for it?"

"No, she didn't." But then came the long-ago echo of his grandmother's voice, saying: *The woods are dangerous, Ilyushka, even in summer and the light. One day, I remember—oh, long before you were born—your mother went out to gather mushrooms and she was so long, Ilyushka, that I thought she was never coming home. And when at last she did, she was mazed, as if she'd spent too long in the sun. . . .*

Wonderingly, Ilya repeated this to Kovalin.

"But what happened to my mother? And what has it to do with me?"

"I would hazard a guess that it was your conception."

"What? The *rusalki* are female. And whatever befell my mother that day took place long before I was born."

"The *rusalki* are not female, despite their appearance, and the gestation of their offspring is not human, either. The *rusalki* do not have a gender. If you were to be so unfortunate—or so lucky, for opinion varies—to sleep with one, you would find that they have nothing that approximates to human genitalia."

"You seem remarkably well-informed," Ilya said dryly. "Have you been so blessed, then, or so cursed, to have a *rusalka* as your lover?"

"No. But I have dissected them."

"I have killed *rusalki*," Ilya said, staring at him. "And they shatter into ice at the touch of a blade."

"If they have time to marshal their illusions, yes. But they can be caught unawares and turned to colder flesh. They are not spirits, Ilya Muromyets."

Ilya rose, stiffly, and crossed to the window. Ice glittered on the Neva beneath the winter sun. Beyond marched the ranks of apartment blocks, made of the grey, crumbling concrete that had been a Soviet speciality. The modern, everyday world, where spirits and heroes did not belong. But he was sure that Kovalin was lying to him. He could almost smell it.

"Then what are they?" he asked, still gazing out across the city.

"Whatever they might be, they have been here for a very long time, hiding out in the silent places, the cold lands where few humans go. There is no sign that they use any kind of technology, yet there is evidence that they experiment on humans. And I suspect that if I was to take a sample of your blood, there would be matching DNA between you."

"What?" Ilya asked, blankly. He swung to face Kovalin. "Are you telling me that I am not human?"

"Of course you're not human," Kovalin said impatiently. "Not as we understand it, anyway."

There was a short, charged silence.

"And what are you?" Ilya asked finally. There was something about Kovalin's eyes that deeply disquieted him. They seemed too dark, too opaque.

"I am a member of an organization formed in the late nineteenth century, dedicated to solving the occult mysteries that seem to weigh so heavily upon us here in Russia. Rasputin was our last study—another man who took an unnaturally long time to die. The changes scattered us, drove us underground. We were persecuted as counterrevolutionaries. Now that the Soviet Union is no more, we have once again emerged. We began the century as mystics, but we ended it as scientists."

"And where do the *rusalki* come from, in your opinion? Another world? Like the little grey aliens of the Americans?"

"In my opinion . . . ." Kovalin considered the question for a moment. "They are from another world, but perhaps not in the sense that you might mean it."

"I don't understand."

"I've said they do not use technology that we are aware of. No spaceships, no ray guns, no robots. And yet they have astonishing abilities—like your own, but much greater—and they are able to slip in and out of this reality."

"What makes you so sure they're not supernatural, then?"

"Did I say that I was sure? They are certainly supernatural, in one sense of the word. They do not obey physical laws as we know them."

"Why are you telling me this now?" Ilya asked.

"Because we have only just tracked you down. I told you, our organization was thrown into upheaval during the last century, persecuted and scattered. Many of us went into the parapsychology programs run by the KGB, but the politicians disapproved of us. There weren't many five-year plans for supernatural endeavors. *Perestroika* has proved a mixed blessing. We have regrouped; we have a measure of governmental approval, but like everyone else, little in the way of funds. I am on your side, Ilya Vladimirievitch Muromyets." He used the patronymic without mockery. "I want to help. But in doing so, you can also help us."

"How?"

"I told you that I have dissected a *rusalka*. In fact, I have had the privilege of examining one of the creatures. We captured it in the forests near our facility; it was weak and sick. In the folds of its clothing—a kind of robe—we found something. It was made of an unknown metal, but shaped like a fossil: an ammonite, perhaps. We removed the object and placed it in a safe container; it spun a hard web around itself, as if for protection. It now resembles a small black ball. A day later, a second *rusalka* entered the compound—we have no idea how, since it is guarded and sealed—and tried to seize the object. It took a great risk, and it was not successful. We killed it."

"How?" Ilya demanded.

"We shot it before it had time to generate its illusions. It was deemed too dangerous to keep the object at the facility any longer, and so a member of the organization was sent south, to Uzbekistan. He has not made contact, and we don't know what has happened to him. We searched the border traffic as best we could, but found nothing. Word has come, however, that traces of the thing have been detected in Almaty, in Kazakhstan. I would like you to find it."

The *volkh's* gaze slid blandly away, and it was then that Ilya realized that Kovalin knew very well what this object might be, but was keeping it to himself. And the story he had just told seemed too glib, too rehearsed. Ilya's long life had left him well able to smell out a lie. "Clearly, it seems to be valuable to them," Kovalin went on smoothly.

"What sort of traces?"

"The object seems to have an *effect* on the world around it. Reality shifts, alters."

"How?"

"Strange weather conditions, curious phenomena. Our information is limited."

"Why should I help you?" Ilya asked, sitting back down on the bed. "Why can't you search for this thing yourself? Why, indeed, should I even believe you?"

"Because I have other duties. And if you succeed, Ilya Muromyets, then we will help you achieve your greatest wish. We will help you to die." His black gaze met Ilya's own. He smiled blandly. "And because, quite frankly, you have nothing else. The tide of time has washed you up, and you have nowhere to go and no one to be. Why you, you ask? Because you are a hero, Ilya Muromyets, a sword for hire. Hopeless quests are what you do."

Interlude

The old man was reading the newspaper when Anikova's men blew his door off its hinges. In his confusion, he dropped the paper, knocking over the samovar and flooding the kitchen floor with tea, but he moved fast enough after that. No doubt he was aiming for the fire escape, in order to drop down onto the monorail tracks and lose himself in the heart of the city, but Anikova was too quick for him. He was halfway out of the window when she caught him by the braces and hauled him back.

Something scuttled out from beneath the kitchen sink, and Anikova glimpsed hot-coal eyes in a mass of dark hair before the thing sank sharp teeth into her ankle. She swore.

"Get it off me!"

The old man gave a high cackle of laughter.

"He doesn't like you, the old *Domovoi*."

Anikova kicked out, sending the creature against the wall. It lay still for a moment, then slid back under the sink. Her ankle burned and she hoped the creature's teeth had not been infected. Insanitary, horrible creatures; Central Command should enforce the regulations more stringently. If the situation had not been so serious, it might even had seemed comical, but Anikova was too angry to see the funny side of things. She held the blastgun to the old man's head and snapped shockwire around his wrists. The old man grew slack and still.

"Against the wall, now! Spread your arms." Swiftly, Anikova checked his pockets, but found nothing except a box of matches and a ragged handkerchief. She threw them onto the table in disgust. "Where is it?"

"Where is what?" The old man turned his head to look at her. His eyes were round and bland, offensive in their very disingenuousness.

"You know very well what I am talking about. The distorter coil."

"What in the world is a distorter coil?"

Anikova could have sworn that the old man was enjoying himself.

"A piece of forbidden technology, stolen from Central Command's laboratories. I know the dissidents passed it to you before they made it over the border. You were seen talking to them. I have a witness who swears that he saw it in your hand. You see? You can hide nothing from us." Anikova mouthed the usual clichés with a confidence that she was far from feeling. *Hide* was what the old man had done most successfully up until now. "Answer my question."

"Or what?"

Anikova stared at him in disbelief. It was impossible that a person should be unaware of the penalties for such a crime: a spell in the *Gulag* at the very least. Perhaps the man was mad, or simple, or arrogant enough to think that such a thing could never happen to him. It occurred to her that any or all of those reasons could explain his involvement with the insurgents in the first place.

The Mechvor stepped forward and put a gentle hand on the old man's arm. "It really would be better if you simply told us," Kitai said. Her dark eyes, whiteless among the soft planes of her face, were filled with concern. "We care for all our citizens. We don't want anything to happen to you."

The old man gave her an arch look. "Then you know what you can do, don't you? You can leave me alone."

"We can't do that," the Mechvor said sadly. "You might fall into bad company. Some of your fellow sympathizers have already gone south, to the horse tribes. You don't want to spend the rest of your days among barbarians, do you?"

It occurred to Anikova that perhaps the old man thought the two women were practicing nothing more than some good cop/bad cop routine, that he was responding with a game of his own. It was not true. The Mechvor genuinely cared, unlike Anikova.

She tapped Kitai on the shoulder. "You're wasting your breath," she said. The Mechvor turned, and just for a moment, Anikova felt a twinge inside her head; a neural toothache, sharp and stinging. She stumbled back.

"I'm sorry," she muttered, hating herself for her weakness in front of the suspect. His face was turned back to the wall, but she knew he was grinning. The Mechvor put a placatory hand on Anikova's arm.

"I know how hard this is for you, Colonel," she

murmured. "Please try not to worry. I'm sure we can sort everything out to everyone's satisfaction."

"All right," Anikova said sourly. "I'll let you deal with it."

"Would you like to stay here while I ask this poor misguided soul a few questions?"

"No," Anikova said. "I'll wait outside."

In disgust, she picked up a handful of samizdat papers from the table and strode to the door. The light streamed into the passage, dappling the white plaster walls. Anikova went over to the window and looked out.

Pre'gorod—First City—stretched all the way to the Northwest Gulf, the Red Star banner snapping over the roofs and golden domes, revealing silvery glimpses of sea. A carrier was coming down to the airport, falling from the sky like a great drop of rain. If Anikova craned her neck, she could see the monorail—aptly named the Bullet—streaking across the city. Down in the street, her own long *siydna,* hovering between the trees, gleamed in the evening sun.

Anikova opened the window and breathed in clean air from the gulf, laden with salt and the tang from the herring fisheries, masked by the headier scent of the limes. Her *siydna* was already dusted with pollen; it danced up in yellow swirls beneath the vehicle's stationing-jets.

From up here, First City was quiet and well-ordered, everything and everyone in its place. But Anikova's ankle still stung where the *Domovoi* had bitten through her boot, and she could hear the murmuring voice of the Mechvor from inside the old man's apartment. From the corner of her eye, she saw the city shift: the buildings shrinking, becoming greyer and smaller, the trees withering. Anikova grew cold. These glimpses of another, lesser reality seemed to be growing, but few people were prepared to talk about it. Except the dissidents. And she remembered with deep unease the heretical thoughts that her father had increasingly begun to voice before he fell into the breach all those years ago: *We are stealing from them, you know. From the Motherland, from Russia itself. We are leaching their dreams, to fuel our world. The better it gets here, the worse it becomes on Earth.* And that was the key to her own long uncertainty. *But now I know it's true. Central Command has told me so. Yet what right do we have? Are we not a nation of dream-stealers, thereby? And are we poisoning our world by our actions, diminishing ourselves?*

Restlessly, Anikova returned to the door and peered through. The old man was now sitting at the table, with Kitai bending over him. In the lamplight, the Mechvor could have been his granddaughter, neat in her dark uniform, but Anikova glimpsed the form of her avatar within her silhouette: a black, twisting embryo. Anikova did not wait to see any more. She closed the door behind her and leaned against the wall.

She could not stop herself from listening, but there was nothing to hear, and that was the worst thing of all.

Part Two

One

Ilya Muromyets' great black sword, concealed in a fishing-rod case, rested at his shoulder. A packet of sunflower seeds weighed down his pocket and a shot of low-grade heroin—the very last, Ilya told himself—sang through his veins. The train rattled through the suburbs of St. Petersburg, gathering speed once it reached the flat whiteness of the steppes.

It was a Tuesday in early March, hardly the best time for traveling, and the compartment was almost empty. Ilya had only one companion: a middle-aged woman with a disappointed face. Her gaze passed over Ilya's shabby appearance with distaste, and for the rest of the day she devoted herself to a pile of true-crime magazines. A hardened soul, Ilya thought dreamily. Russia was full of them, had always been. But a hard soul was almost always the shell for a wounded heart, or so they said. Ilya felt that his head was stuffed full of aphorisms, like a pudding with raisins, the trite detritus of a too-long life.

He felt sorry for the woman and blearily offered her a handful of the sunflower seeds. She declined, which did not greatly surprise him. His face, reflected in the dirty window of the train, was stripped down to its Slavic bones. His eyes were hectic, the pupils pinpricks.

The journey passed in a haze of drugged speculation. It would not have astonished him to learn that he had simply imagined Kovalin's visit. Perhaps he was wholly mad, nothing more than a casualty of a broken Russia, part of the flotsam washed up on time's shores. Maybe he was indeed no more than forty-five, a demented soul pretending to be an eight-hundred-year-old hero. And what had happened to the others over the years: the Nightingale Bandit, Manas of the Kyrgyz Mountains, Mikula, Svyatogor? He had not seen any of these men for years, and it had not been for want of looking.

Perhaps, as he suspected with distant envy, they were dead at last, or had retreated into the wilderness, just as he himself had done for a time before once more seeking life in the grimy, teeming cities of the Ukraine and western Russia.

But Ilya could not imagine what reality he could be fleeing from, what worse thing could possibly have befallen him than that which had happened already. Surely the truth was more terrible than madness. He reached into the pocket of his overcoat and took out the paper that Kovalin had given him. There was a telephone number on the piece of paper, a contact within Kovalin's organization.

We have ended the century as scientists, Kovalin had said, but Ilya wondered if this was really true. The man seemed to reek of sorcery, yet he was the only meaningful thing that Ilya had left. And he had promised death. For that tenuous hope, Ilya was prepared to believe almost anything.

But try as he might, Ilya could not reach a satisfactory explanation as to why Kovalin had chosen him for this task. Surely Kovalin had his own people on which to call? The only answer must be that tracking the object was dangerous—perhaps so dangerous that only an indestructible person could do the job. But the situation reminded Ilya too strongly of a day over eighty years before, when another mysterious official had sent him on a similar quest. And that adventure, not long after the Revolution, had ended in Siberia where, surrounded by death in the bitter winter, he had, as usual, survived.

Memory took him back as though the intervening years had never been. The railway line ran arrow-straight from Moscow to Petrograd, aside from the bend known as the Tsar's Elbow, but the closer they drew to the Gulf of Finland, the edgier Ilya became. When the train drew past Kalinin, crossing the frozen artery of the Volga, the signs of revolution became even more apparent: the artillery forces outside the town, soldiers stumbling through the snow. The train thundered through, leaving the troops behind.

Ilya leaned back in his seat and closed his eyes. The operative, one of Dzerzhinsky's men in the new police force they called the Cheka, had been oblique. The target was engaged in counterrevolutionary activities; he had set up a secret laboratory in the forests and had collaborated with Germans. His eradication was essential to the security of Lenin's new state. Ilya, weary of war, did not care to question too greatly what he had been told.

He felt like a bowstring, nerves tightly wound along the Petrograd line. They passed wave after wave of forest. An officer moved down the train, collecting papers. Ilya handed his over with barely a glance. The officer passed on. The outskirts of Petrograd appeared through the window of the train.

Ilya waited until the train had left Petrograd and headed north. The carriage was crowded now, filled with soldiers. It was past noon, the sun a round coin behind the clouds. Ilya took a slab of bread and cheese from his pocket and ate it, staring out of the window at the white expanse of the Gulf of Finland. They were not far from the border. He recalled the Cheka official's instructions. *You will see a church with a broken dome, then a damaged house. You will have to leave the train at that point. After that comes the forest. The building is perhaps a mile from the ruins of the village, heading northwest toward the sea.* Ilya kept close watch through the window and at last saw the church with the fallen dome by its side. Stained wood showed through the faded gilt. The house was no more than a wall, scarred by fire.

Snow began to fall, whirling in from the gulf, cold salty air gusting through the cracks in the carriage. As the train slowed down and the forest once more began to press in upon the track, Ilya got to his feet and made his way along the train. The soldiers watched him with indifference. The train seemed endless: row upon row of the same grey faces, the same patched uniforms. Ilya stepped over guns, over packs, over men's boots until he reached the last carriage of all. He made his way to the end, conscious of eyes on his back, and hauled open the door.

He stepped out onto the little ledge at the back of the train, into the sudden punch of cold air, and pulled the door closed behind him. He put his hands on the rail. The track stretched away until it became lost in the trees. Making sure that the sheath of the sword was settled firmly across his shoulders, and that the pack containing the explosives was securely fastened, Ilya swung over the railing and dropped down onto the track. The train trundled away. Ilya stumbled over the rails and into the forest, then leaned against a pine to catch his breath. After the musty, sweat-soaked air of the train, the forest was a blessing. Ilya began to track toward the sea, noting fallen branches and the way the light fell, taking care not to circle back.

By the time he reached the facility, it was dusk; a good time, Ilya thought. His superiors had done their research: the target, Tsilibayev, preferred to work late.

"He feigns eccentricity," the man from the Cheka had said. "He works alone."

If Tsilibayev appeared that peculiar, Ilya thought, then it was curious how he had managed to survive the most recent purges. Unusual behavior was a luxury that few could afford, genius or not.

He paused for a moment, to get his bearings. He craved a cigarette, but it wouldn't be wise. Someone might see the light. As he stood ankle-deep in snow, he heard the lightest, softest footstep behind him. He turned, hand halfway to the sword, but it was a hare: winter-white, gazing at him from great dark eyes. It watched him for a moment, then loped away. Ilya chose to take it as a symbol: still the superstitious peasant boy beneath the twentieth-century façade, more easily believing in signs and the stars than in science. He listened. There was the sudden rush of snow deep in the woods, then nothing. Ilya walked on, following the point to where another sound began to filter through the silence: a low humming, like a generator. He was drawing close to the facility.

Soon he could see it: a series of low huts with corrugated iron roofs, standing in a clearing. A cold wind blew through from the gulf, stirring Ilya's hair. He stood still and listened. Someone was moving about in the long building to his left. There were two guards in the gatehouse, dozing over their guns. There was no sign of any dogs. Ilya slunk under the barbed wire, then through the trees to the wall, conscious of the knock of the sword against his shoulder. Merkulov's instructions had been precise. The device lay at the back of the largest building, but was not itself very big.

"It is a coil of black material," Merkulov had told him. "It is very small—it would fit into the palm of your hand—but it is contained in a circular device, perhaps a foot and a half in diameter, attached to a nest of wires. Kill Tsilibayev, and destroy the coil. Blow it up."

Ilya, his back to the wall, glanced through the window. He could see shelves and a low metal table covered with what looked like the fragments of a generator. Ilya waited until a man came into view. It was Tsilibayev; he matched the photograph that Merkulov had shown to Ilya: a short man with cropped, greying hair and blue eyes with an Eastern tilt. A face with humor, thought Ilya. A Siberian face, moreover. With an effort, Ilya put aside his misgivings. The scientist did not look like a collaborator, but Ilya knew, perhaps more than anyone, how little one could rely upon appearances.

Tsilibayev was moving around the lab, attaching wires to a sequence of generators. Ilya thought of Frankenstein: life jerking to its feet at the touch of the lightning strike. But Tsilibayev's equipment was modern, all with its factory stamp. The only anomaly was the black disc in the corner of the room. Ilya could see it now that Tsilibayev had moved out of the way. It hung in a cradle of wires, a spider in a web. Tsilibayev threw a switch and stepped back. Invisible lightning touched a spark to the black coil. It began to spin, yet made no sound. It whirled silently around its own axis, so swiftly that it soon became no more than a blur.

Ilya glanced around. The compound was empty. Ilya moved toward the door and looked through a crack. Tsilibayev stood with his back to the door, watching the spinning coil and occasionally glancing down at a device in his hand. Ilya could not tell what he was doing: taking readings of some kind, perhaps. Very slowly, Ilya tested the handle of the door. It yielded beneath his gloved fingers. It was not locked. He looked again. Tsilibayev was still absorbed in his work.

Ilya drew the sword, stepped through the door, and closed it quietly behind him.

Inside the building, the air smelled of chemicals. His hair snapped with static. *Kill him quickly; no last words, no warning, just send him, unknowing, to God.* But as Ilya raised the sword to strike, a flash of soundless light came from the direction of the device. A bright line appeared in the air, hanging vertically, like the sun glancing down the edge of a sword. Tsilibayev turned.

His eyes widened, but all he said was, "So you're the fool they sent to kill me. I knew it would come sooner or later. It won't make any difference to *that*." He gestured toward the spinning device.

"They tell me you're a traitor," Ilya said, unsettled by the scientist's contempt.

"Of course they do. What I'm doing has nothing to do with Russia's enemies. I suppose they made up some fairy story. What was it? Spaceflight?"

"Time travel," Ilya said before he could stop himself.

Tsilibayev gave a great bark of laughter. "And you believed them? Your accent's Siberian; you should have more sense. Who are the secret police recruiting these days, idiots from the villages?"

"I've seen too much strangeness in my life," Ilya said, stung.

Tsilibayev sobered abruptly. "Do you know, something in your face makes me believe you? But we're wasting time."

Ilya, the sword still drawn, took a swift step forward. Tsilibayev's lip curled. "Destroy it if you like, after you kill me. If you can. You'll find it harder than you think, even with dynamite. It's based on something very old—an ancient artifact, supernatural technology that I came across in Siberia—but that's another story. It may be nothing more than a copy, but it still works well enough to take folks to the other side. After that, who knows?" He snatched a hat from a nearby chair and placed it on his head. "I don't know what it's really like over there," he said, almost conversationally. "I've only ever had glimpses, a few hours at a time. But it can't be worse than Russia, can it?" And with that, the scientist stepped sideways into the air and was gone. The crack closed behind him; the machine whirred faster and faster, then something snapped. The coil spun down to a tangled wreckage of wires. There was no sign of anything nested within them.

Ilya stared open-mouthed, Tsilibayev's words echoing in his head. But he was under orders; it seemed that there was nothing left to do but follow them. Working quickly, he set the explosives, placing the bulk of them at the foot of the now-silent device. When he reached the door, he set the detonator and ran toward the forest, stumbling across the snow. But even as he ran, counting down, he knew that nothing would make any difference now. He could feel that Tsilibayev had been speaking the truth.

He threw himself to the ground just before the blast. A wave of heat boiled overhead, stripping the trees clean of snow. Ilya breathed ash and the smell of burning resin. He listened and it seemed to him then that he could hear voices, the sound of humming, coming from somewhere that was at once very close and yet extremely far away. Tsilibayev's words snapped back into memory: *Destroy it if you like, after you kill me. If you can. You'll find it harder than you think, even with dynamite.* Ilya stirred uneasily, but he had no desire to go back and see what remained of the device, if there was even anything remaining. He waited until there was only smoke and showering snow, then got to his feet and started walking.

The men were waiting for him at the railway track. He saw without surprise that they were Cheka. He could think of nothing to say, and the men, too, were silent. There was little point in trying to escape, for there were too many of them, and so he went with them to the waiting vehicle. As they headed along the remains of the road to Volgograd and the train to Siberia, he sat, staring behind him into the darkness, no longer caring.

That had been over eighty years ago now, but the cold and the darkness were the same. Toward dusk, the train pulled into a small station, and the passengers were allowed out to visit the little kiosk that stood at the end of the platform. Ilya bought bread, and, despite his better judgment, a bottle of vodka. The heroin was wearing off now and he ached for it. There was no chance of scoring. He knew this was a good thing, but it did not feel that way.

The passengers milled about the platform, stamping their feet in the snow. Shivering, Ilya looked upward, but a light mist hung like a veil across the sky, blotting out the stars. They were traveling through the forests now, the deep black woods in which he had spent so much of the last few hundred years. It was good to get out of the city, away from the reek of petrol and pollution. Now, all he could smell was pine resin and snow. He thought again of the forests beyond old Petrograd, the marks of shellfire and revolution and the secret laboratory blazing among the trees. What had really become of Tsilibayev? Where had he disappeared to, and what had become of the thing at the heart of that strange spinning machine? Ilya could hardly believe he had followed his orders so blindly, but at that point, orders had been all that he had left.

Ilya stepped back onto the train. He sank down

and took the sword onto his lap, cradling it like a child. His body ached for heroin. He opened the vodka and took a long, burning swallow. When the dour woman came back into the carriage, Ilya glared at her. Muttering, she collected her possessions and moved into the adjoining compartment so that he had the seats to himself. He could not sleep, in spite of the vodka. Instead, he rested his head against the icy window and sat, staring as the train pulled away toward the bleakness of the Kazakh steppes.

Two

Elena finished cleaning the third-story offices and dragged the bucket out into the corridor, then bent down to wring out the cloth. Her head was splitting: the legacy of a troubling night. Once she had fallen asleep, she dreamed that she had walked into the apartment, only to find it empty: Anna and her mother and even the furniture were gone. But as she looked around her, Elena had realized that it was not the apartment in Almaty at all, but somewhere quite different: known to her, and yet strange. The walls were paneled in birchwood, and the sunlight that fell across them was deep and golden. Wondering, Elena walked over to the window and looked out into an unfamiliar world. Lilies the color of brass nodded by the window, and the sharp, pungent smell of nutmeg wafted in. But the leaves of the lilies were blue and razor-edged, and when she bent toward one, it twisted away from her with a delicate disdain, startling Elena so much that she woke up.

The dream kept returning to her during the course of the day, seeming more real than the dull, corporate surroundings of the oil company. She wondered with dismay whether she might be sick. Perhaps she'd picked up something in Tashkent. A few days off work now would mean a week's wages down the pan—less money for Canada and she would probably have to buy medicine. She'd stick to dosing herself with green tea for a few days and hope it sorted itself out.

Uneasily, she thought again about the object and its heaviness. What if it was radioactive after all, and she was guarding some kind of toxic lump? Perhaps it was just stress. Mentally, she started the familiar calculations: another month's wages for herself and Anna, plus the pension, and perhaps if she could talk Gulnara's brother into another run to Tashkent before he left the country . . .

As she straightened up with the bucket, a familiar voice said in surprise, "Elena?"

She looked up, and there was Fyodor Tereschenko standing in front of her. Instead of the battered leather coat and the old *ushanka* hat with earflaps that he had habitually worn at the cosmodrome, he was dressed in a tight dark suit and he'd shaved off his beard.

"What in the world are you doing here?" Elena asked blankly.

"I've come about a job," Fyodor said. His face crumpled with embarrassment. "Someone mentioned that you were working here. I thought I'd look you up."

"Aren't you working at the cosmodrome anymore?"

"Yes. No. Well, not exactly. I came back to see if there's any work going." He glanced dubiously at the dripping mop as though Elena might offer him a job on the spot.

"So what's happening at the cosmodrome?"

"A lot of changes. NASA's more or less taken over the running of the station, which, between you and me, is just as well. At least they've got the money. . . . We do updates for TASS, and we still service the resupply craft. There are a few launches—we're doing it at bargain rates now: a million dollars instead of three million in Florida. It's all right for the Americans, but we're still getting our salaries from Moscow. Except, well . . ." He shrugged, smiling ruefully. "You know what they say. We pretend to work and they pretend to pay us. I haven't had any money since January."

"Well, you've heard that Georgian curse, haven't you? *May you be obliged to live on your salary.*" She paused. "How are you managing?" Perhaps it was a rude question, but in recent years people had stopped caring too much about that. Delayed salaries were an all-too-familiar story.

"I'm moonlighting as a taxi driver in Leninsk. And we've still got that little garden. It's not much, but at least we get to eat. Mind you, Leninsk's a bloody awful place." He gestured at his clothes and added bitterly, "Hence the suit. I'm applying for other jobs, anything I can find. But I'm not sure if I stand a chance—I've only got a doctorate and ten years' experience in a redundant space program, after all. I thought there'd be more work once the new station went into orbit, but . . ." His voice trailed away.

"Well, you can see the sort of high-level intellectual tasks I'm engaged in these days," Elena said wryly.

"Little Havroshechka in the fairy tale has nothing on me."

"And you haven't even got a magic cow to help you. Elena . . ." He leaned across the bucket and gave her a quick hug, startling them both. There didn't seem to be much else they could say. They were both embarrassed. They made some vague arrangement to meet up for a drink, but Elena knew it wouldn't happen. They were too much of a reminder for each other of what each had lost. After a few halfhearted good wishes, Fyodor left.

Elena finished the cleaning and then walked home down Lenina. The sky was overcast and she could smell snow on the wind. Spring was so late this year. The first heavy flakes were falling by the time she reached the apartment. After the disquieting dream, she was almost relieved to step through and hear voices, but they stopped as soon as the door shut behind her. She went into the lounge.

Anna and her mother were sitting side by side on the couch. Their expressions were identical: a quivering, hidden excitement. The money box sat on the table.

"Mama? What's going on?" Elena asked.

"Look," Elena's mother said, beaming. In silence Elena counted the money inside the box. There was more than there had been last night: almost two hundred dollars more. Enough to get to Moscow. Elena sat down, clutching the box.

"Wherever did this come from?"

Smiling, Elena's mother patted Anna's arm.

"My Anushka," she murmured. "I have such good daughters." She wiped away a tear and Elena stifled her irritation. Her mother meant well, and the years after her father's death had been hard for them all. She should have more patience.

Anna said, "I got the money yesterday. A bonus, from work." Her eyes met Elena's in a sudden, baffling challenge. "I phoned Marina in Moscow. We've almost got enough for tickets and start-up money now. When we get to Moscow, we'll be staying with her for a few days until we find an apartment. And she's heard of a job, too. In an office." Again, the challenging look.

"Anna, that's marvelous," Elena said. She reached out and hugged her sister, and Anna gave an uncertain smile. "Come and help me with the tea, and then— well, I suppose we'll have to start to think about packing, won't we?"

In the kitchen, she pushed the door shut and turned on her sister.

"Where did you get it? Waitresses don't get bonuses." She could see the truth in her sister's face, but she did not want to look at it or let it in. It was like standing on the lip of a precipice. She could hear Gulnara's voice as clearly as if her friend had been standing in front of her. *I saw her in the Business Club. . . . She introduced me to her boyfriend. He seems nice, doesn't he? For a German.*

Anna stared at her defiantly. "It *was* a bonus. Sort of."

"Oh, *Anna*." Elena put her arms around her sister. "If I'd ever thought you'd—we'd have gotten there with the money. We nearly had enough."

"It would have taken ages and you know it. I'm not getting any younger, Elena. I'm twenty-nine and

I'm sick of it here." Anna was stiff in Elena's arms, un-yielding.

"Who was he?" Elena asked.

Her sister's voice was muffled, but Elena couldn't tell if it was with defiance or shame. "An engineer. From Frankfurt. And there were others. I met them in the Business Club. I didn't tell you before because I knew what you'd say." She pulled back and looked Elena in the face. "Look, Elena, it was only a couple of times. Lots of girls do it. The first one said he'd pay me fifty dollars—I thought, that's a *fortune,* it's almost five months' salary. It would just be stupid not to do it. And it was okay. They're just men. They were nice, really."

Elena did not know what to say, or to think. Anna, her little sister, suddenly seemed a stranger. "Mama mustn't know," she said. Her voice did not sound like her own. Anna nodded vigorously.

"Of course not. So you'll back me up? Say you knew about the bonus, and we wanted it to be a sur-prise?"

"All right," Elena said reluctantly. "But what about the rest of the money? You're not—you're not planning to do this again, are you?"

"If we could get another fifty—"

"Anna, no. Will you promise me?"

Slowly, Anna nodded. But a shared girlhood had left legacies: of hidden dolls, borrowed makeup, unfin-ished homework. Elena had always known when Anna was lying, and vice versa. And Anna was lying now. It wasn't the issue of sex with strangers, but the familiar-ity of it that was so depressing. The twenty-first cen-tury and here was Anna, trained as a lawyer, but feeling obliged to do what girls had done for thousands of years to get their families out of a jam. And combined with that was the faintest trace of guilt, that she herself hadn't found the money fast enough, or had the nerve to do what Anna had done. Perhaps she should have joined that dating agency after all, and found a rich foreign businessman. But confronting her sister would be useless; she'd have to think of something else. If she could get hold of a few dollars from somewhere, so that they could just get the tickets sorted out . . .

"Listen," she said, as another thought occurred to her, "this job in Moscow. Is that real, or something else you made up?"

"No! It's true."

"But it's not in an office, is it?"

After a long pause, Anna said, "No. It's in a night-club. But it's just serving drinks. Nothing more than that."

I'll bet, Elena thought. And she'd have more than a few words with Marina when they got to Moscow. She wasn't letting Anna near any nightclubs, if she had to lock her in the apartment. But the damage was done; the main thing now was keeping it from their mother. Anna went back into the living room, and Elena leaned against the wall. The cold kitchen felt suddenly sti-fling. There had to be another way besides prostitution and drudgery.

She thought of Fyodor in his too-small suit; of her-self standing in a corridor with an apron and a mop, and then she thought back to the days of the launches: the rocket blasting up from the grasslands in a great, rosy column of fire. You can't see the stars very well from cities; there's too much interference. You can't see clearly at all, but Elena didn't want to think about that.

She stepped into the hall and went quickly toward her bedroom, to where the jewelery box sat on the chest of drawers. Elena sat down on her bed with the box on her lap, and investigated the contents. The ball was intact. At the bottom of the box lay three gold chains, a locket, the bracelet that her father had given her the year he died, and her grandmother's gold cross. Not much, but maybe enough for a few more dollars. It wasn't yet four o'clock; the place she had in mind would still be open.

"Anna! Mama! I'm just going out to the post office. I forgot to post the electricity bill," she called, wrestling with her coat and boots. She stuffed the jewelry box into her bag and ran down the stairs into the street.

Three

Ilya had lost track of the time. How many days had it been since they had left Moscow? Two, or three? He could no longer remember. The hours passed in a blur, but by the time the train pulled into Almaty, both the heroin and the vodka were long gone. Light-headed and shaky, Ilya dragged the sword out onto the platform and stood blinking in the early morning light.

He had visited Almaty years before, when it was still named Vernyi and nothing more than a Russian outpost on the far fringes of what was not yet an empire. How long ago had that been? A hundred and twenty years, perhaps. Coming out of the station, the grey streets with their lacing of bare branches looked like everywhere else, but then Ilya looked up to see the mountains floating high above the city, the dawn frosting their sides with light. A cold clean wind sailed through the streets, making Ilya shiver. But it was a good wind, bringing no sound other than the small rustlings of animals and birds far away in the rocks. Up there in the mountains, there was nothing for miles.

His brow was chilly with sweat. He had no suppliers here, no contacts, but it should be easy enough to buy smack—Ilya shivered again, this time with resolve. He would not go down that road; it led nowhere. He would avoid the bars and the dealers; he would stay clean until he had found what he was looking for. He swore under his breath. He knew he was lying to himself, and he knew what he must now do. He was aware that he was not thinking clearly, that the first priority should be finding the object, but this was a duty he owed to himself, not to Kovalin. Besides, he had no idea where to start looking. *Strange weather conditions. Curious phenomena.* But the weather here was just the tail end of winter, and the only curious phenomenon in Ilya's immediate locality appeared to be himself. All Kovalin had been able to tell him for certain was that the object was known to be here in Almaty—or had been several days ago. Ilya sighed.

There was a faded map on the public information board outside the station. Ilya peered at it until he found what he sought, then set off through the streets of this familiar, foreign town.

As he walked through the early morning light, Almaty began to wake around him. He saw an old woman scraping snow from the steps of an underpass. A group of schoolchildren gathered at the foot of a bronze statue. Ilya paused to read the inscription: *Abai.* Memory tugged at him. He remembered a man of that name: an old poet, out among the steppe dwellers, the horse clans, who had recognized Ilya for what he was and did not care. Ilya recalled a round face, Orient-eyed beneath a turban. Words echoed in his head: *Everyone who thinks differently is already an outcast, my Russian friend. You are neither alone nor unique. You may have had longer to wait than most of us, but perhaps it is merely that your time has not yet come.*

Abai had been a poet, not a shaman; a seeker of words, not an oracle. But Ilya now stared up at the half-remembered face and wondered whether there was any real difference.

Perhaps it is merely that your time has not yet come.

Ilya mouthed the words aloud, then realized that a group of young mothers was gazing at him in alarm. A woman drew her child closer to her and whispered in its ear. Ilya gave the child a wolfish smile and turned away.

It was a long trudge up the street to his destination, footstep after footstep, shuffling through the snow. He could feel the mountains at his back, a force as strong as the wind, holding him up and driving him on. Before him, past the rows of apartment blocks that lined the street, lay a dark edge of trees. Ilya stepped from the pavement and found himself in the park.

At this time of the day and year, the place was quiet. Ilya made his way between oaks and firs, past a great monument of rearing horses and a man with his bronze mouth open in a silent shout. A flame flickered over the surface of a marble plinth. Ilya stood before it for a moment, head bowed, remembering nightmares of a multitude of wars.

Snow muffled sound and the trees seemed to swallow the light. Ilya walked on until he saw the gleam of gold. The air was freezing, yet his hands and face were suddenly hot. How long had it been since he stood before a place such as this? Two hundred years or more, ever since the priest at the old cathedral of Kiev had cast him out, flung his beads in his face, and damned him for an abomination. Since that day, Ilya had avoided holy ground, and now here he was, seeking it out. Then the need for the drug—its sweetness, the only warmth he had come to rely upon—snatched at him. Ilya leaned, gasping, against the trunk of an oak. What time would the bars open here in Almaty? He was a fool. He should have waited around the railway station. Such places attracted dealers like flies drawn to fresh blood. Ilya swallowed and turned back to the church.

The cathedral floated above the trees, light as a dream. Its walls were painted a rosy pink, the color of a dawn sky. Golden cupolas shone against the clouds. Ilya took a shuddering breath and walked forward. Nothing happened. He was neither beset by priests nor struck by lightning. Moving jerkily, like a puppet, he climbed up the steps and put his hand to the wooden door. It swung open. He stepped across the threshold into a soaring room, and looked up to see gilded stars. They glittered in the candlelight, as though revealed by racing clouds, and the air was heady with incense. Ilya stumbled as if struck, and collapsed into a nearby pew. He was alone in the cathedral. He dragged his gaze upward, to meet the calm golden face of Christ.

The Lord was looking past Ilya toward the door. Ilya had dreaded the thought of meeting Christ's eyes, and that God seemed prepared to ignore him made things easier. He did not think he could cope with being forgiven, not just yet. Holding tightly to the wooden rail, he pulled himself to his feet and fumbled with the sword. If the priest came in—well, Ilya would just have to start praying, that was all. He carried the sword to the altar and knelt before it. He could not look up, in case he caught Christ in a frown. Instead, he stared grimly ahead to where the golden cross sparkled on the altar.

He placed the sword in front of him, held upright by the hilt. This was an old practice, and perhaps unfitting for a Christian place of worship, but it seemed right. Ilya gritted his teeth and clasped the raw blade with his right hand.

Pain seared through him. He gasped, and his grip involuntarily tightened. A trickle of blood ran down the blade of the sword, and through the haze of pain Ilya whispered, "Lord, let this be a vow, sacred to you, that I will not touch the drug until my journey is over. Let me have a single clean death, not many small ones." He thought of renouncing vodka, as well, but that was further than he was prepared to go. He needed *something*, he thought. If God were really Russian, then God would surely understand. He added under his breath, "Bring me to my destiny. Show me what it is." His own words startled him. Years ago, it had been a preoccupation, but it had been a long time since he had considered the question of destiny.

He let go of the blade. It hurt, more than anything had done for years, even the knife in his chest. The whole cathedral swam red, as though the air had turned to blood. But the vow was made. Ilya bound up his hand in the sleeve of his coat and slid the bloodied blade back into its sheath. He would have to clean it later; there was nothing that could be done here. Then he fell back onto a bench and closed his eyes.

His hand throbbed. He tried to focus on the pain, diminish it, but it was overwhelming. Then, through the pain, he heard something. It was not a voice, and yet it spoke to him.

I am here, it said. *I have found you. I am coming.*

Who are you? Ilya asked, puzzled.

But suddenly there was a hand shaking his shoulder, and a very human voice saying, "Friend? Is everything all right?"

The reflex was too strong. Ilya's eyes flew open and his good hand reached for the man's throat. The man stepped back with an exclamation and Ilya saw that it was the priest: a long equine face underneath the tall hat. He did not look old enough to be a priest. His beard was wispy, like coils of black fleece.

"Sorry," Ilya muttered. "Must have been asleep."

"It's my fault," the priest said quickly. "I shouldn't have woken you like that. Is everything all right?"

"I—hurt my hand. I fell in the park on the snow, caught it on a broken bottle."

"People will not use the litter bins," the priest said in distress. "We put up signs, but everyone just seems to ignore them. I sometimes think that no one cares about anything anymore."

"I know the feeling," Ilya said with a thin smile.

"Come into the back office. There's a toilet there, with a sink. I've got a first-aid kit. And tea—that's always good for shock." His gaze fell on Ilya's shrouded sword and he gave a puzzled frown. "You were going fishing? In this weather?"

"Present for my nephew," Ilya said, improvising hastily. "Birthday."

"Oh, I see. Well, come on through."

The thought of the tea was enough to draw Ilya to

his feet. He followed the priest through the incense-laden vault, still echoing with the remnants of his vow. But then there was the sudden drumbeat of rain on the wooden dome above him. A flicker of lightning sparked from the gilded icons. Startled, the priest looked up.

"The weather's broken."

"Sign of spring," Ilya said.

"About time. I thought the snow was never going to leave us."

It felt right, Ilya thought. Whatever storms the spring might bring, winter was passing at last.

Four

ALMATY, KAZAKHSTAN, 21ST CENTURY

Last night's foray to the pawnshop had seen a moderate degree of success: a few dollars from the gold chain and the watch. But the pawnbroker had not been interested in the ball.

"What is it?" he had asked, puzzled. "Is it made of metal?"

"Just a curio," Elena had lied, glibly. "My father said it was some kind of relic."

"I can't see anyone paying good money for it. Sorry."

Elena had then tried some of the market stalls, but though people were selling single boots and unworkable radios, the ball remained an object of curiosity, not desire. It rested once more in Elena's pocket, still heavy, still obscure.

Now Elena stood at the top of Lenina, looking south. The mountains were blanketed in drifting clouds. Her coat was soaked and her shoes were sopping wet, but it was better than more snow. The deep gutters that carried excess water down from the mountains were running brim full, so that it seemed that every street was bounded by a narrow stream. The trees, freed of their weight of snow, were bowed down by raindrops. And the sky was darkening again, heavy with storms.

Elena stepped out into the road to flag down a lift, but everyone was rushing home before the next cloudburst. Perhaps if she hurried, or found shelter . . . Then the thought of the cathedral snapped into her head. It was not far away. Elena set off again and was halfway across the park when the heavens opened. She dodged beneath the branches of a fir to catch her breath. The storm had come on so quickly, it must have raced down from the peaks. She hoped they weren't in for a wet spring.

Above her, something rustled in the branches. Elena looked up, expecting to see a squirrel or a magpie, but there was nothing. A shower of dislodged raindrops scattered across her face, making her flinch. Elena peered into the tree and something hissed. Startled, Elena stumbled back. She saw a face in the branches, upside down: gleaming eyes with pinpoint pupils and a row of needle teeth. It was coming down the tree, sliding along the trunk like a polecat, but the size of a man.

Elena cried out with fright. Then she turned and ran, her feet carrying her away from the thing in the tree. She slipped on the wet path and almost fell, but she did not stop and look back until she reached the edge of the park.

There was nothing behind her. The park was wet and empty. A woman with a bundle of shopping was staring at her.

"*Dyevushka?* You all right?"

"There was someone in the trees. I thought they were going to attack me." She abruptly sat down on the low wall that ran along the edge of the park. The woman clicked her tongue.

"The park's full of drug addicts, drunks, who knows what. Probably after money. Did they hurt you?"

Elena shook her head.

"Well, don't you go through there again, even in the daytime." The woman was clutching her shopping bag as though Elena might try to snatch it away. "I don't know what this town's coming to."

Still shaken, Elena nodded and the woman walked on. But she was right. It must have been some crazy person, driven by the mad impulse to climb a tree. Now that she thought back, the face had appeared female. Perhaps it had been one of the poor souls from the asylum, released because their families could no longer afford treatment. That seemed the likeliest explanation.

It was raining in earnest now, and Elena's hair was plastered to her face. She bolted across the road, dodging the traffic, and into the area in front of the market. The place was lined with stalls selling all manner of things: flat dried fish from the Kyrgyz lakes, batteries, radios, a stuffed eagle. Trying to keep beneath the awnings, Elena hastened toward the main market building and through the door.

She found herself in the vegetable section, in front of stalls covered with herbs, peppers, eggplant, apples. She was instantly assailed by cries from the vendors: "What do you want, *dyevushka*? Sultanas? Oranges?"

Gold teeth flashed. Elena wondered how many of

these women had university degrees. She would have bet that at least half were educated to the graduate level. Smiling, she shook her head and made her way through the vegetable section, past buckets of milk and piles of butter, toward the meat market. Beyond that were stalls selling clothes. She would just take a quick look. Perhaps by then the rain would have stopped.

To the left, high in the roof of the market, there was a sudden quick movement. Elena stared, but there was nothing there. It must have been a trick of the rainy light, filtering through the plastic covering of the ceiling. She was in the meat section now. A row of *kielbasy* sausages hung redly on hooks, surrounded by slabs of mutton. Turning the corner of a stall, Elena came face-to-face with the flayed head of a horse: the ears still pricked, the dark eyes startled against the exposed whites. The woman behind the stall gestured to it.

"Fresh today. You want some?"

Elena shook her head and crossed to the end of the row. She squinted into the dim vault above her head. She could see nothing but shadows. The scene in the park had unnerved her, making her edgy. *Get a grip on yourself,* she thought. *Stop jumping at things that aren't there.*

She went through the doors at the end of the market, to the crowded garment section. Elena looked at the merchandise, but there was little of interest: cheap Chinese goods from over the border, a few things from Russia. She was more interested in the pattern books, which promised a middle way between the shoddy imported garments and the expensive Western-style clothes that were sold in big stores like TSUM. Canadian cities, Elena had read, had more than one big store. It would be nice to have more choices.

Leaving the clothes behind, she went out into the passage that led to the street. The steps were slick with rain, but there was a brightness beyond the glass doors that suggested the storm had passed.

Elena stepped forward. Sharp fingers clamped tightly over her mouth and a hissing presence dragged her backward. She was drowning, going down into the rain, a river closing over her head, blood-red water banishing the distant stars.

Five

The young priest had put ointment on the cut and bandaged it. Now Ilya sat, sipping tea and watching the rain pour down through the pines beyond the cathedral. The priest had excused himself, saying that he had services to perform. Ilya tried to remember what these might be, and failed. He could no longer recall clearly the offices of the Church, only the festivals, and even these were colored by memories of the pagan world of his childhood. But it was all the same thing in the end, Ilya thought, whether you tied a rag to the papery bough of a birch tree or lit a candle beneath a gilded roof.

Restlessly, he got to his feet and went to the door. His muscles ached and his nerves were wire-taut. He wondered how long it would be before withdrawal really began to take a hold. He had faced armies, but he was still afraid of this; scared that need would drive him to break the vow before he had even begun. He had to find a place that was safe, away from dealers and temptation, but he already knew that this was one of the worst cities in that respect. Afghanistan and the border could be no more than a few hundred kilometers away. Give it until nightfall and there would be a dealer on every corner. Maybe the priest knew a place to go—the dormitory of a clinic, perhaps. But then he would almost certainly have to pay. . . .

The sound was sudden, startling him from his reverie: a woman, crying out in terror.

I am here, something whispered.

There was a flicker of movement in the pines, a shower of raindrops. Ilya ran down the steps and into the park.

A *rusalka* was moving through the trees as swiftly as a squirrel. It was chasing prey. At the point where the path branched off toward the war memorial and the eternal flame, a tall blonde in a raincoat was running. The *rusalka* swarmed down the tree toward her and Ilya cried out in warning, but his voice was hoarse. The woman stumbled once, and Ilya's heart skipped, but then she was out of the park and into the street and he lost sight of her. He could still see the *rusalka,* however. It was crouching at the side of the war memorial, beneath a rearing bronze horse, holding its clawed hands out to the eternal flame in a mockery of hearth-fire warmth. Ilya ran down the path, trying to ignore the heaviness in his limbs. He felt as though he were running underwater, and as he panted up to the war memorial, the *rusalka* uncurled itself unhurriedly, like a cat, and slunk over the top, apparently without seeing him.

Cursing, Ilya looked around him. A young couple walked past him, laughing, but when the girl saw Ilya, her face changed and she clasped her boyfriend's arm. He must look alarming, he thought: wild-eyed and disheveled, with the bloodstained bandage wrapped around his hand. No one would be looking to him to perform any heroics in the near future. Slowly, he walked over to the street.

The blonde woman had disappeared. But just as Ilya was starting to think that all might be well, he saw the *rusalka* again, scuttling underneath a market stall. No one else seemed to have seen it, but there was a curious sheen to the air, like a heat haze, and he wondered whether the creature was broadcasting some kind of interference around itself. Or perhaps it had to do with denial: People saw these things more easily in the old days, when they had believed.

Experience told him to look up, and there it was again, upside down on the ceiling. It was not looking at him, but staring into the market below. Ilya followed its gaze and saw the blonde woman once more. She was standing uncertainly among the vegetable stalls, her knuckles white around the strap of a shoulder bag. He was about to call out to her, but thought better of it. After the fright she must have had, the last thing she would want was some bloodstained maniac accosting her in the middle of the market. But why should the *rusalka* be so interested in this ordinary, attractive girl? Unless, of course, she had something it wanted. . . .

Ilya followed the woman through the main hall of the market and into a corridor filled with clothes stalls, keeping a wary eye on the ceiling. As the woman reached the end of the hall, the *rusalka* slid down the wall and disappeared. The woman went through the door. This time, Ilya did not hesitate. He ran to the doors, scattering startled shoppers, and into a passage. He glimpsed the woman as she turned. The *rusalka* was waiting for her.

Six

ALMATY, KAZAKHSTAN, 21ST CENTURY

Elena lay gasping on the tiled floor of the passage. A cold shower spattered her face and she looked up to see a woman's head flying across the vault. Its eyes were empty and its hair streamed out behind it like molten metal. It struck the wall and exploded into shards and fragments that spiraled away through the air.

A hand clasped Elena's wrist and hauled her to her feet, so that she stood in a ringing silence. She looked numbly at the man who stood before her with a blood-ied sword in his hand. A gleam of sunlight shot through the glass doors of the market. Elena backed against the wall.

"Dear God, what was *that*? And who are you?"

To her immense relief, the stranger lowered the sword.

"It's all right," he said quickly. "I'm not going to hurt you."

"I think you just saved my life," Elena said. Her voice was shaking. What kind of person went around with a sword in his hand? It looked like an antique. "And what was that *thing*?"

Her rescuer started to cough, leaning back against the wall, with a hand pressed to his chest. "Sorry," he gasped.

Warily, Elena considered him. His black leather overcoat was scuffed at the hem, and she absently noticed that a button was missing from the sleeve. A pale, angular face—typically Slavic—beneath unkempt, greying hair. The eyes were a chilly, haunted blue, but you saw a lot of eyes like that these days. Looking more closely, she saw that there was a tilt to them, suggesting ancestry other than Russian, a touch of the East. One hand was bandaged. It was also obvious that he was ill. Elena edged away a little. Tuberculosis was rife in the prisons, and this man had the air of a convict.

"My name is Ilya Muromyets," he said, recovering his breath. Odd, Elena thought, that he introduced himself in the Western manner. Didn't he have a patronymic? "And that creature was a *rusalka*."

"A *rusalka*?"

"Yes."

Elena stared at him incredulously. "What, you're telling me that was a water spirit? *Rusalki* are a myth."

"So am I," Ilya Muromyets said, smiling for the first time.

"What do you mean?" Elena asked with the anger of recent fright, but he did not answer. The name seemed familiar, somehow, but he was talking like a crazy person. She started to edge away toward the door.

"Why did it attack you?" Ilya Muromyets asked. "Do you know?"

"I've no idea." But even as she spoke, her hand curled protectively around her handbag and Ilya Muromyets' cold blue gaze fell upon it. Elena felt her face flushing; she was lousy at keeping secrets.

"What's that you've got there?" Ilya Muromyets asked, very low.

"It's nothing. It's something I found ages ago."

"Show me."

"Why?" Elena demanded. Even in these odd circumstances, she didn't see why she should comply with the instructions of a stranger.

"Because I've saved your life once already this morning, and I might have to do so again," Ilya Muromyets said, sounding reasonable enough. Reluctantly, Elena reached into her handbag and took out the black ball. Ilya Muromyets stared at it.

"Do you know what it is?" Elena asked.

"Where did you find it?"

"In the snow," Elena said, determined to tell him as little as possible.

"Here in Almaty? When?"

The cold eyes held her, and compelled. She said reluctantly, "On the road to Tashkent, about two weeks ago. There was a bad freeze, people died. The ambulance men were stealing things from the dead. I think this fell out of an ambulance driver's pocket, but I'm sure he stole it from someone else."

"Do you know who the original owner might have been?"

"There was a dead man in a car at the front of the line; he had a strange look about him. Maybe the thing belonged to him. But I don't really know."

"Strange? How?"

"I thought at the time that there was something funny about his eyes. But it must only have been that he had frozen." She shivered at the memory, wrapping her arms around herself. "I tried to find out what this thing might be. I went to the library and the museum; I phoned everyone I could think of—I used to be a scientist, you see. Anomalies arouse my curiosity."

Ilya Muromyets' eyes narrowed. "Tell me more."

"Stop interrogating me," Elena said. "Who are you, anyway?" Surely he could not be from internal security, not with that down-at-the-heel appearance, not to mention the sword. Unless the armed forces had become too poor to afford guns. But his interest in the object was intriguing.

"I told you my name," he said.

"Which means nothing."

Ilya Muromyets smiled. "True. There's no reason why you should have heard of me, not these days."

"Were you famous or something, then?"

"Or something. And you haven't told me your name, even."

"Elena," Elena said, after a pause.

"Just Elena?"

She did not answer.

"Well, if you don't want to tell me . . . Or perhaps it's Elena the Fair, like the story of the firebird?"

He smiled with sudden charm, and to her surprise, she found herself smiling in return.

"Do you live here?" Ilya Muromyets went on.

"I don't know anymore," Elena replied before she could stop herself.

It was a foolish thing to say, but he answered, "I know the feeling. Listen, Elena. What you are carrying is a danger to you; you've seen that already. Let me take it off your hands and you'll never set eyes on me or it again, I promise."

Elena felt suddenly as though she was standing back at the cosmodrome, gazing up at the stars, and she knew then that she was looking at the future. "If I give you this, it'll come at a cost." To her own ears, she sounded hard, like the new money-grabbing Russians she so despised. It made her add, "I've lost my job, my self-respect, and my family's starting to fall apart. Even my country's been abolished. All I have is a home I don't belong to anymore."

"I know what it is like," Ilya Muromyets said with a curious diffidence, "to lose everything, and not to know any longer who you might be. But I also know what it is like to need to be the hero of one's own life. If you wish, you can come with me, take your object to people who know what it is and what is to be done with it."

She must have looked suspicious, for he added, "If I meant you harm, I'd have let the creature kill you, or done it myself before now."

Elena looked into Ilya Muromyets' face, but could not read anything from it. She did not believe him. She believed in rockets, not *rusalki*. She did not know what she had seen, but she was certain that it could not have been anything supernatural. Surely she had been attacked by some drug addict, and Ilya Muromyets had scared the girl away. She could not have seen that head, flying toward the wall and leaving no trace of blood and bone behind. And Muromyets wanted the black ball, or knew someone who did. Maybe it was valuable after all; an antique, perhaps.

"Then how much will you give me for it?" Elena asked.

Ilya Muromyets grimaced.

"I don't have much money on me. Otherwise I'd buy it from you. But the people I know will be able to pay you for it, I'm sure of that."

"And you don't know what it is."

She saw him hesitate.

"I'm not sure what it is, no," he said. She could not tell if he was lying, or simply uncertain.

"So how much do you think they'll pay me for this unknown thing?" Elena said. Her gaze locked with Ilya Muromyets'.

"I don't know."

"You don't even know if they really will pay, do you?"

"What do you think, Elena? Do you think it's worth a chance?"

There was always the possibility, Elena thought, that it might be some kind of elaborate scam. God knows there had been enough of those over the years; she'd read about such things in the newspaper. What about that organ scandal in Tashkent? People had been told that they were being smuggled abroad to a new life, but they turned up in pieces in some village midden.

"Where are they, these people?"

"They're out of town," Ilya Muromyets said.

That settled it. "Tell them to get themselves into town, then," Elena said. "I'm not going anywhere with someone I don't know."

"I could just take it," Ilya Muromyets told her.

"But you won't," Elena said. "Will you?"

Ilya Muromyets shook his head, saying wearily, "No. I won't take it from you."

"Go to your friends, then. Tell them I'll meet them tomorrow in"—she hesitated, trying to think of somewhere suitably public that had security guards—"the lobby of the Hotel Kazakhstan. Say eleven o'clock. Then we'll talk."

"Where can I find you?" Ilya Muromyets asked. "Just in case I can't reach them?"

"There's a cafe on Mamedova Street, by the old metro vent. You can leave a message there," Elena said. She did not even want to give him her phone number, just in case. You never knew what contacts people might have, the extent to which they might be able to track you down. Ilya Muromyets nodded wearily.

"Very well. I'll tell them."

"Is there any way I can contact you? Where are you staying?"

"I don't know yet. I've only just arrived in town."

"If anything happens, and I can't make it, I'll leave a message at the cafe on Mamedova. Otherwise, I'll see you tomorrow," Elena said.

"All right. I'll see you then." He did not sound happy, but Elena was not disposed to further argument. She turned quickly and went out through the door of the market.

The rain had blown out over the city, leaving a washed pale sky in its wake. A group of old men had already clustered around a chessboard at the far end of the market, and Elena could hear the faint, discordant drift of karaoke from a cafe stall. She felt safer with people around. She walked swiftly across the wet concrete until she reached the edge of the trees, then looked back. The entrance to the market was empty; Ilya Muromyets was nowhere to be seen. Perhaps he had gone inside. Elena fingered the ball in her handbag, relieved to find it still safely tucked away. The whole episode had made little sense: this talk of spirits and strangeness, Ilya Muromyets' gaunt face and fractured manner. She wondered whether he was simply mad, but then she remembered the image of the girl, hanging above her with that needle smile. Involuntarily, her eyes lifted to the surrounding buildings, as though the girl might even now be crouching among the pigeons, but there was nothing.

Elena took a last look around, then hastened toward home.

Seven

Ilya waited behind the door of the market, his eyes closed, until he heard the woman's footsteps resound on concrete. She was walking west, her heels tapping with a swift, decisive rhythm. Ilya paused for a moment, then slipped outside. Sounds rushed upon him: a blackbird high in the trees might have been singing inside his own head. Ilya ignored these noises, concentrating instead upon Elena's heels on the pavement.

She thought he was mad, of course, and he couldn't blame her. He wondered if she would even remember the *rusalka*'s attack the next day. The *rusalki* had their own methods of remaining undetected: confusion, illusion, a pressure in the head. And they were aided by the precepts of this modern age, which, even in Russia, sought to reject the supernatural, and to embrace sweet reason. He had seen the war going on in Elena's mind. He had almost been able to hear her sorting and organizing, convincing herself that what she had seen had been explicable after all. *Rusalka* to runaway; from sword to fishing rod.

But the world was not so easy as these rationalists

would have it. Perhaps the *volkh* was right, and maybe the *rusalki* were creatures from another world, but Ilya Muromyets intended to treat them the same way that he always had: as enemies, and deadly in their treachery and stealth. His job now would be to keep Elena safe until the morning. Thus he looked up as he passed beneath the trees along the street, to see if a white face might be peering down through the branches, and he listened to the sounds around Elena's receding footsteps, to make as certain as he could that she would not be set upon before he could reach her.

He could see her now: her tall, neat figure nearing the end of the market stalls. Ilya moved beneath the scanty protection afforded by the trees; if she looked back, he did not want to be seen. He followed her past the mural of a smiling woman bearing a basket of fruit. That was what this town was named after, he remembered now: Alma-ata, in the Kazakhs' barbarous tongue. *Father of apples*. Elena was vanishing behind a passing tram. Ilya hung back, in case she should chance to glance around, and then he saw it.

The thing was sitting underneath one of the stalls, gnawing on a bone. Ilya's first wary thought was that it was one of the *rusalki* themselves, without the glamorous disguise, but then he saw that this creature was different. It was sinuous and small, its muscles gleaming beneath a translucent layer of skin. It had an unfinished, embryonic appearance. It reminded Ilya of the horse's head in the market, flayed and glistening. But the tissue beneath the skin was mottled, purple and grey like a bruise.

He reached for the fishing-rod case. The thing turned its head and looked at Ilya out of great black eyes. It sucked the bone straight into its mouth. Ilya saw the bone go down its throat with a great painful gulp. Then it was gone, swarming up the wall and into a crack in the concrete. Ilya glanced at the stallholder and his customers. Clearly, they had noticed nothing.

He caught sight of Elena again, walking toward the bus station. Ilya was immediately worried. What if he'd spooked her so much that she was heading out of town? She disappeared behind a plume of exhaust fumes. Ilya pursued, hastening past the line of Tajik refugees in their floral *shalwars,* reading the cards for passersby or selling the last of their pitiful possessions. One of the women looked up sharply as Ilya passed, gave a knowing, gold-toothed grin. Did she see him for what he was, Ilya wondered, or did he merely look like a potential customer? The latter seemed even more unlikely than the former.

Elena was almost at the end of the street, turning left. Ilya followed her down an unremarkable avenue of apartment blocks until she vanished into a dark doorway. He closed his eyes and listened, counting the number of steps that she took. The slam of the steel door was deafeningly final. He could not follow her into her home, but he could still listen. Keeping one ear open, Ilya went back out onto the street to find a public telephone.

It took him two attempts before he found one that was working. Looking up, he saw the broken-tooth vent of the unfinished metro, rising above him. He glanced across at the apartments, wondering whether Elena might glimpse him if she looked out of the window, but the place was half-hidden behind a tracery of branches. Fumbling in his pocket, Ilya extracted a few coins and pushed them into the machine. It took several minutes to accomplish this. A good thing these old machines still took rubles. The brief battle with the *rusalka* and the pursuit through the market had left him breathless. His palm throbbed with the cut of his vow, and his hands were trembling. The cut across his palm burned and stung. *Withdrawal.* It would not be long till it really started to get its claws into him, the sweats and shakes and fever, but he had no choice now. He had made his promise and there was no going back on it. For the first time in centuries, God was watching him.

The phone at the other end was ringing. At least Kovalin hadn't palmed him off with a forged number. But it was a long time before anyone answered.

"Who's that?" said a voice. It sounded very old and querulous, as if woken from sleep. Ilya wondered whether he might not have a wrong number after all.

"You don't know me," he said quickly. "My name is Ilya Muromyets. Kovalin gave me this number to call, if I had anything."

"Kovalin? Ah, yes, the boy," the voice said. Ilya's eyebrows rose. If the dead-eyed, corpse-faced Kovalin was a boy, how old was this person? "So, do you?" the voice went on.

"Do I what?" Ilya said, stupidly.

"Have anything." The voice was patient, as though reasoning with an idiot. *Not far wrong,* Ilya thought.

"Yes. I think so. I think I've found what you're looking for."

"Do you? How long have you been in Kazakhstan?"

"I got off the train this morning."

"And already you have found the thing for which we have been searching? Kovalin told me that you are a desperate man, Ilya Muromyets."

"Nevertheless," Ilya said, as firmly as he could, "I may have what you're looking for." He did not want to say: *I think I drew it to me.* The wordless voice still echoed in his head: *I am here. I have found you.* What the hell was this thing?

"Then come to us now. Show us. I will send a car."

"I don't have the object myself," Ilya was forced to admit. "Someone else has it. She wants to meet someone from your organization, to sell it. Tomorrow, at eleven. In the lobby of the Hotel Kazakhstan."

There was a long pause. Then the voice said, "Very well. I will give you a chance. We will be there. But do not be late."

"I won't—" Ilya started to say, but the voice had hung up. There was only the humming of the phone in his ear. Slowly, he replaced the receiver and focused once more on Elena's apartment. He could hear snatches of conversation, tuning in and out as though molded by static.

"—nothing very much. I went to the market. I thought we'd have the rest of that plov tonight, how does that sound?"

He thought that was Elena. An older, female voice answered briskly. Still listening in on this desultory conversation, Ilya sat down at a nearby table and ordered a shashlik and tea. Bottles of beer stood in the freezer and Ilya was tempted, but thought better of it. It was foreign, imported, and it would cost too much. Perhaps it was unfortunate that Kazakhstan, though Islamic, was not a dry country.

"How long does this place stay open?" he asked the waitress.

"All night."

"Any chance of a cheap place to stay round here?"

"You could sleep out back with the refugees."

Ilya, studying her, saw blue eyes in a dark Persian face. It was likely that she was one of those refugees. She looked no more than sixteen.

"Two hundred *tenge* will get you a bed. And there's a toilet—we built it ourselves." She sounded proud. He'd slept in worse conditions in Siberia, and he could keep an ear out for Elena, at least.

"All right."

"Do you want to see it?" the girl asked, in the manner of a receptionist showing a guest the best bedroom. Ilya stifled a smile and followed her through to the back of the cafe, to a collection of rusty old vehicles and corrugated iron huts.

"We sleep here." She pointed to an ancient bus.

"It'll do."

A boy was cooking plov in a wok over an open fire. He had no face, only a mass of blackened scar tissue. Blue eyes like the girl's were scowling in concentration as he stirred the rice and mutton.

"My brother," the girl said, following Ilya's stare.

"Dear God. What happened?"

"A shell. It fell on the house. We lived near Parchar, in Tajikistan. Everything in the village was destroyed."

"Who did it?"

"I don't know. Rebels, maybe, or mujahideen, or the Americans."

"Why would Americans destroy your village?"

The girl shrugged. "I don't know. Why not?"

Ilya's heart reached out to her, but she did not seem unduly concerned. Perhaps she had been too young to remember properly, or perhaps such events were like bad weather, striking without reason. The girl leaned over her brother, teasing, threatening to snatch the spoon, and the boy gave a happy, lipless grin.

Watching them, the craving for heroin receded until it was no more than a distant tide. Ilya knew that it would come back, but faced with these two, who had so little, he could not bring himself to care about his own troubles. He went into the bus and sat down on one of the stained mattresses, listening as the rain once more began.

Interlude

Early that morning, Anikova drove the staff car back from the dacha to Central Command. It was not long past dawn and she was still half-asleep, so when she reached the curve of the road that led past the lake, she stopped the car and got out. The lake was dim with mist in the early morning light; if Anikova narrowed her eyes, the landscape seemed to blur and swim, as though she was looking through a water-filled glass. Nothing moved in the pines, or among the white-striped birch branches. If she looked at the coils of mist in a certain way, she might imagine that the lost city of Baikal was rising from the water: the oldest place in Russia.

But this was no longer Russia. This was her home of Pergama Province, not far from First City. Strange, Anikova thought, to be homesick for a place one had never known, but Russia must still run in her blood. *This is Byelovodye,* she reminded herself, *the heart of all the Russias, the place where they meet, the hidden Republic. This is the best place of all.* She looked down at her smart dark uniform, its buttons in the shape of snarling bear heads, at the red stars at her cuffs. Yet when she thought of what she and the Mechvor had to do that day, of what they had already done, she felt hollow and unconvinced, as though the uniform was the only thing holding her together.

Anikova rested her forehead on the cool side of the staff car and took a breath of morning air. That kind of thinking was forbidden these days, and had never been entirely wise. She remembered her mother cautioning her against dangerous thoughts. *Be careful what you dream. Look what happened to your father.* And then her mother's face would grow pinched and pale as she screwed her hands together in the shelter of her apron. Anikova had taken good heed of the lesson; an easy thing for a child to learn, but harder for an adult, forced into disquieting compromises. She should forget about hidden cities, forbidden dreams: just get in the car and drive. But it was a long time before she could bring herself to leave the lake.

An hour and a half later, Anikova sat with her hands on her knees, watching as the Mechvor went through the procedure. Kitai's whiteless eyes were closed; her face wore a faint smile. Anikova thought that this was what irritated her most about the Mechvor: The woman never seemed to lose her temper. She remained good-natured, good-humored, even under the most trying circumstances. Anikova could not help feeling, however, that Kitai felt a genuine concern for all her subjects, even when she was so ruthlessly stripping their dreams from their heads.

The old man lay on an operating table, surrounded by equipment. What made it worse was that this was the second case that morning; Kitai had already seen to a girl brought in by Anikova's people on the previous day. She had been found outside the People's Palace, distributing samizdat literature, perhaps the very leaflets that had been printed in the old man's bathroom. Anikova had watched sourly as the Mechvor questioned her, treating it all as a huge secret, as though they were all girls together, gossiping about boys and love. The girl had at first been terrified, but had gradually relaxed, confiding in the Mechvor, forgetting about the silvery bands that crisscrossed her shaved scalp and led downward to feed into the skin of Kitai's hands. And in due course, Kitai had plucked her thoughts neatly from her skull, leaving the girl a passive, empty shell.

"We'll give her something new, later today," Kitai had said that morning. "Something much more appropriate." She had put a hand on Anikova's arm and peered anxiously into her face as they made their way up the marble steps of Central Command. "She'll be a lot happier, really. And it won't hurt a bit."

The wind that blew across the central square was cold and tinged with rain. The classical portal of the Command building towered above them, its façade dull in the absence of sunlight. Anikova, dressed only in her uniform darks, shivered.

"Tell me," Anikova said. "How many people's memories have you altered like this? How many dream-neurons have you bled dry?"

Kitai looked momentarily blank. "Why, I can't remember." She shook her head. "I'm sorry, Colonel. I do keep excellent records—I'm sure I could get the numbers for you."

"Don't bother," Anikova said. She wondered how old the Mechvor really was. She had the appearance of a girl in her twenties, but Anikova had first met her when she herself was a raw recruit, and that had been three decades ago. In that time, the Mechvor had barely altered.

"I started my work among the horse clans." Kitai seemed eager to make up for her inadvertent lapse in knowledge. "It was very different then, naturally. We had not developed the technology; we used drugs and drums. I suppose you might say I was a kind of shaman. But now, with all this new equipment, there's no need for any of that primitive sort of thing." She smiled. "I'm a very modern girl, really."

You are what the State wants you to be, Anikova thought, but she did not say so aloud. The last thing she wanted was Kitai poking about inside her head. The Mechvor was looking at her sharply, nonetheless.

"You do understand how necessary this is, Colonel?" she said. "That dreams and ideas should be controlled? Because otherwise, reality itself is in danger of collapse. Ever since the coil was stolen, the breaches along our borders have been growing, increasing in number and in size. These are no longer just the little natural rifts, Colonel. If we don't find a solution, it's only a matter of time before a major breach occurs. If this coil remains in the wrong hands, and matters reach a point where the tribes and our enemies can freely cross between here and Russia, our national security will be threatened. We have to redouble our efforts if we're to maintain our wonderful society."

"Of course I understand," Anikova said. "I lost my father through a breach. Do you think I'm not aware of the risks?" How many coils did Central Command possess, anyway? She knew that most of the gates on the Byelovodyean side were powered by Tsilibayev's engineered copies and had now been closed, but she could not help wondering as to the number of ancient originals. That information, however, was strictly classified: The only certainty was that there was now one less. With an effort, she forced her thoughts from her mind.

"Colonel, I'm so sorry," the Mechvor said, but she must have known about Gregori Anikov's death. Anikova's background was a secret to no one; Kitai's sympathy felt merely superfluous.

"Well, I should get busy," Kitai went on. "It would be nice to go for lunch later, wouldn't it?"

Anikova muttered something in reply. The Mechvor, feeding the links back into her hands, connected herself to the machine and started work.

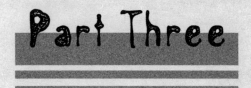

Part Three

One

ALMATY, KAZAKHSTAN, 21ST CENTURY

That morning, Elena found herself applying her makeup with more than her usual care, using the American lipstick that had been a birthday present from her sister, and coaxing the last grains of Clarins powder from its case. Then she stared at herself in the bathroom mirror and frowned. Was she so desperate for a boyfriend that she would dress up for a madman with a sword? She had not had a date in over a year, and there had been no one serious since Yuri had chosen space in preference to her. But she knew that the smart suit and the lipstick weren't for the mysterious Ilya Muromyets. They were for herself, for her future, in a way that she did not fully understand.

The weather was still cold. Elena hesitated between her raincoat and the full-length rabbit fur, eventually deciding on the latter. She did not want to risk it in the rain, but she felt the need to persuade these unknown people that she was someone to be reckoned with, a professional woman with money. The fur coat was over seven years old, but still had its silver sheen. Now that the winter was passing, she would sell it before they left Moscow. She could not stop thinking about Anna and the German. Where was her sister today? In the restaurant or, God forbid, flat on her back in someone else's hotel room? Elena was determined to wring a decent price out of Muromyets' contacts, if it was the last thing she did.

She collected the ball from its place on the dressing table. It lay heavy and innocent in the palm of her hand. There had not been the rustle of something inhuman, bolting beneath the dresser in the night. What had Ilya Muromyets meant, with his talk of *rusalki*? A lunatic, she thought again, or perhaps merely a poet. She remembered, uneasily, the addict in the park and the girl's head flying toward the wall of the marketplace corridor. She could not have seen such a thing; she must have imagined it.

She took a last look into the mirror. Then, making sure that the ball was safely zipped into the inner pocket of her handbag, she checked the gas stove and the locks on the door, slipped into her best pair of heels, and walked down into daylight.

The Hotel Kazakhstan was on the other side of town. Elena found herself looking warily about her as she walked, but the day was dreary and overcast. As she turned the corner onto Abai Street, a plume of cloud lifted up from the mountains, briefly revealing their snowy summits. The wind changed, veering round to the north. The first heavy drops began to fall and Elena decided to take the chance and hitch. She put out a hand, waiting until a car with a single occupant appeared, and flagged it down.

"Kyda?"

"Hotel Kazakhstan," Elena said. If she was lucky,

and the man wanted the fare, he might take her all the way. But he shrugged.

"Sorry. I'm not going down Lenina. I can drop you at the bottom of the park, if you like."

"Thanks," Elena said, though the thought of the park brought back some unpleasant memories. She studied the man covertly as they drove. Charms dangled in the windows of the car; the seats were cracked and cheap. A cheerful Kazakh face, nothing sinister about it. She had a brief, broken memory of the thing in the pine tree, the snap of teeth. She ought to be glad of the prospect of getting rid of the ball, but her lethal curiosity had also been aroused.

That was the trouble, Elena thought. If there was the promise of anything interesting, she always wanted to get involved. Then the doors would slam shut, just as they had during her time in the space program. It wasn't anyone's fault. It was just the way things went, and at least in this case there might be a chance of getting some money out of it. Then Anna wouldn't have to do what she had done. Thinking of her sister, Elena felt a dull, dim bemusement, as though she had been living with a stranger all these years.

The car pulled toward the curb and stopped. Elena handed the driver a hundred *tenge* note and got out into the chilly air. Lenina stretched before her. She could see the lattice of the Hotel Kazakhstan reaching up to the heavens like a crown. The tiny square of the cable car appeared behind it, hauling itself up Koktubye Hill where the radio mast stood. It was perhaps a twenty-minute walk and there was enough time; she was reluctant to spend any more money on car fares. Elena set off toward the hotel.

Despite the chill, she could already taste spring on the wind. There were buds on the oaks along Lenina and the gutters were still running with snowmelt. In the distance, she could see the statue of the Golden Warrior coming into view, high on its immense pedestal, riding on a griffin. Another of Lenin's replacements, overlooking the government square. Elena had seen the original armor half a dozen times; it had been dug up in an archaeological find in the 1920's, high in the mountains. She dimly remembered her father snorting with drunken derision and remarking that an empty suit of armor was as good a representation of the new state as any. But everyone agreed that it was a useful landmark. It meant that she was no more than a few minutes' walk from her destination.

When she reached the concrete forecourt of the hotel, she paused. Ilya Muromyets was nowhere to be seen. Perhaps he was already inside. She made her way to the double doors of the building, stepping aside as a group of businessmen came through. Americans, or perhaps European; she could not tell. They wore expensive coats and their faces appeared freshly scrubbed, as though their mothers had polished them with handkerchiefs. One of the younger men gave Elena a frank, appraising glance as he went by. Elena smiled back. It was good to know that she wasn't entirely unremarkable, sliding into the invisibility of middle age. But then she thought of Anna's German engineer, of international dating agencies, and felt her smile fade.

Then she was through the door and into the gloom of the hotel foyer. It took her eyes a moment to adjust and realize that the shadowy figure standing before her was Ilya Muromyets. His sharp-boned face was haggard. She wondered where he had spent the night.

"Are you all right?" Elena asked.

"Yes, yes, I'm okay," he told her, dismissively. "Do you have it?"

"Yes. Are they here?" Apart from Ilya, herself, and a bored girl emptying the ashtrays, the foyer was empty.

"They're upstairs in one of the rooms. Eighth floor, number 820. I phoned the main guy again this morning. He didn't want to meet down here."

"I'm not going up there," Elena said firmly.

Ilya looked at her, opened his mouth as if to argue, and then seemed to think better of it.

"You can understand why?" Elena asked.

Rather to her surprise, he nodded. "Yes, I understand. And maybe you are wise."

"I'm a woman," Elena said. "I have to think of these things."

Ilya gave a sudden wry grin. "So you do. I'll look after you, you know. But there's no reason why you should trust me. It makes the situation more difficult."

"Just call the person doing the deal. Tell him to get down here if he wants the thing. How long is this likely to take?"

"Do you have a mobile phone?"

Elena did, but the phone card cost money and she was reluctant to use it up. "Ask the desk to call upstairs."

Ilya went across to the bell and summoned a receptionist, a young woman with an elaborate bouffant hairstyle. She looked vaguely familiar. She regarded Ilya with undisguised disdain.

"Room 820," Elena said. "Can you call them for

me? Tell them there are some people waiting for them downstairs."

The receptionist's face relaxed a little as she studied Elena.

"Isn't it Elena Irinovna? I went to school with your sister. I'm Natalya Yulieva."

"Yes," Elena said, and smiled. "I remember you. You used to live on Pushkin Street."

"We still do. How's your sister? I haven't seen her in ages."

Ilya nudged Elena's elbow. "She's fine," Elena said hastily. "Could you make that call for me? Thanks."

"Of course," Natalya said. Ilya melted back into the shadows.

"She thinks I'm a drug dealer," he murmured.

"Are you?"

Ilya shook his head. His face was drawn and pale and his hands were jammed into the pockets of his overcoat. She could not see whether they were trembling. If he was an addict, it would explain his shabby appearance, which didn't make her feel any more secure. Perhaps he'd been in the military: a lot of people had picked up the habit in Chechnya, or perhaps Afghanistan. It was hard to judge his age—late forties?—and she had once heard that heroin made people look older. The thought sealed her decision not to go anywhere alone with him.

The receptionist was frowning at the phone.

"There's no answer."

"No? Maybe they went out."

"I'm sure they didn't. I'd have seen them. Ivan Mikhailovich!" Natalya called. A man at a desk in the corner glanced up. "The three men in 820. Have any of them gone out?"

The man shrugged. "Not to my knowledge." He turned back to his papers. Elena turned away, deliberately ignoring him, and she saw that Ilya was doing the same. "Keeping an eye on the Americans," Ilya whispered. Elena nodded. The presence of the FSB man made her feel a little safer. She leaned over the reception desk. "Can you try again?"

"Sorry, there's no reply. It's just ringing and ringing."

"Look, it's past eleven," Ilya said tightly. His head was on one side, Elena noticed, almost as though he was listening to something. He added abruptly, "Wait there," and vanished in the direction of the lifts. Elena turned away, but from the corner of her eye she saw that once Ilya had gone, the FSB man rose from his place at the desk and unobtrusively followed. Watching American, or dealers, or everybody? Elena paused indecisively. If she lost Ilya, she'd lose all chance of selling the object.

"If my friend comes back, tell him I've gone to the ladies' room," Elena said to Natalya. She slipped around the side of the foyer, to the second set of elevators. The elevator cranked upward, as if it was being winched by hand. There were more buttons indicated on the door panel than there were floors. Elena wondered what would happen if she pressed number 20. Go right out through the roof, probably.

Moments later, she was on the eighth floor. She followed the signs. Rooms 810–820 were around a corner. There was a peculiar musty smell in the corridor, as though it hadn't been cleaned for years. Perhaps they no longer bothered; it occurred to her to ask Natalya on the way back down, see if they wanted another cleaner. She could hear nothing. Cautiously, she peered around the corner. The door to room 820 stood wide open. There was no sign of Ilya or the FSB man. Caution warred with curiosity. She would just look through the crack of the door; she would not go in. . . .

The smell grew stronger as she crept along the corridor, but it was no longer musty. It reminded her of something, like the atmosphere in the launch chambers at the cosmodrome: electric and anticipatory. She put her eye to the crack in the door. She could see a man's hand, lying limp on a red carpet. The fingers were curled and unmoving. Elena stepped back from the door.

"Ilya?" She had not meant to speak, and her voice sounded very loud in the overwhelming silence. Then he was standing in front of her. His face had been pale before, but now it was grey.

"What happened?" Elena asked. She tried to step around him to see through the open door, but he blocked her path.

"They're dead. Don't look. We have to go." He grasped her hand and pulled her down the corridor. For a visibly sick man, he was disconcertingly strong.

Elena, too startled to protest, said, "Where's the man from the FSB? I saw him follow you."

"I don't know. He's not in the room. Although it's hard to tell."

"What do you mean? Let go of me," Elena said and tugged her hand free. "Did you kill them?"

"No. Why would I have done such a thing?"

"I have no idea, Ilya! I know nothing about you."

"You know I saved your life. I think Ivan-from-the-FSB went to fetch his friends. I think he suspects something's happened. He's right. We have to get out of the hotel."

They took the lift as far as the second floor, and then the stairs to the basement. The kitchens were like a dungeon, cavernous and damp. A chef was putting something into an oven; Ilya and Elena waited until his back was turned, and made a dash for the door. They fell out into a yard, surrounded by dustbins.

The hotel towered above them. The mountains lay ahead, mist curling across the distant rows of pines. Elena's mind was racing. Both the receptionist and Ivan-from-the-FSB had seen her in Ilya's company. And they would suspect Ilya of the murder. That lean and hungry look was not one to inspire thoughts of innocence. The receptionist knew who she was, knew where she lived, and even if Natalya was disposed to keep her old friend's sister out of trouble, Ivan must have heard them talking. The foyer had been as quiet as the grave. The FSB was never overly concerned whether one was guilty or not. They liked order, and neat solutions, and a murder pinned on the nearest possible suspects was usually neat enough.

Her earlier words to Ilya floated back into her mind, the mockery of an echo. *I'm not going anywhere with someone I don't know.* Now it seemed that she had no choice.

"Come on." Ilya was already making his way between the dustbins.

"Where are we going?"

"Away from here, for a start."

Elena, deeply regretting her choice of shoes, followed him across a cracked concrete forecourt and into an ornamental garden. In summer this was a pleasant enough place, with umbrellas and fountains, but now the water had congealed to icy mud, broken by twisted willows. They crashed through a line of bushes and out onto a potholed track. And now Elena knew where they could go.

"The cable car!"

Ilya spun around. "What?"

"It leads up to Koktubye Hill. There are villages on the other side."

Ilya nodded. "Quickly, then."

As they panted up to the kiosk, the car was rattling into the terminus. Ilya thrust change into the attendant's hand and there was a brief teeth-gritting wait before the car set off again. Elena felt Ilya's cold fingers close briefly over her own. The bandage across his palm was grimy. Gently, she pulled her hand away.

"Don't worry. We'll be long gone by the time they get their act together."

The ground was already far below: a maze of old houses and bare-branched cherry orchards. The mountains were suddenly very close, as though the cable car was climbing up the rim of the world.

Had Ilya killed those people, back there in the room? Memory was only now beginning to sharpen and clarify. The carpet had not been red, after all, but a dull institutional green, covered with blood. It had been, he had said, hard to tell who was in the room. She looked down at her hands and saw that they were shaking.

"Elena," Ilya said. Tentatively, he patted her sleeve. "Don't *worry*. I told you—I'll look after you." He looked suddenly younger beneath the junkie pallor, and she thought, oddly, that he would have been an attractive man, given half a chance. Perhaps he still was.

"When we get to the top, we'll make our way down the other side, to one of the villages." She was thinking aloud.

"That's a reasonable plan. Then find a car. Hire someone to take us somewhere. Over the border would be best, into Kyrgyzstan. It's the closest city, isn't it? And if it's anything like the rest of the former Soviet Union, bureaucracy will be so bad between the different countries, it'll take time for the police to catch up."

"Ilya, wait," Elena said blankly. She couldn't leave town just like that. There was her mother and sister to think of; there was Moscow and Canada. "I was thinking more of finding somewhere to hide, not leaving the country. I haven't got much in the way of papers—no passport, no travel documents, just my identity cards and my Party card. I haven't got much money, either. And I'm wearing stupid shoes."

Ilya smiled, a real smile this time, not the wolfish grin. "Here," he said. He reached into his overcoat pocket and took out a sticky package. "Take it. If you have money, you probably won't need papers." He thrust the money into her hand and she took it gingerly. The edges of the notes were wet and red. She estimated, dazed, that it was approximately five thousand dollars.

"Where did you get this?" she asked, but she already knew.

"From a dead man's jacket. He won't need it. I'll keep the other half."

"Your contact had ten thousand dollars in his

pockets?" She owed her current circumstances to the pockets of a dead man, back there on the Tashkent road. She nearly asked Ilya if he'd thought to steal the man's teeth.

"It would probably have been yours anyway. I think it was payment for the object." He gave her a sharp glance. "Which is safe, yes?"

"I think so." She scrabbled in her handbag. "Here. You might as well see it for yourself."

Ilya took the ball in his undamaged hand, weighing it. As he did so, the ball split.

"It's broken!" Elena said, dismayed.

"It's unraveling. . . ."

They stared at the ball. Filaments were spinning out over Ilya's fingers. It resembled a spider's web: a matted tangle of glossy dark hairs, so fine that they drifted up into the still air. Within the center of the threads lay a smaller object, like a nested doll. It was roughly in the shape of a small coiled fossil, but made of bronze. A thin groove ran down one polished side. Ilya dusted the filaments from his palm. They floated down onto the floor, where they formed a brief black pattern before melting into ash.

"What is it?"

"Elena, I don't know." He seemed as baffled as she. "Can you hang on to it? My pockets have holes in them."

"What if it's dangerous?"

"I'll carry your bag if you like."

But the fur coat had only a shallow pocket, and she did not want to relinquish her bag and the money. "No, that's all right. I'll carry it," she said.

They were almost at the summit of the hill. Elena

lapsed into calculation. A thousand dollars would be more than enough to get her over the border, stay somewhere cheap for a few nights, then get a train ticket to Moscow or St. Petersburg. She could lose herself there, in the big cities where no one cared who you were or what you had done. She had been standing in the foyer when Ilya went upstairs. They would surely not want her for murder, would they? She was an accomplice in the eyes of the police, she told herself firmly, nothing more. And the rest of the money could be mailed back to Anna and her mother. Four thousand dollars would buy visas and tickets; it would get them to Canada.

But what about the FSB? Her original reasoning had been correct; they wouldn't care whether she was guilty or not. If she was arrested, lawyers would have to be hired, costs met, bribes delivered. All the Canada money would be gone, eaten away into a bottomless sink of red tape and corruption. She would rather become a fugitive than see that happen, but it was beginning to sink in that she might have blown any chance of working on a space program again. Long-term gains, long-term losses. She found herself veering between excitement and despair.

"What about you, Ilya? Do you have any travel documents?"

"Sort of."

That meant any papers he had would be forged, bought on the black market. It was none of her business.

The summit of Koktubye Hill was lost in cloud. She could see the radio mast lifting out of the mist like a spear. Closer lay the dumpy domes of the cafe yurts.

If only they could stop for a moment, get a glass of tea . . . But all of her possibilities had narrowed down to flight. She fumbled in her bag for the mobile and dialed her mother's number. She could, at least, tell them not to worry, even if it was a lie. The thought of the police suddenly appearing on the doorstep, her mother, unsuspecting, shuffling to the door in her slippers—no, it was not to be borne. The phone rang and rang until the answering machine clicked in.

"Mama? It's me. I've had to leave town for a day or so, I've got caught up in something a bit tricky"—*understatement*—"and I need to sort things out. Please don't worry. I'll call you later."

Ilya was watching her, his face unreadable.

"I had to call them," she said defensively.

"I didn't say you did not." He turned his head and stared up the hill to the destination of the lurching cable car. Elena tried not to think about her unsuitable shoes. She knew what lay on the other side of Koktubye: the long slope, heavy with scree and scrub, falling hundreds of feet down into the valley below. And these high hills were only the foothills of the mountains. Beyond lay the great wall of the Tien Shan.

Stop it. So what if you ruin your shoes and your feet hurt? At least it isn't snowing. All you have to do is make it down the slope and then Ilya will find someone with a car. If she started fretting now—if she started *thinking*—she would sit tight in the cable car and wait to be arrested.

Machinery whined and groaned. The cable car had only recently been renovated; Elena tried not to think of all the years it had spent rusting in heavy snowfall. The car swung ominously upon the rail and ground to a halt. Ilya rose shakily to his feet and helped Elena from the car.

"How are your shoes?"

"I'll manage."

"I'll help you." He gave her feet, in their smart high-heeled pumps, a quick, measuring glance. "If it becomes a real problem, you can have my boots, but they will be too big."

"My God," Elena said in wonder. "You *are* a gentleman, aren't you?"

"You might say I was raised in an old-fashioned way."

They slipped behind the yurts of the cafe; no one was around. They passed a dog on a rope, which rose to its feet, growling, and a large, mild cow. Elena took the muddy path through the trees, which ended in a barbed-wire fence.

"We'll have to go over."

"Or under," Elena said, ducking grimly. She felt her fur coat catch on the wire, saw Ilya reach down a hand. After a moment, he pulled her coat free, but his hands were trembling. If he went into serious withdrawal, what was she to do? She knew little about cold turkey. Was it like a bad case of the flu? Or worse? Or was Ilya not an addict at all, but simply ill? The subject would have to be raised at some point, but for now, Elena compromised by asking, "By the way, are you sure you're all right?"

He nodded briefly. "Yes."

If he was a typical man, Elena thought with a mixture of irritation and pity, the last thing he'd want would be a fuss.

"Good," she said, and set off down the slope. It

was not too bad if she went sideways and concentrated on putting one foot in front of the other, but this was the gentler part of the hill. Elena found herself regretting the erosion of the snow. A fall now would result in bruises or worse, in broken bones. She looked up once at the mountains and felt dizziness snatch at her: that old sensation of looking down into the sky. The Tien Shan were so huge that they distorted perspective. From farther down the slope, there was a sudden rattle of movement. Elena frowned, trying to see.

"What was that?"

"I don't know." Ilya's face was set and abstracted, as though he was listening to the wind. He muttered, "I can't hear—" then broke off.

"They keep goats around here," Elena said, but the sound came again and when she looked down the slope she could see something little and dark, leaping among the stones. A cat, perhaps—but then it stood up on its hind legs. "It's a monkey," she said, startled, and Ilya replied, "No, it is not."

"What is it, then?"

"Some kind of ghoul. I saw it in the marketplace yesterday."

"A *ghoul*? I went through the market. I didn't see anything like that until—until that girl went for me." It occurred to Elena that Ilya might have followed her.

"We should hurry," Ilya said. He pointed to the wall of the mountains. "Look."

There was a front coming in over the Tien Shan; a band of clouds trailing streamers: a spring storm coming over the Chinese border, that would be as much sleet as rain. Elena gritted her teeth and slithered down the slope.

Two

Ilya did not like taking Elena with him, but he could not leave her to the mercy of the authorities. If the FSB man had not been so close behind, Ilya would have demanded that Elena give him the object, paid her the bulk of the money, and been gone. With the object no longer betraying her presence to the *rusalki*, as Ilya was now sure it had done, they would leave her alone. But the situation had become complicated by the murders and the consequently certain involvement of the FSB. Ilya had firsthand experience of such people. Those who were not brutal were incompetent and lazy, and could often be bought off over more trifling matters, but murder was a serious crime. He could hardly try to explain to them that the murders had not been committed by anything human. He had seen the marks in the shredded flesh, the bites on throat and rib cage. The men in the room had been killed by *rusalki*, but he did not know why and it was not, in any case, an explanation the police would believe.

Moreover, it looked as though Westerners stayed at the Hotel Kazakhstan, and a set of murders would be bad for business. People would suspect the *Mafiya*. The Westerners would stay away, and he knew that few enough of them came to Kazakhstan in the first place—corruption, red tape, and violence made it a hard place in which to do business, even for the big oil and gas companies. No, the hotel manager would surely insist on the case being treated properly, and the girl at the desk had known Elena. So he had no choice, really. They must both run, and Kyrgyzstan—close, mountainous, with a different bureaucracy—was the most practical choice.

Ilya did not want to respond to the small voice within that told him he would welcome a companion, especially such a pretty one. He had learned to do without friendship over the years, without women other than whores, but it was never easy. He stole a look at Elena, picking her way through the stones, her face set in determination. An intelligent woman, too, and a brave one. *The best thing you can do, my hero, is to stay as far away from her as possible. Such a woman should have nothing to do with the likes of you.*

The storm front was coming in fast over the mountains. He could no longer see the ghoul, but no doubt it was there, hiding among the stones. But he had the sword. If he could slay *rusalki*, he could surely dispose of this one small creature. Unless there were more than one, and they were following . . .

The *volkh*'s voice echoed in his head: *not human. What am I, then?* Ilya silently asked the wind, but there was no reply. He listened for that other small voice, but there was nothing.

At the bottom of the slope, a road led toward a scattering of buildings that looked like one of the old communal *kholkhoz* farms. The city had ended abruptly, far behind them now and cut off by the mountain wall. To Ilya, it seemed as though Almaty huddled against the Tien Shan for protection, seeking shelter from the endless steppes. He remembered the steppes in earlier centuries, still swept by the wild horsemen, the riders with their leather armor, their hunting eagles, their swift and deadly bows. Two generations and Russian guns had put an end to that. The riders were gone, replaced with accountants and car salesmen. Perhaps it was better. Ilya did not know, but he wondered where such dreams might go to die.

He heard Elena's foot slip on loose gravel even before she cried out, but did not manage to reach her before she fell. She sprawled across the slope, hands scrabbling for purchase. Ilya, cursing his own weakness, hurried over and helped her up.

"Are you hurt?"

"I don't think so. Bruised." She stood up. She had dropped her handbag. Ilya spotted it among the stones. He picked it up. "No, I'm all right." She leaned against him, steadying herself as she secured a shoe, and before he could think better of it, he put his arms around her. It was a long time since he had felt so close to anyone.

I am here.

Ilya blinked. A sudden burst of light spilled from the bag in his hand. Ilya saw a space open in thin air, a spark running up it like a fuse. There was a burst of light high in the air above the mountains, then it was gone.

Ilya stared, but there was nothing there.

"What was that?" Elena whispered.

"I don't know." Embarrassed, he let her go. "We'd best get moving."

It was no more than early afternoon, but the sky was already dark with rain. They had reached the road. The village was perhaps half a kilometer ahead. Ilya could see a light in a window, heard voices idly discussing the weather. He paused for a moment and listened further. He could hear the small creatures in the mountains: a squirrel running along a branch, the sudden flutter of a flock of birds flying upward, then the rattle and rush of branches being thrust violently aside. And all the while a pounding sound upon the wet earth, as insistent as a drum. It was a long time since he had heard that sound: the noise of hoofbeats, a multitude of horses, ridden fast.

"Ilya?" Elena asked. "What's wrong?"

He had expected sirens, not horses. "I don't know," he said. "I can hear hoofbeats."

Elena looked around. "Where? I can't see anything."

"They're in the mountains," Ilya murmured, but even as he spoke, it was no longer true, and the hair prickled at the back of his neck. The riders were down from the slopes, and at the head of the road on which they were now standing. The horses, free from the constraint of the trees, ran swift as thought, faster than any normal animal. And they were bringing the storm with them.

"They're coming for us," he whispered.

"My God, Ilya—who? What are you talking about? Where are they?" Elena was looking wildly about her. She would not yet be able to see or hear them, but they were coming. "If someone's after us, we have to get off the road." She pointed to a strip of trees on the other side of the valley, marking the path of a streambed. She tugged at Ilya's sleeve. They stumbled across a bank of stones toward the trees. The drumming noise grew louder, blotting out all other sound and deafening Ilya. He put his hands to his ears, but it did no good. Then the first wave of rain hit them, drenching and sudden.

They had almost reached the trees when Ilya made the mistake of looking back. The riders were coming through the rain. They bore banners the color of blood, and they wore short leather jerkins and close helmets. The front line rode without reins, gripping their horses with their knees, their bows trained upon Ilya and his companion. He had seen nothing like them for over a hundred years. Elena had turned, too, and he saw her face grow blank with shock. As he stared, the riders parted. A figure was riding with them, dressed in a tall conical helmet and armor made of gold, chased and configured with images of leaves, lions, and spirals.

He heard Elena gasp, "That's the Golden Warrior!"

They could not see the face beneath the golden helmet. The Warrior raised a hand, gave a command. Elena said, "No." She grabbed Ilya's arm, dragging him in a zigzag toward the trees. Something small and dark darted between his feet, and the ground seemed to give way beneath him.

He was alone, staggering through a landscape of branches and mist and rain.

Do not be afraid. I am here.

He tasted cloud-cold on his tongue and then, quick as a dream, the sun came out. The warriors were gone. And Ilya was not where he had been.

Interlude

The airships wallowed like tethered porpoises over the refinery, riding the warm forest wind. A pair of boots dangled from an open hatch: Shadia Anikova, completing the afternoon's air detail. Despite the attendant threats, it was work she enjoyed, monitoring the borders of the Republic, checking for breaches. It was proper army work and it got her out in the open air, away from the confines of Central Command and the solicitous, disquieting presence of the Mechvor Kitai. If only she hadn't been posted so close to the southern border this time.

They were high up here, close to the range that divided Pergama from the southern steppe. It was still possible to see the distant heights of the Balchus, snowcapped even in summer, rising in irregular detail above the Pergama plain. First City was lost in the distance, veiled in the afternoon haze. Beyond that, there was nothing but the endless forest, rolling two thousand miles to the north of the Republic. Someone else would be sitting above the forest even now, on the deck of another airship, watching for a breach.

Anikova envied that person, even though the southern detail got extra pay. The south was the province of the *kochebniki*, the horse clans. And the clans were known to kill strangers, calling them devils and worse.

The airship dipped ponderously as Anikova swung hand over hand down the guide rope to the deck. Below, a bulbous dome tethered to a wide platform towered above the surrounding trees. At the edges of the platform, shockwire and trips protected the raised walkways from intruders, in compliance with standard regulations. But the principal intruders here were only the rats that inhabited the underside of the platform barriers. Occasionally goats from the river pastures would wander up and come to grief on the shockwire.

As far as the crags, the pines formed a dense, dark wall, but from this height Anikova could glimpse the tops of the native trees—ezhny, bhul, and dzadra—floating above the line of conifers. Behind her, the dome bulged slowly upward as it filled. A light wind stirred the blue feathers of the dzadra, as though smoke drifted across the top of the forest, and the kited airships bounced on their moorings above the dome. Their shadows fell across the platform as they moved, momentarily hiding the sun.

Anikova was squinting upward into the sky, trying to see whether there was any sign of the returning DK9, the two o'clock, when Arkady Iskakhov came down the walkway to stand beside her. He sketched a salute, though Anikova was never one to stand on ceremony. Having made colonel in her mid-forties, she was content to go no further. She did not like to think that it was because she feared further promotion, perhaps a permanent posting to the south. Even

Central Command was better than that, even Kitai. Or was that really true anymore?

"Two o'clock's late," Iskakhov remarked.

"Yes, I know. I was just wondering why."

Iskakhov shrugged. "Don't know. They said they were coming in early. In fact, they had a head wind. Maybe there was a hitch over Sanskiya."

"Could be. So, are you going off shift now?"

"In a minute, yes. I've got to log the readings, but actually, she's looking pretty good at the moment." They turned to look at the billowing udder of the dome, a khaki bag straining at its moorings. "And then I'm off. Back on Wednesday. Do you want anything from town?" He was a good sort, Anikova thought. Not her type, but a decent soldier all the same.

"No, I don't think so, thanks," she said. "I'm staying till tomorrow night, then I'm returning to First City. *Kak zhal*, eh?—a real shame. I've been working at Central Command for the past few weeks. To be honest with you—" but then she broke off. Iskakhov would understand. Even among sympathetic colleagues, one had to be careful what one said these days.

"*Ladna*. So we won't be seeing each other for a bit?"

"I hope not. Nothing personal, Colonel."

Wind stirred the swelling bag of the dome and it bulged out across the platform. "Here we go," Anikova said, shielding her eyes. Above them, the serene watermelon shape of the two o'clock airship sailed into view.

"Christ," Iskakhov said. "He's a bit low."

"Why is he flying so low?" Anikova said simultaneously, and then the airship turned, revealing a soundless burst of light that tore a vertical strip in the world from sky to forest.

"My God, my God, it's a breach!" Anikova heard Iskakhov cry. "Why didn't the monitors pick it up?"

With horror, Anikova realized that she could see clear to the other side of the breach. It was huge. She had never seen such a rift in the world before. Beyond lay a whirling mass of mist and water. Then, as abruptly as it had come, it closed, but it was already too late for the airship.

The guide ropes of the DK9 brushed the azure plumes of dzadra and then the topmost masts of the pines. From this angle, the airship was immense, foreshortened against the sky. As it approached, it lost height, lurching so that its nose nudged the trees. They could see the truncated front of the cabin, slung low under the base of the ship, and as they watched, there was a sudden, soundless flare of light. The airship burst upward, its sides opening out like petals in a flower of fire, then sank down into the trees. Tinderdry, they sparked and flared.

Anikova and Iskakhov were enveloped in an immense wash of heat, which scorched the throat and eyes, but Anikova was already running for the console comm. She could barely speak. Trying to shout into the comm, she heard her parched voice as a whisper, but the crew had seen the whole thing on the monitors, and in minutes they were out on the platform.

Anikova could hardly see through the smoke pouring from the blazing forest. She heard the siren start up and a rumble as the fireditches opened, but they had left it too late. The flames ran in rivulets along the dry edges of grass toward the platform and licked around its heavy legs, flowing under and around it until the refinery was circled by a burning collar. The crew started up the side ladders toward the kited ships. Anikova turned and came face-to-face with the foreman, ashen beneath the smoke.

"The protocols—" the man managed to say.

"Fuck the protocols," Anikova shouted. "Do you want to die?" Through the sooty haze she glimpsed Iskakhov vanishing up the ladder, and ran after him, the foreman close at her heels.

The fire had reached the edge of the platform, creeping swiftly over and across. As Anikova climbed, she felt the rungs grow hot, and through the smoke she found herself looking out across a sea of fire as the forest caught alight. The flames ran along the platform toward the dome, and then Anikova was up and into the cabin of the kite, hauled over the portal by Iskakhov. She reached for the foreman's hand, but the man's foot slipped on the greasy rung. The foreman fell, going down without a sound into the flames boiling at the foot of the ladder. Iskakhov grabbed at Anikova and pulled her back into the cabin. His face was grey.

"Where's everyone else?" she cried hoarsely. Only a third of the crew were in the cabin, casting off. "We can't leave now."

"If we don't, we never will," someone said grimly. The kite rope was sucked into the edge of the cabin and there was a lurch as the ship detached. They floated upward, rocking on the hot shaft of air, and through the open door Anikova watched, fascinated and numb, as the filled dome expanded and tore. She covered her mouth as the gas welled upward and then they were away, spinning over the burning woods and up into the clear air.

Iskakhov knelt, retching on the cabin floor, and Anikova's legs gave way. She sat down hastily beside him. When she tried to speak, she found that no sound came from her seared throat, and when she raised her hands, they were black with soot.

Below, the forest was on fire.

Part Four

One

Ilya?"

Elena looked frantically around, but her companion was nowhere to be seen. And neither were the line of trees, the road, or the slope down which they had so recently come. She glanced behind her, half-expecting to see the warriors, but there was no one. The wall of the mountains stretched away behind her, but they were higher than even the Tien Shan, and the sky that their snowy summits seemed to reach was a darker blue. There was no sign of the storm, but the ground beneath her feet was wet with the passage of rain. She was standing at the edge of a field. Lines of young wheat marched away toward a break of oaks, their leaves yellow with the first touch of spring.

"Ilya?" Elena called again. There was no reply. It was very quiet. A flock of birds wheeled overhead and she could hear the whistle of their wings. They were white cranes, with long, graceful necks, and as she watched, they turned and flew toward the sun. The air smelled strange, and it was a moment before Elena realized that it was merely fresh, without the acrid tang of pollution that filtered up from the city streets.

Slowly, she began to walk along the edges of the wheatfield, trying to fight down the panic and analyzing the data at her disposal. If the warriors had been some kind of mirage, they had been a very detailed one. She had smelled the sweat of the horses, heard the creak of the harnesses. And what of the Golden Warrior? Even now, a ferocious debate was raging between Kazakhstan's academics as to whether the armor had belonged to a woman. It was, apparently, a woman's helmet, and it was certainly true that the armor was quite small. And it had been a woman's fierce face that Elena thought she had glimpsed beneath the tall, golden cone—but then, she wanted to believe that the Golden Warrior had been female, so perhaps her expectations had engineered her vision.

Yet none of this could offer any explanation of where Elena was now. And a sudden cold thought struck her: What had happened to the object?

Elena scrabbled in her handbag and there it was, as heavy and unyielding as ever. She slung the bag more securely about her neck, undid her heavy winter coat, and slipped off the uncomfortable shoes. Where there was a wheatfield, there would be habitation. She remembered the voices she had heard in the vision. They had sounded normal, ordinary. There had been a child. Whatever this world might be, she told herself, if they grew crops and raised children, it could not be as terrifying as all that.

Two

There was no sign of Elena or, thank God, of the warriors. And he knew at once that this was not the true world, even though the sounds that came to him were familiar ones: birdsong, the noise of small animals in the undergrowth, the rustle of leaves. To his disgust, Ilya found that he was shaking. Some hero, indeed. The first sign of real danger and he stood quivering in his boots. Elena was better off without him, wherever she might be.

Farther off, he could hear voices. Ilya listened.

". . . it's not showing up on the chart. I can't track the mileage without it . . ."

". . . more tea in the samovar, if you want some . . ."

". . . if you can't find the details on the computer, why don't you just look at my ticket? It's simple enough . . ."

Ordinary conversations, thought Ilya, spoken in a curiously accented Russian, but where *was* this place? He thought that he had seen it before, in dreams. It had the same feel. He looked up at the sky, where the bright sun burned, and found no answers. Ilya closed his eyes, listening beyond the ring of voices, seeking the edges of the world.

A voice, very clear, very cold, said, "We ride again, I tell you. Even if it takes us across the border, we ride!"

It was the voice of the Golden Warrior, he was sure of it. He could not tell whether it was the voice of a woman or a man. But in that case, how was he able to understand what the voice was saying? He did not speak Kazakh and the Warrior would not converse in Russian. And what was a horde of fourteenth-century Kazakh horsemen doing in a world where people had problems with their computers and the sky was a darker blue? In eight hundred years, he had never heard of such a place.

"Ilya?" His head snapped around. It was Elena, but he could not tell where she was. He tried to narrow it down, filtering out the great murmur of voices until he found her. Minutes later, it came again.

"Ilya!"

Away to the west, somewhere along the mountain wall. Even if he could not speak to her, at least she was alive. Relief filled him. He started walking west. Fragments of speech washed over him like the waves of an invisible sea, but he was used to that. It was the heroin that was a problem, or the lack of it. Withdrawal made his throat dry and his vision blur. Sometimes he stumbled. His joints were aching, and once it was as though the world's pain had come to greet him. It brought him to his hands and knees, gasping and retching on the dry earth.

I will find you.

There it was again, that unknown voice in his

mind. He struggled up and walked on, listening for Elena. He did not hear her again for some time, and now she was no longer calling his name. She was singing softly beneath her breath. He did not recognize the song, but he knew the sound of her voice. It struck him that he would know it anywhere, and the knowledge brought dismay: the promise of further hurt, for both of them. He followed nonetheless.

The landscape was similar to the country around Almaty: hills giving way to the higher, forested slopes. Far above, toward the glittering summit of the mountains, Ilya saw the carved gouges of glaciers. But the land that fell away from the mountain wall was fertile: long fields of wheat, and apple orchards. High on one of the hillsides was a long, low house, surrounded by trees, but Ilya thought it best to keep away from habitation. And besides, he could still hear Elena's voice.

The sound of her song led him onto a road: not the usual potholed tarmac, or even the dirt roads of earlier years, but a straight trackway made of some kind of smooth black stone. It was unlike anything he had seen before. He bent and ran a hand along its surface. It was cool and seamless and hard, like obsidian. Ilya frowned. He tried to walk more quickly, but the pain was coming in waves and it was difficult even to stand. He should lie by the roadside, he thought dimly, let the world take him. Death was long overdue—and yet, somewhere within, he realized with distant amazement that he no longer wanted to die.

Elena's song stopped. He heard her say, *"Ilya?"*

—and then he saw her at last, a small figure farther along the road.

She ran to meet him, holding her shoes in her

hand. She appeared genuinely glad to see him, and for a moment that realization blotted out the pain.

"Ilya, you're here." She reached out to him and then, evidently embarrassed, let her hands fall by her sides. "Where are we? Where is this place?"

He shook his head. "I don't know, Elena. I've no idea."

"How did we get here?" She was not, it seemed, expecting an answer, for she went on, "I've been looking at the plants. I know some of them, but others—look." She held out a fronded blue strand like a horsetail. "I've never seen this before. And those trees—what are they? Surely we can't be on another planet?"

"I don't think so." A little reluctantly, Ilya told her about the voices.

"They were speaking Russian? Are you sure?"

"It's the only language I can speak well, Elena. A little German, French, Kazakh—I know Russian when I hear it."

"You must have pretty good hearing," Elena said, giving him a puzzled look.

"I have . . . abilities. My hearing is one of them. I can hear a voice from a thousand miles away."

Elena looked doubtful. He could hardly blame her.

"How sure are you that it's actually your hearing? Could it be something like telepathy?"

"It's not just voices. I can hear other things, too. Natural sounds: leaves falling, the unfolding of a bee's wing."

Elena's eyes widened. "I thought your name was familiar. I've *heard* of you. In childhood stories—the legends of Russia."

Ilya gave a wry smile. "Yes, I was famous for a while. A *bogatyr,* an 'elder valiant champion.'" He paused, embarrassed. "A hero, basically."

"Aren't you supposed to have a flying horse?"

He smiled. "I wish. I've had many horses, but none of them had wings. And my sword isn't a magic one, either. It's just a sword. People love to embroider a plain enough tapestry."

"But you weren't the only *bogatyr,*" Elena said. "There were others."

"There were, yes. The Sons of the Sun, they called us." He started to cough at that point, turning away from Elena and burying his mouth in his sleeve.

"Ilya, are you all right?"

"I'll be okay. . . . Not just sons, either, but daughters. Some had unnatural strength, others the sight of an eagle. We passed into legend, became nothing but stories. Mankind outstripped us."

"*Mankind?* Are you telling me that you aren't human?"

"I have been told that I am not. I myself do not know."

She was staring at him.

"Do you believe me?" he asked. He found that her answer mattered to him.

She gestured around her in response. "My views of reality have undergone something of a change, Ilya. This morning it would have seemed preposterous. Now it's verging on the plausible." She paused. "But if you're not human, then what are you?"

"I don't know."

"Do you think you could be from here? Wherever this place is?"

"I don't think so, Elena. I was born in Russia. My mother was an ordinary woman; we were peasants. We lived in a little log *izba* in the middle of the Siberian forest. You were a foreigner if you came from half a kilometer up the track."

Elena said nothing.

"We ought to try to find some kind of shelter. And food," Ilya said, thankful to change the subject.

"There are houses up on the ridge. And you said you heard people speaking Russian. I think we should take a chance."

"I don't like the idea of seeking people out."

"Neither do I. But it's that or sleep in barns, and steal." His face must have been easy to read, for she added after a glance, "You'd rather do that, wouldn't you?"

"I've had a lot of practice," he admitted.

"Then perhaps we should compromise. Hide out for a time, watch whoever we see. If they don't appear dangerous, we'll chance it. And you can listen to them, can't you? What do you think?"

"Very well," Ilya said warily. "We'll see."

A track branched off from the main route, leading up into the foothills. Ilya worried that they might be too visible, but there was no sign that they were being watched. It was unnaturally quiet. They saw no one in the fields; there was no traffic along the road. Ilya tried to filter out the wash of background noise. He could hear the humming of machines all around them. He did not know what they were, but it was a twenty-first century soundscape: washing machines, computers, generators.

Gradually, however, a greater sound began to impinge upon him, a singing through the air. It was coming across the mountains. He stopped, shading his eyes with his hand.

"Ilya? What is it?"

"I don't know. A plane, maybe."

He was wrong. The next moment, the immense bulk of a zeppelin sailed above the peaks. It was silver, its flanks caught the late afternoon light until it shone as brightly as a captive moon.

"It's huge," Elena said in wonder.

As the thing turned, Ilya saw that it bore letters on its side: RT817.

"Does that mean anything to you?" he asked.

"No," Elena said, gazing into the heavens and shielding her eyes from the glare of the sun. "I don't recognize the symbol, either."

The zeppelin did not bear the hammer and sickle, but another sign: a many-pointed star, in ideologically-sound crimson. The air was filled with the sound of the zeppelin's engines, and more craft were soaring above the mountain wall. These were smaller, sharper, like silver arrows. They darted beneath the zeppelin.

"Are they attacking it?" Elena asked.

"I don't know," Ilya replied, but he did not want to take the chance and get caught beneath some aerial battle. Memories of German bombers flashed through his mind. He caught Elena by the arm and pulled her into a nearby hedge. This time, there were no trees among which to shelter. Fields of beets stretched away from the road. A craft flashed by, so close above them that Ilya glimpsed the line of rivets that ran along its underside. The craft roared up, a needle against the sky, twisted, fell back.

But as it came round, Ilya, blinking away the dust, saw a curious thing: a line of light in the sky, splitting the pure dark blue. There was a bitter, chemical smell. He reached for Elena's hand. The world changed once more. He tasted earth, the bitterness of beets, snow. They fell through into a howl of sleet in the darkness beyond.

Interlude

Anikova rejected the offer of a staff car, saying that she preferred to walk instead. She was dawdling, reluctant to get to her appointment on time; she had tried very hard to get out of it, but the Mechvor had insisted.

"I know what I saw," Anikova had told her. "A breach, that was all, and an accident that followed. I don't need counseling."

"You are afraid of me," the Mechvor said, her head on one side. Anikova found the gesture both affected and sinister. She caught a glimpse of Kitai's avatar, coiled within her like the double exposure of a photograph, and thought again: *Bozhie mne. What are you?* The Mechvor's strangeness, her inhumanity, were becoming harder to ignore. Kitai put a hand on Anikova's arm with her customarily delicate concern. "You have no reason to fear me, Colonel. Or may I address you as Shadia Marianovna?"

"If you want," Anikova mumbled ungraciously.

"So. You saw a breach. And you acted responsibly

in a most dangerous situation. You know that Central Command is proposing to decorate you for it?"

She spoke as though offering sweets to a child.

Anikova said, "I have a chestful of medals. I clank like a bucket whenever I stand up. You know as well as I do that it doesn't mean anything." She did not want to add: *What about the men whose lives I could not save? Do I get a medal for them, too?* She knew perfectly well that this was a probe; that underneath the veil of concern, Kitai wanted to find out what else Anikova might have glimpsed in that sudden flickering inferno.

"Look," she said, controlling her distaste with difficulty. "It's very good of you to be so concerned, and I know that Central Command likes people to have a psychological assessment when this kind of situation occurs, but it really isn't necessary. I prefer to deal with things in my own way." *I do not need this endless probing into my psyche, this work of dream-stealers. I need silence and the lake, and my family, that is all.* But to say so might arouse suspicions in the Mechvor, the realization that perhaps Anikova was not the perfect Party tool after all, but had thoughts and feelings of her own. So Anikova took a deep breath and forced the words out.

"Maybe you're right, however. Perhaps counseling might help me to deal with things better."

The Mechvor smiled with relief. "There's often an initial resistance, Shadia Marianovna. It's perfectly normal. Please don't worry. We'll take good care of you."

But it was not what she had seen through the breach that concerned Anikova, but what else Kitai might discover lurking inside her head, what heretical thoughts. Leaving the Mechvor behind, she walked slowly along the street, remembering.

—————

She had been fifteen, and the family had gone to the dacha outside Azhutsk for the weekend. Pergama Province sweltered in the heat and Anikova couldn't sleep. At last she threw the windows open, activating the chemical screen that kept the insects at bay, but outside the evening air was baking. Light lingered in the west, a deep, clear aquamarine, and the moon was rising like a shadow on the sky. Through the nightscreen, the woods shimmered in a haze.

There was a tree outside the window, in which a younger Anikova had sat for hours, hiding from her sisters in the sinking twilight. Now, Anikova turned to switch off the light, and when she looked back, the *rusalka* was sitting in the branches. The creature's almond eyes glowed. She looked like a medieval maiden, demure in the branches of the tree. Anikova stood frozen at the window. She saw the *rusalka's* mouth open, and the sudden, frantic fear made her tug the windows shut. Then the *rusalka* was gone, drawing back through the summery leaves without a sound.

Later that night, lying sleepless and clammy in her bed, Anikova heard someone singing in the woods. The song called to her of the coolness of the forest, and the streams that poured down through the crags, and the great dreaming land. Anikova thought of the mouth that was making that song, and only that image kept her from slipping downstairs and out into the enticing trees. At last, she thought she heard laughter, faint and moving swiftly away.

She knew the prohibitions. It was not permitted to speak of the *rusalki,* or to think about them. They, and the things like them, were the soft heel in the armor of the Republic: the old dreams that helped the world to crack. The Mechvor reminded Anikova of the *rusalka,* yet she knew that they were not the same. Kitai was something else, something ancient harnessed in the service of the State, but the similarity remained, a disturbing echo of difference. Anikova did not know whether the Mechvor would see the *rusalka* looking back at her out of memory, and she was afraid of what might happen in the course of the counseling session.

She resolved to think only of the breach: only of fire and death and horror. She must force from her mind all criticisms of Central Command's most recent actions. Then, perhaps, Kitai would be deceived, and leave her alone.

Part Five

One

To Elena, this felt like the world they knew: Almaty, with a spring storm raging. But they were no longer on the road that led beneath the slopes of Koktubye. There was cold snow under her feet and the sharp smell of pines. She looked up and saw a ragged pinnacle of rock through a break in the clouds. She had lost her shoes. Ilya's hand, painfully clasping her own, was icy.

"We're in the mountains," she cried above the wind. She saw him nod.

"We've got to find shelter. It's nearly dark."

She followed him through the trees, wincing with every step. The snow had already soaked through her tights, biting her with its chill. She brushed aside wet, heavy branches and thought longingly of the world they had left. But it had not been so tranquil at the end, with those swift planes. She thought of the warriors and the hiss of arrows in the dark, and shivered, but there was a more immediate threat. If they could not find shelter, it would be the end of them both. It was still early enough in the year to die of exposure.

She tried to fix their position. Surely that was the peak of Karniznaya above them, seen from behind? But the nearest village, in that case, would be Ozyomy, over a dozen kilometers away, and hard going even in fine weather.

"Elena!" Ilya shouted. "Do you know where we are?"

"I think so. But we're nowhere near a village. Our best chance is to find one of the herders' huts on the *zhelau*. On the pastures," she explained, as Ilya frowned. "We need to head down beneath the snow line."

She could no longer feel her feet. Ilya grasped her arm, helping her when she stumbled.

"Look," he said. "This is foolish. Father Frost isn't going to show up and give you shoes, you know. . . . Take my boots." Before she could protest, he reached down, undid the laces, and stripped them off.

"I don't know about Father Frost—I think I'm turning into the Snowmaiden. What about you?"

"I went barefoot for years. I was a peasant before I was a hero. Don't underestimate me."

It was, she had to admit, much easier with the boots, even if they were several sizes too big. Together, they ducked under branches and kicked aside the snow. At last, the snow grew patchier and then vanished. They came out into a wide expanse of grass, battered flat by the storm. Above the peaks, a scrap of sky showed a livid green: the last of the day's light. On the other side of the *zhelau*, Elena could see a small dark square.

"There's a hut! Look."

She ploughed into waist-deep, wet grass. In minutes, without the protection offered by the trees, her coat was soaked. By the time they reached the hut, her hair was plastered over her face and she could barely see. She fell through the door.

"Is there a stove?" Ilya asked behind her.

"Stove, matches, and kindling."

In these high pastures, where people had been eking out a living for centuries, warmth meant the difference between life and death. There were two bunks, with rough blankets that still smelled of horses. Ilya sank down onto the lower one as though his strings had been cut. Elena, trying to ignore the numbness in her hands, fumbled with the kindling and eventually lit it. The flame flared up, sending shadows spinning across the wooden walls and floor. She struggled out of her wet coat, wrinkling her nose at the odor of sodden fur. Outside, it was now quite dark.

Smoke spiraled up, sending Ilya into a coughing fit. He seemed unable to stop: doubled over, racked for breath. It was another unwelcome reminder of tuberculosis. Even if it wasn't TB, he had still spent hours in the cold and the wet and there could be no doctor in reach, even if he was willing to take the risk of discovery.

"Ilya, you have to tell me. Are you ill?" Feeling inadequate, she found a battered kettle and a water bottle. The water smelled musty and old, but it would be all right if it was boiled. Somewhere, there might be tea. She set the kettle on the stove.

"Not ill," Ilya gasped. "Anyway, can't die. Unfortunately."

She frowned. "You'd better tell me what's wrong. Are you an addict?"

He looked up. His pupils were pinpointed against the pale eyes. He managed to smile. "So obvious, eh?"

Without comment, Elena sat down beside him and took his hand. The bandage had come off; a raw red scar crossed his palm. She rolled back the thick sleeve of his shirt. Needle marks covered the inside of his forearm; he must be running out of veins by now.

"When did you last take it?"

"Few days ago. I swore I'd kick it, in the cathedral." He gave a dry, rasping laugh. "I'm sick of it. I started to bore myself years before you were alive, and now it's finally happened. I'm sick of being sick."

"Why did you start?" she asked; adding dryly, "Was that boredom, too?"

"I wanted to blot out myself, the world, everything. I don't imagine it's an uncommon reason."

"No, I don't imagine it is."

They sat in silence for a moment. Then Ilya said, "Elena, you shouldn't worry about me. I'll be fit to travel."

"Withdrawal's not supposed to be all that quick, Ilya," Elena said doubtfully. "Have you tried it before?"

He winced. "Once, a long time ago." His gaze flickered, shifty and ashamed. "This isn't the first time I've been an addict. It was hard. Right now, my very bones hurt, but I heal quickly."

"Is there anything I can do to help?" There was a flicker of something behind his eyes, a familiar longing, and she thought, *If he wants me to sleep with him, what am I going to do?* She was still holding his hand, his fingers curled cold in her own, and she was sharply aware of his presence and their isolation. The sensible side of her counseled caution, but Elena had a feeling that caution could be overridden at any moment.

The realization of her attraction to him took her by surprise. It was a long time since she had wanted to be held by anyone, and he lacked both Yuri Golynski's flashy good looks and confident air. Still, she thought, Ilya might not be a cosmonaut, but he was supposed to be a hero, wasn't he? It seemed she was still drawn to a particular type.

But Ilya said only, "The kettle's boiling."

She found a packet of black tea. There was no food and Elena was uncomfortably reminded that she had not eaten all day, but there was no help for it.

"It's a good thing we're Russian," she remarked.

"Why is that?"

"We're used to hunger and cold."

Ilya smiled. "Not your generation, surely? Not under these new men: Brezhnev, Gorbachev, Putin . . ."

Names like beads on a chain, or those nested dolls that were so popular with the few tourists who made it as far as Almaty—parodies of politicians.

Elena laughed. "*New* men? Brezhnev's been gone for thirty years, I'm happy to say. That's when the USSR really started to die, if you ask me—during the *Zastoi,* the Stagnancy."

"At least there was a degree of peace. And those men are new to me."

"If you are truly as old as you say you are," Elena said dubiously, for she still did not quite believe him, "you must have seen a host of changes in Russia."

"Political changes, yes. But in reality? In eight hundred years, most of what I've seen has been people having kids, growing turnips, getting sick. They complain about the system—tsars or the Party, doesn't matter what the theory is, the reality doesn't seem to change all that much for most people. They grumble, they endure. And then there are the deaths." His face creased momentarily, as if he did not want to face what he was saying. "All the deaths. Forty million, so they say, in the last century, what with the wars, the purges, enforced collectivization . . . And Communism was still better than the time of the tsars, except for Stalin. Russia is built on death. Yours has been a peaceful time, by comparison. I don't imagine you had to look over your shoulder too much, or watch your words." The irony of what he was saying must have struck him, for he smiled.

"Not in my time," Elena said. "You wouldn't want to say anything too stupid in public, obviously, and you don't want to fall foul of the authorities. That's why you and I made a run for it, after all. I don't see a whole lot of difference before the end of the Soviet Union and now. Things have shifted, that's all. We still have the secret police, but now we've got the *Mafiya* as well. Democracy just means that a few families and their cronies run things rather than the Party, as far as I can see. Everyone's greedy, because they have to be. Everyone steals as much as they can from the State. We've become a nation of thieves. When I was a little girl, you'd have to queue in the shops for food, and things often ran out, or they'd produce too much of one thing. We were too big a country for a command economy to work properly. Now there's plenty of stuff in the shops, but no one can afford it. It all depends on what *blat* you have, what pull, whether you know enough people in power to give you a 'roof.' "

Her colleague's remark echoed in memory: *We pretend to work and they pretend to pay us.* She repeated this to Ilya. "That's all the country runs on now, dreams and air. Perhaps it's always been this way."

"It's the way things are," Ilya said. "You just have to adapt."

"Yes, you have to adapt." But he hadn't done so well in adapting, she thought. The tracks on his arms were a testament to that. He must have read her expression, for he looked away.

"Here's your tea," she told him. She passed him a tin cup and he sipped it in silence. Elena felt suddenly exhausted. "Look, I'm going to try and phone my mother, then get some sleep," she said. "You should do the same."

"I don't need much persuading." But she could still feel his eyes upon her as she reached for the mobile and dialed the number. It rang endlessly, but they had to be there, for the answerphone did not come on. Finally a voice said, *"Da?"*

Elena swallowed her relief. It was Anna, not her mother.

"It's me." The line crackled with static.

"Elena? Is that you? Where are you? We've been worried to death."

"I'm just outside Almaty. Look, try not to worry. Have the *militzia* been round?"

"What? No. Have you been in an accident? We got your message, but when you didn't come in for supper, we didn't know what to think. I waited up, but I made

Mama go to bed. She's asleep. Are you all right?" Anna's voice was sharp with worry.

"I'm fine, but I've run into a few problems," Elena said. Hastily, she gave Anna an edited version of events, leaving Ilya out of the narrative as much as she could. "Anna, I've got some money. One of the men paid me before—well, I got paid, anyway. I'm going to send it to you. When you get it, just take off. Go to Moscow. You've got my mobile number if you need to get in touch, or you can phone one of my friends."

"But are you sure they're even after you?" Anna's voice at the other end of the telephone was distant and puzzled. "I mean, no one's called or been round, and you know what the authorities are like if they suspect something. . . . And there wasn't anything about a murder on the news, either."

"I don't know why the *militzia* haven't contacted you. You'd better tell Mama what's going on, but try not to make it sound too serious or she'll worry herself to death. I—" But then the line went dead. It occurred to Elena that the phone at the flat might have been tapped, but she had not heard any of the telltale signs: the clicking or whistling. She dialed again, but the signal had gone.

"Your mother?" Ilya asked.

"No, my sister."

"You live with them?" He paused, then added, "You're not married?"

"Not anymore."

"No kids?"

She was silent. He said quickly, "I'm sorry, Elena. I shouldn't be prying into your personal life."

"It's okay." She reached out and touched his hand. He nodded, forgiven, and dropped into a doze.

Swallowing the scalding tea, Elena hauled herself up onto the top bunk and covered herself with the blanket, then stripped off her wet hose. There was no lavatory in the hut; she would just have to go outside and manage as best she could if the need arose. She tucked her handbag beside the lumpy pillow, trying to make sure that the object would be safe. The blanket was thick and scratchy, but at least it was warm. The glow of the stove and Ilya's ragged breathing provided the illusion of companionship and comfort.

She was disconcerted by the thought that it would be easy enough to slip down and join him. Something told her he'd welcome it, and the memory of his body so close to her own was sharp in her mind. *You've only just met him. You don't know anything about him, and he might be mad. What about AIDS? You know what they say about addicts.* It was a litany of reasons, the counsel of common sense, but her emotions and her body were dictating otherwise. *Think of something else. Remember what happened to you today, this so-miraculous thing.*

It worked. When she finally fell asleep, it was with the memory of a different world in her mind.

Two

Ilya spent the night in a fitful half-sleep, waiting for the dawn. Even here, high on the *zhelau,* he did not want to rule out the possibility that the *rusalki* might still find him, taste his pain on the wind, and seek him out. He was no longer worried about what they might do to him, but one of them had already attacked Elena and he knew that it had intended to kill. She had their property, and they wanted it back. And what of the *volkh*?

At last, a thin grey haze appeared, high beyond the little window of the hut. Ilya waited until the light had grown and then, stiffly, he swung his legs over the side of the bed and slung the sword across his shoulder. Elena was curled on the top bunk, asleep. He looked down at her peaceful face for a long moment, longing to climb in beside her, then made his way outside.

The storm had passed, leaving a chilly wind in its wake. Ilya went around the back of the hut to piss, then stood for a moment, leaning against the wall until his vision righted itself and the world stopped spinning. Hunger, fatigue, and the drug leaching from his veins were taking their toll. There was a ringing in his ears.

"*Dobreden!*"

Ilya spun round, reaching for his sword. He had heard nothing, but a man was standing by the side of the hut. He wore the knee-high, flat-soled boots that the Kazakhs had proved reluctant to relinquish, jeans, a jacket with an American flag on the breast pocket, and a Kyrgyz hat. His face was round and beaming; his smile revealed a row of gold teeth. He could have been anywhere between fifty and eighty.

"Good morning!" he said again.

"Good morning," Ilya responded, warily. Friend or enemy, this person was cheerful and that was always to be avoided when one had just woken up.

"Lovely day."

"I suppose it is, yes. Are you working up here?"

The stranger nodded. "Took the animals up last week for a bit of spring grazing. Thought I'd get away from the wife. No doubt she's pleased to see the back of me, too. I'm in the hut over the ridge. You?"

"Car broke down," Ilya said, improvising swiftly. "On the Kagornak Road. Over there somewhere." He waved, indicating a vague sweep of countryside. "My wife and I were coming back from visiting relatives. We went looking for help, but then the rain came up."

"What's wrong with your car?"

"I've no idea." True enough. He had learned to drive, more or less, back in the 1940's, but that was about the extent of his knowledge. "It keeps stopping and starting." He tried to look urban and ineffectual.

"Sounds like the timing's gone, maybe."

"I'm sure we can get it going again," Ilya said, trying to discourage any impending offers of assistance. "But in the dark, with the rain—"

"Oh, best to find shelter. That's what the huts are for, after all. Any number of folk have been saved from a night in the cold up here. Summer and spring, you're all right—but winter, it'll kill you, right enough."

Ilya nodded politely.

"You don't look so good." The bright eyes creased with momentary concern. "You all right?"

"I've had the flu."

"Want to watch that. Can turn to pneumonia. Can be nasty. Here." The man produced a plastic bottle full of a white, viscous liquid. "Take it. I've been putting it up over the last week."

Ilya looked dubiously at the bottle. "What is it?"

"What does it look like?"

"Milk?"

"You're Russian, aren't you?" *And unspeakably effete,* the following glance conveyed. "Of course it's milk—of sorts." He laughed at his own joke. "It's *kymiss.* Have it. I've got plenty." He undid the stopper and the unmistakable odor of fermented mare's milk wafted forth. It could be some trick, but the man's face was guileless and there was nothing of the supernatural about him. Besides, there was a comradeship in the mountains. People hung together against more impersonal enemies: wolves and the weather. Ilya thought next of his vow: no more heroin. But he had made no promises to God about drinking, and did this actually count as alcohol? It was practically a foodstuff. He gave a brief nod.

"Thanks." He took a quick swallow. It smelled of meat. It tasted foul.

"Give it to your wife." The gold teeth glittered in the light of the rising sun. "Wonderful stuff for breakfast. And bread. I have more back at the hut. I don't need it, and you'll be hungry." He handed Ilya a half-loaf of flat *lepeshka.* "Good luck with the car. If you want to go to the village, there's a path down along the ridge." He pointed. "Keep heading south—that's that way. Take you about an hour. Ask for a man called Nurzhan Alibek—he's a milkman; he mends cars, too. Lives in a small red house on the left. You'll see the goats. Tell him I sent you. I am Zhanat Bigaliev."

"Thanks," Ilya said. "For the bread, too."

"Good luck," the man said again, and set off across the *zhelau,* whistling and striking aside the wet grass with his stick. Ilya watched him go with envy. *This is what I should do. Leave the cities behind, leave the world to itself and come up here with the foxes and the eagles and the small creatures.* But he had tried that, years ago, and though there had been peace for a time in the silences of the earth, it had not worked for long. He had grown restless, as if designed for action.

"Ilya?" He turned to see Elena coming from the hut, clutching her still-damp coat around her. Her makeup had run in last night's rain, leaving dark circles around her eyes. She looked very pale. He felt a wave of protectiveness. "I heard you talking. Is everything all right?"

"I met a herdsman. He gave me this." He held out the bottle. She looked horrified.

"Oh, God, what is it? *Kymiss?* For *breakfast?* Not that I'm turning it down. I'm hungry enough to eat the original horse." She took a sip and made a face, then handed the bottle back. "*Repulsive*. But it's what they live on up here, you know. *Kymiss* and horsemeat sausages and bread. It's the worst diet in the world and they all seem to live to a hundred and ten." Then she gave him an unsettled glance and stopped, as if fearing she had been tactless.

"There's bread. No sausages."

She wolfed down the *lepeshka*. "What did you tell him?" she asked between mouthfuls.

"Our car broke down. He gave me directions to the nearest village."

"Do you think that's where we should go?"

"If we're still making for the border, yes. Find someone with a car, who doesn't ask too many questions."

"They won't ask questions," Elena said with certainty. "Not if we can pay. I doubt there's a policeman for miles."

"Let's hope they still think we're on the other side of the mountains," Ilya said.

"Which is where we should be, after all." Elena drew closer to him, wrapping herself in her coat. "Ilya—what if it happens again? What if we change worlds?"

"I don't know. We'll just have to see." He had to fight the urge to put his arm around her; he did not think she would welcome it. "You still have the . . . thing? It's safe?"

She nodded.

"We shouldn't stop in one place for too long," he said, though if he was honest with himself, what he really wanted to do was head back beneath the meager covers of the bunk and stay there. Preferably with Elena, but he stopped that line of thought before his unruly imagination got out of hand.

"Give me the bottle," Elena said. She made sure that the stopper was tight, and put it in the pocket of her coat. "It'll keep us going. Maybe we can get shashlik or something in the village. I'd kill for a bath. Does my face look awful?"

"No, of course not," he said, and meant it.

She grimaced. "You're lying. But thanks anyway. I'd kill for some proper food, too."

"Let's hope you don't have to."

"I can skin a rabbit, you know. My dad used to take us camping when we were kids, before he disappeared into a bottle of vodka. Excuse me for a minute. I've got to find a bush."

Ilya waited uneasily until she came back. The sun was now high over the peaks and the sky had the clear, blown look of early spring. With luck, the weather would hold. And they would find a car, someone to drive them over the border, and he could sleep.

He said nothing of his concerns to Elena, suspecting that she had worries of her own. The day before, when she had spoken to her sister, he had been able to feel the tension in her, like a thin steel wire under strain. He ducked under a spray of fir, sending a shower of raindrops to the wet earth. "Did your sister say whether she'd heard anything about the murders?"

"She said there was nothing on the news. And they'd had no word from the *militzia.*"

Ilya frowned. No move from the authorities was almost as ominous as a visit. He still did not entirely understand how the media worked, why certain stories were obsessively picked apart and others neglected. Some of it was political, clearly, yet to Ilya this did not explain the avid interest in actors and celebrities. Perhaps it was no more than the old need for fairy stories.

Elena went on, "If someone gets killed, it's usually all over the news. It's not all that common, even these days. Russia's very violent, but it's not the same here. I think the authorities prefer it if people feel unsafe."

Ilya smiled. "You're probably right. It justifies hard-line policing. It's been the same since the first of the tsars."

"They don't need an excuse," Elena said sourly. "But the papers—*Karavan* or *Pravda*—would all be investigating. *Karavan* has broken some real scandals, even though the authorities keep trying to close them down. Perhaps we can buy a newspaper when we reach the village. And we have to get some more boots."

Ilya nodded. This sudden silence on the part of the authorities spoke to him of the *rusalki* and the *volkh,* of the old and buried secrets of the political past.

They had reached the end of the ridge now, and he could see the track running down through a bank of birches. New leaves shone green and some of the branches were decked with pieces of rag and cloth. A wishing tree. He remembered an old country code: a green ribbon for nature, blue for the sky, pink for the moon, yellow for the sun and the sisters of dawn. He had nothing to tie to the tree, but he tapped a branch as they passed, as if the luck might rub off on him.

They had now come some way along the slope.

The peaks were receding against the morning sky, a pall of fumes marking the presence of the city below. Farther down, past a thick line of oaks and ash, he could see a roof.

"Maybe that's the village," he said, pointing.

Elena's face looked pinched in the early morning cold. "I hope so. I've run out of cigarettes." Realizing that he was not the only one with an addiction made Ilya feel less feeble.

"So have I," he confessed. "Or I'd offer you one."

"I ought to give it up. It costs me a fortune."

"I don't think this would be a good time."

She smiled. "You're probably right."

The track led down through the woods and over a stream heavy with snowmelt and rain. Ilya crouched down by the bank and splashed his face with icy water, but it did little to dissipate the woolliness in his head. They came out onto a potholed curve of road and there was the village below, no more than a scatter of low houses with corrugated roofs and tilted porches, the gardens a tangle of cherry trees and old raspberry canes. Chickens picked along the roadside. There was no one to be seen.

"What should we do, knock on a door?" Elena asked.

"We'll see if anyone's about first," Ilya said. He did not want to contact the milkman, the horse herder's friend. Sooner or later, they would meet and perhaps talk. The stories would not add up, and in country districts people remembered such things, became suspicious. And if their descriptions were circulated at any point . . . It was not worth the risk.

"Look," Elena said. "We can ask there."

A kiosk stood by the side of the road and Ilya could see that the shutters were up. He followed Elena to the little booth and peered in. A teenage girl sat inside on a stool, reading a fashion magazine.

"Good morning," Elena said. The girl grunted. "Ilya, what kind of cigarettes do you want?"

"All we've got are Polyot," the girl said.

Ilya watched as Elena bought two packets. "Better than those American things. They give you cancer, you know."

Ignoring this, Elena said to the girl, "We're looking for someone with a car. We're trying to get to Bishkek. We can pay."

The girl stood so that her face was framed in the opening of the kiosk. She was Kazakh, with dark brows over green, Oriental eyes.

"I could ask my uncle. He's got a car. He does taxi work sometimes." She vanished through the back of the kiosk and reappeared a moment later, tottering on a pair of stiletto boots. Elena frowned.

"Why aren't you in school?" she asked.

The girl looked at her as though she were mad. "It's Saturday."

"Of course it is," Elena said faintly. It was the girl's turn to frown.

"Why isn't he wearing any shoes?"

"She's wearing mine," Ilya said. "I took her fishing. She broke a heel." He looked pointedly at the girl's boots, but her expression had changed to one of sympathy.

"I did that once," she said.

How did women manage with these modern fashions? Ilya wondered, but he already knew. They found men and borrowed their shoes. They followed the girl around the back of a house. Goats looked up mildly, demon-eyed, as they passed.

"Mama?" the girl called. "Some people need a lift."

The mother appeared, dusting flour from her hands.

"Where to?"

"Bishkek."

"That's a long way. Four hours, at least."

"We can pay."

The woman shrugged. "Well, it's up to you. If it was me, I'd catch the bus." *Mad Russians,* her expression implied.

"My wife gets sick on the bus," Ilya said before Elena could protest.

"I'll phone my brother. I don't know if he can do it, mind. But I'll ask."

"Ask him how much," Elena called after her. They were left alone in the hallway with the ticking clock. It had an ominous sound to Ilya's sensitive ears. He had never grown used to this method of marking off time, minute by minute, day by day. What was wrong with a glance at the sun, or the year's rhythms? But it was progress, he supposed. Idly, he eavesdropped on the woman's conversation.

"Yes, to Bishkek. Yes, today—no, I don't know why; they didn't say. Does it matter?"

A man's voice, on the other end of the phone: "Can they pay up front? I'm not doing it otherwise. I told Sultanat I'd take her into town this morning."

"It can wait, surely? Anyway, you'll have to go through Almaty—why don't you drop her off? She can find her own way back."

"Her legs are bad."

"Well, then she shouldn't be walking round town. Has she seen the doctor yet?"

Ilya stifled his impatience as the conversation veered away into a morass of personal detail. At last, the woman returned.

"He'll do it. He's coming over. He wants ten dollars each way."

Elena, despite the money resting in her handbag, managed to look suitably dubious. "It's a lot," she said. Ilya wondered how much she usually earned. He did not understand this foreign currency, this pegging of everything to the dollar. But then, he had never really gotten the hang of money in the first place. As long as you had what you needed, why worry? Perhaps, Ilya reflected, this was why he had found Communism relatively amenable. A pity it hadn't worked.

"It's that or nothing." The woman was apologetic but firm. "He's got the car to keep going; gas is expensive . . ."

"All right. We'll pay."

"He'll be twenty minutes or so. He has to sort out the car. Come in, come in."

She ushered them into a living room, almost buried beneath a horde of knickknacks. Elena vanished into the bathroom for what seemed like an eternity, and reappeared looking different. Ilya supposed that she had done something with her makeup, though he could not have said what.

They were given tea, bread, cakes, biscuits, sliced sausage, processed cheese: Kazakh hospitality, a holdover from the days when a visitor could have ridden days to reach you, when a guest was a gift from

God. Ilya tried not to eat too ravenously as the woman interrogated Elena about their marriage, their children, their work. Elena lied with remarkable glibness, Ilya thought. He supplied hopefully corroborating details around mouthfuls of bread. It was strange to feel hungry again, to want food other than the sugar cravings of heroin. He heard footsteps in the garden; the woman went from the room.

"My cousin Nadia," Elena said in response to his raised eyebrows. "Three kids, works as a secretary. I just pretended."

"I wasn't criticizing. It's a useful skill."

Elena lowered her voice. "Useful or not, I don't like lying."

"Of course you don't." Before he could stop himself, he touched her hand. "You're a good person." Elena looked startled, and Ilya stood up, to cover his embarrassment. "The driver is here."

Three

When Elena set eyes on the car, she wondered if it would even get them as far as Almaty, let alone the Kyrgyz border. It was an old Lada, rusty around the edges, and the seats had long since collapsed. The woman's brother looked shifty to Elena; he had a long dour face. But perhaps it was better to have someone who was a little sly, who might not want to draw attention to himself.

"You want to go to Bishkek? My sister told you about the money?"

Ilya peeled off a ten dollar note from a thin handful and Elena saw the man's eyes widen. She hoped Ilya had judged it correctly: too little, and he might think they couldn't pay; too much, and the man might be tempted to robbery. Although there was something about Ilya, even ragged and shoeless as he was, that did not invite aggression.

"This is for the trip," Ilya said. "I'll give you the other ten when you drop us off."

"*Konechna*, of course. Where in Bishkek?"

"Listen," Ilya said, confidingly. He drew the man

aside, beneath the bare branches of a cherry tree. "The thing is, it might not be a bad idea if you dropped us off before the border. You see, my friend doesn't have proper papers. If they ask for documents, we might have a problem."

"She doesn't have papers," the driver said, a flat, distrustful statement, inviting answers.

"No." An awkward pause. "You see, I'm afraid we've been a little bit deceptive. This lady isn't my wife. She's someone else's."

Brilliant, thought Elena, in spite of the slur on her character. If it got them out of reach of the authorities, she did not care. Light dawned across the driver's long face.

"Oh, I *see.* Everything is clear. But I'll get you to Bishkek, don't worry. I have papers for the car. And you can pay, yes? If they ask questions?"

"No problem."

What if they're looking for us? What if we're recognized? Elena wondered. If she could get Ilya alone for a moment, she would ask. But it was already time to go. Ilya got in the front seat and she found herself oddly disappointed. Surprisingly, the car started at once. They pulled onto the road toward Almaty.

As they reached the outer suburbs, Elena tapped the driver on the shoulder.

"Would you mind if we made a couple of stops? I need to go to the market, very quickly. It'll only take five minutes."

The driver gave a bark of laughter. "Women! Running away from home and all they can think about is shopping."

"I have to get some more shoes," Elena snapped. "I broke a heel."

"Well, in that case—what was the other stop?"

"It's on Furmanova. I have to drop off a letter." The post office would be closed on a Saturday. She would bundle the money up and drop it off at her aunt's. There was the risk that someone was watching the place, but if she just went into the hallway and stuck it in the mailbox, it should be safe. The boxes were locked, after all.

Even at this time of the morning, the market was teeming. Elena leaped out of the car and bolted into the warren of stalls, deafened by Kazakh pop from the cassette decks and the hubbub of voices. She ran past the medical stalls selling bandages, medicines, and syringes. It made her think of the thing that had attacked her, and of Ilya. He had looked even more unwell this morning, and she felt a pang of warmth and pity.

She fled past electrical goods, and into the clothes section. She stopped at the first stall she came to, found a pair of boots in her size, and slapped down the money without even trying them on. She snatched a packet of underwear from a neighboring stall, paying with her handful of change. She was damned, she thought, if she'd go on the run with a strange man without taking spare underwear with her. Then she hurried back, fighting the sudden irrational fear that the car would not be there, and telling herself not to be so foolish.

The car was gone. Elena's heart sank to her borrowed boots, until she realized that the driver had pulled along the block to avoid a bus, which was being cranked into action with a starting handle. Ilya's wan face now stared at her from the backseat. It lit up when he caught sight of her.

"Do you want to sit in the front? It's making me feel sick, watching the road," he said, winding down the window.

"No, I don't mind. I don't like sitting in the front, either," Elena said hastily, wanting his closeness. She slid in beside him.

"Furmanova?" the driver said over his shoulder.

"Please. Then Bishkek. The sooner we get out of Almaty, the happier I'll be."

"So, your husband. What does he do?"

"He's a lawyer." Everyone hated lawyers. The last thing she wanted to do was awake the driver's masculine sympathies.

"No wonder you're running away. You'd have no chance in a divorce settlement. My cousin, she was married to a lawyer, but he left her, went off with some tart from Akmenugorsk. Anyway, *then*—" The cousin's woes lasted all the way down Zhibek Zholu, along Gogola, down Tolubaev, and into Furmanova. And Elena thought she'd had a hard life. The cousin's problems would have graced a soap opera. The driver's dour face and shifty manner were all a con, Elena decided. He was clearly a secret romantic.

She directed him to her aunt's house, raced into the hallway, and stuffed the money into the mailbox. It took only a moment and then she was back in the car. No one seemed to be watching, but how to tell? They could be tailing her even now. She twisted in her seat, squinting through the back window of the car, but the only thing that appeared to be following was an ancient bus, hood propped open with a starting handle to prevent overheating. It was belching clouds of exhaust.

Elena sat back, thankful to be heading out of town. She finally admitted to herself that if the circumstances had not been so stressful, it might even have been exciting to be going into the unknown, leaving family tensions and her dull cleaning job behind. But she would rather have been heading for Canada, or Baikonur and her beloved work—but now there was Ilya.

She stole a glance at him. His head was resting against the window, his arms folded around himself as if to ward off the world. His eyes were closed and he looked gaunt, the lines beside his mouth carved into deep grooves. He needed a shave. What a difference from scrubbed, polished Yuri Golynski—but she longed to put her arms around Ilya, to take care of him.

She thought better of it. Best to leave him be. She turned her attention to the road ahead, taking them out toward the edges of town, past the concrete apartment blocks and the parks with their erratic fountains. High-rises appeared, the ornamental tiling on their sides starting to flake after the winter cold. The mountains reappeared, grew huge. Suburbs of smaller houses, like the ones of the driver's own village, fell behind and they were at last out on the steppe, following the main road to Bishkek.

Here the land was grey and fawn, overlaid by a faint drift of green. Another few days, some more rain and sunlight, and the steppe would be transformed into a sea of flowers. *Thank God,* Elena thought, *it's spring, at last.* Rain was sweeping across the mountainsides, turning them to indigo before they vanished into the streamers of cloud, and she could enjoy the sight now that she was no longer out in it. Beside her, Ilya murmured something, and sank lower in his seat. The driver, moved perhaps by some delicacy of feeling, attached a pair of earphones and sang along beneath his breath. A herd of horses drifted across the road, dark against the grass. There was no other traffic. The city had fallen far behind. Ilya's head slid down the back of the seat until it was resting on Elena's shoulder. Not allowing herself to think, she nudged him awake. He came to with a start.

"Lie down. You'll be more comfortable." She patted her lap.

He looked surprised for a moment, but did not argue. He curled on the seat with his head on her knees, face buried in the rain-tangled fur of her once-best rabbit coat. Unable to stop herself, she stroked his hair from his forehead, finding that it was softer than it looked, a wolf's thick pelt. He muttered something.

"What?"

"I said, you're an angel."

She felt warmth spreading through her. The last time she had felt like this had been at the cosmodrome, standing under that ocean of stars and realizing that Yuri had come outside in the cold to look for her.

"Ilya?" she whispered, but he was already asleep.

Four

Ilya woke, briefly, to find that they were still traveling. He could see a pale square of sky through the window of the car. His head was resting in Elena's lap. Her eyes were closed; perhaps she, too, slept. He supposed that he should sit up and find out where they were, but he did not want to wake her. He could smell the steppe, filtered through the gaps and cracks in the frame of the car: sweet grass, wet earth, the sage fragrance of saxaul scrub. He shut his eyes again and sank back into warm darkness.

He was next woken by Elena's hand on his shoulder.

"Ilya?" Her face was taut and scared.

He struggled up, limbs cramped and stiff, longing for a cigarette.

"Elena? What is it?"

"We've reached a roadblock."

The police officer stood by the side of the road, flagging down the car with a baton.

"Sorry," the driver said. "I'll have to stop. He probably just wants money—they pretend you've been speeding, the bastards. Don't say anything. Just have the money ready. Leave it to me. If he asks, say you're my cousin and her husband."

But when they pulled over, bouncing across the potholes, the policeman put his head through the window of the car. Ilya saw an impassive face: a series of heavy slabs of flesh, a small, pursed mouth.

"I wasn't doing more than seventy," the driver said. "I've got papers."

"I'm not interested in your papers," the policeman said. "I need a lift."

"Sorry?"

"A lift to the border. My colleague took the car. We've only got one, and it keeps breaking down. And then they phone me up, tell me to come down to the customs post, but how do they expect me to get there—walk? You've got room in the front, I can see."

"*Ladna.* Get in, then."

The policeman climbed into the front seat, removed his hat, and began to chat about the weather. Elena's hand was clamped around Ilya's own; she had a surprisingly strong grip for a woman.

At first, he suspected that the policeman's behavior—the request for a lift, the chatty demeanor—was nothing more than a ruse designed to lull two dangerous suspects into security and, ultimately, betrayal. But gradually he saw that the policeman had told nothing more than the truth. He had seen so many people like this over the years: petty officials and bureaucrats, relegated to some sleepy backwater, bored half to death. Or perhaps the policeman was content to be stationed in such a remote place, away from the *Mafiya* and the violence of the big cities. Perhaps the man just wanted a quiet life. It was hard to say, and harder still to judge. But he did wonder why the policeman had been summoned to the border in the first place. A simple matter of routine, or some other reason?

Sleep was out of the question. But Ilya felt better than he had in days, perhaps even years. The craving for the drug had dissipated to a dull ache, just under the level of discomfort. He lit a cigarette. The car slowed down.

"We're almost at the border," the driver said over his shoulder. The policeman gave a grunt, whether of satisfaction or annoyance, Ilya could not tell.

They were surrounded by cars and trucks queuing for the customs post. The car inched forward. Soon they could see customs through the dust kicked up by the traffic: no more than a row of sheds and money-exchange kiosks. Ilya realized that he had no idea what the currency in Kyrgyzstan might be these days. It had been much easier with just the ruble, but now every little country wanted its own money. Men squatted on their heels in the dust, waiting for unknown transactions.

"Our turn next," the driver said. They could see a man in uniform moving slowly down the line. At last, he reached them. Elena's fingers tightened around Ilya's.

"Papers." The official was young, barely out of his teens. Ilya suspected that he had been drafted; police rather than army. He looked singularly unenthusiastic about his chosen duties. The policeman in the front seat got out of the car.

"Thanks for the lift." He added to the younger man, "Look, don't worry about them. They're all right." He thumped the top of the car and wandered ponderously off toward the customs post. The young man waved them on. The car slid through the customs post and onto the highway to Bishkek.

"And we didn't even have to pay," the driver crowed.

"Thank you," Elena breathed. A little farther down the road, she made the driver stop, and ran out to a money exchange. She came back with a handful of tattered notes.

"*Som*, not *tenge*. They won't take Kazakh money here."

"They'll take dollars, surely?"

"Yes, but—" She made a face and said in an undertone, "If people know we've got dollars, it might cause problems. Kyrgyzstan is poorer than Kazakhstan. They think Almaty's like Paris."

"I've never been to Paris."

"I don't think there's much similarity, to be honest."

Ilya could see Bishkek in the distance, a line of haze backed by the mountains of the Kyrgyz Alatau. Something about the steep slopes, the fall of black hills to the steppe, tugged at Ilya's memory. He had come here years ago, early in the nineteenth century, before there had even been a city, nothing more than a little clay fort on the Chuy River. Later—much later—he had skirted what had become a settlement: Pishpek, the town of the churn. There was something else he should remember, something hovering at the edges of his memory. He nudged Elena.

"Do you know Bishkek?"

"I've been here a few times. We came with my dad

once, on the way to Issy Kul—the big lake, you probably know it. It was the year before he walked out on us." Her face was sad, remembering, and he wished he could comfort her. "The last time I came was to a scientific conference at the university. It's a quiet little place. It's a bit like Almaty, only a lot smaller."

"We'll have to find somewhere to stay," Ilya murmured, with a warning glance at the driver. He could see that Elena understood.

"It's still early. We've got time."

The city suburbs gradually appeared, very different to Ilya's memories of the place. This was a modern town, built on the same carbon-copy lines as Almaty. The Soviets had such a mania for order, Ilya thought. Here, too, there would be a TSUM store and a Gorky Park, a Lenin Prospekt. But the names must have been changed to those of Kyrgyz heroes by now. And *that* was what had been circling his memory like a wolf on the prowl: Manas. The great son of Kyrgyzstan, hero of a thousand legends and sagas. What had happened to Manas since Ilya's epic fight with the man? He must surely be dead like all the others. But now that he thought about it, Ilya had never heard anything of the nature of Manas' death; he had simply vanished from history. And now it seemed that there might be a place beyond this world, where one might vanish to. . . . Manas' words rang in his head: *We are born enemies.*

He caught sight of a prancing bronze figure on a horse, and craned his neck to get a better look. That was Manas, surely, that flying, flamboyant figure. Elena touched his arm.

"Look," she said. They were passing a very different icon, at the entrance to the park. "They've still got

Lenin." He could not tell from her tone whether this pleased her or not.

"Never mind Lenin," the driver said over his shoulder. "They've still got a statue to Felix *Dzerzhinsky* in Oak Park."

Ilya thought grimly of the Cheka—Dzerzhinsky's secret police force—and a laboratory blazing in the winter snow. The Kyrgyz seemed to have foregone the current vogue for extinguishing the past. Perhaps it boded well. Or perhaps not.

The driver pulled alongside the curb and turned to face them.

"*Tak.* This is Bishkek. Do you want anywhere in particular?"

Ilya shook his head. "This will do." He reached into his overcoat and took out the money. "Here."

"Thanks." It vanished into the driver's pocket. "Good luck. Hope things work out. Hope your husband doesn't catch up with you."

Elena managed a pale smile. "So do I. Thank you."

They watched in silence as he drove away. "What now?" Elena asked.

"We should find some food. Then somewhere to stay. Do you know anywhere?"

"We want to stay out of big hotels and anyway, there are only two. They'll have FSB or the local equivalent at the desk. Maybe we can find a guesthouse." She pulled her coat more tightly about her shoulders and stood upright in her new boots. "We still don't know if anyone's even after us."

"Best not to take the chance."

"If I can find a public phone, I'll call my mother. My mobile battery is running low."

"There might be a phone in the park. There'll certainly be food." He could smell shashlik, hot and smoky through the thin spring air. They began to walk toward the center of the park. Here, farther south, spring was more advanced. The oaks were hazed with green and the new grass was springing up through the mud. In the center of the park was a small cafe. Ilya and Elena sat beneath a tattered plastic umbrella, ordered shashlik and salad and chai.

"You're drinking tea?" Elena asked. "You don't want a beer?"

He smiled at her. "No. And the only thing I crave at the moment is decent food."

"Do you think you've kicked it?" She spoke diffidently, as if reluctant to embarrass him.

"I don't know. I think it should take longer than this, but it's gone for the moment. It might come back." He grimaced. "I hope not. It's no life, Elena. It's no life at all."

The shashlik arrived, lamb interspersed with lumps of fat. Ilya tore into the meat. Elena looked uneasily about her.

"I keep thinking that we must be being watched."

"Someone will be watching, I'm certain of it. The only question is who." He listened for a stealthy footstep among the trees, but there was nothing, only the occasional raindrop. He was more worried about the *rusalki* and the *volkh* than the FSB. What if Kovalin held him responsible for the murders? But he did not think that it was too likely. It was evident even to a casual observer that the butchery had been done with teeth rather than a sword. Why had the *rusalki* killed Kovalin's colleagues? And why had they not come after

Elena, to retrieve their property? The little cafe suddenly seemed open and exposed.

"Have you finished?" he asked Elena. "I think we should find somewhere to hide."

She swallowed the last of her tea and nodded. "At least we've got something inside us. Those cakes this morning weren't really enough. When we came with my dad, I remember we stayed in a guesthouse on Shevchenko Street—an old couple ran it with their daughter. I was wondering if it's still there. It was years ago."

"It's as good as any, I suppose. Do you know how to get there?"

"I think so." Elena paid the waitress and rose to her feet.

"We should walk. I don't want too many people making a note of us."

"I don't mind, after all that time in the car." Elena looked away. A kind of careful constraint seemed to be growing between them. He wondered if she regretted letting him sleep in her lap. No doubt she only had done so out of pity and now wanted to head off the threat of further intimacies. He did not know how to approach the subject. Better, perhaps, to let it lie.

He got the impression that Saturday afternoons in Bishkek were habitually quiet. There was a brief hum of activity around a building that might have been an employment agency: men sitting on their heels, smoking, chatting. Some of them looked as though they had been there since morning; patience was ingrained in their faces like dirt. Occasionally a woman would come out of the office and call a name, then retreat.

Ilya and Elena left this limited bustle behind and

turned down into a drowsing maze of back streets. Ilya heard children's voices, but apart from this there was only the murmur of trivial conversation behind apartment doors. He paused, listening more intently.

"Ilya?"

A snatch of conversation, close by and plucked from the air.

"It is the same man, I tell you. I have seen him before."

"And the woman with him?"

"We must be careful."

Ilya imagined a finger, laid across invisible lips. The voices receded to a murmur, then silence.

"What is it?" Elena asked.

He shook his head, not wanting to worry her. "Nothing."

They passed run-down civic buildings, weeds growing in the cracks of the paving stones. There was nothing to remind Ilya of the little fort by the rushing Chuy, or the emerging frontier town that he had known so many years ago. The sleepy, dilapidated appearance of the place suited his mood; it was a world away from the rush and violence of the western cities. Elena frowned up at a street sign.

"Trouble is, they've changed all the names. . . . It's as bad as Almaty. *Abdymomunov.* That doesn't ring any bells. I might have to ask someone."

They crossed the street, to where an elderly lady was walking a small tired dog.

"Excuse me, can you tell me if Shevchenko Street is still Shevchenko, or have they changed the name?"

"No, it's still the same. But anyone will know. No one pays any attention to these new names. The old ones were good enough for years. Go to the end of the road, then right."

They found it easily enough after that, and to Ilya's surprise, the guesthouse was still there, half-hidden behind the trees. Inside, there was a woman behind the desk, seemingly asleep.

"Excuse me. We're looking for—" Ilya hesitated, but Elena said, "A room. With twin beds." The woman stared at them doubtfully.

"You're married? I'm afraid I can't let you have a room if you're not. It's against the rules." This was still an Islamic country, Ilya thought, despite the Soviet veneer.

"We're not married. This is my brother."

The woman might believe it, Ilya thought. They were both blue-eyed. The old poet Abai's voice resounded in his head: *You Russians, you all look the same to me. As like as one blade of grass from another.*

"We've just come from Kazakhstan, from Taldy Kurgan," Elena went on. "We're here to see my nephew at the university. His mother died recently, and there are some problems, so . . ." Her voice trailed away, but the woman's face was immediately sympathetic. Ilya wondered where Elena had developed this talent for fabrication. He tried to look appropriately bereaved. Murmuring condolences, the woman shuffled around to the front of the desk.

"Come with me. There is a nice room, looks out onto the street. Very reasonable in price." They followed her along a narrow, dark passage and up a flight of stairs.

"How much?" Ilya asked.

"Five hundred *som* for the room, for one night. How long are you staying?"

"We're not sure. It depends how quickly we can get things sorted out." Elena sounded harassed. The woman clucked.

"Terrible, terrible. I'm so sorry. Maybe it won't take so long. But the room will be available. It's a quiet time of year, this. Very busy in the summer—they all come, on the way to the lake. Have you been to Issy Kul?"

"Yes, a long time ago," Elena said.

The lake. Ilya remembered a shining rift of water, almost a hundred kilometers long, the mountains floating above it like clouds, and a great silence filling the world. He had stood on its shore and a man walking by with a herd of goats had told him its name: Ysyk Kol. It must be the same place. He had been there for almost a month, hiding out in the ruins of a fort that had once belonged to the Scyths. Despite its wildness, it had felt like a place of safety. The water had been warm, even in the depths of winter, the gift of underwater thermal springs.

"Ilya?" Elena was looking at him oddly. "The landlady wants to know if this will do."

They were standing at the door of the room. Wan sunlight poured through grimy windows. He saw two beds, pushed apart, with iron-spring mattresses. The plaster was flaking, but heat was blasting out of a radiator and a television set stood in one corner. "It'll be fine. Do you want us to pay now?"

The woman nodded. "There'll be a deposit. One night's charge. Here are the keys: This big one is for the room, and these two are for the outside door. But I put the chain on after midnight, so don't be late. There's a girl who comes to do the cleaning in the mornings. If you need to ask for me, I am Raisana Akyenbekova."

Ilya handed over the money.

"Sign here."

Ilya inscribed an indecipherable signature. "My name is Ivan Kostlovich. My sister is Natalya." The woman nodded and left, closing the door behind them. Elena sank down on one of the beds. "Do you think the TV works?"

"We can try. You'd better do it, though. I'm not good with these new machines."

After some fiddling with the aerial, Elena got the thing to function. She crouched over it, changing channels until a picture appeared. An old film—some epic set in Soviet times—then a cartoon for children. Ilya eyed the fuzzy, brightly colored images with distaste. He did not like television. It contained too many voices, rang imperiously upon the ear. Elena frowned.

"I was hoping for the news. What's the time?"

"Four o'clock." Ilya said. He lay back against the bolster at the head of the bed and closed his eyes. *Only for a moment,* he thought, but when he opened them again, the sky was blue with twilight and Elena was nowhere to be seen. He was just about to go in search of her, still groggy with sleep, when there was the rattle of the key in the lock and she reappeared. Her blonde hair was wet.

"I had a bath. Thank God; at last. The bathroom's down the hall."

"You should have told me where you were going," Ilya said, not yet forgiving her for the moment of panic when he had woken to find her gone.

"I didn't want to wake you. I thought you could do with a rest. How are you feeling?"

"Not so bad." He grimaced, rubbing his eyes. She had taken her handbag with her to the bathroom, he noticed. She did not yet entirely trust him. "Weak."

"You need food and sleep."

"I've had both. I need a wash." He struggled up from the bed and went to the door. "I won't be long."

The bathroom was some distance along the hall. Ilya shaved quickly, then stripped and stood under the trickle of brown water from the shower. It woke him up, at least. He went back to the bedroom, feeling slightly refreshed. Elena was watching the television. He sat down beside her, maintaining a careful distance between them, and was pulling on his boots when there was a knock at the door. They looked at each other in alarm.

"It must be the landlady," Elena said. She called, "Who is it?"

"It's me. Raisana."

Cautiously, Ilya opened the door. The landlady was standing outside.

"There's someone to see you."

"Who?"

"He didn't give a name. He's waiting downstairs."

"Did he ask for me by name?"

"No. He said, 'The two people who came here this afternoon.'"

"It might be someone from the university," Ilya said, to diminish her suspicions. "I told my son to phone first, but you know what youngsters are like. . . . Perhaps it's one of his friends." Behind the lie, his mind was racing. "What does he look like?"

"I can't really tell—his coat's pulled up. I told him you'd have to come down. My husband doesn't like people who aren't guests coming into the rooms. We've had things stolen. Not that I'm suggesting a friend of yours—"

"It's not a problem. We'll come downstairs." He picked up the sword, still in its fishing-rod case. "For my son," he added, in response to the landlady's puzzled glance. His thoughts were speeding ahead. What if they had to put up a fight in the hallway? Raisana would call the police, assuming they weren't already here. He could not think of a way to say, "Is this man from the FSB, do you think?" without arousing her suspicions.

But when they stepped into the hallway, he saw that it was not a policeman at all. It was Manas the bogatyr.

Interlude

From the heights of the Edraya, Pergama Province stretched below in a blur of heat. The waves of dark green and azure forest were broken only by the little towns, basking in the sun. The smoke of the recent fires still hung above the peaks of the Balchus, and the dim land was marked with a long scorched scar. Shadia Anikova found herself reluctant to look at it, as though she could force it from memory.

"Look, you can see it," Natasha said, destroying Anikova's attempt at denial. "Must have been one hell of a bang." She reached out and squeezed her sister's hand. Anikova gave a tight nod.

"I didn't think we were going to make it. I still can't believe it happened. One minute everything was fine and normal, and the next moment . . . There was a breach. No warning, nothing." She closed her eyes for a moment, trying to blot out the recollection of that great rift of light opening out over the land. It was, however, the reason she was here today. Kitai had insisted that she take a break for a couple of days, and Anikova had been happy enough to agree, though not for reasons of personal trauma: a weekend at the family dacha had won her a brief respite from the Mechvor.

"I didn't see anything in *Novosty* this morning, and you know I always read it from cover to cover."

"Of course not. They don't want information like that to get out." *They?* When, she wondered with bemusement, had Central Command ceased to be *us*? "The *Rad* told the newspapers it was a gas explosion. Who knows, some people might even believe it." It didn't matter whether they believed it or not, Anikova thought, nor how convincing the government-doctored information really was. The important thing was that people wanted to believe that it had just been a gas leak, that their world was not starting to fall apart at the seams.

Only two generations, and already the truth of where they had come from was classified information, available only to the military and the upper echelons of government. And even among those in the know, it was receding into legend. *After all,* Anikova thought, *I was born here, and so was my mother. My grandparents came here for a reason; they were pioneers.*

No one wanted to go back to the mess that was Russia, the swift deterioration of revolutionary goals that should have remained pure, and they had not been given the option. Everyone knew it was a one-way trip. But although she had known no other place, she couldn't help wondering about the *Matraya-Derevnya,* the Motherland: what kind of people lived there now, and whether they spoke the same language, followed the Party, worshiped the same God.

Natasha had parked the *siydna* on the landing spot

immediately above the viewpoint. Now, she leaned over into space to catch the breeze.

"You could fly from up here," Natasha said, hanging over the edge. "You could just jump, and soar."

"God, Tasha, please, could you not do that. Ever since the—the explosion"—it was becoming easier to get used to the fake term—"I've started having a problem with heights. Anyway, you wouldn't soar for long. You'd plummet."

"I'd fly," Natasha said, her voice distant. The breath of wind carried her voice away, lifting her dark hair like a wing. It was not safe to say such things, not even here into the wind's silence.

"So, shall we go on up to the point?" Anikova said, uneasy.

"When does the switchback run? On the hour?"

"As far as I know."

"We haven't been up here since October," Anikova said. "Do you remember? We took Uncle."

"Oh, that's right. Nursultan came with us, too." She gave Anikova a reproachful look for editing her boyfriend out of their personal history, as so much had been revised from their nation's.

"I remember that," Anikova said with a thin smile. She did not like Natasha's boyfriend, whom she suspected of countergovernment sympathies. That she secretly shared those sympathies did not lessen her dislike. And there was the Islamic question, too: Nursultan's grandfather was the Imam of a major mosque.

The switchback began at Voronezh Point, careening across the sharp hills of the Edraya as far as Mariupol. There, the hills dropped in a scarp to the forested plains surrounding Azhutsk. By the time the sisters reached the point, there was already a queue. They could see the returning switchback coming down the opposite slope before crawling back up the ridge to the point. Anikova started to laugh.

"What?"

"So much for exercise," she said. "First we take the *siydna*, then we take the switch."

"Well, we're walking now," Natasha said.

"A couple of hundred meters, yes."

The switchback came in with a thin electric hum. Above it, the air wavered. Anikova could smell hot metal: an enticing, tarry odor. They filed through the gate and strapped in.

"Oh, I'm sitting backward," Natasha said, dismayed. "Change with me, Shadouschka?"

"No, thanks. You can handle it."

"Shadia!" Natasha cried. But her sister's name was lost in the gush of air as the switchback took off, hurtling down the slope and up the other side of the ridge. As they climbed, the pace slowed and the scent of pine, resinous and acrid, filled the car. Anikova could have reached out and drawn her hand along the branches. Blue fronds of dzadra floated out between the clusters of fir. All the roads in Pergama skirted the forests, but the switchback had been carved straight through, to follow the line of the gorges.

They were far enough into the woods at this point for Anikova to feel that a bridge had been crossed, that they were in the part of Byelovodye that belonged only to itself, and not to the colonists. She knew that it was foolish, there on the plunging, plummeting monorail with the pergolas and cafes of Lake Irrin at the other end, but she wished the switchback would stop, that they could get off and wander into the woods' heart. Then she thought of the *rusalki,* smiling behind their mantles, and of the other things that were supposed to live in the forests, and she felt herself grow cold.

As they came up over the last ridge, Anikova caught a glimpse of Lake Irrin lying below, blue and gentle in the afternoon sunshine. The switchback rolled down to a halt beside the lake station. As they stepped down onto the platform, the air was noticeably cooler, with a breeze blowing across the water. Anikova felt as though she could breathe for the first time since the breach. The psychic turmoil left behind by the Mechvor's probing was ebbing away, too. But she did not want to think about Kitai, not today.

They walked slowly along the promenade, to the edge of the water. Irrin glittered in the sun. Carp swam lazily in the shallows, between the green banners of weed. The little town itself reached up the slopes of Drezneya, built in the thirties as a resort and self-consciously charming. It was much favored by the members of Central Command and the *Rad* for their summer homes. It was pretty in winter, but difficult to reach without *siydni* transport, and often walled off by the blizzards.

"Some wealthy people up here," Natasha said, as she did every time they came. At the end of the promenade a teahouse overlooked the lake, and they secured a table on the terrace. Natasha sat looking up at the chalets, each with its balcony and dark curling roof.

"You could afford to live here," Anikova teased. Natasha snorted.

"*I* couldn't. Nursultan's family could."

"That's what I meant."

Natasha raised her dark eyebrows.

"And what makes you think Nursultan wants to live cheek by jowl with Christians? Not that he's prejudiced, you understand, but—"

"How is he, anyway?" Anikova asked.

"His father's influence has put him on the Standards Committee. I haven't seen that much of him."

"He passed selection, then?" It surprised Anikova. She thought again of those doubtful sympathies; of the earnest counseling of the Mechvor.

"I suppose so. Did I tell you he's out in Tatzinsk?"

"No. What's he doing there?"

"There's talk of a joint party summit in the autumn: us, Bakistan, and Uralesk. The Bakistanis want to develop Tahe as a free-trade zone."

"The Uraciks won't like that."

"They're pragmatists," Natasha said absently. "They're willing to concede a certain amount, as long as they get what they want in return, which is a chunk of the southern steppe. That's the trouble with this world. What with the tribes, Christians, Islam, and the Party, it's not big enough for all of us any longer."

Anikova stirred her glass, watching the tea—the color of beechwood—swirl within. God forbid that they should go back to the situation in the fifties. She and her sisters had heard their father's stories over and over again: the spark attack on Akcholai, the firestorms set by the horse tribes. *Place makes you what you are,* Anikova thought, *and when that is stripped away and you are forced to live somewhere utterly new, then you have to revise who you are and where you derive your identity.* Their mother had gained hers from nationalism, but she had watched her father become increasingly disillusioned, until the breach had taken him from them.

And where do I take my identity from? Anikova wondered, staring out over the rippling waters of Irrin.

Voices drifted across the lake from an ornamental pleasure boat, and Anikova could hear the tap of a horse's hooves along the road. The *Rhus* and their horses, she thought, inseparable wherever they went. The sun was skimming the western rim of the Balchus, floating above the Edraya. Soon it would be gone.

Anikova and Natasha walked back along the lakeshore and sat on the station wall to wait for the switchback. Going toward Voronezh, the woods were dim in the fading light. Anikova strained her eyes looking through the shadows, but the woods were still. The scent of resin was still strong in the early evening air. She leaned back in her seat and shut her eyes, and, unbidden, the thought came to her: *We are still here, we Russians. After all this time and all the things that have befallen us, we are still here.*

The thought made her uneasy, as if time was reaching back to them, a breath of future change in the idyllic day.

That was the problem with her people, Anikova reflected, always giving a nod to fate in case something unpleasant waited around the corner, never accepting that life, even for a short while, could be truly untroubled.

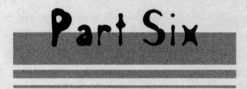

Part Six

One

KYRGYZSTAN, 21ST CENTURY

At first, Ilya did not recognize the *bogatyr*. Manas had been tall, flamboyantly bearded, filled with a nonchalant and menacing elan. Now, Ilya saw only a stooping figure huddled in the folds of a dirty coat. When they entered the hallway, Manas was perched on a nearby chair, staring into space. He started at the sound of their footsteps, then hastened up to Ilya and put both hands on his shoulders, standing too close, with obvious intent. Ilya took an involuntary step back. The long Kyrgyz face was still handsome, though now it was clean-shaven. Manas' eyes were bright and hectic. Ilya felt a momentary gratification that he had not been the only one whom the years had not treated so kindly.

So, Ilya thought. *It seems I am not the last, after all.* The realization made him shiver, like cold rain. *And if Manas is still alive, then how many others of my strange kind? And why has there been no trace of them until now? Why have I not heard them all these many years?* And then, the coldest thought of all: *They used to say only one* bogatyr *could kill another.*

Manas' thoughts were, it seemed, running along similar lines. "Such a long time! When was it we last met?" There was clear challenge in his face. *We are born enemies.* Manas, Ilya recalled, had always loved to walk on the edge. At least the *bogatyr* had the wit not to use Ilya's real name.

"It must be the eighties, at least," Ilya said politely. True enough. The eighteen eighties, anyway.

"Amazing. It seems like yesterday. Listen, I need to talk to you." His eyes slid over Elena with evident appreciation. Ilya bristled. The landlady's eyes were shining with curiosity. "Alone," Manas added.

"All right," Ilya said warily. "We'll go up to the room." He looked toward the landlady. "I'll keep an eye on him, I promise."

"I'll wait here," Elena said. Ilya cast her a mute plea: *Explain this.* As he headed back up the stairs, Manas in tow, he heard her say to the landlady, "Perhaps my nephew's in trouble. . . ."

—and the landlady's reply, "Often it happens, when the mother dies. One minute they're such good boys and then they go right off the rails."

Ilya smiled to himself. His own mother had died hundreds of years ago, but he still felt the loss, even though he could no longer remember exactly what she had looked like. She'd had blonde hair, like Elena's. The recollection was somehow unsettling. He reached the door of the room and motioned to Manas.

"Inside."

"Oh, no," the *bogatyr* said, balking like a horse. He made a sweeping gesture with one hand. "You can go first."

"Very well," Ilya said, but he unfastened the

fishing-rod case and kept Manas in the corner of his sight as he went through the door. The room was as silent and empty as they had left it. A halo of light could be seen through the window: a streetlamp, blurred. It was raining again.

"So," Ilya said, turning. "How was the twentieth century for you?"

Manas gave an indifferent shrug. "Nothing much."

"Oh, come on. Not even Kyrgyzstan's been that quiet."

"I spent most of it in the mountains with my people. They still believe, you know, up in the Alatau. They don't give a damn what happens outside their own valleys. They still sing songs about me." He paused. "Actually, now that the Russian rabbits have scuttled back to their burrows, I'm getting a lot more attention these days. There's even been a TV series about me." He looked up at Ilya with sly pride. "That's something, eh? What about you?"

"Someone wrote an opera," Ilya said. It was hard not to be bitter, harder still not to see the funny side of the matter.

"Oh, but that's wonderful," Manas said with a thin edge of contempt. "As long as they're still singing songs about us, we live on, eh?"

It had occurred to Ilya more than once that there might be greater truth in that than Manas realized. What if they really were no more than phantoms, the embodied dreams of their respective lands, anchored to the world by a tenuous thread of belief? It would explain why he had spent the last decade in a haze of heroin and alcohol. No one believed in anything anymore. Perhaps he was no more than a reflection of that lack. *We are, none of us, individuals. We are only what so-ciety makes of us, humans or heroes.* What was a hero but a collection of valued qualities, in service to his fellow man or the State? It was a central tenet of Marxism and it seemed appropriate to Ilya that a hero should be less real than ordinary men, rather than truly superhuman.

"So why are you here, Manas? Have you come to welcome me to your mountains? And how did you find me, anyway?"

"I followed the people who are following you."

It was a shock, but not a surprise.

"And who are they?" Ilya asked.

"For a man who is a hero, you've certainly man-aged to attract some undesirable characters. Not your lady friend—she's lovely—but you had a party of dream-stealers on your tail, did you know that? You've lost them for the moment, though. Do you know why they're following you?"

"Do you mean the FSB?"

"What? A bunch of petty bureaucrats? No, not them. I mean *dream*-stealers. People who control what goes on inside other people's heads. The people who *run* organizations like the FSB."

"Manas, I have no idea what you're talking about." Best to pretend ignorance for the moment.

"Of course you don't. You're a Russian. You proba-bly don't have anything going on in that head of yours except where the next vodka's coming from."

Finally, the realization hit Ilya. "Do you mean a *volkh*? A man named Kovalin?"

"That's the one. You've met him?"

"Yes."

"And what did he tell you?"

"The same thing that you just did. They are working against the creatures known as *rusalki*. My enemies."

"And so you immediately assumed they were your friends."

"No, I am not completely an idiot. I agreed to help them because Kovalin told me he had the power to give me something I wanted. In turn, they wanted me to find an object for them. Something belonging to the *rusalki*."

"And did you find it?" There was a sudden burn behind Manas' gaze, an eagerness.

"Not yet," Ilya said cautiously. Instinct told him that it was best to keep quiet about the object. "I went to meet Kovalin's contacts. Elena came with me. She's a scientist."

The *bogatyr* was frowning.

"Once you found this object, what were you planning to do? Hand it over to Kovalin?"

"I arranged to meet his contacts, to discuss the matter," Ilya said, "but the *rusalki* got to them first."

"Truly, the Russians are a remarkable people," Manas said, shaking his head. "And you are one of the greatest figures of their folklore. You rival only Prince Ivan the Stupid."

"What have I done to deserve that?"

"Has it once occurred to you that the *rusalki* are your friends, not your enemies? That they have saved your life time and time again not as punishment, but because you are important?"

"Obviously it has occurred to me," Ilya said angrily. The crack about Ivan the Stupid rankled. "But they have not approached me, nor attempted to discuss the matter with me, nor shown any signs of being other than my foes. In addition to this, they have a reputation—which I have witnessed firsthand—of abducting people, taking them beyond the world, never to be seen again. And I have also seen them kill."

"They are not human," Manas said after a pause. "They take folk, it is true, but they do not often kill them. They select. And they do not act according to human principles. By our standards, I suppose, they are ruthless."

"What are they, then?"

"You know about aliens? You watch TV?" Manas' face became reflective. "I love it. Best invention of the twentieth century, if you ask me. *X-Files*. Excellent program. Very exciting."

"It's American," Ilya said.

"So? You think Americans don't have legends, tell stories? The *rusalki* are like aliens—the little grey things who abduct people. Do you know that several thousand Americans claim to have had this experience? Not all of them have come back again. Of course, we in Russia, being superior"—Manas appeared to have abandoned his Kyrgyz origins for the moment—"have beautiful girls instead of little monsters. But I believe they are the same thing. And they are not alien in the sense that they are from another planet. They move between this world and the other."

"The other?" Having been there, Ilya thought he knew what Manas was talking about, but he wanted to hear the *bogatyr* say it, see how far Manas' understanding tallied with what he had already been told by Kovalin.

"The other, indeed," was all that Manas said.

"Say this is true. How do you know all this?"

"Because three months ago, I met a man in the high Alatau. An *akyn*. Do you know what that is?"

"A bard?"

"Precisely. One who dreams for a living and writes poems about those dreams. A man like Kovalin, but from this world."

"What?"

"The *akyn* told me something very interesting about your *volkh*. Namely, that he isn't from this world any more than the *rusalki* are. And he is your enemy and mine."

"Long ago, Manas, you told me that *you* were my enemy."

"Why, so I am," Manas said with sudden charm. "But you know the old Moslem saying, don't you?— 'My enemy's enemy is my friend.' "

Ilya frowned. "Does that make us friends?"

"No. But it does make us allies. I came with a request, Ilya Muromyets. If you are successful in your quest, as one hero to another, I ask you—do not hand the thing for which you are looking over to Kovalin. I do not ask you to *give* it to me, mind, only to keep it safe from him."

"And if I do not?"

"Ah, then—or so my poet tells me—then the world will fall."

Two

Having lulled the landlady's suspicions and made sure that she was safely back in the kitchen, Elena hovered outside the bedroom door, trying to overhear what Ilya and the stranger were saying to each other. Usually, she despised eavesdropping, but she felt that the circumstances were curious enough to override her scruples. As she heard the stranger talk about the *rusalki*, her hands tightened on the strap of her handbag. She also found that she was waiting for the sound of Ilya's voice.

Slow down, she told herself, *slow down. If you are starting to feel so strongly about him, then he almost certainly is not the right choice.* God knows, it had happened before. Her last boyfriend had vanished into space after only two months, and now she wondered how much of that had been simply circumstance, a keyed-up excitement as they approached the start of the mission. Yuri had not been as damaged as Ilya— cosmonauts tended to be stable, once one discounted the madness that made them want to go into space in the first place—but he had undoubtedly been emotionally inaccessible, focused more on his work and on the mission than on her. Elena could understand that, and understand too that it had been part of his appeal.

From within the room, she heard the scrape of a chair as someone rose. Not wanting to be caught listening at the keyhole, Elena slipped around the corner and out of sight. The door opened and the stranger stepped through. He retreated down the stairs. Moments later, he was followed by Ilya, carrying the fishing-rod case.

"Ilya," Elena hissed.

He turned. "I'm going with him. Wait here. Lock the door, push the bed against it, and make sure the windows are bolted."

"Why can't I come?"

"I want to make sure you're safe." His gaze flickered to her handbag and she knew he was thinking about the object.

"I'll look after it," Elena said.

"I know you will. But make sure you stay here."

"All right," Elena said dubiously. She did not fancy the role of damsel in the tower.

"I don't know how long I'll be. If it's a long time, I'll call you. I'll take the number of the guesthouse." At the corner of the corridor, he turned. "Elena. Be careful."

"You, too." She waited until he had vanished around the corner, then went to the window and peered out into the twilight. Two figures, both tall men, were receding swiftly down the street, one behind the other. She held her breath, but the stranger did not turn to see if he was being followed.

Thoughtfully, Elena sat down on the bed. She flicked through the channels of the television and at last found the news. It was in Kyrgyz and she could only understand occasional words and fragments, but she watched the images unfold nonetheless. The news was a litany of car crashes and drug busts. There was nothing about bodies in a Kazakhstani hotel. There had been an earth tremor to the north of Almaty, along the line of the mountains. Elena leaned closer to the set to look at the little diagram. It depicted Koktubye Hill, the place where they had encountered the horse tribe. She stared at it thoughtfully.

The news changed to the wars in Afghanistan and Chechnya, perennial subjects for discussion, followed by a shot of the new space station, like a great wheel above the world. Yuri could be floating clumsily down one of those passages even now. Elena sighed with envy. Then the weather: rain, with sudden dips in temperature and occasional sun, typical for spring. The advertisements came on, then a game show with squealing contestants trying to win a holiday in Cyprus.

Elena turned off the set in disgust and closed the curtains. Opening her handbag, she reached for her mobile phone and dialed her mother's number, but there was nothing, just a hiss of static and failed connections. She must be out of range, or perhaps the mountains were blocking the signal. The region was full of such black spots. She put the phone back in her bag.

The object was still within, nestled in a handful of tissues.

She stared down at it, half-expecting something to happen, half-fearful. She was not entirely willing to admit to herself that she resented being left behind, that she wanted an equal share in any adventures.

She took the object from her bag, weighing it in her hand. It was the same as ever: heavy, cold. At first the chill of it froze her down to the bone, but then it grew warmer, seeping into her palm like sunlight. She sank down onto the bed, still holding the object. She thought of that strange land and the hope rose within her. It was what she had always wanted, after all: the chance to be part of the reach for the stars, for other worlds. She had never hoped to visit one, and there was little chance that she would ever have children. The descendants of others would travel out beyond the solar system, not her own blood, her own genes. And she wondered now whether that was why she had pinned so much of her life on the success of the space program: It was the only dream left available to her.

The warmth of the object flooded through her. It was comforting, like another presence. She thought back to Baikonur, to the excitement before the launches, the rockets blasting up into the burn-blue sky, mission control working like a single entity, a gestalt. The rockets still traveled, but from a shattered country, and she had been sidelined. She felt as though she had fallen from a great height, burning out on reentry. Her eyes snapped open. The object was as cold as old ashes.

Restlessly, Elena put it back in the bag and turned back to the television. But as she flicked the switch, light flooded out across the room, so bright that she flung up an arm to shield her eyes.

This time, there was no sense that she was being drawn into the strange world on the other side of the light. It faded, until it was nothing more than a long opening, suspended in the air. Elena stood, blinking as her eyes adjusted, and found that she could now see through the gate. The world beyond was plunged into twilight.

She was standing before a garden fragrant with fruit trees. High above, snared in the branches of a cherry tree, she saw a single burning star. A wind drifted through, laden with the fragrance of grass. A shadow moved behind the trees. Elena waited, watching.

Slowly, a figure stepped out onto the grass and hesitated.

"Who's there?" it called—a woman's voice, brusque and speaking in oddly-accented Russian. Elena, seized by panic, nearly did not reply. But it was the closest she had come to meeting a person from this other world and she did not want to lose the chance.

She called out, "My name is Elena. Don't be afraid. I'm on the other side of the—the hole in the air."

"Oh, my God," the woman said. "It's a localized breach."

Somehow the term, with its technical connotations, was reassuring.

"I don't know what you mean," Elena said. The woman was coming close now, striding swiftly across the damp grass toward the gateway. She was tall and dark-haired, perhaps fifty or so, dressed in some kind of military uniform with the jacket undone. Elena could see an insignia on the shoulder: a scatter of stars.

Something about the woman's face was oddly familiar, yet Elena was certain that she had never set eyes on her before.

"How long has this breach been open? How long have you been using the distorter coil? Where did you get it?" The woman's voice was sharp, accusing.

"A what? Look, I don't even know where you are."

"Where are *you*?" the woman demanded in turn. "Earth? Russia?"

"Yes. Well, I'm in Kyrgyzstan. Not Russia, not anymore."

"Kyrgyzia? That's in the southeast, isn't it? Toward Pathan territory."

"Pathan? Do you mean Pakistan?"

"I don't know that name," the woman said. She ran a hand through her hair and Elena saw that her arm was strapped up in a bandage.

"Who are you?" she asked.

"Colonel Shadia Anikova. Pergama Provincial Military. It won't mean a lot to you."

"It means nothing," Elena said. "I'm Elena." She could see something at the base of the trees, scratching about. It was the size of a pheasant. "What's that?"

The woman glanced over her shoulder. "Just a *kikimura*," she said dismissively. "Listen to me. The coil—"

But at that moment, the room in which Elena stood began to shudder. Outside, she heard the sudden, protesting creak of branches. The gap in the air sealed shut with a snap; the bag rocked on the nightstand. Elena snatched it up, preparing to run from the room, but there was no need. The tremor had passed as swiftly as it had come. There was no sign of the gateway in the air. Elena gave the object a narrow-eyed look, thinking fearfully of the earthquake on the news.

But the object sat in the middle of her handbag, silent and impenetrable.

Three

Manas was heading toward the park. The streets were empty, but Ilya could see lights in the windows of the apartment blocks, catch snatches of mealtime conversation. He had spent many evenings like this, wandering the *prospekts* of St. Petersburg and Moscow, looking enviously in on the warm world of ordinary people. But this time he had a room of his own to which to return, and Elena instead of a syringe. The thought of sleeping once more in the same room glowed within him like lamplight.

Manas had disappeared into the trees. Ilya paused and listened, then caught the sound of uncertain footsteps. After a few minutes they stopped. Ilya peered into the dusk. Surely that was a statue, standing so still at the edge of the trees? But then the statue moved. Ilya saw a man in a business suit and black-and-white *al-kapak* hat. He was middle-aged, unremarkable.

"Did you find him?" he heard the stranger say in Russian.

"Yes?"

"And then?"

"He seemed to believe me. He claims not to have it."

"Is he lying?"

"I do not know."

"Can't you tell? I thought you said you would be able to detect this thing if he had it."

"Well, I did not." Manas' voice tilted into arrogance. "If it is here, it has not spoken to me. But take my word for it—he is Russian, a simple sort, not good at dissembling."

"*Panimyu,* I understand. But we should not talk here. We need a place where our voices will be masked."

"What about your office?" Manas asked.

"Don't be naïve. You know it is bugged, like all government buildings."

Ilya saw Manas nod, then the two men turned away and began walking swiftly across the park. Neither said anything more. He followed them until they reached a small street lined with bars and restaurants, evidently the cheerful equivalent of Moscow's Arbat. Manas and the stranger headed into the nearest bar. Cautiously, Ilya followed.

The bar was crowded and noisy, filled with youngsters and not the kind of place that Ilya would normally have sought out. He had to stop himself from performing the search-and-locate that had, during the time of his addiction, become second nature. He had come forth from the twentieth century with two new skills: a familiarity with modern weapons and the ability to recognize a dealer at twenty paces. He made his way to the end of the bar, ordered a vodka, then slid into a cubicle. From there, he could see Manas and the

stranger, who sat with their backs to him. He took a
fiery sip and settled back to listen.

"—sure that we have not been followed?" the
stranger was saying. Manas shrugged.

"Very likely." He glanced around the bar. Ilya
shrank farther into the cubicle. "So I suggest we keep
the conversation to matters of more common knowledge for now. *Tak*. You had questions for me?"

"Of the nature of the place where you and this
man Kovalin come from. Does it have a name?" the
stranger asked.

"Byelovodye. The land of white waters. Its gates
were supposed to lie somewhere in the Altai, not so far
from here. Did you know that?"

"Yes. It's like Shambhala. I thought it was a fairy
tale."

"It is. So am I. So is our heroic Russian friend."
Manas' voice was edged with contempt. He added,
"Actually, I'm an epic."

Ilya smiled to himself as Manas went on, "It is a
place that has a more fluid and flexible relationship
with our dreams, with our stories and legends, than
this world will ever possess. Entities come from it—the
rusalki, for instance. Ideologies change it. There is reason to believe that at the demise of the Soviet experiment, its nature substantially altered—indeed, it may
be that this alteration came first, and was the cause of
that demise. It is a kind of parallel dimension that affects, and is affected by, our own ideas."

"Are you saying that it is some kind of imaginary
world?" the stranger asked. He sounded incredulous;
Ilya could not blame him.

Or some kind of collective unconscious? Ilya wondered. A few weeks with that *Gulag* psychiatrist all those years ago hadn't gone entirely amiss.

"No, it is quite real. But it works according to different laws. Memory has a slightly different function there, for example."

"Do many people live there?"

"Folk have wandered in or been taken there by the *rusalki,* over the centuries. There have been ways through before—gates opened by ancient, unknown technology—and it seems that sometimes there are little natural rifts. But in the 1920's—not long after the Revolution—Byelovodye was colonized. A man called Tsilibayev found a way to replicate the equipment that can create a gate. We don't know where he found the means—he kept his sources very close to his chest. What is clear is that he didn't fully understand the technology he was trying to copy and his equipment was never very stable, but it worked nonetheless. The early Bolshevik authorities sent groups of people through, in case Russia fell. It was a top-secret project, a way of preserving national identity if all else failed. Felix Dzerzhinsky, the old monster, put a stop to all that—thought it was counterrevolutionary, or some such nonsense. The Cheka had the laboratory destroyed. But Tsilibayev's technology is still being used within Byelovodye, by those who understand even less than he."

The room seemed to echo with guilt. Ilya thought back eighty years, remembering a bilious green office and the look on the Cheka operative's face. He remembered the expressionless visages of the men waiting for him by the railway track, to lead him to the next train east and Siberia. These men were like beads in a black rosary, another link in a chain of destruction.

"Does *anyone* fully understand it?" said the stranger. "Do you?"

"I am no scientist, any more than you are. But I know that this device can be *used*. That is all I need to know. It is a key. It is not even necessary to be near a gate—the thing can open rifts in the air itself—but that is too dangerous."

"How so?"

"You might not find yourself on solid ground, or find yourself in the middle of a sea. Byelovodye is not a geographical replication of Russia, you see. The device must be used responsibly."

"But can anyone use it?"

"Certain folk can activate it by their thoughts alone. Otherwise it requires complex equipment and, as Tsilibayev discovered, that is not always stable. But don't worry—I'm here, and I'm on your side."

Ilya wondered whether the stranger could hear the slyness in Manas' voice. *Certain folk.* Did Manas mean all the *bogatyri,* or something else? It made him wonder anew about the coil, about his own relationship to it, and the still small voice in his head.

"Can you activate it?" the stranger asked. "Do you possess that ability?"

"I can do many things," Manas said, and laughed.

He isn't going to tell him, Ilya thought. But did that mean that Manas had the power, or not?

"What happened to the colony?"

"It survived, and grew. People had families, married some of the descendants of the folk who had drifted in over the years. They established their own state. Ideas from the outside world—what we are pleased to call the real world—slipped through the barrier, affecting what happens in Byelovodye and vice versa. I am talking about *all* ideas, by the way—all dreams—Central Asian as well as Russian, Islamic as well as Christian. This is not some fantasy land, some bucolic Russian idyll. Dreams of technology and the future are as powerful as any fairy story ever was. Byelovodye is now a modern socialist state. Over time, the colonists decided that they wanted nothing more to do with the 'real' Russia. They are as insular and introspective, as repressive and repressed, as the Soviet Union ever was." Manas' voice was thick with hate.

To whom was Manas lying? Ilya wondered. The Kyrgyz hero seemed to know much more than he had told Ilya, which was hardly a surprise.

The stranger said, "And it is the key to the gates between these worlds that Kovalin and his kind are now seeking?"

"It is *a* key, yes. One of the few remaining pieces of the old technology."

"And the gates themselves? Where are they?"

"Here, too, there are few that remain. One lies in Samarkand itself and is very old. It's been lost for centuries—my allies have only recently discovered it. But there is another, not far from here—a newer opening. It lies at the far end of Lake Issy Kul, in an abandoned military facility. I have arranged to meet the *akyn* there, my poet, tomorrow at sunset. He says he has valuable information for me."

"What kind of information?"

"I do not know." Manas rose. "I will keep you informed."

"Do so. If an advantage can be gained for Kyrgyzia, you know I will want to hear of it."

"Of course. You are a politician, after all."

Ilya waited until they left, straining to hear their conversation as they went out onto the street. But Manas and the stranger remained silent, with only their footsteps echoing along the wet road. Ilya threaded his way through the bar, ignoring the impulse to stay, to drink, to score. Elena was waiting for him.

Four

To Elena's great relief, it was not long before Ilya returned.

"Ilya? Something's happened."

He sat down on the bed beside her and listened with attention as she described the garden, and the woman within it.

"She spoke of a breach?" Ilya said. "Do you know what she meant?"

"I don't know, but I can guess. A breach between their world and ours?"

"Perhaps. But what could have caused it?" There was a new unease in his face. He went on, "What else did she say?"

"She asked me if I was using a distorter coil."

"A what?" But they both looked toward Elena's handbag.

"She said something about the Pergama military. Have you ever heard of a place called Pergama?"

"It sounds Greek."

"She'd heard of Russia and Kyrgyzstan. She knew

where they were. It must be a parallel world, Ilya. An alternative."

Briefly, Ilya told her of what he had overheard.

"So I was right. What a wonderful thing, Ilya!"

He nodded, slowly. He did not seem as excited as she was by the news.

"Don't you agree?" She touched his hand. "Ilya, this is what I've been looking for all these years. Another chance for us, for Russia. A different future."

He grimaced. "From what the stranger said, they seem to be making the same old mistakes."

"We don't know that. We've seen some of it for ourselves. Did it look all that bad to you?"

"No," Ilya said slowly. "But if you stepped into the middle of the Russian countryside on a spring day, it might look good to you, too. You're the scientist. What do you think?"

She sighed, not wanting to admit it. "You're right. We haven't seen enough to judge."

"Elena, you want so much to believe and so do I, but we have so little real understanding."

"This world that Manas spoke of. It's called Byelovodye?" she asked.

"So he said."

"Strange," Elena said. The name brought memories flooding back. "My father used to tell me stories of Byelovodye, the land of white waters, when I was a kid. When he wasn't too drunk. They were so real—almost as though he had been there. He used to say that the entrance was up in the Altai. There was even an expedition to look for it, he said, but they didn't find anything."

"I remember stories, too. The shamans used to talk

about it in Siberia. They spoke of it as a kind of first place, an origin. But I wonder if it really existed, or if their belief brought it into being."

"But the place we saw was so real. So solid."

"Elena, I don't think we should separate from now on if these rifts between the worlds are going to happen." Ilya paused, adding, "I don't want to lose you."

Elena glanced at him. He was staring at the wall.

"No," she said carefully. There were nuances in that last remark that she was not sure she had interpreted correctly. "We should stick together. It'll be safer."

They sat in silence for a moment. She was very conscious of his presence next to her, of the scarred, bony hand resting on the coverlet between them. The prospect of launching into an awkward discussion, with room for so many misunderstandings, was a dismal one. Instead she said, "I'm glad you came back." Then, not giving herself time to think, she leaned over and kissed his cheek. Ilya turned toward her like a drowning man and they fell back onto the bed.

With Yuri Golynski, her last lover, there had always been the sense that he was doing her a favor. He would glance up with a kind of abstracted arrogance in the middle of sex, suggesting how fortunate she was that he—cosmonaut, Soviet hero—had selected her. It had almost certainly been unintentional, but this trace of smugness had done nothing to enhance the experience. Ilya, however, seemed to have trouble accepting that it was really happening. She could see the disbelief in his face. He kissed her over and over again, burying his face in her neck, then her breasts. When she put her arms around him, she found that he was shaking.

"Ilya, when did you last . . ."

His voice was hoarse. "A very long time." She slid her hand between them and found how hard he was. He cried out as she touched him. She rolled on top and kissed him again, surprised by the extent to which she was taking the initiative. Usually she was more passive; men were said to prefer it, as it demonstrated a becoming modesty, but she could not hold back.

Ilya did not seem to have any complaints.

"Elena, my darling . . ." His voice was strained and hoarse. "Very soon I'm not going to be able to stop."

She sat up, straddling him. "Oh, God, we don't have any condoms."

There was a familiar, mute male plea in his eyes: *Can't we do it anyway?* And she nearly gave him what he so clearly wanted, but the old fear of pregnancy was too ingrained, and the needle tracks on his arms were a grim reminder of more recent dangers.

"Lie still," she told him. She unbuttoned his shirt, sliding it over his shoulders. The muscles were tense beneath his skin; she kneaded them until he relaxed. Then, reaching down, she undid his fly and took him in her hand. Ilya writhed, hands moving back to grip the bars of the bed. It was only then that she realized he was afraid of hurting her. She stroked him, running her free hand up and down his chest with an exhilarating sense of ownership. But she could have counted his ribs, and one of the scars looked red and recent. His hand returned, to press her palm against the damaged flesh. Seconds later he came, quickly and hard, shouting out and causing a vicarious pang deep within her. Elena hoped there was no one in the room next door. Especially since they were supposed to be brother and sister.

Ilya's eyes fluttered open. "Elena . . ."

If she could not have him inside her, there was the next best thing. She climbed down from the bed, took off her clothes as he watched with exhausted contentment, and slid in beside him. He held her carefully: too thin for his build, but with an unnatural power in muscle and sinew. She tensed for a moment, then relaxed. *Human enough where it counts,* she thought, smiling to herself.

His hand drifted between her legs.

"Ilya?"

"Your turn," he murmured. "I've learned a few things in eight hundred years."

He was very gentle and she was surprised at how little time it took. She fell asleep almost immediately, without even reaching for her cigarettes.

Interlude

BYELOVODYE, N.E. 80

Shadia Anikova drove her sister back to First City late on Sunday afternoon. She thought they were never going to get out of the dacha; Natasha kept forgetting one thing or another and running back indoors. Anikova sat impatiently in the driver's seat, trying to appear unconcerned. She was watching the light, still a pale brightness in the west, but soon evening would fall and Anikova would not have confessed to any member of her family that she was afraid of driving back in the dark. She kept remembering the second breach, that unnatural hollow in the air and the shadowy room beyond.

As soon as she had realized what was happening, Anikova had to fight the urge to step through the gap and see what lay on the other side. She once again recalled what she had been told by Central Command about the Mother Country: that it was degenerate, falling apart, finished. That its influence could no longer be tolerated upon her own world, that all gates between them must be sealed, except one, and that the

means to control that gate—the stolen distorter coil—
must be retrieved so that Russia's dreams could be bled
through it. A pity for the government's sake, she
thought, that Tsilibayev's duplicate coils had not been
more stable. If they had functioned more successfully,
Central Command could have relied upon one of them
to power a gate, rather than chasing down this old, lost
piece of technology. But Central Command would still
have wanted the original coil retrieved, in case it fell
into the wrong hands.

Their agents were working on that retrieval even
now, dispatched into what was fast becoming hostile
terrain. She had seen the latest report this morning:
that they had hired locals to help them in their search
for the coil, but also that they believed Byelovodyean
insurgents had slipped through the gap and were
working against them. Anikova's sympathies slipped
and slid; she concentrated grimly on the road ahead.

The road to the city took the vehicle past the long
lakeshore and back through the forest. Though they
were well within the boundaries of Pergama here,
Anikova could not suppress an atavistic shiver. The
rusalki kept to the deep woods, along with the northern predators—zhuren and packwolves. Pergama was
supposed to be a safe and gentle province, but Anikova
did not like the way that the trees bowed close to the
sweep of the road, fading away into the darkness that
covered half the world.

Finally, the glow of First City and its ring of refineries appeared through the falling darkness, familiar
and comforting. Anikova pulled up outside the compartment, and the doors of the *siydna* whispered open.

"There you go," she said to her sister.

"Aren't you coming in?" Natasha asked.

"No, I ought to get back. I've got work tomorrow." More sessions with Kitai, a dismaying prospect.

"Well, thanks," Natasha said, leaning in through the car door to kiss her sister. "It's been good to see you." In the heights of the compartment block, a blind twitched. Anikova pulled away in a whirl of dust. On the wall of the compartment building, a word had appeared in fluorescent paint: *Pamyat*. It gleamed wanly through the twilight, the name of a dissident group. Anikova supposed that she should report it, but they usually used fadepaint and in the morning, she knew, it would be gone with all the rest of the dreams.

One

Elena awoke and lay blinking at the ceiling. A pale dawn light illuminated the room. Beside her, she could hear Ilya's quiet breathing. She rolled over and raised herself up on one elbow. In sleep, his face seemed untroubled, younger. She regarded him with desire and tenderness and dismay. She knew what her mother would think: to sleep with a derelict off the streets, a madman. But if you could walk between one world and another, who was to say what was or was not possible? She believed Ilya's story, and that was the disturbing thing. *Love will make you do this, believe all manner of lies. . . .* Perhaps madness was infectious.

Ilya twitched like a dog, dreaming. Elena thought: *eight hundred years. That's a lot of ex-girlfriends.* Or wives, even? The thought that there might be some *babushka* somewhere, still remembering the lunatic she had loved as a girl, was somehow a terrible one. She had seen a Hollywood film once, which also featured immortal men. Their relationships had, of necessity, become very complicated. All men had history, but surely never so much. It would take getting used to. Best to live in the present as much as possible.

Ilya, stirring, smiled when he saw her. It was the smile of someone who has woken up to find that he has won the lottery, and all at once Elena knew how much she had fallen in love.

She leaned across and murmured into his ear, "We'll have to buy some condoms today." He looked at her oddly and it took her a moment to interpret his expression. She sat up. "Did you think this was only for last night?" Or maybe that had been his intention after all, and she had been wrong. Like so many men, perhaps once was enough to move him on. She felt cold, but he said, "To be honest, Elena, I wasn't sure if it was just out of pity."

She lay down once more, her head on his shoulder. "No. No, it wasn't."

Don't tell him how you feel, her inner caution counseled. Early morning declarations of love were the one thing designed to bring masculine walls back up again. She had made that mistake with Yuri. The moment you let your guard down with a man, they began moving smoothly away. She slid an arm around him, trying to sound matter-of-fact and sincere at the same time. "I really wanted to. I still do."

He made love to her again, with a new assurance in his touch: the gradual return of sexual confidence, and a kind of gratitude that ended in release for them both. When it was over, Elena lay thinking. She had heard that heroin could induce impotence as well as all the other losses it brought in its wake. She wondered whether that might have contributed to the sense of defeat in him. And she was as prone as anyone else to thinking that she could be the one to make it better. *All he needs is the love of a good woman. . . .* But it wasn't as easy as that and she knew it; she had fallen into that particular trap before now, and it always ended badly. *Because it always brings resentment, and if you need them to need you, what happens when they stop?*

"Elena? You're frowning." His voice was half-worried, half-amused.

"I'm hungry."

"Well, then." He kissed her, lingeringly, and reached for his clothes. "Let's find some breakfast."

Downstairs, they ate bread and jam in silence. Elena found that, despite her best efforts, her gaze kept straying to Ilya's face, studying the sharpness of its planes and angles. When she discovered that she was becoming obsessed with the way he chewed, she told herself to snap out of it and looked out of the window instead, watching families heading to church. She could hear the bell ringing out over the town and wondered how many people would have attended the Friday service at the mosque as well. She knew a number of folk who went to both, hedging their bets. Not for the first time, she wished that she could believe in God; if ever she needed prayer, it was now. Her thoughts returned to the magnet sitting opposite her.

Men were supposed to have greater visual acumen, but if that was the case, why weren't they the ones who sat staring like sheep at the women they'd just slept with? She turned abruptly back to the table and found that he was. It was his turn to flush and look away. He said carefully, "I need to know what you want to do."

"About what? About us?" Her voice was too sharp.

"About us, and about the thing in your handbag. Do you have a pen?"

"Here."

On the back of a paper napkin, he wrote: *I don't know who's listening, following.*

Do you think we should go to the lake? She wrote in reply. When Ilya had spoken of it, she had realized that she knew where Manas might mean. It had been a military base, the kind of secret that everyone knew about. It had been said to test torpedoes for the Soviet Navy, and she remembered her father joking about how the Navy couldn't afford an ocean, only a lake. She looked at Ilya.

He said aloud, "Elena—you have money now. That's originally why you wanted to do this. You could go on to Moscow, take your family." She could tell that it cost him to say this.

"I gave them most of the money. I can always follow on." A tangle of feelings: responsibility; duty to her mother and Anna warring with this new, fragile love; a consuming sexual need; sheer curiosity and the allure of something glimpsed on the other side of life. It was unlikely that she would ever work on a space program again, and yet now there was this improbable chance of a new world just around the corner. Unless she had simply gone mad.

"Well, we can be mad together," Ilya murmured, and she realized that she had spoken aloud. She took his hand, weighed it in her own.

"What do you want, Ilya?"

"I have more purpose now than I've had for years. A world to protect and someone to—" He hesitated.

"To what?"

"Someone to be with."

She wanted to think that he had been about to talk of love, but perhaps it was no more than her own desires putting words into his mouth. But his fingers tightened around her own. With his free hand, he wrote: *Could be trap, we must be careful. But even so, I think we should follow Manas, go to Issy Kul.* And Elena agreed.

Before they left the guesthouse, she rang her mother from the telephone in the hall, but there was still no reply. Elena was torn between wanting to go back, to find out what had befallen her mother and sister, and not just because of the *militzia.* She hoped that they had gotten the money and were on their way to Moscow by now, though heaven alone knew what Anna would get up to in the capital. But her sister wasn't the only one sleeping with men she'd just met. Perhaps Anna should be keeping an eye on her and not the other way around. Or maybe it was just that Elena was tired of the responsibility of keeping the family together and wanted, selfishly, something of her own. She went back to the room and found Ilya, putting her arms around him and resting her cheek between his shoulder blades.

"We need to plan. How to travel, which way."

"I suggest the bus station or a private car."

"If we're going into the back country, I might need to cover my head. Some of these parts are very Islamic."

Ilya gave her an odd look. "You come from an Islamic country."

"I come from a Soviet one. Kazakh women have never worn the veil." She smiled, thinking of the miniskirted girls that thronged the streets outside the mosque. "Anyway, I don't usually pay attention to that kind of thing. I don't like all this talk of God."

"Because it isn't rational, defies all evidence?" He was teasing her, but there was an edge to his voice all the same.

She smiled. "Religion is the opiate of the people, you know."

"But they never complete that quote, do they? *Religion is the opiate of the people, the heart in a heartless world.* And isn't it also said that when people stop believing in God, they don't believe in nothing, they believe in anything? . . . Do you believe me, Elena, when I tell you what I am?"

"Over the past few days I have seen a lot that defies evidence. Including you." She stood abruptly and held out her hand. "We should get going."

The bus station was crowded with people bound for the villages; there were no free cars. Elena and Ilya had to wait for the bus, perched on a bench next door to a chai vendor. Ilya was looking about him, tight-mouthed and wary, scanning the crowd for the glimpse of a familiar face. She knew he was looking for the *volkh,* or for the man she now knew as Manas. Ilya glanced at her and shook his head.

Perhaps it was only her imagination, but he seemed less pale, and the trembling that had accompanied withdrawal had gone. She wondered if he had really managed to drive off the drug, and what circumstances might serve to turn him back to it. It was so seductive to think that all would be well as long as she stayed with him, but she knew that she was not a match for heroin. No love—that of her mother or Anna or herself—had been able to keep her father alive. Drowning in vodka or sleeping in the embrace of morphine, it was all the same in the end. She thought that human love was never enough. But maybe a world could compensate?

She checked her bag again, obsessively, for the object, which now lay next to a newly purchased packet of condoms. Elena smiled. And now the bus was rumbling along, spewing exhaust and passengers. A mass of people surged toward the open doors. Elena elbowed her way forward, with Ilya at her heels. She found a seat near the back and collapsed into it, searching for a tissue to wipe the grime from the window. The bus smelled of sweat and food. Ilya leaned back against the seat, still scanning their fellow passengers. His mouth turned down with evident frustration and he closed his eyes. One hand gripped the sword in its traveling case, the other reached for her own and held it. Ilya, it seemed, had found some sort of anchor. Elena, in turn, clutched the bag. A short wait, turbulent with people fighting for the remaining seats, and then the bus was pulling out again, trundling through the suburbs of Bishkek toward the mountains.

Two

Ilya dozed, waking to a glimpse of the high peaks. It was raining again. He could see it streaming down the windows of the bus, blotting out the view. If he did not close his eyes, he thought, he would do nothing but stare at Elena. *She is a flame, and I am already too close.* He might have lived a foolish life in these last few years, but he was still not entirely a fool and he knew what would happen. She would take the place of the drug for a little while, become the center of his world, and then she would grow tired of trying to love a hopeless cause and leave. Self-indulgent perhaps, but he had watched it happening in the bars along Leninski Prospekt: the arguments, the recriminations, the women walking out for the last time and the men turning back to the vodka with a curse and a sigh. He did not know if he could be better than he was, and he owed it to Elena to find out before too much damage was done. It was not likely that she would fall in love; she was being kind, that was all. But he knew that it was already too late for him.

The bus was limping up the mountainside. Finally, it coughed and stopped. There was a murmur from the passengers: part anger, part resignation.

"What's wrong?" Elena asked. "Have we broken down?" She did not sound surprised.

Ilya went with some of the other men to look. The driver had pulled into a space by the side of the road. Smoke poured from beneath the hood. It was evident that they would not be going any farther for some time. Ilya glanced uneasily around, wondering whether this was a normal fault or sabotage.

"Don't blame me," the driver said, catching Ilya's eye. "It's nothing to do with me."

"Can you fix it?" Ilya asked mildly.

"What do you think I'm trying to do? There's a place up the road; they sell food if you want some." He turned his back on the assembled passengers. Ilya went back onto the bus and explained the situation to Elena.

"He says there's a cafe nearby. I'll get you some tea, if you want."

She smiled at him. "Thanks. Yes, please. But be careful." Other passengers, clearly Kyrgyz, were retrieving flasks and bundles of food from the roof racks, and opening their paper to the crossword puzzles. There was nothing to do but wait.

"Don't let the bus leave without me," Ilya said to Elena. She gave him a look: *What, are you mad?* It was immensely reassuring.

He made his way down from the bus. Outside, the road was slick with rain. The mountains towered above the little yurt of the cafe: a shadow of white upon whiteness. He could see the high chasms of glaciers, carved into indigo rock. It made him long for the enclosed confines of the bus, for the everyday. The yurt was as fragile as a mushroom against the vastness of the world.

Ilya listened as he walked toward the yurt, keeping an eye out for the slinking forms of the *rusalki* or the dark shadow of the little ghoul. Manas' words echoed in mockery: *They are not your enemies.* But he still did not know what to believe. It would not have surprised him to see the *volkh* spring up from the ground like a dark spirit, but the land was empty. He could hear nothing. The mountains swallowed sound. He bought tea and bread and carried it back to the bus.

"Are we far from the lake?" Elena asked, huddled in her fur coat. The heating inside the bus was gone, and the windows steamed like a *banya*.

"I don't know. I think we'll have another few hours to go. If we ever get moving." He handed her the tea. Both of them, he knew, were thinking of what might lie ahead. Ilya leaned back and closed his eyes, and found himself remembering once more.

He did not recall much about his early childhood; only the long pain-filled nights, and his mother bringing a handful of snow to cool his hot forehead when the fever struck. The worst of it was being unable to move, having to be carried everywhere, seeing nothing but the wooden ceiling of the *izba* because he could not turn his head. At least he could hear, and he spent most of his time listening, giving forms to the creatures he heard deep within the forest, that he had never seen.

Ilya, having no brothers or sisters, thought only that this was what it was like to be a child. When he grew up, he told his mother, he would run as fast as the little dog that crept under the *izba* at night to sleep, as fast as the wind. He did not understand why, when he said this, her face would grow still and fearful and sad. And then the visitors came.

They arrived at the end of autumn, after a day of storms. Ilya liked the thunder, the pattern of light and shadow across the ceiling, the sudden flicker of lightning, the sound of rain on the walls of the *izba*. But this storm was different, terrifying in its intensity: the thunder rolling across the land and the wind snapping trees before it. Ilya might have expected it to deafen him, but in fact, it did not. It was so loud that it seemed muffled, like distant drums. But when the visitors arrived, everything became quiet.

It was the silence that first attracted his attention. His mother had gone into the yard, taking advantage of the lull in the storm to feed the frightened chickens, and Ilya had been idly listening to her movements. Then, she was simply gone, and so was everything else. He could hear nothing. It was as though someone had thrown a blanket over his head. Then the door of the *izba* creaked open.

"Who's there?" Ilya asked, hearing his voice—high and frightened—and hating it. "Who is it?"

There was no reply. Gradually he became aware of a strange singing note that shook the *izba* and made the walls rattle. He felt it travel all the way through his bones, moving up through his legs, making his flesh twitch and crawl. The inner sound reached his skull. There was a burst of light, so bright that Ilya cried out.

A voice said, "Boy? We need water. Fetch it." The voice rasped, as though forced out of a distorted throat.

Ilya said, "I can't move."

"Fetch it," another voice said, soft and dreadful.

And Ilya Muromyets found that he could stand up. His legs were weak, and he had to hold himself upright by clutching the few sticks of furniture, but he could stand and walk. In a daze, he fetched a horn cup of water. He tried to see who was speaking to him. There were three of them—all women, all beautiful—and the light bent and twisted around them. And something else was there, too: a glowing unseen presence that spoke to him without words.

You have been born for me. We belong together; we are part of the same dream. I will wait for you.

He held out the cup of water and something took it. He felt hot, dry fingers brush his own. There was again the high singing note and then they were gone. The cup fell to the floor. And Ilya's life as he now knew it, began.

He opened his eyes. The bus was moving, grinding up the mountain road once more. Elena was peering out of the window. Ilya's thoughts, when he could wrench them from the wonderful distraction of Elena, turned again to the past: to Manas, to the Nightingale Bandit, to all the old heroes. And, finally, he listened to the instinct that had been nudging him ever since he had stepped through that rift in the air, to another world, the instinct that told him that Byelovodye was where his origins lay. The rift was not an anomaly. He himself was anomalous—he and all the other *bogatyri*, and the creatures that pursued him.

After all these years, ironically thanks to Manas, he finally understood what Tsilibayev had been trying to achieve. Not a time machine, or some nonsense cooked up by the NKVD, but a way to enter a dream-world by mimicking older technology. But where had that technology come from? Ilya had destroyed his chance to find out, by following orders blindly and firing the lab. He wondered what had become of Tsilibayev, how long he had lived in Russia's parallel. Was time even the same there? Could Tsilibayev still be alive? He'd surely had a better deal than Ilya, whatever had happened to him—and yet, perhaps Tsilibayev had still missed out, for the Great Patriotic War had made Russians what they were, had created the unity, the love of nation and of one another. Ilya sighed. But perhaps there was a nightmare dimension, too: nation-alism, insularity, paranoia. *Perhaps it is they who are real, and we who are nothing more than their dark dream.* And what about the coil? For now, Ilya knew what had spoken to him all those years ago in the *izba*.

We belong together; we are part of the same dream. I will wait for you.

But if that was the case, how had that breach opened up in the hotel room, when Ilya himself had been across town, eavesdropping on Manas? He could find no answers.

Elena dozed, her head on his shoulder. It was midafternoon by the time they reached Balykchy at the easternmost end of the lake. Issy Kul snaked into the distance, splitting the mountains with a marbled rift of water. The rain had swept down into the passes, leaving a pale spring sky in its wake. They left the bus at Balykchy, waited an hour, then caught the next bus to Karakol.

Three

Karakol had changed little from Elena's childhood. Here were the apple orchards, faint with the first haze of leaf, and the tall poplars overlooking gingerbread-carved houses. Some of the roofs bore sculpted dragons, a reminder of how far east they had come. After the concrete monotony of Bishkek, the town looked welcoming, in a shabby kind of way, and the air was fresh.

The military installation lay some distance beyond the town; it was unlikely to be signposted, but anyone would know where it was. It had been shut down some years before, and there had been talk of selling it to a Canadian company for development into a leisure complex. She did not think anything had come of this.

They found a room in a sanatorium, not far from the center. There was no sign that anyone was following, but that meant nothing. They had no reason to trust Manas. He could have set up the whole thing, spun a plot to lure them here. Perhaps it was a way of flushing them out, to draw Ilya into a situation where he would reveal whether or not he possessed the object. There could be a dozen people on their trail, all unseen. There were plenty of folk in Russia who had the opportunity of a great deal of practice over the years. She felt exposed and raw until she was inside the illusory sanctuary of the room.

At first, Elena meant to do necessary, responsible things: wash her hair, go out and buy bread and a toothbrush. But after the long journey and two cramped buses, she found herself edgy and impatient. She did not know how much that related to the prospect awaiting them or the enforced proximity to Ilya, but as soon as they were through the door of the room, she reached for the packet of condoms. He did not need to take the lead. She made love to him with a relentlessness that afterward alarmed her, as though she had been possessed. It had not been like this with Yuri. It had not been like this with anyone.

After, she looked at the needle tracks along his veins and wondered about the nature of addiction. He was holding her too tightly, as if he could not bear to let her go, but after a while she found it hard to breathe.

"Ilya?"

He murmured something in reply. He sounded half-asleep.

"We ought to think about finding the place."

He sighed, releasing her into a tangle of sheets. "I know. Do you know where it is?"

"I think so. It's near an old fort of the Scyths, but it's not close. It's up on the hillside at the western edge of the lake, perhaps twenty kilometers or so."

Ilya peered at the bedside clock. "If we set off now and hitch a lift, we'll make it before dark. I want to take a look at this place we've been invited to walk into. I do not want to take you into a trap. I don't want to walk into one myself."

"I wish we had a gun," Elena said.

He squinted down at her. "What, me and my sword aren't good enough?" It was a moment before she realized he was teasing.

"No! I trust you, Ilya." She did not want to deal with hurt masculine pride, and besides, it was true. It was not from these situations of uncertainty and danger that she wanted a man to protect her, it was from *trudnosti byta*, the tough scramble of everyday life, and then they just didn't seem to want to stick around. She added, "I'd like a weapon of my own."

"It should be easy enough to get hold of a gun," Ilya said. "But we don't have time. You'll have to rely on me for now. And on your own wits."

Thanks for the concession, Elena thought. But he went on, "Elena, please don't think I'm being condescending. I know how strong women can be. I've seen them in war, in famine, in times of great change, and they are always the strong ones. Men just don't want to admit it. But now—I don't know what we're dealing with. I know how much I can take, but if anything happened to you . . ." His voice was muffled in her hair.

She said, "Nothing's going to happen to either of us," and wished she could believe it.

They found a car in the central square and asked to be taken to the village nearest to the installation. The driver was Tungan, not Kyrgyz, and he spoke of the lake by its Chinese name, Ze Hai. He seemed unsurprised to be asked to ferry two strangers to such a remote spot, but Elena chattered on anyway, talking about how they were to meet her sister at one of the sanatoria around the lake edge. She did not know the name of the place, she said; she would recognize it when she saw it. Ilya was watching the road. When he touched her hand, she waited until they came to the nearest sanatorium and told the driver to stop. They stood at the entrance until he drove away.

The wind that blew down from the mountains was piercing, and the sky was deepening into green. Ilya and Elena made their way through apricot groves to the lakeshore.

"Where's the fort?" Elena asked.

"I saw the ruins from the road. There's not much left of it now. The installation lies behind it, in a little valley. I'll keep an ear out. If Manas is here, I don't want to be seen."

"*Do* you think it's a trap?"

"It's possible."

They made their way along the shore of the lake, their shadows thickening in the last of the light. Elena could hear water running and bubbling over the rocks. She crouched for a moment and dipped her hand into the lake. It was tepid, heated by deep thermal springs. She knew that the lake never froze, but it gave her hope, somehow, that winter was really over. Something cried high in the heavens and she looked up to see an arrowhead of wild geese arcing toward Karakol. The sound made her shiver, but Ilya was striding ahead toward the ruin of the fort.

When he reached the little grove of firs that lay just below the fort, he stopped.

"Can you see anyone?" Elena whispered.

"No. I can't hear anything, either." There was the gleam of metal in the twilight. She had not seen him draw the sword.

"Elena," he began.

"Don't tell me to wait here. I'm going with you."

Even in the growing dark, she saw him smile. "I was about to say, watch your footing, that's all."

"I'll be careful."

The fort was no more than a jumble of stones. Elena tried to imagine it as it must have been in its heyday: a round tower, perhaps with a scarlet banner snapping from its turrets, surrounded by harebells and the brittle grass. And below, the long line of the lake, a wound in the mountains, as deep and silent as a captured sea. She looked back. The sun had long since fallen behind the western peaks, but the lake still shone, reflecting the sky. Lights were scattered along the shore: sanatoria or local dachas. They seemed a world away from the old stones of the fort. *We should never have come here, we Russians. We should have left this place to the ghosts and the geese and the silence.* Yet she had always believed in the dream of Soviet progress, the steady march of civilization. It seemed that the tide was drawing back, and taking her heart with it.

There was no sign of movement around the fort, and a person would have found it difficult to hide among the scattered rocks. Elena followed Ilya up under the ridge. Far to the east, the summit of Khan Tengri, Lord of Spirits, glowed rose-red, catching the last of the sun. But the rest of the world lay in shadow as far as the Chinese border.

Something rustled in the grass. Ilya swung around.

A man was standing at the edge of the fort, among the stones.

"Where did he come from?" Elena whispered. It was as though the figure had sprung out of the ground.

The man held out empty hands, calling, "Come down. I'm not armed. I just want to talk to you." It was not Manas.

"Who are you?" Ilya called.

The man stepped forward. Elena discerned a thin, humorous face with a wisp of beard.

"I am an *akyn.* And you must be Elena Irinovna and Ilya Muromyets, *bogatyr.*"

"How do you know that?"

"We've been keeping track of you," the *akyn* said. He reached out and touched Ilya's arm, as if reassuring himself that Ilya was real. With the flat of the sword, Ilya moved the *akyn's* arm aside. "It's only been in the last couple of days that we found you. *What a wonder.* I thought this when I first learned of Manas. The greatest legend of the Kyrgyz people, alive and strolling about in the modern day. Who would ever have thought such a thing? And yourself, too—though you're a Russian myth, of course, and therefore not quite so interesting."

"Thank you," Ilya said dryly. "You don't seem surprised to see us."

"I am aware of your remarkable powers of hearing. If I had been in your shoes, I would have followed Manas, listened to what he had to say. I know about the meeting with the politician, you see. I was the one who set it up. I know you and Manas have been foes in the past; if he had simply asked you to come here, would you have done?"

"I do not know. Probably not."

"It was partly a setup. But you can trust him, you know. He fights for a just cause." The *akyn* pointed toward the ruined installation. "Do you know why Manas has such an interest in this place? Do you know what that used to be?"

"Some kind of military base," Elena said.

"And do you know why someone would put such a base there, in this remote spot?"

"Strategic considerations," Elena said. "We're close to the borders of China and Tajikistan, and that means anyone who's interested in Afghanistan has an interest in this region, too." She steeled herself for the usual response: the jocular put-down of the Soviet male, about how she was clearly more than just a pretty face.

But the *akyn* said only, "Like so much of our history, this place, too, is a combination of reality and illusion. It was a guard post, true, but not only of the obvious borders."

Turning, he began to walk down the slope toward the installation. Elena, with a doubtful glance at Ilya, followed. He had shifted the sword; she could see the faint gleam of its hilt above his shoulder.

"You're talking of Byelovodye?" Ilya said.

"You've had at least a glimpse of this other land, haven't you? You've both seen it?"

"Yes." Elena was cautious.

"What do you think it is? Where do you think it lies?"

"I do not know. But I know that it is Russia. The air smells of home."

The *akyn* snorted. "A typically Russian thing to say. It belongs to all of us. The Russians have tried to claim it, as they have claimed everywhere else. I should have met you in Manas Park, not Gorky Park as they call it now."

"Maxim Gorky was a great writer," Ilya said, stung into national defense.

"And Manas is a great man. What I am trying to tell you, my fine Soviet hero, is that there are many dreams and visions, not just Russian ones. And that other world, of which we receive such tantalizing glimpses, is where all those dreams lie."

"Dreams? Like the *rusalki*?" Ilya asked.

"The *rusalki* are its guardians. Your *volkh* and his colleagues, on the other hand, want to control the gates between the worlds, bleed off our dreams drop by drop. Typical of the secret police everywhere. You look skeptical," the *akyn* added, turning to Elena.

"I am skeptical. I'm a scientist, after all. And I don't know who to believe."

"I suppose that is natural," the *akyn* remarked, blandly. "Why should you believe a know-nothing, goat-herding Kyrgyz poet?"

"What's your agenda, then?" Elena asked.

"Byelovodye needs rescuing; it's beginning to atrophy. And this world needs rescuing, too. We need to get our dreams back."

"And that?" Ilya pointed to the installation.

"I have something to show you."

"A gate?"

The *akyn* turned to face him. "I don't expect you to tell me immediately whether or not you have a key. I know I must earn your trust. See what I have to show you and then you can decide."

The remains of the installation huddled in the valley below, dimly visible as a collection of domes and cubes behind bare branches, surrounding the central polygon. They made their way slowly down, skirting the perimeter and keeping to the trees. Finally, they came to a line of bushes and then barbed wire, rusting and ancient, decorated with warning signs.

"We'll have to go under," the *akyn* murmured.

It's a trap. I don't want to go in there, Elena thought. But the *akyn* was already ducking under the wire and she did not want to stay out here in the darkness. Besides, she was curious. Cautiously, she followed. The wire snagged on her coat and she pulled free, expecting the sudden shrill of alarms, but the installation was quiet and dead, almost as much a ruin as the fort had been. *Graveyards,* she thought, *monuments to dead dreams.* The polygon looked like the dome of a cathedral: new faith replacing the old. She waited as the *akyn* peered through the broken window of one of the perimeter buildings.

"Can you see anything?" she asked.

Ilya tried the door, but it had rusted shut.

"We can get through the other side of the dome," the *akyn* said.

The second entrance of the polygon had once been padlocked, but now the lock had been twisted off and the door swung open on its hinges. The *akyn* paused for a moment, then stepped through. A torch flickered into life. Elena and Ilya followed.

The dome was huge, an expanse the size of an aircraft hangar, but little remained inside. Either the installation had been cleaned out when the military left or locals had looted the place, for the only things remaining were a set of iron girders stacked against the wall.

"What are we looking for?" Elena hissed.

The *akyn* led them to a metal plate in the concrete. A ring was set into it. Ilya reached down and tugged with both hands. The plate shifted, but did not rise.

"It's rusted shut." Delicately, with the point of the sword, Ilya freed the plate. It came up with a teeth-aching scrape, revealing a dark hole below. "Hand me the light."

"What can you see?" Elena said, craning over his shoulder.

"Nothing much. Wait." He sank to his knees.

"Don't go down there."

Visions of a descent into the earth and the plate slamming shut above them were haunting her, but he said, "I can't see anything if I don't."

"It's at the end of the room," the *akyn* said. "I'll go first, if that would make it easier to trust me."

"I'm staying here," Elena told them. She wished they had managed to get hold of a gun. The *akyn* lowered himself into the opening. Ilya turned to Elena and pressed the fishing-rod case into her hands.

"What if you need this?" she whispered.

"I may not be the hero I used to be, but I think I can tackle a frail old man if he tries anything. Keep a watch on the door."

Ilya swung down into the hole. There was the gleam of torchlight on metal walls. She heard him whisper, "My God."

"Do you see it?" the *akyn* asked.

"Ilya? What is it?" Elena called down.

"I haven't seen anything like it for eighty years, but it looks like Tsilibayev's machine."

"It's based on that device, which was a copy of something much older." The *akyn*'s voice, reverberating from the underground room, sounded pleased, as if presented with a particularly promising pupil. "We didn't discover it until recently, when the installation was closed down. I want Elena to take a look at it."

"Why me? I was in astrophysics. I know nothing about machines like this, whatever it is," Elena said. She had no intention of going down into the chamber.

"You're a scientist. You have a better chance of understanding it than either Ilya or myself."

"I'm surprised they didn't destroy it when they closed the facility."

"A lot of places like this were simply abandoned. Lack of funds, the Soviet withdrawal. There's a bioweaponry plant in Kazakhstan that was just left—they took the samples, but not the equipment. And the number of nuclear installations that remain are notorious. Remember that submarine base in Archangelsk, where the electricity company cut the power off because the Navy couldn't pay the bills? The subs were just about to go critical when some admiral came up with the cash. . . ."

"If it is a gate," Elena asked, "can it be opened?"

"If you have the means," she heard the *akyn* say softly. But Elena was listening to another sound. Someone was walking around the wall of the polygon.

The footsteps were soft and deliberate.

"Someone's coming," she hissed. The torch was abruptly extinguished. Elena pressed herself back against the wall. She could see the door between the thick lattice of the girders. It was opening. A whistling sound began: a single sustained note, singing along the girders until they began to vibrate. Elena's ears hummed and rang, and through the sound-filled air she heard Ilya make a small noise of pain and protest in the chamber below. Someone stepped through the door. She saw a dark figure dressed in military fatigues, a gun in one hand. The *akyn* scrambled from the hole. The man was striding swiftly forward, heading for the metal plate.

Elena's head rang; she felt as though someone had stabbed a needle in each ear. She cried out from the shadows. The man raised the gun and it was aimed directly at her, but Elena was already throwing herself flat, still clutching the sword, rolling over and over as the muffled whine of a bullet sang past her ear. The light of the torch swung upward and she recognized Manas.

She had no time for thought. She struck out with the sword, aiming at Manas' knees. She felt the blade cut through flesh and strike bone. There was a sudden smell of blood. Nausea rose sharp in Elena's throat. Manas fell backward, toppling in silence. Two figures swarmed up from the ground: Ilya, followed by the *akyn*. But the whistling was growing louder and louder. The polygon began to shake, entering destructive resonance. *Some kind of sonic weapon,* she thought with distant analysis. *Sounds like it's going out of control.* Above them, a girder twisted and fell, pinning Manas to the floor.

Elena, clutching the sword, scrambled to her feet and slipped on slick wetness. Ilya was flat against the wall, hands pressed to his ears. The *akyn* was bent double at his side. Manas was writhing like a fish beneath the girder; she saw a white flash of bone as he moved. Elena fought back another wave of sickness. Grasping Ilya's arm, she hauled him up, and dragged him toward the door, with the *akyn* close behind. As they reached it, the roof tore open and crashed down, bringing the walls of the polygon with it and enveloping them in dust. Elena, looking back, saw the floor cave in, burying the machine. She heard the crunch of metal as it gave way. They stumbled out beneath a cold, moonlit sky.

There was a dark trickle of blood down each side of Ilya's face and Elena's hand was wet, too. She looked at it, puzzled, until she saw that it was Ilya's blood. His sleeve was torn open and there was a gouge in the flesh beneath where the bullet had grazed him.

"You're hurt!"

He frowned at her. Through the ringing in her ears, she heard him say, "What?"

"Out," she mouthed and pointed to the perimeter fence. He nodded, grim-faced. They were halfway there when the *akyn* stumbled and fell. Elena dropped to her knees beside him. "We have to get him to a hospital."

"*Joq,*" the *akyn* murmured. *No.* His hands went to his chest and she thought he was exploring the wound, then realized it was the old Kyrgyz gesture of apology. "*Esseq.*"

She thought that meant: *I'm hot,* but the night was bitter.

Then the *akyn* said more clearly, "I'm dying. Give me my rosary—in my pocket."

Elena reached into blood-wet cloth and found the beads. She pressed them into his hand and his fingers closed around them.

"What *happened*? I thought Manas was on your side?"

"Manas has betrayed me. I don't know why." The *akyn*'s voice was bewildered. "But it's not the only one, the only gate between this world and the next one. The other—the oldest one—it's in Samarkand, in his tomb." The *akyn* was gasping now, barely intelligible.

"In whose tomb?"

"The marauder's. Go to Samarkand, protect the gate, stop Kovalin." He seized her hand, pressing the bloody rosary into her skin. "Keep dreaming," she thought she heard him say, and then he died. But she kept hold of his hand until she was quite certain that he had gone.

Ilya picked up the *akyn*'s skullcap and put it over the quiet face, hesitated, then made the sign of the cross. They headed for the perimeter fence and clambered up the hillside. When Elena looked back, there was no movement from within the compound. The polygon lay in ruins, like a broken shell. She reached for Ilya's hand and did not speak again until they reached the shore of the lake.

Interlude

From where Anikova stood, the white dome of the mosque seemed curiously out of perspective, foreshortened into a squat mushroom. It had been one of the first buildings in Azhutsk, assembled in the early, heady days of the colony. The current imam had showed Anikova the photographs, and so she knew that beneath the crystalline nanoplastic tiles and ribbing of the dome lay the nose of an ordinary C-21 transport zeppelin. It seemed that the mosque had remained in this sketched stage for a decade or so: the muezzin ringing out each day from a minaret made from a geological testing shaft. Now, the dome rose like a pearl among the drab compartment blocks and refineries, and below it lay the little garden in which Anikova now stood, waiting to question the imam.

She did not relish the task, but she had been afraid that Kitai might volunteer in her place. The news of the imam's possible involvement in the insurrectionist movement had come only a few days before, and there were very personal reasons why Anikova did not want the Mechvor to set her mind on the man. The imam was the grandfather of Natasha's boyfriend, and though she did not particularly like Nursultan, he was still associated with her family and any disgrace he suffered, could affect her. It was all creeping too close to home.

Imam Socdian came from Earth itself, from Samarkand. He was well past ninety, but in his youth, it was rumored among those of the *apparatch* who were aware of the colony's true origins, he had made a pilgrimage to Mecca. An observant and reflective man, he had taken copious notes, and when he had crossed the dimensional boundary to Byelovodye he had spoken at length with the rector of the Architectural Institute of Pergama and commissioned the garden.

It was shaded by genetically enhanced trees: a persimmon-apricot cross with small red flowers. The walls were plastered in white stucco, but at the end of the wall that abutted the mosque lay a covered portico divided by three arches, with a fountain at the center. Each arch had been decorated with the azure faience tiles that Imam Socdian had seen and admired on his travels, so that on stepping into the building one felt as though one had plunged into a well. The cool blueness reached the pinnacle of the dome and across the watery expanse raced gilded inscriptions taken from the Koran.

Imam Socdian had mostly complied with the old dictat against representation, but at some point he must have rebelled, for at the back of the portico lay three panels: a phoenix rising from a fiery city; a tiger nose to nose with a deer; and a curvaceous, cavorting horse.

Anikova waited for the imam beneath the tawny

flowers of the persimmons and wrestled with her conscience. She did not know where it would end, this
hunting down and interrogation of suspects, this theft
of dreams. The garden was a representation of a paradise in which Anikova did not believe. But paradise
was what the first colonists had tried so hard to create,
in a dangerously imperfect world. Byelovodye was not
heaven, but it could still be a dream made real, and
places like this were a part of that. If she handed over
the imam to the Mechvor, would he ever create such a
garden again? She looked down at her dark uniform,
with its crisp creases, a black scorpion among the
thorns of a rose.

Immersed in coolness, she closed her eyes and listened to the murmur of the bees in the persimmons
and the liquid notes of the little fountain. A discreet
cough announced the imam's presence. Anikova
looked up.

"You look very comfortable," the old man said. "I
hardly like to disturb you."

"I was waiting for you," Anikova told him.

"Would you like some chai?"

It would have been rude to refuse. Anikova followed him to the table beneath the portico and
watched as he poured a careful stream of tea into two
glasses. Anikova had one spoonful of sugar; the imam
took three.

The gilded ribbing of the dome momentarily
caught the light and blazed against the sky. Anikova
blinked.

"What did you want to see me about?" the imam
asked.

Normally, Anikova would simply have issued a

warrant and a request that the suspect present himself for questioning. But these circumstances were a little different. She heard herself say, "Did you know that there are rumors about you?"

From the corner of her eye she saw the imam become very still, but when he spoke, his voice sounded as mild and pleasant as ever.

"What kind of rumors, Colonel?"

"Not fortunate ones. You see, the story of your pilgrimage in your youth is known, and there are those among my colleagues who claim that the few who are still alive, who have lived on Earth, want to keep the dream-gates open. The suspicion is that they cannot be entirely trusted."

"The climate has changed," the imam said, still mild. "A decade ago, that would not have been such a problem."

"As you say, the climate has changed."

"What do you intend to do about it?"

Anikova should have handed him the warrant at that point, but she thought instead of Kitai's blank dark gaze and she leaned forward to put a hand on the old imam's arm.

"Leave. Get out of Pergama, go back to Earth while you still can."

"I don't think that's an option any longer. I know nothing of these new republics, and from what I hear, their brand of Islam isn't what I was brought up to believe in. Fanaticism grows, fundamentalism grows, or so I hear—" He gave her a sidelong look. "Too many of my coreligionists have turned murderers. It is not the true faith. I will not be branded a terrorist when all I wish to do is to encourage minds to turn toward God.

This is our colony, our sanctuary, just as much as it is of your people."

"Then at least go into hiding," Anikova said, recklessly.

"Why are you warning me, Colonel? We all know who you work for. Is it because of your sister and my grandson?"

"No," Anikova said. "It is because—" She did not know what to say. "Because of a crisis in faith."

They looked at each other in silence. The dome of the mosque seemed as fragile as a shell now that the light had gone. An evening breeze lifted the glossy leaves of the persimmon.

"I should go," Anikova told the imam.

"I will think about what you say," he murmured. He walked with her to the garden gate, through the gathering shadows.

Part Eight

One

Are you planning to finish that?" Elena asked warily.

Ilya tapped the half-empty vodka bottle. "What, this?" It was now close to midnight. It had only been over the last hour that his hearing had properly returned. His ears still rang.

"Yes."

That look, he thought, must be one that mothers passed down to their daughters: a practiced, repressed resentment. And he resented it in turn, with its connotations of control and disappointment, but he knew that all it really evoked was his own guilt. When it had come down to it, he had not been able to protect either Elena or the old *akyn*, and that was why he was drinking.

At least his impulse had been to reach for the bottle rather than trawling the unlit streets of Karakol in search of the nearest dealer. The weight of it fell on them both: generations of broken promises to women and to God. He knew he was reminding her of her father. The realization made him push the bottle away and go to sit beside her.

"No, I'm not going to drink it all," he said. "I want to make love to you. And I'm so sorry."

"Your hearing is abnormally sensitive, isn't it? No wonder you couldn't do anything." Her face was creased in sympathy and, with astonishment, he realized that she did not blame him.

"It hurt enough," he said. "Elena—what happened back there? I could not see."

"I struck Manas with the sword, across his legs. I must have hurt him badly." Her face crumpled and he held her tightly, murmuring reassurances. But there was nothing he could say that would make it any better, because it was hard to kill, and should never be an easy thing, and the consequences had to be faced. He bitterly wished that he had been able to save her, not from the violence, but from the horror of having to commit it.

"I'm all right," she muttered, and reached for a tissue. After a moment she added, "Do you think he's dead?"

"I don't know. His kind—my kind—seem to be hard to kill."

"I think we should assume that he is not dead, then." This time, it was Elena who reached for the vodka and poured herself a measured shot. "That thing in the chamber, beneath the polygon. You told the *akyn* you knew what it was."

"I've seen such a thing only once before, years ago. I was working for the Cheka. They sent me to kill a man."

He gave a brief version of the events of eighty years past, glancing at Elena to see how she was taking it. There was interest in her face, not judgment. "They told me that he was trying to develop a time machine."

Elena's eyebrows rose. "And you believed this?"

"You have no idea—or perhaps you do—*what* the security services have experimented with over the past fifty years. Telepathy, clairvoyance, farseeing techniques, hallucinogenics . . . The KGB has always been professionally credulous."

"Russians are obsessed with the parapsychological." Elena frowned. "If they do their experiments in a proper scientific way—well, that's all right. But often they don't."

"Any rumor—that the Americans were using farseeing to spy on documents in Moscow, that they had developed over-the-horizon radar—anything was enough to send the Lubyanka into a flurry like a bunch of chickens. During the Great Patriotic War, the very notion of putting a man into space would have gotten you a one-way ticket to Siberia. Rumors work like dreams; they feed off need, and the security forces are obliged to investigate these claims just in case one of them happens to be true."

"And some of them are, aren't they? Other dimensions, eight-hundred-year-old heroes . . . What *must* they have made of you?"

"They just thought I was good at my job. I never told them what I was; I falsified my records over and over again. I think I always secretly hoped that someone would find out, just to see what might happen. I have a self-destructive streak, Elena. You may have noticed. And the device that I saw underneath the polygon—it was the same thing. There's been a long-term project to open the wall between the worlds. That thing you're carrying is a part of Tsilibayev's machine, or something very similar." He paused. "Tsilibayev had copied older technology. Perhaps this is an original component."

"It had some kind of shell around itself when I found it. I don't think it's something that a twentieth-century scientist could have made. It seems too—alien." She paused. "So what part do you think Kovalin plays in all this?"

"I know what I've been told, but I don't know what to believe. Manas said one thing; Kovalin said another. It's likely they both lied. But I think the key to all this is control of the dream-gates. Different forces, vying for power. What else is new?"

"I don't understand why Manas didn't try to kill us in Bishkek. I'm assuming he was after the coil."

"He wasn't sure that we had it. Perhaps he wanted to kill several birds with one stone: destroy the machine and the coil. Or perhaps he had another plan."

"I'm not sure that he intended to destroy the installation. It sounded to me as though that device he had went out of control."

"I don't know."

"What happened after you dynamited the lab?" Elena whispered. He was very conscious of her nearness, her warmth.

"Siberia. Originally it was a ten-year sentence, but I knew they never expected me to come back. Not many people did in those days. But I survived, as you see."

"God, Ilya, you must have been through hell."

"I am a Siberian peasant. I'm used to it. It was hard, but at least it was quiet. Chechnya was worse."

"You fought in Chechnya?"

"Chechnya, Ingushetia, Afghanistan. I've fought everywhere. It's the only thing I really know how to do." He knew that she was staring at him and he did not want to see what might be present in her face, so he said, "The *akyn* spoke to you before he died. I could not hear. What did he say? Write it down for me."

When she had done so, he read the scribbled note carefully before touching it to the little flame of the cigarette lighter.

Samarkand. The place of the battle with Manas that had passed into such improbable legend. He had not been there for many years, but the knowledge that it contained a gateway to Byelovodye did not surprise him. Of all the cities in this region of Asia, surely Samarkand—domed with gold and azure, ruined and rebuilt again and again over the centuries—was the true home of dreams. And the tomb of the marauder must be that of Timur the Lame, nightmare son of the steppe, whom the West knew as Tamerlane, and who was rumored to have been one of the first of the *bogatyri*. Tamerlane, whose army reached St. Petersburg and who, if history had been a little different, might have conquered Russia itself. Ilya considered: Was this the key to Manas' involvement? Was Manas, out of Central Asian nationalism, working with the Byelovodyeans with the aim of bringing Tamerlane's ancient dream to life and causing the downfall of Russia? But how?

"I still don't have proper papers," Elena said aloud.

"But we can pay. We got into Kyrgyzstan, didn't we?" He spoke with a confidence that he did not feel. She accepted it, but he could tell it was just that she wanted to believe him.

Two

They had decided to leave Karakol that morning, but found that the bus was not due to leave until ten. So Ilya and Elena walked down to the lakeshore road to wait. Elena could not dispel the prickling at the back of her neck; she jumped every time a bird began to sing. The memory of the sword striking flesh was as fresh within her as a new wound. She had not told Ilya this, but she had awoken in the night with it still sharp in her mind: of the sword hitting the bone and the shock running electric up her arm, the sudden stink of blood. The memory had sent her running to the sink, to stand trembling and retching over the basin. Now, in the early morning sunlight, she shivered again. Surely Manas must have been killed when the complex came down . . . but she did not really believe it.

She kept a sharp eye on the hillside, but the land soared up toward the passes in a series of ghostly steps, too shadowed to see properly. The lake itself was very still. Its edges were as pale as glass; she could glimpse the lakebed. A few meters from the shore lay a ridge of rock like the beginning of a wall, vanishing into the deeper water.

"They say it's a city," Ilya said. "There's an old story that it drowned."

"Did you ever see it?"

He shook his head, watching as a line of ducks veered over the water, hiding the wall beneath a veil of ripples and fractured light. Ilya sat down on a nearby stone and lit a cigarette.

"How are you feeling?" Elena asked. She had told herself to stop badgering him about his health, but it was hard. Women were supposed to be solicitous, caring, concerned, but men seemed to get tired of it after a while. It had always irritated Yuri, as though she was questioning his competence, but she knew that he would have been offended if she'd failed to show an interest. You couldn't win.

But Ilya smiled up at her.

"Not so bad, thanks. I still want it, you know?" From the shadow that crossed his face, she knew he was referring to the heroin. "But it isn't so strong." He looked down at his hands. "I thought it would never let me go."

"That's the trouble with we Russians," Elena said. "We're a nation of addicts. Not just drugs, but vodka, too. And ideas."

"I sometimes think we just want our dreams to come true, but we want it too much and we drive them away so that there's a gap between us and our dreaming, and we need something to fill it. But nothing ever can. I don't think it's just Russians, though. I think it's all of us."

"The Kyrgyz say Manas is only a little lower than God," Elena said.

"I wonder if he's found it as hard as I have, to live up to being a hero. It would seem that he has."

She wanted to say: *I think you are a hero,* but it would have sounded false, so she said nothing.

"And you, Elena. What are your dreams?"

"Science. Space. The future. At least, those were my dreams. I don't know anymore." Now, she realized that her dreams had become more nebulous: a glimpsed, unreal land and a damaged man. But in the next moment, she thought that perhaps this wasn't entirely true. The hope for the space program had merely gone underground, running through her unconscious like water seeping through rubble. They sat in silence, staring at the vanished world beneath the lake, until the bus rumbled along the road.

The journey was slow and uneventful as far as Kyzyl-Suu, where Elena got off the bus and bought more water and a newspaper, as well as a Russian translation of the *Manaschi* epic that was prominently displayed on the bus-station counter. Evidently the Kyrgyz were losing no time in promoting their national *bogatyr.* It was an odd thought, that the down-at-the-heels man in the battered leather coat, now dozing by her side, fell into the same legendary category.

She read the newspaper, a day-old copy of *Kazakhstanskaya Pravda,* from cover to cover. There was no mention of the murders at the hotel. The front page was filled with news of the earth tremor and subsequent fire that had swept through woodland beneath the slopes of Koktubye Hill. Meteorologists were mystified by the fire, but Elena again remembered that great rift in the air and could not help but wonder.

She finished the newspaper and turned to the epic, reading with care as the bus trundled along the mountain passes, through scattered settlements and the pointed columns of the roadside graveyards.

> *"Not a space there was between flag and standard;*
> *the range of the Altai could not be seen. . . .*
> *Black plains, grey hills, the face of the earth was*
> *   beaten down . . ."*

Very Kyrgyz, thought Elena, all earth and struggle and death, very far from her dreams of space and a shining tomorrow. But that was the tension in Russian dreams, too: the love of land and the need to escape from it. That was all *prostor* was, the word held to best express the Russian soul: vastness, expanse, space itself. Who, then, were the heroes? It seemed that they were everyone—a return to the proletarian ideal, in the end.

She looked up. They were passing yet another military installation, part of the buildup of recent years. A man in uniform sat at a guardhouse, dozing over a gun in the spring sunlight. Then a street of low white houses, electrical repair shops, a garage. They had reached Barskoon. She nudged Ilya awake.

"We'll have to change buses here."

At the bus station, she tried to call her family, but there was no reply. She called her sister's mobile, only to find that it had been switched off. She left a message anyway, not knowing what to say.

The day wore on. The bus came, taking them down to Naryn. They kept passing unfamiliar traffic on the road: military trucks bearing the American flag, probably en route for the Afghan border.

Elena became bored with the *Manaschi* tales. There was something relentless about the epic, which made her feel short of breath. She wished she had something Russian to read—Dostoevsky or Turgenev—something classical, with its reassuring darkness and familiarity. She missed reading, as she would have craved a drug. That thought made her glance at Ilya, but he was still sleeping. He seemed to have an infinite capacity for sleep; she wondered if it was a legacy of the heroin or whether he was simply exhausted. She wondered, too, if they had any kind of future together. A moment later, however, Ilya was pulling her down between the seats.

"What—?"

"Someone's shooting at us."

The bus was a sea of confusion; people bundling down into the central aisle, a woman's voice frantically trying to calm a wailing child.

"Bandits?" Elena mouthed. It was still a problem in Kyrgyzstan, but not usually on these main roads.

"I don't know." Ilya's voice was ragged. "Keep your head down."

They waited. Gradually, by degrees, the bus fell into a kind of anticipatory hush. There was no more gunfire. Elena fought the urge to look up and see what was happening. She imagined Kyrgyz gunmen, raiders from the Tajik side of the border, about to storm the bus and kill everyone. It had happened before, but it was difficult to imagine it befalling her. She felt as though she had stepped from one nightmare into another. She swallowed hard and stared toward the front of the bus, but nothing happened. The driver got back in his seat and started the engine.

"It's all right, get up. We'll be in Naryn in fifteen minutes."

The passengers rearranged themselves in a storm of questions, but the driver just shrugged.

"Some incident with the Americans. Don't ask me. I don't know anything."

Ilya, leaning across Elena, was trying to look out of the window, but after a moment he shook his head. "Can't see a thing. It all looks quiet enough." He squeezed her hand. "Are you all right?"

"I think so," Elena told him, but she was lying. She was certain that the incident had been related to them, that they were the eye of a traveling storm. She did not understand how she knew this, but she was sure of it. She thought again of Manas, falling under the bite of the sword.

Soon after that they reached Naryn: a dismal collection of army barracks and featureless breeze-block housing. The river thundered alongside the road, grey with mud washed down from the mountain slopes. Ilya and Elena left the bus and walked across the weed-strewn central square opposite the administrative Akimyat building. The streets were filled with soldiers: Russian, Kyrgyz, and a detachment of men in foreign uniforms, all wearing sunglasses.

"Americans," Ilya said, and his mouth turned down.

"You said you were in Afghanistan," she prompted, diffidently.

"Once in the 1830's, trying to do something about British spies." He gave a brief, reminiscent smile. "Very enterprising young men. Very fond of disguises. But I was there again in the seventies, with the Soviet Army."

"That must have been grim."

His face was bleak. He caught hold of his wrist. "First introduction."

"To heroin?"

"They grew so much of it. There were fields of poppies in the mountains above Herat. The flowers were beautiful, like suns in the grass. But the army ran out of medicine, and I was injured—got shot by a sniper—so . . . That's really where it started. I kicked it when I came back to Russia, but it was always there in the back of my mind, and things got bad after Afghanistan. I think we brought a dark wind blowing in our direction. The Soviet Union started to break down, and then it collapsed and so did I. That's when I started using again."

She looked at him. His chin was tucked into his collar, against the wind. His pale eyes were narrowed. He seemed suddenly quintessentially Slavic: closed, stubborn, not quite broken. She tucked her arm in his and walked on.

The only place they could find to stay was a former Pioneer Hostel with dormitory beds. At this time of year, they had the dorm to themselves, but it was drafty and echoing, with too many shadowy corners for comfort. Neither of them felt inclined to stay in it for longer than they had to. They went out to buy shashlik, which was marinated and tough. *Even sheep must find it a hard life on those high, stony pastures,* Elena thought. When they finished eating, it was still only eight o'clock. In tacit collusion, they went in search of a bar.

Naryn, all too clearly, was not known for its nightlife. There was a bar not far from the Pioneer Hostel, filled with soldiers and local prostitutes. Elena attracted stares from both sexes: hostile wariness from the women, frank interest from the men. Ilya's mouth tightened. They found a rickety table in the back and ordered a bottle of vodka. Kyrgyz pop blared from the speakers. It was too noisy to have a conversation. They held hands on the beer-stained tabletop and drank in silence. A group of Americans came in to sit behind Elena. She listened, idly, but they spoke fast and her English was rusty. A single snatch of conversation managed to catch her attention.

"Man, when that guy in your truck started shooting, I thought you were going to go nuts."

"I thought I *was* going nuts. One minute he was asking for a light, the next, he was firing into the fucking air. I couldn't see a goddamn thing—and then there it was, real quick."

"What did it look like?"

"Like a shadow—a little, dark thing. Probably an animal. Marmoset or something. Only saw it for a second, then it just disappeared."

"What are they talking about?" Ilya murmured.

"I don't know. I think they're talking about the shooting on the road. One of the men thinks there was something strange about it." She thought of the thing they had seen on the slopes of Koktubye; the thing that Ilya had called a ghoul.

Ilya knocked back a shot of vodka in evident disgust. "That's the way it's been all along. Something strange. Shadows in the darkness, old ghosts. I want to deal with something real. Let's go back to the hostel and get some sleep."

His mood seemed to have changed for the worse. He was silent on the way back.

At last she ventured to ask. "Ilya? What's wrong?"

"It's nothing."

She did not press the question, but he must have taken her silence as a reproach, for he said, "Those Americans. You had your back to them, but I could see how they were looking at you."

"They didn't mean any harm, Ilya. They'd have looked at anything female."

"But I kept thinking: What's she doing with *me*?"

Mythical forces were one thing, old-fashioned male jealousy was another. It was almost good to have something normal to confront.

She said, "I didn't notice them. I was looking at you. I'm falling in love with you, Ilya." She hadn't meant to say that, either. It seemed to echo around the main square. He kissed her, on the windblown steps of the Akimyat, and for once she did not care who or what might be watching.

Three

They had an uneasy wait at the bus station the next morning. If there were not enough passengers, the driver told them, the bus would not run. The wind was still whipping down from the slopes, freezing the skin. Ilya pulled the collar of his coat closer and turned to Elena.

"I don't want to hire a car," he said in an undertone. "I don't trust these people."

There were no Russian faces in sight, only Kyrgyz and Tungan, and Ilya caught no more than fragmented snatches of conversation. He did not hold anything against the locals, but this was not his country. They were less than a day's drive from the Chinese border.

"If the bus goes, we could be in Uzbekistan by tomorrow," Elena said.

"Do you know how long it will take?"

"Andjian's only two hundred kilometers from here, but it depends on the weather. I spoke to the driver. He says the Naryn road is reasonable, but then it heads up into the passes on the border and it can take ages. He told me to buy food." She held up a parcel.

"Thank you. I'll give you the money."

She shook her head. "We'll sort something out." She chafed her hands. "It's still so cold. I won't deny it, Ilya, I'll be happy when we get farther south."

Ilya agreed with her, partly at the thought of sunlight and spring thaw, but partly just to keep the peace. *I am a Northerner,* he thought, *and I like a colder light, a paler day.* It was well enough in these high passes, but he disliked the prospect of Uzbekistan; its subtleties, its proximity to the countries that had once formed the Persian empire. He admired its people, even though they had matched the Russians, cruelty for cruelty, over the years, but the region had brought him nothing but unhappiness. Tamerlane still cast a long shadow over anyone Russian.

Elena nudged him. "Ilya? Come on. The bus is going." A family had appeared, enough people to make the journey worthwhile. Ilya watched them as they boarded the bus before him. They were Uzbeks, going home. A man in a shabby suit, two women in patterned floral frocks and slippers, a slender girl of ten who gazed at Ilya with a somber hostility that dismayed him. He wondered if she looked at all Russians in that way. The women, chattering like birds, herded the child onto the bus and vanished into its depths.

Ilya and Elena took a seat near the front, away from the petrol fumes. For once there was plenty of room, but there was little to see: only the mud-colored road ahead of them, with occasional glimpses of the rushing Naryn River. The road followed it, snaking around the hills. The monotony was broken only by small settlements, a herd of goats roaming along the road, an occasional herdsman on horseback.

To alleviate the boredom, Ilya began to question Elena about her time on the space program. It seemed as magical a dream as any he had ever come across. He listened to her stories about Mir with as much wonder as a child listening to fairy tales.

"And then, of course, they had the fire—one of the guys, Lazutkhin, lit an oxygen candle and instead of just releasing the stuff, it went up like a little volcano. The trouble they had putting it out—he said he thought they were all done for. And then there was the crash. One of the docking modules came in too fast and the commander couldn't bring it in properly."

"It hit the station?" He remembered reading something of the sort in the newspaper, but it was still so hard to know what was true and what wasn't.

"It nudged it, which was enough to do damage, of course. It was an awful day. Everyone going around with long faces . . ."

"They must have been afraid for the cosmonauts."

"Yes, naturally—but they also thought the Americans would pull out, you see. Because NASA was always so worried about safety—as though you could put men into space without risk."

"The Americans never want to make sacrifices," Ilya said.

"No, they don't. Although sometimes I think they might have a point. Americans—Westerners—value life in a way that we don't anymore. I sometimes think we've stopped caring, become too hard. Ilya, I wouldn't say this if we weren't in a half-empty bus in the middle of nowhere, but I got the impression that

Star City would rather have someone die than be found out. They were running a whole set of experiments up there that the Americans didn't know about, and it wasn't really safe at all. Ground control took some crazy risks with those cosmonauts. When the crash happened, NASA wanted to know why they brought the docking modules in so quickly, why they didn't steer them in slowly so that they could control the speed. But Yuri told me that if you brought the thing in too slowly, the docking mechanism malfunctioned—it made all sorts of compensations that would put the module even farther off course. Whereas if they brought the modules in quickly, they didn't have time for it to go wrong." She paused and took a drag on her cigarette. "It's amazing no one died."

As casually as he could, Ilya asked, "Who's Yuri?"

"One of the cosmonauts." She stubbed the cigarette out in the ashtray on the side of the seat. "Actually, I went out with him for a bit. He was my last boyfriend. It wasn't serious." But her glance flickered and he knew that this was another of her white lies, the kind women told so easily to men. He could not blame her. "He broke it off. He was going back to Moscow. I think he had someone else there. They usually do."

"He was a fool," Ilya said, and was rewarded with her smile. But he could not stop himself from asking, "And others?"

"Other men, you mean? I was married for a short time. He was an engineering student. We were nineteen—much too young, but everyone did it then. They'd say you were left on the shelf if you weren't engaged by twenty-two."

"It was much the same in my day," Ilya told her. *Whenever that had been.*

"It's different now. The divorce rate's so high, they're waiting longer. Some girls don't get married at all; imagine that."

Ilya did not want to get drawn into a conversation about social customs, though he knew that he should let the matter drop. How old did you have to be before you started taking note of all these lessons?

"Why did your marriage end?"

"I left him. He drank, of course, everyone does, but it was getting ridiculous. What can you do? And he wanted to end it, anyway." She was staring out through the grimy windscreen of the bus. "We couldn't have kids. I mean—*I* couldn't. Something wrong with me . . . But it's the same with so many girls round here, and anyway, you can't be sure how they'll turn out. When I was little, the Chinese were still doing atmospheric testing at Lop Nur—you heard about that? And we were doing nuclear tests as well, so . . . It's bad in the north of the country. Children born without eyes, without proper bones. It's probably just as well." She sounded matter-of-fact. He could not tell from her voice whether she really believed it, or whether it was simply too old a pain. He squeezed her hand. After a moment, she said, "And you?"

"What about me?"

"With women."

"Well, I got married in sixteen hundred and thirty-two and she was killed eight years later, by the Tartars. I have no children that I know of." And that had been a perpetual surprise, given the number of women he had slept with. The refrain echoed in his head: *not human.*

Elena looked perfectly blank. She said, "I'll say this for you, Ilya, it's not like any relationship I've ever been in before. Just tell me: there's no *babushka* somewhere, wizened like an apple, who's still cherishing fond memories?"

"God, I hope not. I've always tried not to get too involved. Except once."

"What did she look like? Your wife?"

"I barely remember," Ilya said, and was disconcerted to realize that it was true. She had died in the days before photographs, and memory grew as faint and distant as a faded icon if there was nothing to refresh it. He was about to say, "I think she looked like you," but instinct told him that this would not be well-received. He took Elena's face between his hands and kissed her instead, long and slow. The driver gave a reproving cough. The bus trundled on.

Four

She dreamed that she was back at Baikonur, sitting tensely with the rest of ground control as the Kvant module neared the station.

Something was nagging at her. Surely Mir had long since fallen from orbit? But she could see it on the screen, a spinning web above the world, and now the module that was drawing closer to it was no longer the familiar squat shape of Kvant, but the gleaming structure of the new international station. Elena found that she was gripping the side of the control module so tightly that her hands hurt.

"*Ladna*, Elena. Ready?"

"What?"

"We're all waiting, Elena." Yuri Golynski was beaming at her. "Bring her in."

"But I've never done this before. I'm in astrophysics."

"Not anymore." They were all looking at her expectantly. "It's all up to you now."

She looked down at the instrument panel and it had changed to a garden. Blue-fronded ferns had replaced the levers, cushions of moss sprouted where the console buttons had been.

"I don't understand," Elena said, but she began to move her hands in a sequence of dreamlike passes between the ferns, so that they drifted apart. Slowly, the new space station began to glide toward Mir, spinning as it went. Elena felt as though she was conducting an orchestra. She waved her arms, not having the faintest idea what she was doing.

"Gently, Elena . . ." It was Ilya's voice in her ear. She looked up at him, puzzled.

"What are you doing here?"

"I've made you some tea," Ilya said. He took her hand and guided it across the console.

"No," she said. "I can do it on my own."

The two structures nudged one another and merged. Elena watched in fascination as the solar arrays slid across one another, meshing the two stations into a seamless whole.

"Well done," someone was saying. "A perfect match." And Elena woke up.

Five

It was dark when they reached the border: a huddle of huts alongside a checkpoint on the Andjian road. The bus stopped and an official climbed aboard to check papers. Elena handed over her scanty identity documents; Ilya delivered his greasy bundle of assorted forgeries. He made sure that the official got a good look at the folded packet of dollars.

"Don't you have proper papers?" the official asked.

"Aren't those good enough?" Ilya said.

"We have to cross," Elena added. She plucked at the official's sleeve. "My mother's ill—we only found out last night." The official looked down at her, expressionless, and spoke the words that Ilya had been dreading.

"Come with me, please."

"Look, can't we sort this out?" Ilya moved the packet of dollars from one hand to the other.

"Just come with me."

There was nothing for it but to comply. As they stepped down from the bus, the driver leaned across.

"I'm sorry. I can't wait, you understand? I don't know how long they're going to keep you."

"When's the next bus due, then?" Elena asked.

"There'll be another one along in the morning, the eight-fifteen."

"But we can't stay here all night."

"I'm sorry," the driver said. Ilya heard the words as clearly as if the man had spoken them aloud: *It's not my problem*.

"All right," he said. "Elena, come on. We've no choice."

They were taken into a small cubicle, partitioned off from one of the huts.

"I have to make a phone call," the official said.

"Can't you just let us through? You might be making a mistake, you know. You wouldn't want to do that." Ilya spoke mildly, but he took care to catch the official's eye as he did so. With chilly satisfaction, he saw the man's face grow pale.

"We have to check. We've had people coming over the Afghan border, running drugs and arms."

"But you can see we're Russians," Elena pleaded. Ilya watched the official's face begin to close down with a familiar bland, blank denial. He knew that they would get no further with this line of talk, and he did not have to look at Elena to see that she understood it, too. It was how things were.

"All right, all right," Ilya said. "Make your phone call."

The official left the room, shutting the door behind him. Ilya listened.

"Who is he calling? Can you hear?"

The official was describing them. "A man and a

woman. The man's tall, got a thin sort of face, doesn't look too good to me. The woman's a blonde—no, not dyed. Blue eyes, about thirty-five. Pretty enough. Wearing a fur coat. Yes, they're Russians. No, no one's searched them yet. Do you want me to do it? What?"

Ilya strained to hear the voice at the other end of the telephone line, but there was only the crackle of static.

"I don't . . . even if that's the case, then I can't just . . ."

Ilya made a sudden decision. "Elena. Give me the bag."

After a doubtful moment, she handed it over to him. He reached inside it for the object, cupped the heavy fossil in his hands.

"Ilya? What are you doing?"

He closed his eyes. "Seeing if I can get us out of here." In imagination, he conjured forests, meadows, still lakes. He tried not to remember Manas' words: *You might not find yourself on solid ground, or in the middle of a sea. Take us away from here,* he prayed to the thing in his hands. *Take us somewhere safe.*

I hear you. That familiar, small voice. He knew, now, that it was the coil.

Dimly, he was aware that the official's voice was breaking up, as though the connection was a bad one. But the official was only standing in the next room. It was working. He frowned, concentrating. Behind his eyelids the world grew bright, then dark. For a terrible moment Ilya felt as though the walls were closing in on him, slamming forward to crush him between them. He thought he cried out. Then everything was quiet.

Elena said, "Has it worked?"

"I don't know." They were still sitting in a room. But looking around him, he could see a difference. The paint on the walls was a dull green, rather than blue, and surely the bench was in a different position? Rising, he moved silently across to the door. He could hear nothing beyond it. Ilya waited a minute, then tried the door. It opened easily. He stepped out into twilight. They went through the door of the hut, expecting to be stopped at any moment, but there was no sign of life beyond.

"I can't see a soul. Come on. Let's go while we can."

Elena needed no persuasion. They ducked into the scrub by the side of the road. A ditch ran along the roadside, running with a trickle of water. It was easy enough to traverse. They went along it for several hundred meters, then dodged back onto the slope. The hut lay behind them in a blur of faint light. The road was quiet. They started walking, but they had gone no more than a couple of kilometers before Ilya had to rest.

"Are you sure you're all right?" Elena's face was creased with worry. He looked away.

"Sorry. I just don't seem to have much stamina." He could date to the hour how long he had been clean. How long did it take before withdrawal started to ebb? He had felt all right for the last couple of days, but now it was back, as though the drug's lack was eating through his bones. He would have done anything for a shot. Elena sat down on the dusty earth beside him and put an arm around his shoulders. Her touch was somehow irritating, even uncomfortable, but he did not want to push her away. He wished that they had found somewhere to stay, that they were back on the bus, that he could lose himself in her and try to block out the insistent summons of the drug, but it was no use. He would just have to ride it out. He put his head on his knees and said, "Give me a moment."

———

When he woke, the sky was pale behind a tangle of sage. He was lying uncomfortably on his back on stony ground, his coat tucked beneath him and his head resting on Elena's shoulder. Her eyes were open. She was staring at the sky.

"God, Elena, what time is it?"

"Nearly dawn, I think." She sat up, grimacing, and rubbed the back of her neck.

"What happened? Did I pass out?" Shame came in a hot rush.

"Yes, you did. Are you certain that this really is the other place? Byelovodye?"

He looked about him.

"Look at the road," he said. It was the same black substance that they had seen before. It reached into the distance, snaking through ochre hills dusted with snow. The air smelled of sagebrush and cold.

"Do you think you can walk?" Her voice was tentative, considerate of his pride, but he did not think he had much left.

———

There was no traffic. Soon, the stony land fell away and the road led down through groves of apricot and almond, lacy with blossom. They saw no sign of habitation, though once a herd of horses flashed across the road. A bridge led over a mass of foam. Ilya and Elena, in unspoken agreement, climbed down the embankment to a scatter of sand and stones, to wash as best they could. The freezing water made Ilya feel slightly more human. Elena perched on a rock above the current, vigorously scrubbing her face.

"That's better. Ilya, when we go round the next bend, I want to see a first-class hotel with a proper bathtub. . . ." She grinned at him. "Arrange it for me, would you?"

He smiled back. "I'll speak to the serfs directly."

But when they clambered back up the embankment, and followed the curve of the road, they found only a huddle of buildings, eaten away by fire.

"What can have happened?" Elena asked, shocked. "This looks recent." The air smelled of smoke and soot. Treading gingerly over the wreckage, Ilya turned his ankle on something smooth that rolled beneath his foot. It was a blackened bone.

"Bandits wouldn't do this, surely?"

"Maybe there's been a raid," Ilya said.

"But to burn a whole village out like this. . . ." She fell silent. They both knew how many times it had happened before in their own world: the squads sent in, a quick flurry of death in the night, then the world closing over tragedy like the waters of a pool after a stone has been hurled into its depths.

"We shouldn't stay too long," Ilya said.

Three kilometers along the road, they came across another village. This, too, had been burned. All that was left were ruined walls and the fire-swept branches of an apricot tree, its remaining blossom still crisped by heat.

Ilya was looking up the slope. "Look."

The poles sprang up from the hillside like a grove of trees. They were ten feet high, tied with red rags. A horsetail banner had been nailed to the top of each pole; the long hairs stirred in the wind.

The sight made Ilya uneasy. "I haven't seen anything like this for a long time. This is a very old custom."

"They still do it out on the steppe sometimes. They mark the dead in the old way, just as the hordes used to do."

"But this is a Moslem region," Ilya said. He pointed to the regular graveyard down the valley: the pointed stones each bearing the etched face of the dead, encased neatly between white plaster walls. "Why didn't they bury their dead down there?"

"Maybe it wasn't *their* dead."

He knew she was thinking of the Golden Warrior, the horde sweeping down. The back of his neck prickled.

"Ilya? I think we should go."

He felt as though the poles were watching them, spirits rising from the dust. He did not look back. They walked alongside the road, keeping close to the almond groves. Ilya kept listening, but it was as if a blanket of silence had fallen over the world.

Interlude

Y ou have to find them," the General said. He leaned
back in his chair and gave Anikova a narrow look.

"I'll do my best, sir."

Outside, spring rain was gliding over the city, casting the mountains into shadow and stormcloud.
Anikova had come into Central Command at a run,
but she had still been too slow to avoid a soaking.
Now, she sat on the edge of a silk-upholstered chair,
trying not to scatter rainwater over General Umarov's
immaculate office. The carpet alone must have cost a
fortune. But she was not supposed to take note of
things like that. She had already taken care to comment on the austerity of his office, dropping a word in
the right circles, knowing it would get back to the General and that he would understand. It was not the first
time her tact had been rewarded.

"You'll do more than that. The breaches have been
increasing in number ever since the coil was stolen.
There has been too much chaos already and those we
have sent to deal with it are failing to report back. I
have heard nothing from the Mechvor Kovalin or his

local recruits for three days now. We need stability. If the coil falls into the wrong hands, that's precisely what we will not have. We need one gate open, under central control."

"I understand," Anikova said. She thought with a vague, unfamiliar wistfulness of the woman she had seen, the woman from the other side. *I would love to know what is really happening there. I would like to see it with my own eyes.* But, of course, that was impossible.

"Do we know where the latest breach occurred?"

"We have it down to a ten kilometer radius on the Pergama border, just south of Irzighan." The General's fleshy mouth pursed in irritation. "Ever since the coil went missing, it's these regions that seem to be affected most."

"How big was it?"

"Not too large, luckily. More like a crack than a breach, according to the reports. It sealed itself almost immediately, but if any interventionists came through, they must be found." He leaned across the desk. "Colonel Anikova, this isn't the first of these minor rifts in the area. There was another one a few days ago, not far from your own family's dacha. I had it checked out and nothing was reported, but we need to make it clear to people, to keep their eyes open."

"Understood," Anikova said. *I know there was a breach. I saw it. I spoke to someone from the other side.* The General was looking at her; she was suddenly certain that he could read her knowledge in her face. She said nothing.

"I want you to leave right away. Go to the border."

"I'm ready, sir," Anikova said, knowing that it was a lie.

Part Nine

One

The day wore on toward noon. They were having to rest more frequently now, and not only on Ilya's behalf. Elena could see the pinched lines of fatigue in his face, but she could also feel them in her own. Her feet hurt and they had long since run out of the food she had brought for the bus ride. Moreover, the burial poles had awoken within her an atavistic fear, a sense of something cold and ancient, that she had thought long dead. Rationally, she knew this to be nonsense. Why shouldn't the locals bury their dead in the manner of their choosing? They were entitled to their customs, after all. But somehow she could not help thinking of Tamerlane's horse hordes, sweeping across the country almost as far as the Dneiper and the Don, inspiring an old terror.

As she had reminded her sister, she was not even a native Russian. The land of the horse clans was where she had been born; it was her country. And yet she knew that was not quite true. The old refrain: *My country was the Soviet Union, and they abolished it.* The familiar sense of not belonging swept over her. But if she felt this way, how must Ilya feel? Or had he seen so many changes that it was all the same to him in the end? Slightly breathless from an uphill climb, she asked him. He looked at her askance.

"This is not my kind of country," he said, with finality. "Russia is my country."

"But where does Russia begin and end? Borders change, you know." Elena found herself mildly put out, as though he had disowned her.

"Russia—real Russia—is the land where I grew up: Siberia, the North. Birch trees, black earth, ice on the water in the morning, white cranes that are said to dance. I can't leave it for long, I know this. I could have traveled the world these past years." He smiled. "I've often cursed the fate that keeps me here. Why couldn't I have been born a Hawaiian hero, I ask myself? But the country pulls me. *Your* Russia—" He stopped, turned her to face him, and put a gentle hand across her heart. "Maybe that's in here. Whatever it is."

A typical Slavic gesture, she thought: sentimental, sincere. She replied in kind. "Then that means you, Ilya."

He bent to kiss her, then his head went up. She saw it in his eyes before he spoke. He said, *"No."* She did not have to ask him what he meant; she could hear the hoofbeats herself, coming too fast.

"Quickly," Ilya said and pulled her toward the trees. They raced over the stony ground, gaining the illusory shelter of an apricot grove just as the horsemen swept around the curve in the road. Elena ducked beneath foaming blossoms. The horsemen halted, milling alongside the road. She could see the Golden Warrior among them: straight-backed, on a mare as white as the apricot flowers. There were perhaps twenty of them; too many to outfight or run.

"Keep still," Ilya murmured in her ear. She did not need to be told. She thought: *One man I might be able to handle, but I can do nothing about so many. And Ilya isn't well.* She felt icy cold. Her heart lumped along in her chest. Somewhere, a bird was singing: a lark, high in the pale air. The Golden Warrior was riding swiftly around the perimeter of the horde, gathering them together. The sunlight glittered over the scales of armor. One of the men slid down from his horse. He threw a handful of red dust to the ground, then prostrated himself on hands and knees. He smelled the earth like a dog and raised his head, crying something in a harsh language. He pointed in the direction of the apricot grove. Ilya's arm grew tight around Elena's waist.

"Elena, when I tell you, *go.*"

"Where to? There's nowhere—"

"Up in the rocks behind the grove. I'll be right behind you."

The horsemen, tightly grouped, were riding toward the grove. As they approached, they fanned out.

"Now," Ilya hissed. "As quietly as you can."

They glided back through the grove, breaking out into open ground.

"*Run.*"

But the horsemen had seen them. There was a shout from behind and the sudden rattle of hooves on stone. Elena was already bolting toward the rocks: high slabs, with a crack running vertically between them. Ilya pushed her against the rock and stood between her and the horsemen. The white mare outstripped the flanking riders and galloped up the slope. The Warrior's golden armor flashed in the light, blinding Elena. The mare reared above them and she saw directly into the shining helm. She saw a girl's face, fierce and cold, then the visage of a Mongol rider. Then there was nothing, only a blank and cloudy oval. Ilya struck out with the sword. The mare danced back. Elena saw the Warrior's head turn from side to side. The Warrior kicked the mare forward; Ilya went down under its hooves.

Elena was seized around the waist and dragged up, to be slung across the Warrior's saddlebow. She saw the flash of a knife as it sliced through the shoulder strap of her bag and then the bag, containing the object, was flying through the air as the Warrior threw it to a waiting horseman. But she was more worried about Ilya than the bag. She struggled in the Warrior's grip, kicking and punching, but the Warrior wheeled the mare around and galloped toward the trees. She heard Ilya's voice, calling her name, and went slack with relief. At least he was still alive.

She turned her head as the Warrior's grip slackened. It plucked an arrow from the quiver at its shoulder and slotted it into a bow as Ilya ran forward.

"No!" Elena shouted. She slid over the mare's shoulder, half-falling to the ground. The bow came up. There was a whirring hiss past her ear, but the Warrior had not yet loosed the arrow. It took Elena a moment to realize that the attack had come from behind. A bullet glanced off the golden armor and ricocheted into the rocks. The mare screamed and wheeled around, hooves sliding in the dust. The Warrior cried out, grasped Elena by the arm, and dragged her back over the saddle. The horsemen, moving like a tide, turned and headed for the road.

Elena looked back. Ilya was picking himself up from the earth. Someone was standing on the rocks above them, lowering some kind of gun. Elena saw a visored helmet, booted feet, and a khaki uniform. The figure was visibly female. As Elena opened her mouth to speak, the woman raised her hands and took off the helmet. Elena recognized her immediately: Colonel Anikova. She saw the gun come up again, the woman aiming down the sight, but the mare was into the trees and away. The ground flew past until all Elena could see was a cloud of dust, and then nothing at all.

Two

Ilya was sitting on a bench with his head in his hands.

"I'll ask you once again," the woman said in her curiously accented Russian. "What's your connection with the horse clan? Why did you go to them?"

"I'll tell you again," Ilya said wearily. He had managed to resist giving her his name: a petty triumph, even though she probably knew it already. He had been forced to hand over the sword; that was enough. He wondered how far, if at all, she might be connected with the *volkh*. "We did not go to the horse clan; they came to us. They found us along the road and attacked us. As you saw, my friend has been captured. I have to find her."

The woman smiled. "I remember reading of the old days in the Kazakh and Kyrgyz lands, how a girl might be snatched up over the saddle of a horse and galloped away to be married."

Ilya looked at her. If she was trying to bait him, she was doing an excellent job of it.

"A barbaric custom, or so it seems. But often, I

read, the girl would collude in her own abduction, entice a young man to carry her away so that she could tell her family it was none of her doing, and it would be too late for them to do anything about it."

"Elena's not Kazakh. Are you suggesting that whole scenario was a setup?"

"Why didn't they take you?"

"I'm not as pretty?"

The woman gave him a contemptuous glance and abandoned the game.

"They took her because she has something they want. Something in the bag she was carrying."

"Look," Ilya said. "Of course she had something in her bag. It was some kind of device that came into her possession entirely by accident. I understand people like you. I know how you think; I know what games you expect to play, and I'm sick of it. I got sick of it eighty years ago, so you can imagine how I feel about it now. Just let me explain and give me the fucking truth."

The woman appeared taken aback by this outburst. "Very well, why don't you tell me what you know?"

"If you'll let me have a cigarette, I will." He did not think she would comply, but after a moment she reached into her pocket and took out a packet. He did not recognize the brand: a white box with a red star embossed across it. She took one for herself, then lit his own. It tasted ordinary and wonderful.

"So," she prompted him.

"So. In the early nineteen twenties—" he glanced up, unsure whether she would understand the date, but she nodded.

"I know," she said. "Go on."

"I was involved with the secret police just after the Russian Revolution—the Cheka, under a man named Dzerzhinsky. They sent me to kill someone, a scientist named Tsilibayev. They told me he had invented a time machine, which probably sounds less ridiculous to you and me than to most of the Russian population, and he was going to turn it over to the Germans. I did not manage to kill him, but I destroyed his equipment and his laboratory. As far as I understand, the thing that fell into Elena's hands is an original piece of technology, a device that Tsilibayev copied. I understand also that it is a kind of key, to open a gate between worlds." But he did not want to tell her that he seemed able to activate it, that it spoke to him and that he believed it had sought him out.

The woman was looking at him, her expression unreadable. "Tell me something. If you had known what the equipment was, that it opens a way through into this world of Byelovodye, and if you had seen a little of this world, would you still have destroyed the laboratory?"

"I don't know."

"An honest answer, if a weak one."

"I don't believe in simple solutions. I've seen where they lead."

"What happened after you destroyed the lab?"

"I was sent to Siberia, to one of the camps. Later, in Stalin's day, twenty thousand died in that region, in Kolyma and other *Gulags*. The Trans-Siberian Railway is built on their bones. That is why I no longer believe in simple solutions."

"We have nothing like that here," the woman said. She stubbed out the cigarette, as if for emphasis.

"That's what I would have said about Russia, once."

"But *this* is a better world. Byelovodye is the sum of Russia's lessons." She leaned forward and he could see the belief in her eyes. It was, he realized, a long time since he had been witness to that particular brand of faith, perhaps not since the advent of *Perestroika*. But unless he was greatly mistaken, there was still a trace of doubt behind her eyes, like a pike in a pool.

"That's what I would have said about Russia," he echoed.

"Byelovodye—the Secret Republic—is Russia's heart. How can I make you understand?"

He understood well enough, he thought, but he could not yet believe, however much he wanted to.

"You can help me find my lover," Ilya told her. "That's the only convincing I'll need."

"I will see what can be done," she said very grudgingly. Ilya recognized her reluctance. Their goals might coincide, but she did not want to appear to be giving him any quarter. As she reached the door, she turned and said, "Anikova. Colonel, to you."

"Ilya Vladimirievitch," Ilya said in the old manner. He was not admitting to heroic status, not just yet. He saw a twitch of annoyance in her face, then she went through the door.

Three

They had carried her up into the hills above the apricot groves. The land was stony and cold, still fringed with snow. Elena's head was ringing with the ride and with the discomfort and indignity of being held upside down.

A collection of yurts rose like growths out of the hard ground, from which children ran to meet the horde. The horsemen greeted their fellows with triumphant cries, shrill as wolf pups. There were many women as well as men; all wore pointed caps and carried bows. The Golden Warrior slid down from the saddle as soon as they arrived, and stalked into a yurt. Elena was hauled from the white mare's back like a sack of potatoes and dumped unceremoniously before a narrow strip of fire dug deep into the earth. The horsemen left her there, and went to tend to their mounts. She stank of horses and sweat. She held close the knowledge that Ilya was not badly hurt; she had seen him rise.

Something roared overhead. She saw a slender craft like an arrow, starred with lights. Then it was gone, down over the horizon. The horsemen gave derisory laughs; someone spat into the coals with a hiss. Elena stayed where she was. If she tried to make a run for it, she would be caught and dragged back. If by some chance she managed to escape, she would freeze. She longed for Ilya, with an ache that alarmed her, and longed also for his sword. She should, she thought, have followed her instincts and bought a gun on the black market. But superior weapons had not prevented her abduction.

An old woman thrust a plate in front of her. Elena looked down at something frosted and bloody, cut into strips.

"Eat, eat," the woman said, in fractured Russian. Elena picked up a sliver and tasted it gingerly. It was horse liver. It might be all she was going to get and besides, this stuff was a delicacy back in Kazakhstan. The realization that she was being treated well warmed her more than the fire. She smiled up at the woman, intending to try out her paltry Kazakh vocabulary and see how that went down.

"*Rakhmat.*" The old woman gave a beaming smile, which vanished almost as soon as it appeared.

"Eat," she said again, and went back into one of the yurts. She was wearing stout Russian boots beneath her woolen skirts. So much for ethnic purity, Elena thought, even here. She could do with a pair of those boots herself. She forced down the rest of the liver, then accepted a flat round of *lepeshka* bread and a cup, a fragile thing made of birch-bark, containing herb tea sweetened with honey. At least she would not go hungry.

When she had finished, she rose to her feet and

looked around her. It was now quite dark. A sheaf of stars was scattered across the sky, and Elena looked eagerly upward, but to her dismay, there were no constellations that she recognized. She stared and stared, willing the heavens to take on their familiar configuration, but the stars burned distant and unknown. A great rim of moonlight was spreading just above the ledge of the mountains. The moon looked closer, somehow, and brighter.

The horsemen were milling around, seeing to tack and food. No one looked at her directly, but she had the feeling that all eyes were upon her. Slowly, making it plain that she had no plans for escape, she made her way toward the yurt into which the old woman had disappeared.

As soon as she reached the flap of skin that formed its door, a warrior stepped in front of her: a girl, no more than sixteen or seventeen, with a fierce dark face.

"Joq, joq. Marhamet—oturunguz." Then she paused, adding carefully, *"Nyet."* But Elena's Kazakh, though basic, was good enough. "No, no. Please. Sit down."

"I want to speak to the old lady," Elena said in Russian, racking her brain for the correct words. The last thing she wanted to do was cause inadvertent offense. *"Quaise jerde apam?"* Was that the word for mother or father? She couldn't remember. The girl frowned. *"Apam?"* She pointed across the fire pit, to where a tall woman in her thirties was standing.

"Joq. Keshiringiz, echtem et." Never mind.

"Apam? Mama? Ili babushka?" But the girl was catching on.

"Yes, the grandmother." Elena gestured to the yurt.

The girl put her head around the flap and spoke. *"Minute."*

"Rakhmat," Elena said. *"Rakhmat."* Perhaps if she repeated her scattering of words often enough, she would start making sense. But at that point, two of the horsemen strode across. They clasped Elena's arms, repeating, *"Joq, joq,"* and laughing as they did so, as if she were a naughty child. Elena tried to pull away, but their strength was intimidating. Their hands encircled her wrists like steel bands; they smelled strongly of horses and earth and meat.

"All right, all right," she said, sagging in their grip, and let them lead her to a nearby yurt. They pushed her through the door, not roughly, but with implacable firmness, and she heard the straps of the door being knotted behind her.

The yurt contained only a carpet patterned with birds and beasts, some cushions, and a stove. Elena made a thorough investigation, but there was no gap between the edges of the yurt and the ground; it was like being imprisoned in a drum. The dim red light from the stove flickered across the walls of the yurt. Outside, the shadows of the horsemen were reduced to striding ghosts. Elena curled up on the cushions next to the stove, grateful for its warmth. She could think about nothing but Ilya.

Four

Ilya slept fitfully, having made sure that there was no way out of the room in which he was being kept. The place was spartan: bare green walls with wooden skirting, very Soviet-institutional. A pallet lay across a bench. It was hard, but he had slept on worse and the room was at least clean. There was, however, no doubt in his mind that it was a cell. The door was double-locked and unyielding; the green paint hinted of the Lubyanka. He wondered whether the room was bugged, but a cursory search revealed nothing. Lying back on the pallet, he listened, but the sounds in the building were muffled. He could hear voices, but there was an underwater quality to them: a resonant echo that made it impossible for him to discern what anyone was saying. It occurred to him that the room might be sealed in some way. Perhaps they were used to people with his kind of abilities. But he was too worried about Elena to speculate.

He had seen what the horse clans were capable of firsthand on the Kazakh steppes, all those years ago: terrible refinements of cruelty as barbarous as anything that the Russians had come up with. Men buried to their necks in sand, their heads encased in the stomach sack of a camel so that when the sun fried down, the sack tightened, to drive them mad before suffocation. He had stood at the edge of the steppe, himself a prisoner, watching men die as the buzzards circled. He had been unable to save them. The clans would treat him differently, they said, because he was a Russian. He never discovered what they had in store for him. He had taken pains to escape before that. Siberia had been a picnic in comparison.

Ilya rolled onto his back and rubbed his eyes. Women were more equal among the Kazakh tribes than elsewhere: unveiled, performing the same work as the men. But he could not help thinking of what they might do to a female prisoner. The thought filled him with a terror that he had rarely felt for himself. He dozed a little, but his dreams swooped on him like kites, sharp and clawing.

He woke with a start, to find someone sitting by the side of the bed. At first, in confusion, he thought it was the *volkh,* but then the figure leaned over him and said, "You've been having nightmares, you poor man. We could hear you shouting. I've brought you something to help you sleep."

The voice was gentle, female. Ilya sat up and saw a young woman's narrow face, the delicate sloping lines of Chinese ancestry beneath a coil of black hair. But her eyes were not human; they had no whites. They were like the eyes of a deer. Like the eyes of the *volkh,* he realized with a shudder of shock.

"What are you?" Ilya whispered.

"Hush." She put a warm hand on his shoulder, filling him with a sudden, half-sensual comfort. It reminded him of heroin. He wanted only to bury his head in her lap, but forced himself to pull away.

"Don't worry," she told him. "I'm here to help you. My name is Kitai. I am a Mechvor, a dream-decider. I've brought you this."

She was holding a slip of paper, which she opened to reveal a pale powder.

"What is it?"

The woman tipped the powder into the water glass on the floor. "Drink it. It'll make you sleep. There's no point in worrying about what-might-be. We'll go in search of your friend in the morning; Colonel Anikova is already working on it. You'll need your strength."

Her voice was soothing, verging on the hypnotic. He had not heard a voice like it since his childhood. But it reminded him so much of the drug: the half-sexual, half-maternal whisper heard inside the head in the depths of morphine dreams.

"No," he said, his voice sharp, and knocked her hand away.

"You don't understand." Still soothing, tinged with reproach. "You *must* drink it."

And suddenly he already had. His mouth was fresh with water and a chemical aftertaste, and he was lying down on the pallet without a murmur of protest. Her hand brushed his brow and he realized with dim surprise that she was singing beneath her breath, the same ancient lullaby that his mother had sung all those years ago: *Bayushki-Bayu; I spell you into sleep* . . .

"Sleep now," she said, and he did.

When he next awoke, Colonel Anikova was standing over him. She was neither gentle nor smiling. It came as a relief.

"Drink this. Get your boots on. We leave in half an hour." She thrust a glass of tea into his hand.

"Where are we going?"

"Where do you think? To find your friend, assuming there's anything left of her." She did not wait to hear his reply, but was already striding through the door. He wondered whether a guilty conscience accounted for her manner, after her failure to save Elena and the distorter coil from the Warrior, or whether she was simply always this brusque. Whatever the case, it was better than the insidious kindness of the Mechvor.

He frowned as he sipped his tea, remembering the incident in the night. Why had that strange woman been so insistent? And "Mechvor" did not mean "dream-decider" in modern Russian; the closest translation he could come to was "dream-thief." Even if he had been shouting out, convulsed by nightmares, one man couldn't have been making all that noise, especially in a room that he was certain was soundproofed. But at least there was now the prospect of getting out of here, of actually doing something. His worst fear had been that they would simply leave him in here, while Elena . . . Best not to think about that.

Minutes later, Anikova returned, with the sword slung over her shoulder. It was like seeing an old friend.

"I'm not returning this to you just yet," she said in response to his glance.

"When, then?"

"If it comes to a fight." She patted the gun at her hip. He could not tell what kind it might be. It had a smooth, molded grip. "But I want to make sure you understand something. My priority is not Elena. I might wish it was so, but it isn't." She spoke with stilted correctness; he wondered what emotions she might be concealing, if any. "My priority is the distorter coil. If I have to retrieve it from her corpse, then that's what I'll do."

"I understand," Ilya said. He did not like it, but he could appreciate her position.

"Good." She held open the door. "After you, Citizen Muromyets." There was a trace of a smile on her face. "Yes, I know who you are. And what."

"More than I do," Ilya told her, and was bitterly gratified to see her look of surprise. It strengthened his suspicions about her possible connection with the *volkh,* but he still knew too little to be certain.

She led him through a maze of corridors. He had not seen a great deal of the place on the previous night, when they had brought him in, but it reminded him powerfully of the Lubyanka. Anikova whisked him through a series of swinging doors until finally they came to an atrium. Statues supported the ceiling in an explosion of Soviet brutalism: massive shoulders, faces composed of slabs of stone. The light was dim and filtered, coming from far above, as though he stood in the home of giants.

"Through here," Anikova said, and led him toward two great bronze doors. They stepped out onto a square. He looked back to see a rose-marble façade, fronted with columns. It reminded him of Lenin's tomb. He wondered whether a waxy body might lie encased at the heart of this edifice, then thrust the thought away. Such notions seemed to have unsettling repercussions in Byelovodye.

"Where are we?" Ilya asked. This place could have been anywhere in the former Soviet Union, from St. Petersburg to Vladivostok, but the marble blocks beneath his feet were free of dust and weeds and the gilt facing on the surrounding buildings glittered in the sunlight. Church domes gleamed between the leaves of oak and lime. This was a green city, as tree-lined as Almaty, reflecting the old Russian love of the woods. Then, from the corner of his eye, he found that he was witnessing a different scene. The buildings were tumbled, half-finished, with rough plaster walls. The gilt was tarnished, the marble cracked. It was like the old stories of enchantment, where gold turns to nothing more than a handful of leaves. But which was real? Perhaps both, or neither. Ilya took a breath and kept silent.

"It's the city center," Anikova told him, unhelpfully.

A vehicle was standing at the bottom of the steps: something streamlined, riding low on the ground and as smooth in its contours as the gun at Anikova's hip. It did not look like a car. There were no wheels, for a start. As they approached, the door hissed open and the Mechvor jumped out, her night-dark gaze filled with concern.

"Citizen Muromyets! Did you sleep well? How are you feeling this morning?"

"Get in the back," Anikova said. Ilya did so, followed by Kitai. Anikova swung into the driver's seat and the car glided soundlessly away. Ilya watched the passing scene with interest, having been unable to glean much from his journey of the previous night. It looked like a typical Soviet city. Traffic slid noiselessly along the wide roads, and the air was fresh. Whatever else these people had accomplished, a solution to environmental pollution appeared to be one of their achievements.

Ilya craned to look at the crowds: uniform suits reminiscent of Mao's China, for the men, but many of the women were wearing dresses, longer than those of their Russian contemporaries. Ilya, for whom the miniskirts of the more relaxed Brezhnev era had come as something of a revelation, disapproved of this return to concealment. But the people seemed clean and well-dressed. They all wore shoes, and they did not look hungry. He wondered what he might glimpse from the corner of his eye, but the vehicle was moving too fast for him to see what lay beneath the surface of the city.

"That's the cathedral," the Mechvor supplied as they drove past. "Isn't it beautiful?"

It looked exactly like St. Basil's, down to the bulging crimson domes. A flock of doves wheeled up, hiding it behind a scatter of wings. Ilya looked back, but it was gone. The vehicle swung out onto a smooth black highway. He leaned forward and tapped Anikova on the shoulder.

"Where exactly are we heading?"

"Out onto the steppe. They'll have taken her there, if they wanted her alive."

The Mechvor twisted to look at him. "I'm sure they

won't have harmed her," she said anxiously. "Please try not to worry."

"I'll try," Ilya said. He could see that she meant to be kind.

They crossed a river, and downstream he glimpsed the spines and curves of military gunships, as well as a wallowing hulk that looked like the remains of a sailing vessel.

"Those are the naval yards," the Mechvor said.

"He can see that," Anikova said, shortly.

"But we want to make him feel at home," the Mechvor said. Once more, her voice was filled with reproach. "After all, he is a guest, and guests are sent from God."

"I know, I know." Anikova gave her companion an uneasy glance that Ilya was unable to interpret. He wondered what the relationship really was between these two, where the power truly lay.

The road took them past a series of buildings that the Mechvor described as the state university. The complex was vast: three central polygons surrounded by low halls. The roofs were festooned with a tracery of satellite communication; he could see the dishes from the road. He tried that sideways glance again and found that there was simply nothing there, only a wasteland of grass. It was more comforting to look at it directly. The place was set in a parkland of manicured lawns and groves. The sight of the birches gave Ilya an unexpected pang of homesickness. Yet he was not sure whether it was for the world he had left behind, or for the one through which he was now traveling. He may not always have known what his role was, but he had known where he belonged, and now even that was slipping away from him. He leaned back in his seat for a moment and closed his eyes. *Elena*, he thought. *I belong to Elena.* But he did not even know if she was still alive. That thought returned him to the practicalities of the situation.

"So it's just you, me, and her?" he said to Anikova. "Against a horde?"

"Don't be ridiculous. We're meeting my team at Bhalukishoy. I'm not going in there without armed personnel."

"That's a relief."

"You should know," the Mechvor said gently, "it's most unusual for the tribes to venture this far north. Usually they keep to the southern territories. So there is a great need to drive them back."

"This is just one clan," Anikova said. "A raiding party. And they can't be acting alone."

"Why not?"

"Why would a bunch of barbarians take it into their heads to get hold of a distorter coil? No, they're working for someone. Somebody operating against the State has hired them—or more likely, persuaded them, since the tribes don't use money—to get hold of this thing. So that leaves major questions. Who, and why?"

"How resistant are the tribes to interrogation?" Ilya asked, surprising himself. He thought he had left KGB mode behind him long ago.

Anikova gave a thin smile.

"Good question, Muromyets. They can't be interrogated without a great deal of trouble. They would simply rather die. Hunger strike, suicide . . . We've seen it all."

As he had surmised, the apparent perfection of this State, too, possessed darkness at its heart.

"And they won't talk? At all?"

"No. But the 'who' and the 'why' has a local answer. Even here, we're troubled by dissidents. They're crazy, of course."

Again, Ilya thought he detected a faint unease in her face. It made him question the strength of Anikova's convictions. It was disappointing to see that the old Soviet approach still had its hold: anyone who disagrees is simply mad; the truth is so self-evident, that to deny it is tantamount to a denial of reality itself. But what did that really mean in a world in which reality was so malleable and fluid?

"What do they believe, these dissidents?"

Anikova frowned and said nothing, so Ilya changed the subject.

"The tribespeople, then. Where do they come from?"

"Originally, from Earth. Before we did, long ago."

"Then one might say that this is their country?"

"It is not. They have their own lands. This is *our* country."

Hearing the fierceness in her voice, Ilya thought: *Do I sound like that when I speak of Russia?* No doubt he did. But it was a familiar refrain: the necessity of being right, merely because one was powerful, and guilty.

They were leaving the city now, heading up through scattered villages toward the heights. Ilya watched a Russian idyll passing by: the neat log *izbas,* the white froth of cherry and apple blossom, the new shoots in spring gardens. It would be so easy to stay here. He wondered how content they really were. But the contrast between this bucolic scenery and the barren, wild lands that they had entered, made him restless.

"How long before we get to where we're going?" he asked.

"Another half hour, perhaps less."

"Why are we driving, anyway? I thought you people had aircraft?"

"We do not want to be seen, and they may have weapons to bring down a plane. The dissidents have been arming them; we don't know how far it's gone."

"I've seen planes that look twice as sophisticated as the ones we have in Russia. Don't you have the resources to bring down a handful of tribesmen?"

Anikova gave a snort of frustration.

"It depends on the terrain, not the equipment. And on the land itself. If they were out on the open steppe, it would be a different matter. Guerrilla warfare is always hard."

"True enough," Ilya admitted, thinking of Afghanistan. "Might they have ground-to-air missiles? Rocket launchers?" If that was the case, then where were the dissidents getting their arms from?

"They have weapons," Anikova said. "But if they have the coil, they might be able to use it."

"How?"

"There are people who can activate it with their minds alone," Kitai said. She was watching him closely; Ilya did his best to empty his head of thought. "There is a possibility that the Golden Warrior is one of them."

"But you don't know that."

"No." The Mechvor's gaze was hypnotic.

"What manner of people are these, then?" Ilya asked, as casually as he could.

"Ancient breeds, from the Byelovodyean long-ago. There are suspicions that the *rusalki* ran a genetic program before they eschewed technology. Or perhaps they are merely sports, dreamed up by the land itself."

The word *bogatyr* hung between them, unspoken. But Ilya was beginning to realize why they were taking so much trouble over him. In some way, he was of use to them. He could not help but ask himself where Manas fitted in. He glanced at the Mechvor and saw the trace of a smile upon her calm face.

Ilya sat back in his seat, watching as the villages fell behind. They were out in the wild country now, on the steppe, covered in grass that rippled under the wind like water. Far along the horizon, he could see a dark line of forest. He recognized nothing of this countryside from their brief earlier foray. He wondered whether the landscape bore any relation to the former Soviet Union, or whether it was entirely other.

Whatever the problems Anikova had mentioned might be, they did not manifest. Within half an hour, the road turned past a rocky outcrop and down into a shallow valley. Anikova's people were waiting.

Five

Shortly after dawn, Elena was taken to see the Golden Warrior. She had managed to get a little sleep and the old woman had brought her water, slopping against the sides of a bronze basin. Elena put it on top of the stove and washed as best she could.

"Jagdainiz kalai?"

She thought that might mean, "How are you?" so she nodded vigorously and smiled. It seemed to satisfy the old woman, who held out an armful of clothes. Elena looked askance at the heavy skirts, the overtunic and boots, but it was better than the travel-stained stuff she had on. She dressed under the approving eye of the old woman. The garments smelled of sage and horses, but they were clean and roughly the right size. Then the woman took her hand and drew her toward the door of the yurt.

"Where are we going?" Elena asked, but the woman did not seem to understand. She stepped out into a clear morning, with the sun riding just above the edge of the mountains. The camp was already stirring into life, and to Elena's dismay, it was clear that they were packing up. Three of the yurts were already folded and loaded onto horseback, and a fourth was in the process of being dismantled. Two men and a girl had reduced it to its slotted side screens, folding the lattice into narrow panels.

"We're leaving?" Elena asked. She could not remember the Kazakh. She pointed and raised her eyebrows, but the old woman said only, *"Iye, iye"*—yes, yes, as one might soothe a child—and pulled her forward. Guards stood outside the door of the Warrior's yurt: gold gleamed at their belts and collars. They continued to gaze straight ahead as the woman propelled Elena through the flap of the door.

The Warrior sat cross-legged on a pile of cushions. Its hands rested on its knees; the helmeted head did not move as Elena came in. A smaller person was sitting at its side. She could not tell, at first, whether this figure was male or female. It was dressed in a motley, indiscriminate collection of garments that could have belonged to either sex. A necklace of feathers and small bones was looped about its throat, and its hands were blue with tattoos. Its eyes were blank black ovals. Elena inclined her head in its direction. It was easier to simply ignore the Warrior.

"You are from the other side?" the person asked, in reedy Russian. The voice was high, but male. She had read that shamans cross-dressed, or even that they were sometimes eunuchs. She did not greatly care; the relief at speaking her own language was overwhelming.

"I am from another world," Elena said. "Is that what you mean by the other side? Or are you talking about the mountains?"

"Your world is not this one?"

"No."

"Then you must come from the Motherland that is also Yelen Tengri, the Land of the Dead."

"It is a world of living people," Elena said. The Warrior made a sudden convulsive movement, rattling its armor.

"There is debate," the shaman said, "whether it is this world that is real, or your own, or both. We know your world as Yelen Tengri, but that is just a name."

"Do you believe that we are ghosts?" Elena asked. "That you travel to my world when you die, or in dreams?"

"What do you do?"

"What do you mean?"

"What is your work?" the shaman asked.

"I am a scientist," Elena said. "Do you know what that is?"

The shaman's ancient face creased into a smile. "Look," he said. He rolled up a deerskin sleeve. A substantial watch was strapped around his tattooed wrist. "Would it surprise you to learn that I also have a university degree?"

Trapped. "I'm sorry," Elena said again, sincerely. "I should know not to make assumptions."

"Especially here. This is a world where assumptions are even more dangerous than they are in your own. Assumptions can create facts, where people struggle to control dreams, because dreams can manifest in reality."

"I have no understanding about the nature of this place," Elena confessed.

"That is a good point to start learning, then. What

about this?" The shaman gestured to the silent figure of the Warrior. "What do you think this is?"

Now that Elena had learned that the shaman was an educated person like herself, her view of the Warrior had also shifted. She found that she had, over the course of the last few minutes, started to view it less as an inimical supernatural phenomenon and more as some kind of artifact, a robot, perhaps, or a trick. From the amusement in the shaman's dark eyes, her revised beliefs must be evident in her expression.

"It is exactly what you see. It is a suit of Scythian armor, apparently empty, sometimes with faces glimpsed in the depths of that magnificent helmet, that moves of its own volition and occasionally speaks. Who do you think controls it?"

"You?" Elena asked hesitantly.

"No one," the Warrior said, with such booming suddenness that Elena jumped.

"The Warrior is under its own control," the shaman said.

"But what is it? I mean, what are you?" Elena said to the Warrior.

"I am Chosen—the Warrior, my people's champion."

Well, that was a lot of help, Elena thought, but this time she had the wit to keep silent.

"You see, people seem to need him," the shaman explained. "And so he is there, a kind of animated dream. Just like the rest of the *bogatyri.*"

"It's a *bogatyr*?" She did not want to say that the Warrior seemed far less human than Ilya.

"Of a kind. They vary in their natures and abilities.

I imagine you've seen glimpses of a girl's face underneath that helmet." Elena confirmed that this was so. "If we had any use for money, I'd put good rubles on the possibility that your friend saw a man. The Warrior is, to some extent, subject to people's expectations, not to mention their desires. I see it as male and choose my pronouns accordingly."

"But do you follow—it?"

"The clans follow him. I am an advisor, but still an outsider, like yourself."

"What are you?"

"Well, I am supernatural, too, I suppose. I am what the locals call a Mechvor, though that's a title rather than a name. My kind don't have a name for ourselves. There aren't many of us and most work for Central Command. Among the tribes, we have the role of shaman. We are like the *bogatyri*: real but unnatural, human but not entirely."

"Mechvor means—'dream-stealer'?"

"Something like that. Witch doctor would do just as well. We have abilities, can see to a limited extent into other people's minds, influence their behavior, that sort of thing. But don't worry on your own account. I am bound by a strict code of conduct."

"You said you went to university," Elena said. "Did you mean here, in this world?"

"Yes. Byelovodye works in much the same way as your own, in some respects, but not in others. We become used to losing time, losing memory, our borders and boundaries shifting and changing. The processes of historical revision that took place in your own society are just as real here, though in a slightly different way. Byelovodye responds to changes in your world.

Believe me, there are a host of research departments dedicated to finding out how this is so."

"And the *bogatyri* themselves? What are they? Where do they come from?"

The Warrior, perhaps bored with the turn that the conversation was taking, rose abruptly and strode to the door.

"We ride," it said.

The shaman looked ruefully at Elena.

"Well, that's that. When the Warrior speaks . . ."

"It speaks Russian," Elena hissed. "Why is that?"

"It doesn't, actually. Kazakh speakers hear Kazakh, Pashtuns hear Pashto. To me, it speaks in my own language of Evenk, which is originally a Siberian tongue. Only—occasionally—those who have married into the clan hear its voice in their second language. I like to think that it speaks the language of the heart." He gave an apologetic smile. "Not very scientific, I'm afraid."

"Perhaps poetry is the best science to use here," Elena said.

"If you continue to think like that, you may come to understand Byelovodye itself," the shaman said with approval.

They followed the Warrior out into the camp. By now, the Warrior's yurt was the only one that remained standing, and within minutes, it, too, had been dismantled.

"Where are we going?" Elena asked the shaman.

"Now that they have the device you've been so obligingly carrying around, they'll head north."

"Is that where the tribal lands lie?"

"No, their lands lie in the south. But they have

friends in the north. People who want the distorter coil."

"Listen, I can't go with them," Elena said urgently. "My friend—I have to find him."

"Forgive me, but he's more than a friend, I think?"

"Much more," Elena whispered. Being without Ilya was like missing her own right arm, and yet a week ago, she had never even set eyes on him.

"I'm truly sorry," the shaman said. "But I don't think you have a choice. The Warrior has been sent to find the coil and bring it back. He is relentless in pursuit. He even crossed over into your world, to find you, summoned though a rift that I think your friend Ilya must have opened."

"But why? If you have the distorter coil now, why do you need me?"

"Because it isn't just the coil that's important. It's Ilya. And you matter to him, don't you?"

Elena felt herself grow cold. After all that, she was nothing more than a lure, and she had walked right into the trap that the shaman had set only a few minutes before. *He's more than a friend, I think?* "That doesn't mean he'll come for me."

The shaman smiled. "He's a hero, Elena. That's what they do. I think he'll try to find the coil, certainly. Think of yourself as additional security."

"But why do *you* need *him*?"

"I think you already know that he's been able to establish a relationship with the coil. It is ancient quantum technology made by the *rusalki* when they were still at the flowering of their powers; it is close to sentient. It can be activated by him, by his dreams. It—"

The shaman broke off as a group of warriors rode

up. One of them was the girl with whom Elena had spoken on the previous evening. The shaman rose to speak to her, leaving Elena free for a moment to sit and think. And she brought into the light, with mingled exhilaration and dismay, a thought that had been brewing ever since the incident in the hotel room. It wasn't just Ilya who could activate the coil. She must have done it herself.

The Warrior was a distant, gleaming figure at the far edge of the camp. Its yurt was now a pile of panels and skins being loaded onto the back of a pony. She and Ilya weren't the only ones who could influence the coil. The other person who had such abilities was the Warrior, and Ilya was competition. As long as Ilya was around, he was a danger to the Warrior, and so would Elena be if they realized this.

The girl spoke.

"You are to ride with her," the shaman explained.

"I can't ride very well."

"You'll just have to hang on," the shaman said.

Elena was making plans, but she had no idea whether any of them would be feasible. If they approached anything that resembled civilization—houses, roads—she would try to run. But the thought of an arrow in the back was not appealing, and neither was the prospect of wandering about on the barren steppe. She trusted that Ilya would try to find her, but she did not necessarily want to wait to be rescued. What if something had happened to him? She also kept an eye open for her handbag, though they might have transferred the object to another carrier. A trivial thing, but her lipstick had been in there; she felt naked without it. But it was obvious that her whims were not the principal concern of the clan. She did not want to ask too many questions.

The Warrior rode up. The girl patted the back of its saddle, wheeling the horse around. Elena's handbag was tucked into one of the saddlebags and fastened with straps.

"You're to get up behind," the shaman said. In the end it took the two of them—the shaman pushing, and the girl hauling her by the arm—to help her mount. Humiliated, Elena perched on the horse's back. Clutching the saddle—she did not want to touch the Warrior until it became absolutely necessary—she leaned down.

"What's your name?" she asked the shaman.

"My name is Altaidyn Tengeri. After the sky, you see."

The girl urged the horse away. They rode in the middle of the horde, traveling fast toward the mountain wall. The rising sun was behind them, casting their shadows over the dusty earth and striking the rocks with hard morning light. Elena did not dare look back, in case she shifted position and lost her grip on the rider's waist. But when she became more accustomed to the motion of the horse, she reached down as if to steady herself, and with one hand began to stealthily pick at the straps that fastened her handbag.

Six

The vehicle stopped at the head of a pass, close to a narrow opening in the rocks. Sunlight filtered down, striking the motes of dust cast up by the vehicle's power supply and throwing a haze over the fierce blue of the sky.

"Stay here," Anikova said. She climbed out of the car and strode up to the waiting team as Ilya peered through the window. Anikova's men were dressed in dun fatigues; they reminded him of the soldier he had once been in Afghanistan. But their weapons were like nothing he had seen before. They carried guns that resembled Anikova's, but they were gathered around a device on which sat a thing like an immense shell. It gleamed in the sunlight, like dark polished bronze, and it was surrounded by a cradle of wires. It reminded Ilya of a much larger version of the distorter coil.

"What is that thing?" Ilya said to the Mechvor.

"That? It is a Concet—a dream-net."

"And what does a dream-net do?"

"Stops people in their tracks," the Mechvor said with unaccustomed ruthlessness.

"Are they planning to use that against the horse clan? Is the plan to kill them? Capture them? Neither?"

"Things here do not work in the way that you are used to. We cannot simply kill the Warrior and retrieve the coil. The Warrior cannot be killed."

For the first time, Ilya felt a fleeting sympathy for the being.

"The dream-net will be used to disorient the Warrior, prevent it from activating the coil—if, indeed, it is able to do so. We do not want to take that risk," the Mechvor went on.

"How are you planning to retrieve the coil?"

"We won't. You will."

Ilya stared at her. "And what makes you think I'll help you? Or even that I can?"

"The coil responds to you," Kitai said.

"If it does, I am not aware of it."

"Stop stalling," the Mechvor told him. "I could see the truth in your face when we discussed the matter. I did not even need to reach into your mind."

For the first time, Ilya saw the gentle façade fall completely away, leaving arrogance and something else, something hungrier and more ancient, that he did not want to understand.

"Anikova has asked me to make a bargain with you," Kitai went on. "Retrieve the coil for us, and we'll help save Elena."

"Oh?" He did not believe her. "And then?"

"We keep the coil. You will be free to go—return to Earth, if that's what you want, or to remain here in Byelovodye."

Ilya smiled. "You won't allow that, will you?"

Kitai's rueful serenity was back. "Perhaps not. But you will be free. I give you my word."

Elena, he thought. He was certain that the Mechvor's word was worth nothing, but he kept his face blank and his thoughts in the back of his mind. He had the beginnings of a plan.

"Just try to keep your mind as empty as possible," the Mechvor told him, with more than a trace of irony. "It wouldn't be a good idea to activate the coil by accident."

"Wouldn't we just end up back on the Kyrgyz border?"

"Or between." The Mechvor's face was pinched. He remembered Manas commenting on the dangers of traveling between the worlds. Ilya was about to ask the Mechvor about this when Anikova returned to the vehicle.

"Out. Go and join the rest of the team. Do whatever they tell you."

"Where will you be?"

She gestured toward the rocks. "Up there, with Kitai."

Ilya watched as the vehicle glided to a ledge on the cliff face, then went to join Anikova's team. The team—three men, two women—looked at him with neutral acceptance. He stood a short distance from the dream-net, watching and waiting. The dream-net was moved into position, gliding over the loose earth, to rest behind a bank of rocks. From this angle, it looked like an immense fossil: something dug from the heart of the earth and burnished. Ilya could see no sign of any external workings, nor, aside from the wires, any indication as to why the Mechvor had called it a net. It hovered over the ground, inscrutable, impenetrable, and somehow alien.

"Here," someone said. "You'll need one of these."

He was handed a square of what appeared to be black cloth. When he examined it, he saw that it was made of a fine mesh, and as he shifted it in his hands it became alternatively very heavy and extremely light, depending on the way he held it.

"What do I do with it?" he asked.

"Put it over your head."

Ilya, frowning, did so, and immediately the mesh clung to his scalp, contracting inward. He thought of the Kazakh torture: the bag of skin tightening in the sun, and fought back claustrophobia.

Since he had gotten out of the vehicle, Ilya had been listening, but the surrounding district seemed quiet enough. There were faint traces of sound, occasional snatches of conversation, but nothing that he could pin a warning on. He found that he was conscious of a perverse desire to pull his weight in this new world, convince Anikova that he could be a part of it, but he could not help feeling that here, too, he was an anachronism, not part of the new dreams of Russia. At least this line of thought was helping him to avoid worries about Elena.

Then, all at once, a voice spoke into his ear. He whipped round, but no one was there. It was the coil.

I am coming.

It was followed by a familiar, ominous sound: the beat of hooves. He turned to the nearest person, a girl with a wide Slavic face beneath her mesh helmet.

"They're on their way," he said.

"I didn't hear anything—" Then she gave him a

sudden appraising glance. She spoke rapidly into a device at her collar. Ilya heard Anikova speaking in response.

"We can see them now. They're coming down the pass. Aim for the woman, the blonde."

"No," Ilya said, but the word was drowned in the sound of the horde. Hoofbeats and cries echoed from the walls of the canyon. The girl touched a sequence of switches beneath the dream-net, which began to emit a distant, disquieting hum. Ilya felt as though it was reverberating through his bones; he thought of the sound that had accompanied Manas. Ilya's vision blurred. Through a haze of dust, he saw the horsemen approaching.

The dream-net had become both the most solid thing in the world, and an insubstantial confection of spun glass and frosted wire. To Ilya, it was as though he was standing in two places at the same time, seeing the dream-net from different angles. Then that double perspective itself altered to transform the world into a multitude of viewpoints. Ilya watched, frozen, as an edifice began to build itself up around the dream-net: a towering palace of white stone. A golden cupola gleamed briefly at its pinnacle, surmounted by the double Russian cross, followed by the crescent moon of Islam and a single five-pointed star. Then it was gone, no more than a sequence of shadows upon the air.

"Muromyets! Go! Go now!" Anikova's voice cut through the confusion.

Ilya took a faltering step forward. The people around him were blurred and unreal, ghosts in snow, as the air broke up into a static haze. The dream-net was changing the channel of reality, taking it to the limits of broadcast vision. Ilya glimpsed nightmares in the whirling world, things from the depths of Russia's stories: *Leshy* with its greenleaf hair and root-knotted hands, at once no bigger than a bird and yet pine-tree high. He saw *Domovoi*, the ancient spirit of the house. *Bannik* running on her hen-clawed feet. Old myths for new: Chernobyl's radiation ghosts marched by; chained Chechen dead shuffled forward. He caught a brief image of a cosmonaut, hand raised to an invisible crowd, and he thought with a stab of jealousy and loss of Elena's Yuri. Soldiers, workers, a woman with a sheaf of grain . . . Then the static was scattering like hail as the Golden Warrior's white mare charged through. There was no chance of finding the coil; he wondered how Kitai had even expected it. He was looking for Elena.

He turned to see her by his side, hands held out, and then she was gone, snatched away with such speed that he was not sure if she had ever been there at all. He cried out and found Anikova's vehicle hovering at his elbow. Its top was down. Anikova stood with legs braced apart, squinting down the sights of her weapon. But the white mare leaped forward, knocking the dream-net to one side so that it spun and tottered. A plethora of realities folded in upon one another. Ilya stood knee-deep in grass, underneath a cherry tree, but the blossom was falling first as snow, then as a white roar of water, thundering down out of the rocks to Baikal Lake, then as a flock of swans heading into the setting sun. A single feather touched Ilya's cheek, cold as a kiss.

But one thing remained constant: the *rusalki*, more

than Ilya had seen at any one time before. They appeared as women, gracious and beautiful, then as creatures with sharp claws and teeth, then something stranger that Ilya's mind could not grasp. They stood in a circle, which gradually began to move toward the Warrior. Ilya saw Elena stir across the saddlebow. Her hair streamed behind her as the mare leaped, her mouth gaping. But midflight, midair, the Warrior, its mount, and Elena were as still as a Russian miniature, captured and frozen. The *rusalki* closed in, swift as wolves. Trapped in dreams, Ilya felt the presence of the coil. It sang out to him, connecting.

With a sound that reverberated from the walls of the canyon, the dream-net fell. Realities split. The ground car was thrown onto its side. Ilya dropped to the ground, down through earth and air and stone.

He landed on a tarmac forecourt, with a jolt that knocked the air from his lungs. Beside him, a woman cried out. Blindly, Ilya reached for her hand. Relief flooded through him, until he looked up and saw that it was not Elena who had tumbled down by his side. It was the Mechvor.

Seven

Elena caught sight of the *rusalki* for only a few moments, but it was enough to snatch her back to the memory of the thing in the park, swarming down the rough pine bark toward her, and the attack in the market. The mare trembled beneath her, muscles straining with the attempt to move. The *rusalki* glided forward in a menacing crescent. Elena thought of claws reaching for her throat and, with a great heave, threw aside the Warrior's restraining arm and fell from the mare's back, clutching her bag.

"Get me out of here!" She directed all her longing toward the coil in the bag. She thought of space, of freedom, of flight.

There was a singing pause.

"Please! Help me . . ."

The walls of the canyon, the horse clan riding behind, the Warrior perched on the bunched, leaping back of the mare—everything slid softly past her, leaving a stir of air in its wake, and was gone. The sky was dark. There were no stars. Elena sank quietly down on the ground and closed her eyes.

When she opened them again, it was daylight. She lay curled in the middle of a forest, like a child in a fairy tale. She could see the sky through the branches of the pines and it was once again that darker, stranger blue. She reached for Ilya, but he was not there. She tried to stifle the fright and panic into something more manageable, but then she remembered the coil. Frantically, she opened her bag and there it was, wrapped in leather. It had heard her. It had saved her.

"Thank you," she breathed.

Rising to her feet, Elena looked about her, but there was no one in sight. There was still snow at the foot of the deeper pines, but it was eroding into pale patches and the new grass was pushing through. There were catkins on a nearby grove of birch and the air was mild, fragrant with woodsmoke. And that meant there was a fire not far away. A curl of smoke snaked above the trees. Elena began walking toward it.

She had not gone far when her skin prickled. She turned and saw nothing, but the conviction that something was following her grew. She continued to walk, wheeling around at odd intervals. The forest was quiet and still, and full of eyes. She turned again, and this time there was a rustle in the undergrowth and a hare moved from beneath the brambles. It was still in its winter white; its eyes were huge and dark.

"Hello," Elena said, enchanted. The hare looked at her for a moment, then bounded away. She walked on and minutes later, came to the house.

It stood in a clearing in the forest: a traditional

Siberian *izba*, a cabin made of logs, with a pipe for a chimney.

"Dobreden?" Elena called. There was no reply, but she could hear movement from the back of the *izba*. She walked around it, to find a narrow pen ending in a series of burrows. She frowned. It looked as though someone was keeping rabbits, but a sheaf of corn had been placed in the middle of the pen, which indicated chickens. Then she saw that two eyes, bright as hot coals, were looking at her from the depths of one of the burrows. Elena stood very still. A long beak emerged from the burrow, followed by a narrow, skeletal head. The creature had two little hands, folded across its breast: she saw delicate fingers, bird-boned, half-buried in a mass of downy chestnut feathers. The creature hopped forward on long, thin feet and looked at her with its head on one side. She recognized a *kikimura*.

"Who are you?" said a voice behind her.

Elena, startled, stumbled back against the railing of the pen. The *kikimura*, equally alarmed, bolted for its burrow. There was a girl standing in front of her, holding a bucket. She looked entirely ordinary, perhaps sixteen or seventeen, long red hair in a ponytail, a wide Siberian face, and the tilted eyes of Evenk ancestry. She wore jeans and a rubber apron.

"I'm sorry," the girl said. "I didn't mean to scare you."

"It's all right. You made me jump, that's all." Elena's heart was pounding, but underneath that was relief. The girl spoke excellent Russian. If she was still in Byelovodye—and given the presence of the *kikimura*, she did not see where else it could be—then possibly she was in the north, away from the Warrior and the horse clans.

"*Kikimura*," she said. She remembered the old illustrations in the books of her childhood. "I thought they were hen spirits."

The girl shrugged. "I don't know about spirits. We keep them for the eggs, and they make a good soup, too." The matter-of-fact manner was disconcerting. Elena found herself glancing at the *izba* as if it might sprout chickens' feet.

"There's no one in," the girl said. "My grandma went to see someone, but she'll be back soon. Did you come to see her?"

"I'm lost," Elena said, deciding that for once, honesty was the best policy. "I've no idea where I am."

The girl frowned. "What are you doing wandering in the forest? We're far from anywhere."

"Do you have a map?" Elena asked. The girl's frown deepened.

"A what?"

"A plan, of the region?" Surely the child knew what a map was?

"I don't know what you're talking about. Maybe you should wait for my grandmother. She'll be able to set you straight." The girl spoke with absolute confidence, making Elena smile. She pictured some ancient, forthright *babushka*, a wrinkled face beneath a headscarf and no teeth. As long as it was *babushka* and not *baba yaga* . . . But she did not have a great deal of choice.

"All right," she said. "I'll wait."

Inside, the *izba* was larger than it looked. The girl led her into a long, narrow room running the length of the building. A stove sat in the middle of the room, with a samovar set up in front of a horsehair couch and a low table.

"I'll make you some tea," the girl said. "My name's Masha, by the way."

"Elena Irinovna." She sat down on the couch and looked about her. Pictures occupied the walls: oils of mountains and forest. There were a few small miniatures, including a particularly lovely one of the Swan-maiden. Apart from this, the work looked amateur, probably done by an artistic relative rather than purchased. The cushions of the couch, and the rag rugs on the floor, were clearly homemade, worn through by years of occupation. She could have been anywhere from Vladivostok to Kiev. But there was something missing in this homely, pleasant room, and after a minute, Elena realized what it was. There was no crucifix, no rosary hanging on the wall, no sign that this was a Christian country. But perhaps, Elena thought, remembering the *kikimura* as well as the horse clan, Byelovodye was not Christian.

Masha came back into the room, carrying a tray.

"Here. Tea, and some cake."

"Thank you," Elena said, genuinely grateful. Anything was better than raw liver. Masha disappeared once more. Elena sipped her tea, ate some of the cake, and tried not to worry about Ilya. She leaned back against the couch. There was a prickling at the back of her neck. She reached up to find that her hair was coming loose. It was, moreover, full of twigs and moss. No wonder Masha had glanced at her so strangely. She must look as though she had been dragged through a hedge. She rose and went in search of a bathroom.

She met Masha in the hallway.

"The washroom? It's through the door at the end, out the back. There's a basin and a dipper. We used the *banya* this morning, so the water should still be warm. If you hear a noise, it's only the *bannik*. Rattle the wash-pan—it scares him off."

Elena thanked her and went in the direction that the girl had indicated. A washroom had not been quite what she had had in mind, and what was the *bannik*? She remembered it vaguely from the old tales: a thing that haunted the washroom, all bony legs and a wrinkled face. It was said to rake your back with its claws if you had a troubled future. Elena shivered. The less time spent in the *banya*, the better.

She opened the door at the end of the hallway. It was a bedroom: the walls paneled in pale, glossy birchwood, and wide windows leading out onto a veranda. Slowly, walking as if through a dream, Elena went to the window and looked out. There were lilies, folded up now in the cold shadow of the *izba*. What kind of lily, she wondered, bloomed when there was still snow on the ground? To one side of the room, she could see the open door of the *banya*.

She stepped into the *banya*, keeping an eye open for the *bannik*. The *banya* seemed empty and she washed quickly in the basin, keeping a close eye on her bag. There was no mirror. She picked leaves from her hair and pinned it up as best she could. A small sound came from beneath the stand with the basin.

Elena stepped swiftly back. She had no intention of bending to see what might be crouching underneath the basin. She could see something in the shadows. She moved to the door and opened it. Sunlight fell through. There was a scuttle of movement from beneath the basin; the *bannik,* it seemed, preferred darkness. She caught sight of a hand, long-fingered with tapering ivory nails, covered in coarse dark hair. It made no move toward her, but Elena went backward through the door and pushed it swiftly shut.

"He won't hurt you," someone said.

Elena jumped, and turned to see a woman standing before her.

This must be Masha's grandmother, but the headscarfed *babushka* of Elena's imagination was entirely absent. This woman was no more than fifty and straight as a birch tree. White hair fell to her waist; her eyes were as icy blue as Ilya's. She wore a long woolen skirt and a blouse. Both were the color of her eyes. She made Elena think of water and winter sun. She looked almost Nordic, and Elena briefly considered Masha's parentage. There must have been a Siberian marriage at some point.

"My granddaughter told me you were here," the woman said. "My name is Mati."

"I'm Elena." *Mati.* It meant nothing more than "mother" in old Russian. Perhaps it was a family nickname of some kind.

"She also told me that you were lost," Mati said.

"Yes. That's right. To be honest, I've very little idea how I got here. And your granddaughter didn't seem to have a map."

"No, we have none. There is no need," Mati said serenely. Maybe they simply didn't go anywhere. There were plenty of people, even in Elena's day, who barely set foot beyond their own villages. Her anxiety for Ilya was now wire-sharp.

"I have to find out where I am," she said. "I'm looking for someone."

Mati nodded. "We'll do our best to help you."

Elena followed her back into the main room.

"A moment," Mati said. "My granddaughter is a good girl, but like all young people, she needs to be reminded what to do. I sent her out to feed the *kikis,* and half an hour later I find her daydreaming on the step." With a fleeting smile, she disappeared.

Elena opened her bag and searched for her cigarettes. Only two left. She wondered whether Mati was a smoker. She would save them for later. Instead, she fished the hand mirror from her bag and took a quick look at her hair. Not too bad, though a long lock of it had come free from its pins and now snaked down her cheek. Elena tucked it back again, dimly aware of footsteps behind her. A corner of the room was visible in the mirror and she glanced at it, expecting to see Mati.

"The child hasn't done a thing I told her to do," Mati's voice said behind her, but the figure that Elena could see in the mirror was not Masha's white-haired grandmother.

It was a *rusalka.*

Eight

Ilya and the Mechvor sat in the dim confines of a roadside yurt, listening to the rain beat down onto the canvas.

"You see," the Mechvor was saying, almost apologetically, "I have no way of returning to Byelovodye. And there are people here who wish me harm."

"What sort of people?" Was she talking about the *akyn's* bunch, or the *volkh?* Or Manas?

"Those who work to hold our worlds in an incorrect relationship to each other." The Mechvor's dark gaze shifted, sliding away like oil. Ilya considered this oblique statement. The Mechvor wanted him to know that she was in danger, and the touch of her hand against his suggested that she was not above using a few subtleties to obtain his protection, but clearly she did not want to tell him where her sympathies lay. That, in turn, suggested that she did not know what he was seeking to do. If he was in the Mechvor's place, Ilya thought, he would play his cards close to his chest and find out as much as he could without giving his own game away. He would also be reluctant to let the other person out of his sight. He smiled at the Mechvor, as if weakening.

"Don't worry," he said as reassuringly as he could. "I won't let any harm come to you."

"Thank you," the Mechvor whispered. Her eyes widened until they looked like wells in her face, and he was instantly drawn.

"I can't keep calling you by that outlandish title," he said, to cover his momentary confusion. "Your name's Kitai—is that a Siberian name, by any chance? It sounds familiar."

Kitai nodded. "I am from the region that corresponds to Siberia. The heartland."

"I was born in Siberia," Ilya said. She looked up and smiled.

"I know." Again, the soft touch against his hand. He thought of Elena, steeled himself against dreams. "I knew that we understood each other," she went on, hesitantly.

"I'm sure we do," Ilya said. If his past experiences with her were anything to go by, she could make him do whatever she wished. It was a frightening thought. But perhaps her powers were different on this side of the border.

The Mechvor rubbed her palms over her eyes. "I have to find a way back."

"So do I." His voice sounded colder than he had intended. "I left Elena there." It was hard not to sound accusing.

"There are gates here, in this world. Ones that were created in the last century, but there are also said to be more ancient openings." Her voice held the trace of a question.

"I don't know of any." It was also difficult to know how much to tell her and how much to conceal. But he had to find Elena.

"So you don't know where the nearest one might lie?" Kitai asked.

Samarkand. Ilya stifled the thought as soon as it occurred. He said, "No. I do not."

The Mechvor was staring at him. He thought he saw a trace of satisfaction in her face, and he wondered whether she had plundered information from his mind, or simply confirmed her suspicions.

Nine

Elena sat very still. She could hear Mati moving about behind her, chatting amiably enough about her granddaughter. The woman sounded entirely human. She did not dare turn around.

"Is there a village nearby?" Elena asked as casually as she could. "I was wondering where Masha goes to school."

"We educate her here," Mati murmured. *We?*

"Do you live with your family, then?"

Mati laughed. "Oh, yes. There are lots of us."

Elena, seeking escape, looked around at the amateur oils and the threadbare rugs. It made an unlikely supernatural stronghold. She thought of the *bannik* underneath the basin, of hairy, clawed hands. Mati's own hand came to rest on the back of the couch. As she leaned to adjust a spray of thorned flowers in a nearby vase, Elena looked sideways at the long, human fingers, the short unpainted nails. She wondered what she might see if she looked through the mirror. Mati's hand flexed, convulsively, as she straightened up. Was it Elena's imagination, or did the nails seem just a little longer?

Elena glanced up and met Mati's eyes. They had become colorless, pale as water when a cloud passes overhead, leaching the blue from the sky. And Elena saw that Mati knew, saw the horror reflected in Elena's own face. Mati began to change: the face sharpening, nails lengthening, the glitter of razor teeth. Elena bolted from the couch to the opposite wall, but the *rusalka* was between her and the door. Then Mati was standing in front of her, no more than a foot away. Elena had not even seen her move. Before Elena could react, the *rusalka* reached out and tore the bag from her hand. Elena snatched at it, but the *rusalka* was already across the room.

Mati sat down on the arm of the couch with a sidling motion that turned Elena's stomach. In a raw voice the *rusalka* said, "Try not to be afraid. Fear will change me, make a monster of me. I don't want that."

It was the first indication she'd had that she might possess a power over the creature, but if so, it was a chancy kind of power, at best.

"One of you attacked me in the market in Almaty. I thought I was going to die."

"No one attacked you. She was one of my kind, a wild cousin. She was trying to take the coil, it's true, but she was also seeking to save you."

"From what?" Elena asked, then thought with absolute dismay of Ilya.

"From something that wished you ill."

"Ilya?" Elena whispered.

"Ilya Muromyets, slayer of devils. A good man who does not understand what he is dealing with. Not one who wishes you harm. No, my cousin sought to save you from a ghoul, a dark creature, the avatar of something in this world, which was pursuing you," Mati said, and Elena noticed that, now that she had become more absorbed in what the *rusalka* was saying, the nails had once again receded, the eyes were once more blue. "My wild sisters have great understanding, but little speech. We are not human. We do not think in the same way, act in the same way."

Elena, looking pointedly about the room, said, "It all seems human enough. Or is this just illusion, too?"

"No. This is real."

"Why have you been hounding Ilya all these years?"

"We have not been hounding him," the *rusalka* hissed. "He draws us to him. We are at his mercy, not the other way round."

"What do you mean?"

"Every time he is injured, dying, even simply in danger, he summons us. He has the power to open gaps between the worlds."

"But you've been appearing to him for years, long before he had the coil."

"He is like the Warrior. He does not need the coil to open up a small gap. With the coil, his abilities are amplified." Mati's long fingers closed protectively around the bag.

Don't let her know that you can use the coil, too. Elena tried to keep her face carefully blank. Or did the *rusalka* already suspect? Elena prayed that Mati would think that it was Ilya who had opened the world and helped her escape.

"We had no choice but to help him," Mati said.

"He called us to him in Almaty. He summoned my sisters to the place where Kovalin's men were waiting to slay you both."

"But he said—"

"He does not understand his own power; he does not know. I'm sure he told you what he believes to be the truth."

"Where does his power come from, though? What is he?"

"He is Russia, Elena. He and all the *bogatyri*. The spirits of a country, the embodiment of its dreams. They are at the heart of the great mystery, the relationship between land and mankind. But they're the ones with the real power, not us. That is why everyone has been trying to keep Ilya in the dark. Because everyone is afraid of that power."

"So what are you? What are the *rusalki*?" *And if I can activate the coil, too, what am I?*

"Indigenous inhabitants. Aborigines. Natives— like the Kazakh, the Entsy, the Evenk—all the tribes who make up Russia in your world. But there are legends that we were once nomads who crossed from dimension into dimension, changing as we went, taking on different customs, different forms. We built gates across the worlds. We must have come here thousands of years ago, by your reckoning, building two gates between here and Earth: one in Siberia, and one in Samarkand, and there may have been others that are now forgotten and lost. And then we settled, as nomads do, became both more and less civilized, rejected the technology that had enabled our progress. But it is still important to us to keep those routes open. When a human, Tsilibayev, finally found a way to duplicate our ancient technology, it gave the humans of Byelovodye the means to build gates of their own and control them. Since then, everyone has been battling for power. What happens in your world affects this one. And besides, we have nowhere else to go. We need an escape route, if anything should happen to Byelovodye."

"I can understand the need for a way out," Elena said, thinking of Canada. "But you said what happens in Russia affects Byelovodye. Why should the *rusalki* be in favor of that?"

"Because the Mechvors of Central Command are poisoning this world. In recent years, they have sought to control everyone and everything, they have closed down all the newer gates and locked the technology away. They want to open one great gate, then bleed the dreams of Earth through it. You are a scientist. Think of dreaming as a kind of energy, a force that can be channeled and siphoned. Rather than a balance between the two worlds, Byelovodye will have all the power. I might be in favor of that, but the price is too high. Central Command and the Mechvors want one dream only—their own. The ideals and visions of others, of *rusalki,* of the horse clans, used to matter. We were equals, and now we count for nothing. Martial law was declared throughout the Republic seven years ago. Since then, things have gotten steadily worse—a repression with which you must be familiar."

"I know the kind of thing. Is this why things have been gradually worsening in the former Soviet Union? Is this why so many people seem to have lost their faith in everything?"

"Humans always seek to control their dreams," the *rusalka* said. "They try to nail things down and make them safe, revise history. But the world—all worlds—change too quickly for that to be possible. This is why the distorter coil is of such importance."

Elena was silent.

"You don't know what to think," the *rusalka* said. It was a statement, not a question.

"No. If Ilya were here—"

"You need a man to think for you?" Mati said with thin scorn.

"I need someone whom I know I can trust, to discuss my options," Elena said with equal coldness. "I am a scientist. I have to look at whatever evidence is at my disposal."

"I'm sorry," Mari said after a moment. "Around here, I am used to being an elder. I forget that others may have knowledge of their own."

Elena sighed. "It's an easy mistake. Wanting a man to think for you is one of Russia's greatest problems. First the priests, then the tsars, then the Party. It's a need that encourages the creation of monsters."

"It is the same everywhere," Mati said. "Here as well as your world. But in Byelovodye, if you let someone else do your thinking for you, they can change your reality."

"My world as well as here," Elena said, and the *rusalka* smiled.

"So, you need to choose which side to belong to, Elena, based on what you have already seen. If you accept what I have to say, you will be choosing *rusalki* over human, the horse clans over civilization. The Mechvors of Central Command cannot be allowed to remain in power, and we are no longer willing to grant them a voice."

"What power do I have?" Elena asked.

"None. But you are a guest, and guests are sent from God, they say. We are not entirely monsters. We would rather you rode with us."

If she listened to the *rusalka*, Elena thought, there would be a sense in which she would be choosing dreams over reality. But what about Ilya? How far might her choice be a betrayal of him?

"If you had known nothing of any of us, if the choice had been an abstract one," the *rusalka* said, "which would you choose?"

But Elena did not think of forests and fairy stories, of Golden Warriors and ancient tribesmen. She thought of Valentina Tereshkova's image on the Tashkent Metro, with the daisies like a necklace of stars around the rim of her helmet. She thought of the rockets blasting up from the steppe, melting the snow at the foot of the tower, to be lost in the blazing dark. She thought of Ilya, not as a hero, but as a man, knowing again what it was like to be in love. And she remembered her dreams of Canada, a different land, yet somehow part of the same ideal.

Ilya's dreams were all of the past, she realized, what Russia had been and would never be again, but her dreams were of the future, tomorrow, what Russia might yet prove to be. And she knew that, whatever dreams the *rusalka* had in mind, Elena had already made her own choice.

Ten

UZBEKISTAN, 21ST CENTURY

On the pretext of visiting the lavatory, Ilya hurried to the back of the yurt and flagged down a passing car, making sure that he could not be seen by the Mechvor. The farther he got from this strange, manipulative creature with her weird eyes, the better. An Islamic rosary of black beads dangled across the windscreen. The driver was a taciturn man who spoke little. It suited Ilya. He sat in the front seat, watching the road unfurl between the sway of the beads as they left the yurt, and Kitai, far behind.

Soon they were halfway down the Fergana Valley, not far from Kokand. The Tien Shan were no more than a bright line far to the northeast; to the south rose the distant peaks of the Alai. Cotton fields, hazy with new growth, stretched out across the basin. It had changed little from the last time Ilya had been here, when the Fergana Valley had been split into a succession of bickering khanates, ruled by madmen. He doubted whether that had greatly changed, either. The region had always been a law unto itself. He remembered hearing of a local ruler whose gardens had been bright with peacocks and cranes, a man who had held court from a throne beneath a tree and who had thrown all who opposed him into the dungeons beneath his mansion and subjected them to refined forms of torture. That, Ilya recalled, had been in 1986. They were a long way from Moscow. Investigative Soviet officials had simply vanished. Ilya thought of Byelovodye and was again aware of that faint, dislocated sense of homesickness.

The endless cotton fields rolled by; there was little evidence of any other crop. Ilya mentioned this to the driver and the man spat out of the window.

"There are no other crops. The cotton has bled us dry and now it is starting to fail. No rain, you see, and what falls is poisoned."

"From the Aral Sea?"

"From the Aral, where else? The wind picks up the dry sea dust and sends it down again as rain. And it's polluted, of course. Radioactive, toxic with Allah knows what kind of chemical—no wonder the cotton is failing. And the politicians keep telling us that we've had a bumper year."

"They are all fools," Ilya murmured.

"Yes, they are fools. They do not ask the farmers; they just want to hear the sound of their own voices, like the donkey in the fable. The Russians were as bad—no offense—but these are our own people."

"Politicians are a nation apart. No allegiance to any except their own." The driver touched a hand to the rosary. Close to nightfall, they reached Kokand.

Kokand had altered beyond all recognition since Ilya's last visit. Then, the city had been filled with mosques and *madrasas*; the golden crescents of Islam filling the sky like a hundred new moons. But the city had been sacked in 1918 by the Tashkent Soviets; thousands had died, and the holy buildings had been torn down. Now, as Ilya and the driver walked through the twilight streets, the faces that were turned toward them were still full of resentment and a dull anger. Ilya could not blame them. He put a hand on the driver's shoulder.

"Where is this place?"

"Not far, not far."

The tenuous rapport that had been established between them during the journey had gone. The driver seemed nervous and edgy. He darted through the streets like a thief. Ilya wondered if the man had other designs upon him than the simple scam of a bed for the night, doubtless in a place owned by one of his relatives. He still had the sword, Ilya thought. He wondered where the Mechvor might be now.

"It's on Abdulla Nabiev. I told you, it isn't far. Look, I know what you're thinking. You're right to be suspicious around here—they don't like Russians. But you'll be all right with me. I'm an honest man."

In Ilya's long experience, people who made such a claim were almost invariably lying, but shortly afterward, they reached Abdulla Nabiev and a grubby hostel owned by the driver's second cousin. A price was arranged at a level more satisfactory to the driver than to Ilya, who was certain that he had been overcharged but was too exhausted to argue. He lay down at once, curled around himself like an animal, but it was a long time before he lost consciousness.

Eleven

Toward the end of the afternoon, the golden sunlight faltered and was gone. Rain spattered across the roof of the *izba* in a sudden squall.

"The horse clan comes," Mati said. She stood at Elena's elbow, holding the leather bag that carried the distorter coil and watching the drops beating the furled heads of the lilies into submission. She had taken care to keep a close hold on the bag, and Elena wondered just how much Mati suspected. But perhaps she feared only that Elena would try to steal the thing, not use it. Elena tried to reach out with her mind to the coil, but the voice was silent.

A wind passed through the clearing, bending the branches before it. The next moment, a restless line of horsemen stood beyond the *kikimura*'s run. The Golden Warrior was riding forward, with the Shaman Altaidyn Tengeri on a pony at its side.

"So, I see we have found you," the shaman called to Elena. But the Warrior sat tall on the back of the white mare and Elena could not see inside its helmet. It remained silent and formless. Mati and the shaman began to speak, in a quick guttural tongue that Elena was unable to follow, or even identify. She wondered if it might be Evenk, or another of the Siberian languages. The girl, Masha, still in her jeans and apron, wove between the horses' legs with a bucket of feed. She seemed determined to ignore the strangers that had so unexpectedly landed in her backyard, but perhaps she was used to it. She clucked and the *kikis* scuttled from their burrows.

At the edge of the clearing, the horsemen were dismounting. Mati glanced at the Warrior, inclined her head. The Warrior nodded, as though they had communicated in some manner. She determined to ask Mati about the Warrior as soon as the opportunity arose. She followed Altaidyn and the *rusalka* inside. The Warrior lingered for a moment, looking back, then strode up the steps into the *izba*.

Mati and the shaman had spent over an hour inside the house, closeted in some inner room with the Warrior. It was a conference to which Elena had not been invited. She was now sitting back out on the veranda, watching the *kikimura* scratch among the stones and growing increasingly annoyed.

She could understand the stake that these people had in the distorter coil, in keeping open a gate between Byelovodye and the world, but they were not the only ones to consider. There were the millions of folk in Russia and its former satellite colonies, who would surely be affected by such a course of events. How far did Byelovodyean dreams affect Russian ones,

Central Asian ones, and alter the course of what she still thought of as the real world?

Elena did not resent the conference itself, but she resented her exclusion from it. Was it to be only Byelovodyeans, of whatever human or half-human persuasion, who were entitled to a say in matters?

As if resonating to her thoughts, Mati appeared behind her on the veranda.

"The decision has been made," she announced. Elena, looking up at her, saw that her *rusalka* appearance was now more pronounced. Mati's hair streamed down her back like moonlight; her face was skeletal. Elena swallowed a small lump of fear and said, as coldly as she could, "I'm glad you've managed to come to a decision without my input."

"We have been planning for this eventuality for years," Mati said, frowning. "It is a decision in which everyone has a voice."

"Then why wasn't I asked what I thought about the matter?"

"The human world—Earth—can't be the decider. And I would remind you that you are only here on our sufferance."

By which she meant *alive*, Elena thought with a chill.

"We have to protect ourselves," the *rusalka* went on. "We need an open gate."

"And what about us? I'm not saying you're wrong, Mati—I basically agree with you—but I'm the only real Russian here. I think I'm entitled to make some contribution."

"You *will* be making a contribution," the *rusalka*

said. Perhaps she did not mean to sound so condescending, but Elena bristled nonetheless. "A human
from Earth, from the other side of the border, with the
dreams of your world to throw into the balance," Mati
said. "You are a person with strong ideals, aren't you?"

"I used to think I was."

"Some people are better at hanging on to their
dreams than others. You are one of them, I think." She
reached down and took Elena's chin in her hand; Elena
jerked away. "I see more in you than just a love of
money or power."

Elena smiled. "I thought money and power were
powerful dreams."

"But they are not ideals, they are short-term goals.
This human rush toward an imaginary progress—it
has to be curbed, Elena. The machines that the humans have brought with them and invented, this drive
to overcome nature—it must be turned back."

"I agree that some balance has to be set," Elena
said, thinking of the irradiated steppes, the sad salty
hollow where the Aral Sea had once been. "But you
can't just get rid of all technology in one fell swoop.
How will people live?" The realization dismayed her.
She might be an idealist, just as Mati had said, but her
ideals differed from their own. She wondered whether
the *rusalka* truly understood this.

For answer, Mati gestured around her: at the quiet
forest, the neat rows of new vegetables, the *kikimura*
pecking for corn.

"We've been nothing but peasants for generations," Elena said. "Do you want to bring us back to
that, to some imaginary Slavic idyll?"

"You should know by now not to use the word

'imaginary' lightly around here. Whoever controls the distorter coil controls imagination itself."

"What will happen to Byelovodye, if you're successful? Will the machines just crumble and fail?"

"Slowly, over time, they will decay."

"And what about Russia?" There was already a burgeoning environmental movement in the former Soviet Union, to which Elena was deeply sympathetic, but she did not believe that green totalitarianism was better than any other kind. She said as much.

"You will see," Mati said, serene once more. "It will be better. The steppes will be restored, the forests renewed . . ."

"And we'll all be living in huts and yurts. What about the people who don't want that?"

What about the people who want to reach for the stars?

But Mati was already going back inside the house, to summon the Warrior.

Twelve

UZBEKISTAN, 21ST CENTURY

When Ilya awoke, it was morning. He showered and dressed quickly, picked up the sword, and went downstairs. The driver was waiting dourly in the hallway. Their journey, so he told Ilya, would take another few hours. Once they were in the car, he demanded more money.

"No," Ilya said.

"I'll need more gas. And there's the wear and tear on the car as well."

"We agreed on the price." Ilya gave the driver the coldest, blankest stare that he could summon up and flicked the rosary with a finger. "What about this?" If Ilya on his own couldn't intimidate the driver, perhaps the allusion to Allah might do the trick.

"All right, all right, we'll keep it at the original price. You're a decent man; I can see that."

"I appreciate it," Ilya murmured.

Little lay between Kokand and the south. An endless panorama of cotton fields and bare earth unscrolled along the road, alternating patterns of aridness and fertility. They stopped for food and gas at a place called Jizak, which was no more than a scatter of houses. A group of men sat on the raised platform of a *chaikhana*. Their dull tunics were belted with scarlet and orange sashes that glowed like coals in the shadows. Ilya was reminded that this was fire country, the land of Zoroaster and his followers. There were still said to be temples in the hills, with flames that had been burning for thousands of years.

The driver ordered shashlik and tea. The men stared at them with unblinking eyes, their gazes devoid of hostility or approval, as though the strangers were of no more significance than the passing clouds.

Past Jizak, the road ran arrow-straight through twisted apple orchards. They ran into police checkpoints every twenty kilometers, regular as the beat of a metronome. At each one, Ilya paid a dollar, with poor grace. The driver glanced at the bundle of notes and his mouth tightened.

The flat plains trailed away into dust. To the south, Ilya could see the blue rise of the Fan Mountains, blocks of shadow in the late-afternoon sunlight. The villages through which they were passing grew poorer. Uzbek tunics gave way to Tajik dress. Near the last checkpoint, Ilya saw a group of women in long floral skirts and trousers; they stared at him as the car slowed down, blue eyes in dark faces, betraying Iranian ancestry. Chickens rooted about in the dusty earth at the foot of the checkpoint. The policeman who took Ilya's dollar had a face like a Persian miniature: a mobile mouth, curls of black hair.

They were waved on. The road wound up through

black hills, past outcrops of stone. Ilya thought of bandits, of wolves. The land rose sharply, heaved upward by the distant presence of the Fan. Beyond lay Afghanistan; they were not so far from the border.

At last the road dipped, cut sharply over a white torrent of water, and continued over the crest of a hill. The driver pointed.

"There you are."

Samarkand. A hundred memories jolted him.

Domes rose golden against the blue hills. The modern city was barely visible through the afternoon haze. Samarkand stood untouched by the everyday world: shadowy, seized from time. The road took them down past low houses and secret courtyards. Acacia and jasmine hung over the white walls.

"Where to now?" the driver asked, as if he could not wait to be rid of his passenger.

"The Registan, the great square. Leave me there."

"You don't want to find a hotel before you start sight-seeing?"

"No," Ilya answered. "Take me to the square."

Thirteen

It was explained to Elena that Mati and the Warrior had chosen the site of the gate. Rather than trying to take the coil all the way south, to the lands of the horse clans, the gate would be opened on the steppe, at a special place at the edges of the forest.

"We don't have time to take it south," Mati said to the shaman. From the fraying note in her voice, Elena surmised that this had been no small point of contention.

"It would be safer in the south," Altaidyn Tengeri argued. "We have the means to guard it there; we hold those lands safe against the Pergaman military." It was clearly a point he had made a number of times already.

"Maybe so, but you almost lost the coil in your last encounter with that military. If my wild sisters had not saved you—at great risk to themselves—if Elena had not seized the coil and been sent here to safety—"

—at this, Elena's ears pricked up. Mati continued, "—you realize that Colonel Anikova will be leading a *rusalki* hunt right now?"

"We should not allow ourselves to be panicked into action."

"Who is panicking? No one knows the coil is here—yet."

"Is there a way of tracking the coil?" Elena asked.

"Traces of it can be picked up, but it isn't an exact science. Unless someone is attuned to it, it can only be tracked by the effects it leaves behind it. Central Command uses scanners, but they're not very good, especially if the coil chooses to protect itself. But they'll be searching for the horse clan, and a group of people will be hard to hide."

"My friend Ilya was told that in our world, the coil was taken from the body of a *rusalka*. Is that true?"

"As far as we know," Mati said impatiently, "this is true. The coil was stolen from the military and taken to your world for safekeeping. But the sister who carried it was killed, and it was once more seized by our enemies. Then it disappeared."

"I think I saw the man who took it," Elena said. "It was on the border, on the road to Uzbekistan at the end of winter. He was dead."

"What did he look like?"

As best she could, Elena described the dead man. "And he had strange dark eyes, with a bloom upon them."

"Mechvor," the shaman murmured. "One of Kovalin's men. Maybe heading for Samarkand, trying to get back. We're not sure of the way they took to get to Earth."

"And that is where you found the coil?" Mati asked.

"Yes—I think one of the ambulance drivers stole

it, but then I found it in the snow. It's a long story. I took it home, kept it safe."

"We could not trace it for some time. When we picked up the trail again, your friend Ilya was already on his way to Almaty. The coil found him and he summoned us. He was injured."

"We are running short of time," Altaidyn Tengeri said. "If we set out now, with half the clan sent in different directions to draw off any pursuit, we should have a clear run to the edge of the steppe—no more than a few hours. There, we have prepared a safe place to activate the coil. Once we are there, I and the Warrior will open the gate and seal it." His gaze flickered over Elena and away, generating an unease that she did not understand.

"How will you seal it?" she asked.

"You will see." But there was a sadness in the shaman's face.

This time Elena did not ride on the Warrior's white mare, for which she was grateful. That honor was reserved for Mati, and Elena watched anxiously as the mare shied and balked in the presence of the *rusalka*. If the mare could carry the Warrior without flinching, then the animal's disquiet at bearing Mati was troubling.

Elena herself rode with Altaidyn Tengeri on an old grey pony that reminded her of the shaman himself. It seemed a curious way to transport a piece of cutting-edge technology, though in the light of the allies' beliefs, it made a certain kind of sense.

"Don't worry," Altaidyn Tengeri said into Elena's

ear. University education aside, he smelled strongly of horses and blood, and she was not entirely happy at being so close to him. "I'm sure they won't let anything happen to you. You can watch it all from a safe distance."

Yuri had said something very similar to her just before the last launch. It had irritated her then, too. She was tired of being at the mercy of well-meaning men—with the exception of Ilya.

The forest passed by. Once more she saw plants and trees that she did not recognize, and she wondered whether this was no more than a peculiarity of this other dimension, or if this unknown flora had itself been conjured from the material of dreams, to take root and grow.

Gradually, the forest thinned. Bramble gave way to golden grass and young birch. They rode through a glade of trees and the forest ended. Elena looked down a long slope of grassland to the steppe: folding itself away to blue, distant hills half-lost in cloud-shadow.

A line of grassy mounds rose out of the steppe, marked by tall poles with horsetail banners.

"What are those mounds?"

"Barrows. The burial places of our earliest dead. This is the place where our dreams will come true," Tengeri said, and his face was somber.

Fourteen

By the time he reached the square of the Registan, the sun was boiling down behind the mountains and the air was growing colder. Ilya, who had begun to feel sweat trickle down the back of his neck, was relieved. He looked about him.

The square of the Registan had hardly changed. If he half-closed his eyes, he could imagine himself back in the days when this was the center of the world—one of the greatest cities of the East—instead of some Uzbek backwater. The great gate of the Sher Dor *madrasa* rose above him: gold and azure, heretically emblazoned with lions and deer. The suns above each lionback bore faces: surely an affront to Islam, Ilya thought, and emblematic of a much older religion.

Here in Samarkand, ancient crossroads of the world, the different faiths seemed to coexist peacefully enough: Islam, Zoroastrianism, perhaps even Christianity. And the newest faith of all, Communism, was evident in the roar of traffic from the modern Soviet city that lay behind these old walls. He thought again of Manas: how greatly must the Kyrgyz *bogatyr* resent these Russian incursions, this Soviet presence.

Across the huge expanse of the square, the Tilla Kari mosque mirrored the Sher Dor, gleaming with the light of the sun and the sky until the world seemed inverted, swung into a sea of blue and gold. The turrets—built, Ilya had once heard, to withstand earthquakes—seemed to loom and reel above the square. The sight made him dizzy. He looked down, shaking his head.

There was a tiny scratch of sound, and he turned to see a sparrow fluttering in the dust of the square. But it was the only thing he could hear. The outside world, the noise of the traffic, was gone, as though a great lid had been clapped over the Registan.

The sparrow whirled up in a puff of dust, and with a jolt, Ilya caught sight of Kitai. She was standing at the edge of the square, looking back. But she was curiously insubstantial. He could see the blue tiles of the wall through her body, as though she had become part of the sky, and there was a second shape contained within her own: something small and dark. Ilya recognized the ghoul that he had seen in the market, and again on the hillside. The shape moved as he watched, lying within her form like a seed. She took a step back and disappeared.

Ilya raced toward the place where she had vanished. There was no sign that she had ever stood there, only a sunlit patch of stone flags with celandines growing between the cracks and dust motes sparkling against the blue tiles. Ilya searched the wall, but there was nothing, no evidence of secret exits or entrances. He shut his eyes and listened. The world was silent.

Fifteen

The horse clan rode down the slope toward the barrows, sweeping wide across the steppe in a fan. Elena kept an eye on the skies, but there was no sign of hostility or pursuit.

"I thought they'd try to stop us," she shouted to Tengeri over the beat of the horses' hooves.

"They surely will," the shaman called back.

"Then where are they?"

"I do not know."

Elena could hear the hiss of the horsetail banners in the rising wind. As they reached the bottom of the ridge, the Warrior and Mati rode up beside the shaman's horse.

"We have work to do," the *rusalka* called.

"Elena should stay here," the shaman said. "I—"

But then the world was filled with the roar of aircraft. Elena, looking up, saw that Central Command had found the horse clan.

Zeppelins drifted across the steppe like rogue moons, casting dark shadows beneath them. An arrowhead plane darted between, down, raced overhead, and was gone. *Reconnaissance,* thought Elena. The open steppe was horribly exposed.

"Get back!" the shaman shouted to the clan. "Get back to the trees!"

The Warrior's mare had wheeled around and was heading down toward the barrows. Tengeri kicked his horse in the ribs and, ignoring Elena's cry of protest, followed. She clung to Tengeri as they bolted down the slope. A nearby sagebush went up in a fragrant ball of flame. This time, there was no evidence of dream technology. Central Command had, it seemed, decided to do things the old-fashioned way.

The Warrior's mare turned, spooked by noise and smoke, and stumbled, colliding with Tengeri's mount. Both horses went down, thrashing. As she was thrown clear, Elena saw the Warrior pinned beneath the mare; the *rusalka* scrambled free. Elena got to her knees. Tengeri lay still. But the bag containing the distorter coil lay only a little distance away, among the scrub. Without stopping to think, Elena hauled herself to her feet and ran toward it.

"Elena!" the *rusalka* shouted. "What are you doing?" They reached the bag together. Elena snatched at it but her wrist was gripped by razors. The *rusalka's* eyes were fiery-cold. Her claws pierced Elena's skin, but Elena did not let go of the bag. She reached out and thrust the *rusalka* away. Mati clawed at her, drawing blood, spitting and hissing. Elena struck the *rusalka* across the face as hard as she could, knocking Mati to the ground. Clutching the bag, she raced for the barrows.

Sixteen

SAMARKAND, UZBEKISTAN, 21ST CENTURY

At last he could hear Kitai's faint footsteps, pattering across the flags of the old square. Ilya followed, running along the wall to the corner of the courtyard. He glimpsed a dark shape vanishing into the shadows. She was heading for Tamerlane's tomb.

He chased her past the southernmost *madrasa* and out into the road. Here, all was normal: a twenty-first century afternoon with the traffic rumbling past on its way to the city center. Dodging trucks and taxis, Ilya crossed the road and found himself in a graveyard, surrounded by the etched faces of boys. All dated from the 1970's and early 1980's; it was a graveyard for the Afghan dead. He could almost feel the presence of their ghosts, accusing him, the eternal survivor, as he made his way between the pointed stones and up the hillside.

Up on the hill, the fumes were not so overpowering. The scent of earth seeped through, baking in the sun. He came over the ridge and found himself at the end of a corridor of medieval tombs, fronted with tiles and ochre brick. It was the place where he had fought

Manas, all those years ago. He paused, memory snatching him back. He could almost see the blood, spilling glossy over the stones. He remembered Manas' words all those years ago: *Russians are not welcome here. This place is sacred.* But Kitai's footsteps were slipping on gravel, hissing through dry grass. He followed her onto the brow of the hill.

Kitai led him past the dome of an ancient observatory. The blue-tiled roof and the long sweep of a ruined sextant raised further memory. This was the memorial to Ulug Bek, the most famous of Eastern astronomers, murdered by his own fanatical son, who had considered his father's work an affront to Islam. The place reminded him sharply of Elena: another gazer-at-stars, but please God, not another victim of tribal superstition. Ilya drew a sharp breath and hurried on.

He could see Kitai clearly now, still in her double form. She had discarded the coat, and the shape of the ghoul was running beside her like a shadow. It reminded him of the *rusalki*. Was she the same kind of being, dual-natured, both lovely and repellent depending on dreamer and dream? He had no real desire to find out.

He followed the figure of Kitai across a wide courtyard of stones. A building lay ahead: a round tower crowned with tiles the color of the sky, and he recognized the tomb of Tamerlane. Kitai's double figure slowed and seeped through the stones of the wall. Ilya ran around the building until he found a door. He wrenched it open and fell through into the mausoleum. Window slits lay up in the dome of the roof. Light splashed down the walls, ran over the marble floor like water. The place was lined with gold, thick and glowing. He could smell incense, smoke, polish. In the center of the room stood a tall plinth covered with a slab of cracked black jade, twice the length of a man. A pole stood at its head, bearing a scarlet horse-tail banner.

Beyond the tomb stood Kitai, hands spread on black jade, and beside her was Kovalin the *Volkh,* staring at Ilya with a dead black gaze. But as he stared, a third person limped from the shadows. It was Manas.

Seventeen

Elena risked a look back. The horse clan had melted back into the trees. Beyond, the zeppelins moved like great ghosts. The plane had disappeared, presumably sweeping around for another pass. The *rusalka* was nowhere in sight. Elena emptied her bag onto the grass and seized the distorter coil, then paused. She had no firm plan, other than flight, and that was clearly out of the question. It was Ilya who had the connection with the coil, everyone said so.

And yet the coil was sentient, in some respect, and it had listened to her before. She looked down at it as it lay in her cupped hands. Perhaps, Elena thought, it was itself a dream-artifact, something conjured to fulfill a goal. She glanced around her.

This land was so similar to the steppes around Baikonur. There was the same smell of sagebrush and saxaul, the same thin earth beneath her feet, between the stems of long grass. Memories flooded back: the excitement before every launch, the air of comradeship and shared purpose. She looked up. She could almost *see* the launch site, like a great shadow upon the air.

The coil grew warm in her palm.

"I remember Baikonur," she whispered to the coil. "Won't you listen to me again? Won't you read my dreams?"

Nothing.

"Please," Elena whispered.

You have their blood in you, but you are yet not my kind.

"But you helped me before." What blood did it mean?

That was different. You sought a lesser thing—to rift, not build.

"I did not know what I sought. Not the first time, anyway."

If I am to build your dream, you must send me into it. Even then, without a mind to aid me, your dream may not last.

"What am I to do to make it last?"

Stay.

"Stay where?" Elena asked.

Stay here, in Byelovodye. Help to maintain your dream.

"Not to go back to Earth? But I have family there— my mother—I . . ." What would become of Anna without her?

You will be needed here, the coil said, small-voiced, implacable. From above the forest came the roar of aircraft. If Byelovodye stole the world's dreams, what would happen to Baikonur? What would befall the new space station? She thought of rockets, rotting on the launchpad.

"Then I will stay," she said, and forced her mother's face from her mind.

Another pause, then familiar blue light spilled out to fill the air in a spiral: azure, electric. Dazzled, Elena closed her eyes.

In her imagination it rose out of the steppe like a skeleton: a great bracket of metal, glittering in the afternoon sun, a settlement of polygons, gantries, support buildings. It cradled a ship. But the gantries were rusted and worn, twisted into shards of shattered metal. The walls of the support buildings were pitted and unplastered.

Then Mati slunk around Elena's peripheral vision, more animal now than human, claws visible.

"No," the *rusalka* hissed. "Not that. That is the wrong dream. Give me the coil."

She tried not to look at the *rusalka,* to steer her gaze away from those eyes, but they had captured her and held her tight. Her head felt as though it had been clamped in a migraine vise. With effort, she turned her head away, feeling her sinews stretch to the breaking point.

Beyond, the drifting zeppelins had all gone. Only the skeins of blue light from the distorter coil and the *rusalka* remained. Why did Mati not attack? But the light now fell between herself and the *rusalka,* rendering Mati indistinct, as though glimpsed through heat or static.

The *rusalka* began whispering to her, insidious. "Forget your dead dreams. Technology has failed you; let it go. Give up the coil to the Warrior; let a new dream begin. Return the world to this grass, this earth." The *rusalka*'s voice hissed and murmured inside Elena's head.

For a moment, it was almost seductive. She thought of the steppe in spring: the flowers blooming out of the black earth, the larks rising above the grasslands. Peace as far as the eye could see and the ear could hear. No more radiation, botched experiments, seas turned to dust, ideals dying on their feet.

She thought of the children she would never have, the infertility she had never properly faced and of which she had only ever spoken of once to Ilya, when it had seemed safe to do so. The doctors had never been certain whether her sterility was to do with atmospheric nuclear testing, the background radiation that was much too high throughout the whole region, or the work she had undertaken in laboratories as a girl. One of them had told her that it could have been caused by toxins in the rocket fuel itself, and that was the cruelest possibility of all, that her beloved work had been responsible for her childlessness. She had accepted it with the fatalism that was expected of her, swallowed despair, and moved on.

"Let it go," the *rusalka* murmured sweetly. "Let us help you." Compassion wielded like a scalpel.

"But without dreams, I am nothing," Elena said.

"Nothing? You still have the wind over the earth, the sound of rain, the green of spring . . ." The *rusalka*'s voice was gentle, persuasive, and Elena thought, *That is all they are. Creatures of nature, resenting humankind.* Elena had no doubt that the *rusalka* thought she was doing the right thing: helping humanity, returning it to the old ways. And there was something in that dream of nature that spoke directly to her Russian soul: always the pull of the earth, the turn of the seasons. But something different was tugging her away.

She looked up, and her vision darkened. It was no longer day and she could see the stars. They burned and blazed, as brightly as they had always done. She thought, *They, too, are part of the natural world. Our dreams are not mutually exclusive. The mistakes we make, the price we pay, are part of being human, as long as we learn from them. And I want the dream of the stars, not only of the soil.*

She looked back. The *rusalka* was gone. Elena stood alone in the middle of the steppe, her feet freezing in a sudden gust of snow, the stars curling above her head.

She closed her eyes and thought of Baikonur.

She imagined the gantries knitting together, the tongues of rust circling back, to shine in a great mesh of shining metal. She dreamed that the buildings around her were newly plastered, filled with equipment and regularly paid technicians. Slowly, as she focused, the gantry became sharper, brighter, and the rocket that rested in its metal cage glittered in a sudden shaft of sunlight. A figure walked across her peripheral vision, wearing a lab coat and as fragile as a ghost.

Lastly, she concentrated on the rocket: something slick and sleek and futuristic, something that present-day Russian technology could never emulate. It rose high on the launchpad, and for a moment the curve of its engines blotted out the stars.

Send me to it.

The coil was light and insubstantial now, and she

thought, strangely, *Why, it has itself been nothing but a dream all along.* She raised the coil high above her head, saw it stream and melt and vanish against the rocket's side as though she had cast it into a pool. Blue light stretched and spread to fill the world.

Eighteen

Kitai took a step back as soon as she saw Manas. Ilya drew the sword. Kovalin stared at it, expressionless. "A typical Russian response. The moment you're faced with something you don't understand, you reach for the nearest weapon."

Manas laughed.

Ilya flicked the sword toward Kovalin, again seeing an echo of the *volkh*'s flat black eyes in those of Kitai. "For example, you're not part of any secret scientific society, are you? You're Byelovodyean. They sent you to get the coil back. You told me what I wanted to hear. And that stuff about the *rusalki*—that was a lie, too, wasn't it? But what I want to know is, why me?"

Kovalin turned sharply. "Something's happening in the Republic. We don't have much time, Kitai."

"You were right, my hero," Manas said. "The gate is here, beneath the tomb, powered by another ancient coil and more besides. Tamerlane's people knew of it. When he appeared to die, they thought he would travel through, be reborn in the next world. They must have known that he was not himself human, that he was *bogatyr*—and one of the greatest. And now he keeps the gate open, but even Tamerlane's time is ending. Why you, you ask? You're his replacement. That's why they sent you to fetch the coil: They knew it would listen to you. And once you had it, they were going to use you, wire you into the machine, fuse you to its coil. If I'd been the first to find it—well, I had other plans."

Kitai reached out and placed both hands on the tomb. The slab of black jade slid apart. Blue light poured through. Through the azure haze Ilya saw a figure.

It wore a leather jerkin and a pointed helmet. A horsetail streamed from the peak of the helmet as if caught in an unnatural wind. The figure's hands gripped a familiar, coiled form: bright lines ran beneath Tamerlane's skin, tracing arteries and bone, a mesh of flesh and ancient technology. Yet Ilya could see through it to the golden walls beyond, a double image of imposed realities.

"*Tamerlane.*"

The figure's eyes were open, agonized, aware.

"Did you never wonder what became of him?" Manas asked. "He sacrificed himself to keep the gate open. He's like you, like me. All of us have the ability to use the coils, open little chinks and gaps between the worlds. But if you want to maintain a gate—ah, then the price is ultimately high. He failed to conquer Russia. And so he came here, to conquer another land, but not by force this time. To keep the way open for his hordes to travel through down the centuries. Pity no one told him that times have changed. He's been in here for centuries, but not even the greatest hero can last forever."

Kovalin was edging around the tomb toward Ilya.

"The gate needs the power of a mind as well as that of the coil," Kovalin said. "Look." Around Tamerlane's feet were strewn bones, as small as those of a bird, and a single elongated skull.

"*Rusalki?*" Ilya asked. *Keep them talking, buy time.*

"Just so. Byelovodye needs a single, open, stable gate. This will be it, with you to power it."

"But not under your control," Manas said sharply. "This is *my* people's gate."

He reached into his jacket and took out a gun.

"You think we don't have weapons of our own?" Kitai said incredulously. "That won't help you."

Slowly, the figure of Tamerlane was diminishing, growing ever more faint. Golden lines snaked into empty air, detached from sinew and skin.

"It's powering down," Kovalin said sharply. "He's dying at last."

Kitai swung to face Ilya. There was a pressure in his head, compelling him toward the gate. He took a tottering step forward. A gunshot echoed from the golden walls. Kovalin dropped. As he did so, Ilya threw the sword through the blue and sparkling air. The sword struck Kitai in the chest, slicing into rib cage and lung. The Mechvor fell forward without a sound. Manas stood, gripping the gun.

"I knew you would behave with honor," Ilya managed to say. He felt fragile and shaky, dislocated from his body. "I understand *bogatyri.*"

"You understand nothing," Manas said. He wrenched the sword from Kitai's body and strode around the gaping tomb. "Why do you think I killed the *akyn*—a poet, espousing idle dreams? What good are dreams without power? I and my people have dreams of our own. I wanted the gate to lie in Kyrgyzia, by the lake—that was why I guided you there. But your damned bitch was too quick."

"Your people?"

"The horse clans of Byelovodye. I was born among them. If they can control the gate, they will use it to weaken Russia."

"But the gate is here in Samarkand. Won't it weaken Central Asia as well?"

"Central Asia can withstand it. Our people are strong, they will undergo a new Renaissance once the Russian influence is diminished. You saw this city before the Soviets came in to ruin it with office blocks and apartments; you saw its magnificence. Control of the gate will purge the region of the last remnants of Soviet power. And when it is in chaos, weakened as you say, I will become its new khan, to see the region rise again."

"It's a bit late in the day to turn yourself into yet another local warlord, isn't it? The myth of the strong man, all over again? I've stopped believing in heroes, Manas. I believe in people."

"People? Most of them are barely worthy of the name 'human.' Sheep and chickens, more like, running round in a panic because no one will tell them what to do. You're a fool. You're better off dead. And this time, I don't think anything's going to come and save your life."

He swung the sword. Ilya dodged back. The blade struck sparks from black jade, and light flared across the golden walls of the mausoleum. Manas struck again. Ilya twisted away and the sword caught the sleeve of his coat and tore. He felt the sting along his arm. He did not know if Manas was trying to drive him into the gate, or simply kill him. He did not think Manas possessed Kitai's mind-wrenching abilities, but neither fate was appealing. He feinted, dodged again, reached the other side of the tomb.

The gate was flickering, sending shadows across the golden walls, and growing fainter as it did so. *The gate is dying,* Ilya thought. But might it still be possible to travel through it, without becoming ensnared? For if the gate shut, then he would be trapped on Earth, with Elena still in Byelovodye.

And then he heard a voice.

It was coming up from the pit of azure light that streamed from the tomb. It was not the voice of God or Tamerlane, nor that of a *rusalka,* nor of anyone he recognized.

It was a faint, small voice.

It said, "Have you fed the goat?"

As Manas swung the sword high, Ilya rushed forward and caught him by the arm. The sword came down, biting deep into his side. Ilya staggered, tried to turn from the gate. They both fell over the lip of the tomb, into the light. The gold lines reached out, snapping, electric, seeking Ilya's skin, and missed. He and Manas were falling free.

Nineteen

Elena stood, looking up at the ship. It towered into the heavens, dwarfing the launchpad and the surrounding buildings. Its white sides caught the spring sunlight; the red star on its flanks glowed like blood. She turned and saw that the flowers were blooming out across the steppe, enjoying their brief spell of life before summer came to wither the grasses and scatter the seeds. There was no sign of the *rusalka*, of Altaidyn Tengeri, or of the Golden Warrior. The horse clan had vanished. The air was filled with a faint blue haze, sparkling with lights like the sun on water. Colonel Anikova of the Pergaman military was striding toward her across the black earth.

"What happened?" Elena asked. "Where is the horse clan?"

"Gone. They turned tail; they ride south to their own lands. I've issued orders to let them go." Anikova spoke brusquely, but her saturnine face was close to smiling.

"They wanted to create a dream," Elena said. "And so did I. But we didn't have the same dreams."

"No," Anikova said, squinting up at the launch-pad. "I don't imagine you did. It's a new gate, I'm sure of it. We'll have to wait and see what it lets through. . . ."

Two men walked along the base of the gantry, clad in white lab coats, heads close together.

"The world has adjusted around you," Anikova murmured.

"Won't they be surprised to find themselves working here?"

"In the first few seconds. Then memories alter, transform, adjust. Life here isn't quite like life on Earth. But I suppose you know that already."

"It's something I've come to learn," Elena said, and only when the words were out of her mouth did she realize their double meaning.

"I should arrest you. But one learns to be careful, and I don't know what effect this new opening has had back in the city, in Central Command. I might get back to find an entirely new hierarchy in place, or familiar faces who swear that the whole purpose of our endeavors has been to open the floodgates between Byelovodye and Earth, to establish a Byelovodyean space program."

"Is that what I've done?"

"I don't know. But you've let through a whole world of dreams, whatever else you might have accomplished. You must have believed in this very strongly. I think," Anikova added musingly, "it's best not to risk an incident. I'll take you back to the city, and then you're free to go."

"I don't think I'm free," Elena said, thinking of the coil. She took a deep breath, wondering how much and who she might be betraying, and told Anikova what it had said. "I think I'm going to have to come back here. Keep the dream alive."

Anikova frowned. "You know how the gates are kept open, don't you? Someone who has the right connection needs to be hard-wired into them, fused with the machine. Otherwise they can fold."

"I'm not prepared to go through that."

"No one's asked you to."

"Not yet. But surely there has to be another way. I'll find it, if I can. Go back to Tsilibayev's work, question the *rusalki*—if they'll talk to me, which I doubt."

Anikova was staring at Elena.

"Do you know, there's something about you that reminds me of my sister."

And now that Elena looked at the Colonel more closely, she realized who Anikova had reminded her of, when she had stood before the garden in that hotel room breach: her father. She wondered about the stories that her father had told her with such conviction, of the land of white waters, how he had told them so little about his youth. But it was not the time to voice any suspicions.

Elena turned to face Anikova, finally able to give voice to her fears. "I lost someone here. Will you help me find him?"

Anikova looked sideways at her. "You helped me realize my dream, though I never could admit it—an open gate between the Republic and Earth, a changed society. I have a certain obligation to help you realize yours. Yes, I'll help you to find him."

Epilogue

He was lying very still, eyes closed, when she came into the room. She looked for signs of breath and saw none. Slowly, she went to sit by the side of the bed, but he did not stir.

It was now three days since the incident at what was now the launch site, and three days, too, since two men had fallen out of a crack in the air at a startled farmer's feet. The report had finally reached Anikova's desk and, recognizing the description of one of the men, she had acted swiftly. She had flown Elena to the far south of Pergama Province; she now sat outside on the low wall of a farm.

The farmer's wife had told Elena that she believed the man to be dying. The other one—the one who looked like a tribesman, with the tilted eyes of the East—had fled in the night, and been spotted crossing the border into the lands of the horse clans. The farmer's wife said that she had been glad to see him go. Both men alarmed her, she said; there seemed something wild about them. But the remaining one was too badly hurt to do any harm.

Now, Elena sat by Ilya Muromyets' side and watched him sleep, or perhaps, finally, die. At last she could bear it no longer, and though the local doctor had instructed her that he was not to be disturbed, she reached out and touched his hand. It was cold, but his eyes opened. He smiled up at her.

"I've been waiting for you," he said.

"We didn't know where you were, what had happened," Elena whispered.

"I was on Earth. I made it to Samarkand. There was a gate, Elena. It was buried in the ground, within the tomb of Tamerlane. He was there within it, keeping it open. But I think it died with him. And you? What happened to you?"

"I found a dream," she said.

"Space? The stars?"

"Yes. But I can't help wondering where one would get to, if a ship was sent up from here, from this hidden republic."

"Maybe you'll be the one to find out."

"I've been finding out a lot," Elena said. She felt that if she could only keep him talking, she might hold him here for a while longer. "Kovalin, Kitai, others— they were very old beings. It's believed they were descended from humans who came through the natural breaches, and indigenous *rusalki*. Anikova let me see the records. The later colonists were in favor of the proletariat, not the development of supermen. They made a number of bargains. The half-breeds had knowledge, but there weren't many of them, not enough to enforce their desires. They needed *rusalkan* technology."

"Their sisters saved my life. Over and over again."

Until now. She could see resignation in his face. "But not this time, I think. This time, I have to go it alone."

"I think the *akyn* was right about the *rusalki*. They aren't evil, but they don't have a human agenda. And the failure of their plans for the gate seems to have thrown them into disarray. They have retreated north, Anikova believes, into the deep forest, and separated from the horse tribes. From what I've seen of them, they may not want to have more to do with humans. Superstition says that they're a kind of nature spirit. That's probably as accurate a description as any."

"Does Anikova know what will happen now? How a way through will affect Byelovodye, and Russia?"

"She says we're going to have to be very careful what dreams we adopt. On both sides of the curtain. The Byelovodyeans have the advantage there. They know the power dreams can have."

Ilya smiled. "So do Russians. Believe me."

"This time, we really do have to get it right. No more botched political experiments, no more environmental disasters, no more erosion of science."

"It's not up to us, Elena."

"I know. It's up to everyone." She sighed. "And our track record isn't good."

"Don't look so downcast," he whispered. "You can only be a hero; do the best you can."

If she was a hero, she thought, then she was one with a splinter of ice in her heart. "Ilya? Are you going to be around to help?"

"When I embarked on all this, I did so because I wanted death at the end of it. That was my plan, until you appeared."

"And now?"

"Plans have changed." He sat up against the rough flock pillow, grimacing with pain. "My own sword, too. At least the bastard left it behind. I'm intending to live. I want revenge on Manas." He looked at her, reaching out. "And there are other things worth living for, as well."

"Like quests, and slaying dragons?" She was smiling.

"I was thinking of love."

Later, when he was once more asleep, Elena went out into the sunshine. Anikova was still sitting on the wall, idly teasing a goat with a blade of grass.

"Do you think he'll make it?" she asked, still abrupt.

"We've both seen the future," Elena said.

"And how does the future look to you?"

Elena looked along the slanting shadows of the farmyard, over the wall to the distant heights of the mountains. In the late sun, the snows were golden. It reminded her of the land that swept down from the Altai, or the mountains above Lake Issy Kul. Ilya lay a step through the door. Perhaps she would find a way to keep open the gate that she and the coil had created. Maybe one day she could return to Russia. Dreams could be found in both, and neither world was very far away. She stifled her misgivings, for his sake.

"Future looks good enough to me," Elena said.

About the Author

Liz Williams is the daughter of a stage magician and a Gothic novelist, and currently lives in Brighton, England. She received a Ph.D. in philosophy of science from Cambridge and her career since has ranged from reading tarot cards on Brighton pier to teaching in Central Asia. She has had short fiction published in *Asimov's, Interzone, The Third Alternative*, and *Visionary Tongue*, among other publications, and is coeditor of the recent anthology *Fabulous Brighton*. She is also the current secretary of the Milford UK SF Writers' Workshop. *Nine Layers of Sky* is her fourth novel. She is currently working on her fifth.

Don't miss the next riveting novel by

Liz Williams

Banner of Souls

Far-future Earth is a flooded, shattered world. Its history is lost, and it is governed by the iron hand of the Martian Matriarchy. And the last thing one of the infamous Martian warriors wants to do is to return to this troublesome world to safeguard a young girl from an unknown threat. But even in a world where children are force-grown in garden laboratories, Lunae is no ordinary child. Instead, her extraordinary heritage has left her with the ability to alter time. So now Dreams-of-War must travel to the half-ruined city of Fragrant Harbour, where Lunae lives. And when an assassin comes to Lunae's home of Cloud Terrace, Dreams-of-War, Lunae and the kappa are forced to flee to the flooded northern islands of what was once Japan.

But Lunae goes missing en route, and Dreams-of-War finds a dubious ally in the form of Yskatarina: a mutated woman from the world of Nightshade. Now, stripped of her rank and her armor, Dreams-of-War struggles to return to the plains of Mars to discover the truth about Martian rule over Earth, and the nature of the intrigues that lie behind it . . . In her inimitable style, Liz Williams crafts yet another tale packed with exotic details, absorbing characters, and fascinating socio-political explorations that should continue to cement her reputation as one of SF's hottest new talents.

Coming in Fall of 2004